Anatomy of a Murder

ROBERT TRAVER

ANATOMY OF A MURDER. Copyright © 1958 by Robert Traver. Copyright ©
1983 by Robert Traver. All rights reserved. Printed in the United States of
America. For information address St. Martin's Press, 175 Fifth Avenue, New
York, N.Y. 10010.

www.stmartins.com

Library of Congress Cataloging-in-Publication Data

Traver, Robert, 1903–1991
     Anatomy of a murder
     ISBN 0-312-03356-4
     EAN 978-0312-03356-9

 St. Martin's Griffin ♏ New York

to my friend Raymond

Acknowledgments

For permission to preprint the following, grateful acknowledgment is made to:

Harper & Brothers for a selection from THROUGH THESE MEN by John Mason Brown.

Callaghan & Company for a selection from Callaghan's MICHIGAN PLEADING AND PRACTICE.

The Lawyers Co-operative Publishing Company for the selections from 70 American Law Reports.

ANATOMY OF A MURDER. Copyright © 1958 by Robert Traver. Introduction © 1983 by Robert Traver. All rights reserved. Printed in the United States of America. For information, address St. Martin's Press, 175 Fifth Avenue, New York, N.Y. 10010.

www.stmartins.com

Library of Congress Cataloging-in-Publication Data

Traver, Robert, 1903–1991.
    Anatomy of a murder.
    ISBN 0-312-03356-7
    EAN 978-0-312-03356-9

P   83-2977

D 30 29

Introduction

After serving for fourteen years as district attorney of the northern Michigan county where I was born, one chilly fall election day I found myself abruptly paroled from my job by the unappealable verdict of the electorate. The thing was almost painless: a few punches and pulls of the "wrong" voting gadgets and—presto—I was an ex-D.A.

I also found myself in a bit of a bind. I was fast approaching fifty, two of our three daughters were in college, and between prosecuting criminal cases and pursuing the elusive trout, it seemed I had neglected anything as mundane as building up a private law practice.

Moreover, after the spot-lighted thrust and swordplay of the public courtroom, I seemed to have developed an allergy to crouching in an office all day drafting legal documents full of such luminous phrases as "said party of the first part as aforesaid."

For a spell I tried varied strategems to avoid all those lurking aforesaids. At the time prospecting for uranium was high on the achievements list in our granite-strewn mining area, so I quickly bought a Geiger counter—only twelve easy payments—and resolutely marched off to the granite hills to serve both Mammon and my country. There I soon collided with the whole mountain of radioactive thorium, which, it also soon developed, nobody wanted, evidently much preferring to be blown up, if and when, by scarcer and therefore far tonier uranium.

Next I wrote my second book about my D.A. experiences, which was duly accepted and published and generously reviewed but which nevertheless raced the first one—along with an interim book of short stories—to a blissful out-of-print oblivion, where all three still slumber.

By then another election year had rolled around, so I threw my hat in the ring for Congress (a fate common to unemployed ex-D.A.s, I have since observed), but I barely carried my own county in our sprawling northern Michigan district.

Since neither prospecting nor spinning yarns nor free trips to Washington seemed to be in the cards, I pondered my next move on how I might duck those pesky aforesaids.

Then a rare intruding client interrupted my meditations, an aggrieved citizen who, it seemed, had inadvertently sneezed while rounding a highway curve and had been picked up by the cops for drunk driving. Would I defend him against this crass miscarriage of justice? I would and did, and though I forget just how justice fared in that one, I soon began popping up in scattered justice courts defending similarly aggrieved citizens.

Then a series of felonies began sweeping the county, like an invasion of locusts, and, apparently since I hadn't quite lost the courthouse and jail during my D.A. stint, I suddenly found myself up to my ears acting as defense counsel down in the old stone courthouse overlooking Lake Superior.

With the approach of winter came a lull in the crime wave, and I briefly considered writing a deep think-tank piece—complete with both footnotes *and* footpads—on the eerie effects of changing seasons on human behavior. I already had the title: "Weather to Steal or Not to Steal." Instead I had a sudden impulse to write my first novel. After all, I reflected, I'd already written books of yarns, so why not for a change tackle and concentrate on one single story, say, about one single courtroom trial?

Since I now bore the scars of fighting on both sides of the courtroom barricades, I finally decided to write about a murder trial. The courtroom was one arena I knew something about, and by now I'd appeared on both sides in some pretty bang-up murder trials.

About then I recalled the farewell words of the teacher of the only "creative writing" course I'd ever taken. "Remember, kids," the man had said, "writing about people and places you know can help give your stuff the ring of authenticity." He paused and smiled. "And never forget that old saying: 'An ounce of authenticity is worth a pound of windgassity.'"

Another reason I wanted to tackle a single courtroom trial was that I had a small ax of my own to grind. For a long time I had seen too many movies and read too many books and plays about trials that were almost comically phony and overdone, mostly in their extravagant efforts to overdramatize an already inherently dramatic human situation.

I longed to try my hand at telling about a criminal trial the way it really was, and, after my years of immersion, I felt equally strongly that a great part of the tension and drama of any major felony trial lay in its very understatement, its pent and almost stifled quality, not in the usually portrayed shoutings and stompings and assorted finger-waggings that almost inevitably accompanied the sudden appearance and subsequent grilling of that monotonously dependable last-minute witness....

In what other forum, I asked myself, could a battle for such awesomely high stakes—freedom and sometimes life itself—be fought in such a muted atmosphere of hushed ritual and controlled decorum, one so awash with ancient rites and Latinized locutions, one so filled with such obeisant rhetorical antiquities as "If it please Your Honor" and all the rest?

So I scribbled the winter away, doggedly expunging all aforesaids, finally putting down my pen and taking up my fly rod and bundling my story off to the New York publisher of my last book. Then I folded my arms and impatiently awaited his ecstatic response. One day it came, puzzlingly accompanied by my manuscript, of all things. By then I'd learned to label my rejections, and this one was of the variety I kept in a special file called No, But with a Heavy Heart.

Rallying, I tried another New York house and once again waited for courtroom authenticity to prevail. Prevail it did not, but instead my manuscript, along with a terse mimeographed rejection slip, almost beat me back from the post office, at least establishing a new speed record in my mounting collection of rejections.

Then one evening while I was out fishing, amidst the hum of insects and the swoop of nighthawks, I suddenly remembered an editor who'd worked on my last book and liked it. So the next morning, almost apologetically, I baled the manuscript of *Anatomy of a Murder* off to Sherman Baker at the new New York house where he worked and—presto—both he and St. Martin's grabbed it—and doubtless saved me from a lifetime bondage to said aforesaids.

After that things began happening at a furious pace. I can't possibly remember all but I do recall a few. Thus, the very weekend Sherman Baker phoned the book's acceptance, Governor G. Mennen Williams phoned his appointment of me to sit on the Michigan supreme court. Then the Book-of-the-Month Club nodded and beamed as the book soared off and away and got itself glued to the best-seller lists. A grinning Johnny Carson mispronounced my name on television. My split infinitives appeared in seventeen languages. Elihu Winer made a play out of my story....

Then Otto Preminger and, it seemed, half of Hollywood descended upon the old stone courthouse in which I'd postured and pirouetted before so many juries for so many years. While I may lack a certain critical detachment, I thought and still think Otto did a grand job of picturing what I'd tried to write. If I'm right I also like to think that part of the reason is that contrary to the usual Otto-the-Autocrat legends, he not only consulted both Joseph M. Welch and me on the filming, especially of the courtroom scenes, but listened closely to what we said.

Mature movie fans may recall that Joseph Welch played the part of the presiding judge, masterfully I may add. Between takes he also taught me to play gin rummy, and though his tuition was high, we became close friends, later touring Israel and part of Europe together with our wives, and even planned doing a book. Then in Rome he was forced to fly home with a sudden illness from which, alas, he never recovered—and our book alas, was never born.

Looking back, I find our friendship one of the high rewards of the whole *Anatomy* adventure (I almost wrote "ordeal"). We talked of many things: of our shared interest in the concern over the changing role of lawyers in our society; of our almost guilty feeling, also shared, that the office part of the law had mostly bored us, just as the dramatic kinship of the public courtroom to the stage had always beckoned; and, on a loftier level, how friendship itself was such a curious mixture of chemistry and propinquity, of the almost scarily fortuitous quality in kindred souls occasionally being lucky enough to find each other.

On some days, parched by a particularly grueling session of gin rummy, we'd raise a glass to Otto for bringing together two bewildered wanderers groping their way in the blinding glare of publicity: Joseph's the result of a long and distinguished career culminating in the historic Army-McCarthy hearings (in their day rivaling even the more recent Watergate hearings); mine the unexpected result of a lone shot-in-the-dark attempt by a restless country lawyer to relieve office boredom by spinning an "authentic" courtroom yarn and perhaps, with luck even winning the price of a new fly rod—along with the golden chance to play hooky more often (a guy could dream, couldn't he?), to go wooing those sensible office-shunning trout with his new fairy wand.

Somehow I managed to survive the trauma of best-sellerdom by still clinging to a few shreds of humility. But it was a narrow squeak, and perhaps some evidence that I may have made it is that I still haven't found that writing has become any easier. Nor have I succumbed to the illusion that seems to afflict many of its victims that my idlest scribblings should henceforth be carved in bronze or that my most casual rhetorical burps have now become worth a buck a burp.

One thing that almost surely helped save me was the memory of those two earlier rejections, tough as they were to swallow at the time. Another was the enthusiastic acceptance by the old *Saturday Evening Post* (after *Anatomy* appeared) of the very same fishing story (for which it now paid through the nose) it had earlier swiftly rejected before *Anatomy* appeared. And I hadn't changed a single blooming comma! When the same yarn shortly appeared as the lead-off piece in the annual bound *Best of the Post* my humility ranneth over....

Humility got a further boost when the unpublished book from which the fishing story was taken, *Trout Madness* (and which prior to my novel I couldn't sell or give away, in whole or in part), was promptly grabbed and published and became and remains a sort of piscatorial best-seller of its own. As my stock of humility rose I continued to marvel over how high notoriety alone could so remarkably whet and sharpen the critical faculties of our tribe.

Since *Anatomy* I have written two other "courtroom" novels, *Laughing Whitefish* and the recent *People Versus Kirk,* all three of which now roost under the same publishing roof. All three were either based upon or drawn from or inspired by actual litigated courtroom cases, and I continue to be surprised that six of my eleven published books were drawn from the law.

All of which may suggest that more of my fellow writers ought to explore the neglected boneyards of the law and pay far more heed to that busiest of all stages in our society, the public courtroom. For it is there, and only there, where some of the most moving dramas of our times regularly unfold. Skeptics are invited to marvel and look back over just a few of the so quickly forgotten "front page" trials of recent years—and then take up their pens.

Robert Traver
December 1982

prologue

This is the story of a murder, of a murder trial, and of some of the people who engaged or became enmeshed in the proceedings. Enmeshed is a good word, for murder, of all crimes, seems to possess to a greater degree than any other that compelling magnetic quality that draws people helplessly into its outspreading net, frequently to their surprise, and occasionally to their horror.

Murders must happen some place, of course, and this one and the subsequent trial took place on the water-hemmed Upper Peninsula of Michigan, simply U. P. to its inhabitants. The U. P. is a wild, harsh and broken land, rubbed and ground on the relentless hone of many past glaciers, the last one, in its slow convulsive retreat, leaving the country a jumble of swamps and hills and rocks and endless waterways. Lying as it does within the southernmost rim of the great Canadian pre-Cambrian shield, the region is perhaps more nearly allied with Canada by climatic and geological affinity; with Wisconsin by the logic of geography; but a region which, by some logic beyond logic, finally wound up as part of the state of Michigan; this after a fairy-tale series of political blunders and compromises that doubtless made the angels weep.

Nobody had wanted to adopt the remote and raffish U. P. and Michigan was at last persuaded to take it reluctantly, coveting instead, almost to the brink of civil war, a modest parcel of land along the Ohio border known as the "Toledo strip." This wry political fairy tale unfolded in all of its lovely irony when large copper and iron deposits were shortly discovered on the U. P. rivaling in richness any then known on the hemisphere. The unwanted ugly duckling had turned into a fabulous golden-haired princess. The resourful politicians in lower Michigan were equal to the strain; they quickly congratulated themselves on their wisdom and shrewd foresight. *They'd* wanted the U. P. all the time. Of course they had.

It was here that this murder took place.

R.T.

PART ONE

Before the Trial

chapter 1

The mine whistles were tooting midnight as I drove down Main Street hill. It was a warm moonlit Sunday night in mid-August and I was arriving home from a long weekend of trout fishing in the Oxbow Lake district with my old hermit friend Danny McGinnis, who lives there all year round. I swung over on Hematite Street to look at my mother's house—the same gaunt white frame house on the corner where I was born. As my car turned the corner the headlights swept the rows of tall drooping elms planted by my father when he was a young man—much younger than I—and gleamed bluely on the darkened windows. My mother Belle was still away visiting my married sister and she had enjoined me to keep an eye on the place. Well, I had looked and lo! like the flag, the old house was still there.

I swung around downtown and slowed down to miss a solitary drunk emerging blindly from the Tripoli Bar and out upon the street, in a sort of gangling somnambulistic trot, pursued on his way by the hollow roar of a juke box from the garishly lit and empty bar. "Sunstroke," I murmured absently. "Simply a crazed victim of the midnight sun." As I parked my mud-spattered coupe alongside the Miners' State Bank, across from my office over the dime store, I reflected that there were few more forlorn and lonely sounds in the world than the midnight wail of a juke box in a deserted small town, those raucous proclamations of joy and fun where, instead, there dwelt only fatigue and hangover and boredom. To me the wavering hoot of an owl sounds utterly gay by comparison.

I unlocked the car trunk and took out my packsack and two aluminum-cased fly rods and a handbag and rested them on the curb. I shouldered the packsack and grabbed up the other stuff and started across the echoing empty street.

"How was fishing, Polly?" someone said, emerging from the darkened alley alongside the dime store. It was old Jack Tregembo, tall and lean and weather-beaten as a beardless Uncle Sam. Jack had been a night cop on the Chippewa police force as long as I could remember.

"Fine, fine, Jack," I said, rubbing my unshaven neck. "I ate so many trout the past few days I suspect I'm developing gill slits."

"S'pose you heard about the big murder?" Jack said, moving closer, plainly hoping that I hadn't. "We even made the city papers."

"No, Jack," I said, pricking up my ears. "Just got in—as you see. No newspapers, radios or phones, thank God, up in the big Oxbow

3

bush. Talkative Old Danny could never stand the competition. Trust you caught the villain and got him all hogtied, purged, and confessed for Mitch."

Jack shrugged. "Tain't our headache, Polly. Happened 'way up in Thunder Bay. Friday night. Some soldier stationed up there blew his top and drilled Barney Quill five times with a .38. This Barney ran the hotel and bar there. Claims Barney'd raped his wife. The state police have this baby, thank goodness."

"Hm. . . ." I said, the legal gears beginning involuntarily to turn.

Just then a car wheeled around the corner on two wheels, dog tails flying fore and aft, the car awash with shouting juveniles, brakes and tires squealing like neighing stallions. It narrowly missed piling into the rear of my parked car and then roared away down the street. Seconds later two police cars followed in hot pursuit, sirens away, the last one pausing long enough to pick up Jack, who leapt in like a boy. The scene was invested with a curious quality of Keystone comedy and I thought wistfully of the brooding calm that must prevail at this moment over my favorite trout waters up in the Oxbow bush. Creeping mist, a coyote wailing on the ridge, the cackle of a loon, the plash of a rising trout. I stood looking up over the Miners' State Bank as the big waning yellow moon swam out from behind a jagged dark cliff of cloud. "My heart will always *ble-e-e-e-d* for you," the juke box wailed, "out of my crying *ne-e-e-d* for you. . . ."

"Crime," I reflected tritely, as I trudged up the creaking wooden stairs, "crime marches on."

I heard the monotonously insistent robot ringing of a telephone before I reached the top of the stairs. The waspish buzzing continued. I did not hurry; after all, it could be for the chiropractor, the beauty operator, the dentist, or even the young newlyweds down the hall. It could have been, but I was certain it wasn't. For with one of those swift premonitions one cannot define I knew it was for me; it would be, I was sure, my invitation to the waltz—my bid to accept the retainer in Iron Cliffs County's latest murder. I lowered my duffel and fumbled for the key to my private office. My phone had ceased ringing.

Paul Biegler
LAWYER

read the sign on the frosted-glass door. Underneath was a horizontal black arrow pointing toward Maida's door, accompanied by the words, "Entrance next door." It was surprising how few people ever learned to follow the arrow and instead stood there gripped by a sort of dumb enchantment, pounding stupidly on my private door.

The Chippewa branch store of a national dime store chain embraced the entire main floor of the two-story brownstone building built by my German brewer grandfather in the 1870's. For many years before they died he and Grandma used to live upstairs, and my combined law offices and bachelor's quarters now occupied their old parlor, sitting room and dining room.

Law is one of the last citadels of wavering conservatism in an untidy world and the offices of most lawyers reflect it. My office did not fit the common mold. In fact my mother Belle reprovingly claimed it looked like anything but a law office. Indeed, one of my former opponents for prosecutor had told people that for me it was a perfect place in which to tell, if not make, fortunes. . . . The combined waiting room and place where Maida did her typing—the old dining room—looked more like the reception room of, not a club, but a comfortably old and rather down-at-the-heel fraternal lodge. There was an old black leather rocking-chair and an even older brown leather davenport to accommodate the overflow. Maida had a new desk, it was true, but it was the kind that was designed to look more like a library table than a desk, and completely swallowed her typewriter except when it was in use. There were no magazines, not even *Newsweek*, and no pictures on the walls save an enlarged framed snapshot of Maida's favorite saddle horse, Balsam. Most of the legal files and cabinets and office supplies were kept stashed away out of sight in Grandma Biegler's roomy old pantry. There boxes of carbon paper, ruled legal pads and brown manila envelopes and all the rest had taken the place of Grandma's steaming platters of pig hocks and sauerkraut.

My own office—Grandma's old sitting room—was even more informal than Maida's. The Michigan supreme court reports and all my other law books stood on narrow shelves against an entire wall, completely hidden by drawn monk-cloth drapes—largely, I suspect, because it made me nervous to contemplate so many religiously unread books. My library table was Grandma's old long wooden dining-room table, kept as bare and shining as an ad for spar varnish. Over against one wall was a black leather couch—not a davenport, not a settee, but simply a battered old leather couch. I was determined that the psychiatrists couldn't hog all the comfort. My waggish Irish lawyer friend Parnell McCarthy occasionally teased me that here was where I tested the virtue of my lady divorce clients.

In one corner was an overstuffed black leather rocker with a matching footstool, flanked by a floor lamp and a revolving bookstand for my nonlegal magazines and books. Beyond it was a Franklin stove with an unabashed black stovepipe rising up to Grandma's old chimney outlet near the high ceiling. On the walls were some small color prints and photographs of trout and still others of men—mostly of a tall, thin, balding, prow-nosed character called Paul Biegler, exhibiting or fishing for trout. In the opposite corner stood a combination radio and phonograph and alongside it a television set.

Ostensibly I lived at my mother's house on Hematite Street, but by tacit agreement I usually slept at my office—in Grandma's old parlor—and used my old quarters in the family homestead mostly for storing my fishing gear in the winter and my guns and snowshoes and skis in summer. So my mother Belle dwelt alone in her big empty house like a dowager queen, re-reading her Hardy and Dickens and fussing with her water colors and listening to endless soap operas. It did not seem to bother her that I practically lived at my office. She had always felt strongly that growing boys should have a certain amount of freedom before finally settling down. After all, there was no rush; boys would surely be boys; and to her mind I was, in my early forties, still little more than a fumbling adolescent.

Belle had equally firm views on the seriousness of matrimony. The contract was a long one and sensible people did not marry in haste and repent at leisure. One day, and all in good time, I would doubtless marry and move my lucky bride in among all the clanking curios and relics in the old house on Hematite Street. She had it all planned, even to giving me her rusty old wooden icebox, the kind that used pond ice and drained into a pan on the floor. As for myself I had never married for the simple reason that I had never yet in my travels encountered a woman in whose company I cared to remain more than a few hours at a time, whether day or night. Well, maybe there had been one but she, sensible girl, had instead married a wholesale drug salesman and had presented him with two sets of twins before I lost count.

The telephone began to drone again and I answered it largely because it was the only way I knew to make the damned thing stop. My fishing trip, I saw, was officially over.

6

"Hello," I said into the telephone. "This is Paul Biegler."

"This is Laura Manion," a woman said. "Mrs. Laura Manion. I'm sorry to be calling you so late, but I've been trying to get you all weekend. I finally reached your secretary and she said she thought you might be back tonight."

"Yes, Mrs. Manion?" I said.

"My husband, Lieutenant Frederic Manion, is in the county jail here at Iron Bay," she went on. "He's being held for murder. He wants you to be his lawyer." Her voice broke a little and then she went on. "You've been highly recommended to us. Can you take his case?"

"I don't know, Mrs. Manion," I answered truthfully. "I'll naturally have to talk with him and look into the situation before I can decide. Then there is always the matter of making mutually agreeable financial arrangements."

It was funny, the fine suave marshmallow phrases a lawyer learned to spin to let a prospective client gently know he must be prepared to fork over some heavy dough. Mrs. Manion was an alert student of marshmallow phrases.

"Yes, of course, Mr. Biegler. When can you see him? He's awfully anxious to see you."

I surveyed the clutter of mail, mostly junk and routine stuff, that had accumulated during my absence. "I'll go see him around eleven in the morning. Will you plan to be there?"

"I'm sorry, but I have to go to the doctor's. I don't know if you've heard the details, but I—I had quite an experience. I'm sure I can see you Tuesday, though—that is, if you can take the case."

"I'll plan to see you Tuesday, then," I said, "if I enter the case."

"Thank you, Mr. Biegler."

"Good night, Mrs. Manion," I said. Then I switched out the lights and sat in the darkness watching the reflection of the changing traffic lights below dancing on the opposite wall. The room was stuffy so I opened the window and sat looking down upon the silent and empty city square, watching my smoke drift lazily out the window, brooding sleepily about the tangled past and future.

The town of Chippewa lies in a broad loamy valley surrounded by bald low-lying granite and diorite bluffs, about a dozen miles west of the town of Iron Bay on Lake Superior. Iron Bay is the county seat of Iron Cliffs County. I used to be prosecuting attorney of Iron Cliffs County. Perhaps the simplest definition of a prosecuting attorney is a D.A. who lacks a comparable press and publicity; otherwise their jobs are the same. There are no radio or TV programs exalting the real or imagined doings of "Mr. Prosecuting Attorney." I held the prosecutor's job for ten years, until Mitchell Lodwick beat me. You see, Mitch used to be quite a football star both in high school and later at the university. The boy was good. He was also a veteran of World War II while I was a mere 4F from an old scar on my lung caused by an almost losing bout with pneumonia while in law school. The combination for Mitch was irresistible; I was a hero in neither department so I got beat. Alas, I couldn't run with the ball or tell a corporal from a five-star general. And still can't.

Iron mining is the red lifeblood of Iron Cliffs County. The raw iron ore is mined and coasted downhill by rail from Chippewa to Iron Bay, on the Lake, and thence boated down the Great Lakes to the distant coal deposits and blast furnaces. This makes a handy money-saving arrangement, and for once even Nature seems to have conspired on the side of free enterprise. If it weren't for mining I suppose the county'd still belong to the Indians. Instead it now belongs mostly to the Iron Cliffs Ore Company and the other smaller mining companies and, what's left over, to the descendants of the Finns and Scandinavians, the French, Italians and Cornish, and the Irish and handful of Germans (including Grandpa and Grandma Biegler), who luckily landed here many years before an all-American Senator named Patrick McCarran, ironically himself the descendant of immigrants, had discovered that these yearning peoples were henceforth more properly to be known as quotas, and had run up a tall legislative fence around Ellis Island.

So at forty I had found myself without a job, my main assets consisting of my law degree, a battered set of secondhand law books and some creaking old fly rods. Mitch had been a veteran and a hero; I had been a mere 4F and a bum. For quite a while I was pretty bitter about being beaten by a young legal fledgling who hadn't even tried a justice court fender case when he knocked me off. For a time I indulged in wistful fantasies about the plight of the poor left-at-home 4F in America. Nobody seemed to have a kind word or vote for him; he was the country's forgotten man—he who had remained at home and kept the lamp lit in the window; he who had patriotically bought all those nice interest-bearing war bonds with his time-and-a-half for overtime, who had stayed at home and resolutely devoured all those black-market steaks; he who stayed behind and got a purple nose instead of a Purple Heart; yes, he who had occasionally reached over and turned down the lamp in the window and attempted to console all those lonely wives and sweethearts. . . .

For a spell I even dabbled with the heady notion of organizing a sort of American legion of 4F's. We'd have an annual convention and boyishly tip over buses and streetcars and get ourselves a national commander who could bray in high C and sound off on everything under the sun; we'd even get a lobby in Washington and wave the Flag and praise the Lord and damn the United Nations and periodically swarm out like locusts selling crepe-paper flowers or raffle tickets or so ne damned thing, just like all the other outfits. "Arise and fight, ye 4F's!" their leader Paul Biegler would cry. Were we men or were we mice?

By and by the pain went away, however, and as I sat there in my open office window looking down upon the deserted street I reflected that I wouldn't take my old D.A. job back again if they doubled the salary. No, not even if they threw Mitch in as an assistant. Being a public prosecutor was perhaps the best trial training a young lawyer could get (besides being a slippery stepping-stone to politics), but as a career it was strictly for the birds. I fumbled for and ignited an Italian cigar (one never merely *lights* them) and fell to musing about my old Irish friend Parnell McCarthy.

I have called Parnell McCarthy an Irishman and perhaps I had better explain. In the polyglot Upper Peninsula of Michigan calling a man, say, an Irishman is rarely an effort to demean or stigmatize him—black eyes lie richly strewn that way—but rather an effort at description, a painless device for swiftly discovering and assessing the national origins of a person's ancestors to the simple end of getting along together. Offense is neither intended nor taken. Thus a man named Millimaki is generally known and indeed more often describes himself as a Finn, though his mother may have been a Cabot and his ancestors on both sides have fought at Valley Forge;

and thus a Biegler is hopelessly stamped a German, as often called "Dutchman," though some of his ancestors may alternately have toiled and prayed in the leaky galley of the *Mayflower*.

So Parnell McCarthy was an Irishman, though he was born in the shadow of a mine shaft in Chippewa, and had once possessed, so my mother Belle had told me, one of the loveliest soprano voices of any altar boy in the history of St. Michael's parish. Parnell's "Irishness" lay more in certain word patterns and in the subtle lilt and cadence of his speech than in any vaudevillian *Erin go bragh* Mr. Dooley talk. So Parnell McCarthy was an "Irisher," as many Finns and Swedes might call him, and an Irishman he would proudly remain, to the despair of all visiting sociologists and bemoaners of hyphenated Americans. And all of the U.P. folk were fiercely American, as any rash doubter ruefully and swiftly found out—as all-American, say, as Rocco Purgatorio the Italian, who had once broken up a memorable Liberty Bond rally in the Chippewa High School by abruptly getting up and waving a tiny flag and singing fervently: "Eef you doan lak your Unka Semmy, den go backa to da lan' w'ere you fromm—you—you *son-a-beech.* . . ."

Of late years and largely because of his drinking Parnell had lost most of his clients and had become a sort of lawyers' lawyer, grubbing a fitful sort of living in the exquisite drudgery of looking up land titles and interpreting abstracts for the other lawyers and some of the smaller mining companies. Our intimacy had dated from my first year as prosecutor and had begun with a typical Parnellian flourish. A perplexed young state trooper had phoned me the first thing one Monday morning.

"Mr. Prosecutor, we got a seedy old character over here booked on suspicion of drunk driving. Found him early this morning standing beside on old Maxwell wrapped around a tree, drunker'an a skunk. He insists upon seeing you—alone."

"Who's the villain?" I inquired.

" 'Parnell Emmett Joseph McCarthy,' he says. Claims some dame called Dolly Madison was driving the car."

"I'll come over," I said, wincing.

"But who's this here Dolly Madison character?" the young trooper persisted. "I thought we knew all the old hookers around here."

"I'll be right over," I said. "It's a little complicated to explain over the phone."

Parnell and I were finally alone over at the jail. "Let's have it, Mr. McCarthy," I said respectfully. "And please omit Dolly Madison."

Parnell finally focused his inflamed eyes on me. "All right, all right, young man," he said with great dignity. "I'm drivin' down this road, see, all nice as pie, see, mindin' me own business, when all of a sudden it happen. . . ."

"What happened?" I asked a little shrilly.

"As true as I'm settin' here, young fella, I'm blinded by the lights of an approachin' dragon," he said, and forthwith fell asleep.

After I had rallied sufficiently the officers and I conferred, following which certain arrangements were made whereby we promised to give Parnell the benefit of Dolly Madison if he in turn would promise to voluntarily give up driving. Parnell and I had shaken hands on it, and both promises had been solemnly kept. And that was how I first got to really know my old friend.

I remembered that it had been Parnell who had kept the lonely vigil with me on my last day as prosecutor on that blizzardy day before New Year's nearly two years before. I had bravely determined to stick out that last day in my office if it killed me. Nobody would be able to say that Polly Biegler had cut and run when the going got tough. But no one had been much interested in saying anything; there were more alluring prospects afoot; one had resolutely to get ready, for one thing, to greet the festive new year in an appropriate state of alcoholic coma.

The morning had passed without a single phone call or a caller except the postman, with a heart-warming New Year's card from my insurance agent, which I dropped thoughtfully in the wastebasket, and who was followed shortly by an earnest bow-legged little Cornishman with the *War Cry*, who popped his head in my door with his Salvation Army cap awry and said in a voice quavering with fervor, "May the Lard bless yew an' 'Appy New Year to yew, Sire."

"Ah, Happy New Year to you, General Booth," I croaked morosely, feeling very noble and very sorry for myself. "Please take the typhoid sign off the door as you leave."

"Typhide sign, typhide sign?" the General murmured, mystified, as he picked up his weekly quarter and fled. I grinned evilly at my framed law-school diploma on the far wall.

I was learning the hard way something that people who have never held public office can perhaps never adequately realize: the feeling of utter forlornness and emptiness that sweeps over a man when he is finally beaten at the polls. And the longer he has been on the job the worse, not better, it is. This morbid feeling is beyond all reason; it is both compulsive and a little daft. One's last friend has deserted him; the entire community has conspired to ridicule and humiliate him; everyone is secretly pointing the finger of scorn and hate at the defeated one. All day long desolation was mine and I wallowed in it. By mid-afternoon I sighed and pressed the buzzer for Maida.

"I thought maybe you'd taken the gas pipe," Maida said cheerily as she came in all pert and sassy and shook out her curls and plumped herself across from me with her stenographic pad and a battery of stiletto-sharp pencils. "Are you about to dictate Biegler's Farewell Address?"

I laughed, hollowly I hoped, and slid a winkled twenty-dollar bill across the desk. "No dictation, Maida, rather an errand of mercy. Go over to the liquor store and fetch me a fifth of my favorite pilerun. If Socrates could have his hemlock, I shall have the solace of my whisky." I waved benignly and looked out at the howling blizzard. "Buy yourself a new roadster with the change. Take the rest of the day off to break it in. I'll hold the fort."

"That's the old fight, Boss," Maida said, rising. "Such lonely courage is touching. The boss and his faithful bottle. Whisky for Captain Biegler's chilblains as he stands alone on the bridge and goes down with his ship. His last words were: 'Saw sub, glub glub.'" Maida had been in the Wacs and she gave me a smart salute as she made ready to go.

"Pile it on, Maida, pile it on," I said. "'None but the lonely heart shall know my anguish,'" I quoted stoically.

"Don't forget in your travail, Boss," Maida said, "that the voters of this county have bought and paid for an elegant ten-year graduate course in criminal law for you—and all for free. Where's your gratitude? Just think, for defending just one big case now you can get almost as much as you got for prosecuting criminals for an entire year. And no more legal free loaders on your neck reminding you that 'Yass, I pay my taxes'—anyone who comes in to your office now must be prepared to pay through the nose. And I don't have to be nice to them. Boy, I can't wait. I'll be back in ten minutes with the booze. Thanks for the roadster."

Sensible Maida was probably right, of course, as she has an irritating habit of being, and I saw that my main trouble was not so much that I would shortly be an ex-D.A. but rather the blow to my pride in losing the job to an amiable young fellow barely out of law school, one who didn't know a bail bond from a bale of hay. Why not face it? I was smarting largely because I hadn't been smart enough to quit as the retired champ, like Rocky Marciano, but instead had gone to the well once too often, like good old Joe Louis, and had finally, like Joe, been knocked out by an inexperienced newcomer, a newcomer inexperienced in everything, that is, but youth.

I had sat listening to the howling wind and wondering what had happened to Maida and my twenty bucks when I heard a knock on the door. It couldn't have been Maida because she would have characteristically railed and shouted and pounded or else used her key. It would doubtless be some thoughtless character who'd lurked all day in some tavern, polishing his nose, and then come to gloat over the fading D.A. Lord, it would be good to at last get away from *that* servitude, the thoughtless headlong rush of the great aggrieved multitude. . . . Well, I'd show him what an alert on-the-ball public servant he was losing. I moved over and opened the door.

There stood my old Irish friend, Parnell McCarthy, another Chippewa lawyer, covered with snow and gently drunk. He was holding a damp brown paper bag, top and bottom, balancing it delicately, as though it contained a piece of priceless statuary. With his bulbous red nose and twinkling gray eyes he looked faintly like an erring Santa Claus. He also smelled very good.

"Ah, good afternoon, Paul," he said gravely in his wheezy voice, with its trace of Irish accent, in which the "Paul" rhymed faintly with "awl." He moved into the room with his bumpy dignified walk, talking all the while. "I come as courier, not a Greek bearing gifts. Met Miss Maida at the foot of the stairs just as I was coming up. She asked me to deliver this—this here now package to you." He studied the bag. "Haven't the foggiest notion what it might contain, that I have not." He shook the bag and listened. "Though some mild curiosity, you will observe." He blinked his eyes and shook it again, smiling craftily. "Well, now maybe I've got a dark suspicion. Or perhaps a wee intuition. There," he said, placing the bottle on the blotter in the middle of my desk, his plump hands hovering solicitously. "Always glad to be of service to an attractive young woman." He surveyed the paper bag and shook his head. "Perhaps a farewell token of esteem from one of your desolated constituents," he ventured. "And then again, perhaps a cabbage, who knows."

I grunted. "Suppose the courier takes a peek in the bag, Parn, while I go get some water and glasses. And whatever you find, uncork it." As I stood at the corner washstand in Maida's room letting the water run cold I heard old Parnell rattling the bag; his squeals of simulated surprise and his sighs of wild delight, which I suspected were not quite so simulated. "Oops! My oh my. . . . May the Lord save us. . . . 'Tis a bottle of spirits, that it is. . . . What a remarkable coincidence. . . . An' me just after cravin' a little snort. . . . What a fine gleamin' thing it is, too, an' old Parnell McCarthy just in time to have a ceremonial drop with his old friend and colleague, Paul Biegler. . . . Ah, 'tis a small world, that it is, so full of delightful surprises. . . ."

"The old boy is really wound up," I thought as I stood in Maida's doorway silently watching him. He was holding the bottle up to the light, now, humming the "Kerry Dance," executing a few steps of a grave little dance, chuckling softly to himself. At that moment I envied the man. For Parnell McCarthy possessed that rarest and most precious of human talents, a talent so elusive that it receded only the faster before those who wooed it with more gadgets and toys: the capacity for participation and joy, the enviable ability to draw vast pleasure and enjoyment from small occasions and simple things. For all the old man's show of cynicism, he possessed the sense of wonder and soaring innocence of a small boy flying a kite.

"Ready or not, Parn, here I come," I said.

I filled the jiggers, making a highball out of mine, while old Parnell stood watching the proceedings as rapt as a child on Christmas morning. He took his jigger in one hand and water glass in the other. He leaned over my desk and ceremoniously touched my glass with his, spilling never a drop. "Here's to one of the best prosecuting attorneys Iron Cliffs County ever had," he said softly. "And here's to a brilliant future for her newest criminal defense lawyer."

I shook my head in wry disagreement. "Happy New Year, Parn," I said, and we drank. Parnell, as always, took his whisky straight and followed it with a quick gulp of water. For a man suffering from chronic arthritis, and a little drunk, too, I thought the movements were incredibly swift and dexterous. But then, I reflected, the man had had years and years of practice. Practice, in fact, was Parnell's big trouble. For here was probably the smartest lawyer I ever knew, both the smartest and least successful.

"Ah," Parnell said, smacking his lips. " 'Tis a fine concoction—for peasants bent on extinction, that is."

Parnell and I had then talked of many things, past, present, and future. As he usually did when we were alone and feeling mellow,

14

he had spoken briefly and tenderly of his wife Nora, who had died during childbirth many years before. Old Judge Maitland had told me that Parnell had never been the same after he'd lost his sweet Nora. After a long silence I had asked Parnell what he thought of my prospects for taking any criminal defense work away from old Amos Crocker, the county's leading criminal lawyer. "Do you think there's a chance?" I repeated.

My question about old Crocker was not idle. Amos Crocker was a spread-eagle lawyer of the old school who lived and practiced in Iron Bay, the county seat. Ever since I was a kid he'd been stomping around in and out of court, florid and perspiring, a roarer and fighter from hell. He'd been a constant thorn in the side of my predecessors in office and by the time I became D.A. the only noticeable change in him was that he'd lost all his hair and had acquired a red wig (from Weber or Fields, I suspected) and a hearing aid—along with a reputation for professional infallibility that was legendary.

"Humph," Parnell grunted, shifting in his chair and, I hoped, pondering my question.

Old Crocker was known more familiarly to the rest of us lawyers simply as The Voice or else Willie the Weeper. Besides his booming bass voice, tears were the secret of his success; he wept his way through every trial; and for many years sniffling, lachrymose jurors had been rewarding him and his amazing tear ducts with verdicts of acquittals. He was said to set his fee by the amount of tears he shed, and by the time I had first tangled with him as a young D.A. his rate was reputed to have been $500 a pint. And he seldom contrived to weep less than half a gallon.

"Polly," Parnell had finally said, leaning forward against my desk on his forearms, "on any comparative assessment of the relative legal ability and general intelligence between you two there'd be no question but that old flannel-mouth Willie the Weeper'd never get another criminal defense." He shook his head. "And that's no great compliment to you, either. Why, that flatulent old wind bag!" he went on. "He's like an old-time Chautauqua lecturer addressin' a full tent. All he does is roar and splutter and bawl. In my considered judgment he's a dummy and a faker. He's a man of few words, yes, but he uses them over and over. When he gets through arguing to a jury, when at last the relentless torrent of his stout boiler-plate rhetoric is turned off, all—the judge, the jury, his client, opposin' counsel—all are reduced to a state of cataleptic trance. I said arguing his cases. I take that back; he never made a real jury argument in his life—all he conducts are filibusters. That's how he wins the cases he does, with that and his crocodile tears."

Parnell was warming to his subject and he stood up. "Can't you just hear him carrying on in front of a jury, Polly? Pointing with pride and viewing with alarm? You know yourself he's got only one stock jury argument in a criminal case—and he's been using that for almost forty years. Listen to him!" Parnell had an unusual gift for mimicry. He hunched up his shoulders and blew out his cheeks and in a thrice an indignant old Crocker stood before me, even, it seemed, to the flaming red wig. He pointed a scornful finger at an imaginary panel of jurors. "Ladees an' gen'emen," he thundered, "you can't guess this man into state's prison! Why, folks, I wouldn't send a yaller dawg to a dawg pound on this here evidence!" Parnell grinned and became himself again. "Surely, Polly, you recall those deathless phrases?"

I nodded glumly. "Yes, Parn, I know them all by heart."

Parnell reminded me that old Crocker had defeated me only once in the past six years. In fact the biggest thing he held against the colorful old practitioner was his colossal stupidity. "All that man really knows anything about is common arithmetic—he sets big fees an' gets 'em.

"An examination of the motives that move people in trouble to select the lawyers they do, Polly, would probably fill a five-foot shelf," Parnell continued, more slowly. "Not to mention an insane asylum. You see, the guiltier they are, the tighter their fix, the more apt they are to hire a fulminatin' old fire-eater like Crocker. Don't you see?—if they must ultimately go to prison, as some of them must dimly suspect, they want to go down with colors flyin'. They want desperately to be sent there under the best auspices, on an expensive tour conducted by a hired professional mourner, as it were, roaring and fighting on their behalf. It somehow seems to restore their waverin' self-respect, to bolster them to face the ordeal of their confinement."

"Very interesting, Parn," I said, nodding. Only Parnell could have doped it out this way.

Parnell shook his head. "In any case, Polly, I've watched this dreary business for many years, too damned many years, and it seems to me that most people in trouble tend to equate clamor and noise with astute criminal defense. It's a sad thing. But the Lord save us, it's not only confined to the law. There is a kind of intellectual smog abroad in the land. In nearly all walks of life we betray our insatiable lust for the mediocre, our terrible hunger for the third rate."

"You don't suggest I try to imitate old Crocker?" I said. "Tears and all? I can stick a bean in my ear, of course, but I doubt if I could ever find another red wig to match his. Anyway, I'm rather afraid the only person a wig deceives is the wearer himself." I felt my receding hair line. "I know, Parn," I said, "because lately I've been faced with the problem myself."

"Imitate that old fraud!" Parnell snorted. "Hell no, Polly! You shouldn't have said that, boy. You asked me an honest question and I've tried to give you an honest answer. Or did you prefer me to rub your back with this here horse liniment we're after drinkin'?"

"I'm sorry, Parn. I didn't mean it that way. Talking about liniment, let's have a drink. Here's mud in your eye." I filled his empty jigger.

Parnell stood up and leaned over and clinked my glass. "Perhaps the surest way for you to break in, boy, is to get a big case, somehow, someway, and then win it. Show the bastards how a criminal case should really be defended—with the head and the heart instead of the arms and lungs. But you got to get and win that first one. Ah, there's the rub. Everybody understands success—especially when it's shouted from the front page of the papers. In the meantime it's going to be tough, boy. But keep your chin up, Polly. And your sights, too."

Parnell gulped his drink and his water, one, two—I shuddered involuntarily—and walked resolutely to the door. "I'd like to stay and condole with you, Polly," he said, shaking my hand. He pulled on a pair of dark cotton gloves, the kind that workmen buy at corner groceries. "You know I'd like to stay and heist a few more with you and keep the vigil. But I—I've got to get home and take me a little nap. I'm attendin' church late tonight—my annual visit, you know—and perhaps it's only fittin' that such a poor communicant as I should turn up at least halfway sober. Good night, boy. Happy New Year and good luck."

I stood in my open doorway and watched him walk with dignity to the head of the stairs. He did not look back. I heard him creaking down the wooden stairs and I stood there until I heard the street door squeal shut on its frosty hinges. Then I went back and sat at my desk and poured the remainder of the bottle into a tumbler. "To Parnell Emmett Joseph McCarthy—one of the world's obscure great men," I whispered, downing my drink.

Parnell had been right. After the first of the year when Mitch Lodwick had taken over as D.A. and the county road commission trucks had transferred the last load of accumulated loot from my office to Mitch's, things turned out pretty much as he had predicted. All the important (and lucrative) criminal defenses still went to weeping, bull-roaring old Amos Crocker. There was this important difference, and one which only made matters worse—worse for me, that is: old Crocker began rather regularly to beat Mitch in his criminal cases. Not in all of them, of course, but in most. The net result, naturally, was that the old man became even more firmly entrenched as the county's leading criminal defense lawyer.

Since in the meantime I had occasionally to eat and pay Maida, I finally found myself messing around with divorces and padding discreetly into probate court to assist in whacking up decedent estates between the various taxing authorities and the surviving loved ones. Now there is nothing professionally wrong with a lawyer pursuing a divorce or probate practice, and several things that are right, but there was little or nothing in this practice that drew in the slightest upon my long training in criminal law. I found that the work was placid, moderately lucrative, and safe. But after the drama and conflict of being D.A. I also found it to be boring and dull, infinitely and wildly dull. During that time the only circuit court criminal defense that came my way I got by court appointment for an impecunious defendant, a young camp breaker with a record as long—well as long as his face and mine following his conviction. I'm afraid my defense of this case was somewhat less than brilliant. My heart wasn't in it. In fact I think I saw several more reasons why he should have been convicted than even Mitch or the jury did.

I stirred in my seat by the open office window. A cool breeze had risen—the first touch of approaching autumn—and I closed the window and groped my way to the bedroom. So bored and restless had I lately become that I had announced that I would run for Congress that fall. Things had become *that* bad. But boredom seemed as good a reason as many I had heard for anyone wanting to go to Washington, that Grand Central Station of American politicians, about which, as Woodrow Wilson had once wryly observed,

"In Washington some men grow; others merely swell." I had few illusions about the job, and none about my statesmanship, but at least in Washington, if I got there, I could occasionally shout and wave my arms and perhaps, who knew, chase the daughter of some foreign ambassador 'round and 'round the mulberry root. Or would it be those conveniently chameleon Japanese-Korean-Japanese cherry trees? Then Mitch Lodwick had announced that he would oppose me for Congress on his party ticket. But now it looked like we might first meet in the trial of a bang-up murder case. The chips were down; once again the young veteran and the aging 4F were to collide head on.

"Go to bed, Biegler," I thought, yawning prodigiously. "For tomorrow may be your first big murder case."

All jails stink and the Iron Cliffs county jail is no exception. Despite the annual—and, during his campaigns for re-election, much advertised—citations that Sheriff Battisfore had won for the cleanliness of his jail, neither he nor any other man had yet found a way to make the combination of crowded unwashed men, stale sweat and urine smell like a bunch of roses. The full force of this regrettable state of affairs smote my nostrils as the big outer jail door breathed shut behind me. I was fairly caught. During my nearly two-year vacation from crime I had forgotten how bad it was.

"Sweet violets," I murmured, crinkling my nose and trying to breathe lightly. Jailer Sulo Kangas, the Finn, was on duty. He sat nodding in a chair, his hands folded palms up in his lap, fast asleep. It occurred to me fleetingly that he had been overcome by his environment and swooned. His wispy blond hair was swept up in a Kewpie lock, and he sat under a side and front F.B.I. portrait of one of the country's ten most wanted criminals. "Hello, Sulo," I said gently, not wanting unduly to startle him. "I came to see Lieutenant Manion."

Sulo shook his head, like a man emerging from a shower stall, and slowly swam back to consciousness—"Ya, ya, ya." He rubbed his eyes and patted down his hair and heaved himself to his feet. It was really a shame to disturb him. He had only a few more years to go until his retirement and all who knew him were hoping he would make the grade. For many years he had been a good and loyal jailer, but now he was mostly a tired one. "I'd like to see Lieutenant Manion, Sulo," I tactfully repeated.

"Sure, sure, sure, Polly," Sulo said, reaching for a big brass key which hung from a metal ring as big as a basketball hoop on the wall over his roll-top desk. "You like see him in his cell?"

"Can we use the Sheriff's office for our huddle, Sulo? I see it's empty."

"Sure, sure, sure," Sulo said, opening the barred steel door separating the jail office from the cell blocks, carefully locking himself in, and then shuffling away upstairs to one of the upper tiers of cells, the brass key draped over his arm.

I lit and furiously puffed on an Italian cigar, out of self-defense, and stood idly studying the picture of one of the country's ten most notorious criminals. Hm. . . . The fugitive reminded me faintly of a former scoutmaster I'd once known, a hell of a good man, a verita-

ble pyromaniac, with two dry sticks. I leaned closer and read a portion of the fugitive's criminal record. It was a brief Who's Who of
crime, in its way as drearily predictable as the announcement of a
society wedding. Prepared at Downstate Reformatory; finished at
Sing Sing. . . . I read on. Here was indeed a fine broth of a boy.
One wondered how so young a man, one who had spent so much of
his life behind bars, could possibly have got himself into so much
trouble during his brief intervals outside. If one could only learn
to channel and direct such energy, such single-minded devotion to
mischief, one could surely power a battleship.

I wondered whether he was proud, wherever he was hiding, of his
standing among this elite of criminals, the Big Ten of crime. Ten, I
reflected, was getting to be quite a symbol of achievement through-
out the country. Let's see, there were the annual ten best-dressed
dames, the weekly ten top tunes, and, during football season, the
ten top teams. Always the superlative ten; the best, the biggest, the
flashiest, the loudest, and now, dear Lord, the crookedest. There
were also the ten most—

"Yes, sir," a quiet voice said at my side. "I'm Frederic Manion."

"Sure, sure, sure," Sulo said, mindful of his manners. "Dis is Polly
Biegler, he used to be our D.A. He's the bucko."

"Thanks, Sulo," I said gratefully. "Nice to meet you, Lieutenant."

As I looked at my man the wry thought flashed over me that despite our dearly hugged illusions of civilization and culture, all our
talk about tolerance and fair play and detached social objectivity,
most of us have but two reactions to the people who cross our lives:
we either like or dislike them on sight. It is as simple as that. And I
found myself disliking Frederic Manion on sight. Tolerance, fair
play, objectivity, all could be damned; I didn't cotton to this guy.
An aura of absorbed self-love clung to him like a cloak; he wore
his ego like a halo. He went to work at once to confirm me in my in-
tolerance.

"Hello, there," he said, swiftly taking and dropping my out-
stretched hand. "I've been waiting for you."

The faint air of annoyance and reprimand was not lost on me.
"Yes, sir," I said, gesturing toward the sheriff's office. "Suppose we
do our talking in there."

We sat facing each other in the Sheriff's office, I in a swivel chair
at the Sheriff's desk (where I'd sat through many a tense session as
prosecutor) and Lieutenant Manion at the side of the desk. He

was about to smoke a cigarette and it was an absorbing ritual to watch. The honored cigarette was selected as though each in the pack was unique; it was carefully tamped and some fugitive threads of tobacco were removed; it was deftly fitted into a long, ornately carved ivory holder; it was dry-puffed to see that the flues were opened (they evidently were); a common kitchen match was produced and suddenly struck down across the side of the Sheriff's desk (thank goodness the Sheriff knew I used a lighter); the match was permitted to burn so that all the sulphur fumes were dissipated; and then—then—the holder was clenched in two rows of strong white teeth under the little Hitlerian mustache, and lo! the man was smoking. It was something like watching a crucial place kick in the closing seconds of a tie football game. Good God, the man had made it. . . .

My prospective client sat back and regarded me calmly, with eyes that were neither black nor brown, but bafflingly dark; an expression that was neither interested nor disinterested, but aloof, aloofly detached to the point of scorn. His attitude seemed to say that now, damn it, I was his lawyer; it was up to me to carry the ball. "Mister Cool," I thought to myself. Neither of us spoke for some time and I am certain that had I not broken the silence we might have been sitting there yet (the Sheriff permitting) like two figures trapped in Madam Tussaud's waxworks.

"Where did you get that fancy holder?" I said.

He smiled faintly and glanced at the holder. "China via Burma Road, World War Two," he said. "Hand-carved ivory, Ming Dynasty, mid-sixteenth century."

"Hm. . . . Ripley never told me they had cigarettes or holders that long ago, let alone tobacco."

"They did," Frederic Manion replied, thoughtfully puffing on his Ming holder. I sensed that the discussion was closed and thought perhaps I had better talk about something more properly down my alley, something say, like the possible defenses to a charge of first degree murder.

The Lieutenant turned away, with his air of cool detachment, and looked slowly around the room. I followed his gaze. The dominant motif of the Sheriff's office, like that of the jail proper, was battleship gray: gray walls, gray ceiling, dirty gray outside bars over gray-trimmed sooty windows. I blinked. There was even a gray cement floor. What unsung genius of a paint salesman, I wondered, had thus seduced the county purchasing agent? The gray walls were mostly mercifully overlaid with a lush mural of commercial calendars variously depicting and advertising handcuffs, leg irons, straitjackets, riot guns, tear-gas bombs and similar adjuncts to institutional decorum. There were still other calendars devoted to the more gracious aspects of jail living, such as seatless toilets (warranted absolutely unbreakable), roach powders, various insecticides and delousers, and—I found my gaze lingering—a miraculous spray compound guaranteed to make any jail in the world smell like the middle of a pine forest. . . .

"Can it be possible?" I thought, wistfully skeptical. Maybe I could wire for a supply if I took this case.

Stuck against the far wall was the inevitable optical chart to test the vision of applicants for drivers' licenses, and about which some of the Sheriff's political detractors claimed darkly, I suddenly recalled, that all but the most myopic applicant would pass if he could but discern the chart itself.

"P-L-U-T-O," the Lieutenant was repeating glibly, "5, 0, 7, 8, 4 . . ." and so on down the list. I tilted my horn-rim glasses up on my forehead and was greeted by a blur. I walked over to the chart. "Once more, Lieutenant," I said. "Please. I can't believe it."

The Lieutenant again read rapidly and accurately down through the list.

"Well," I said, returning to my chair, "there goes one possible defense out the window."

The Lieutenant's dark eyes bored into mine. "What's that?" he said.

"I'm afraid," I said dryly, "that you can't very well claim that your shooting was a case of mistaken identity."

The Lieutenant grunted unsmilingly and resumed his cool inventory of the room. Here was one murder defendant, I saw, who did not like to joke about the fix he was in.

One entire gray wall, like a sort of shrine, was devoted to the great man himself, Sheriff Max Battisfore. It was all but covered with photographs, all framed under glass, of the Sheriff as a Public Man, all testifying mutely, in various brotherly attitudes, of his undying love for his fellow citizens—and voters. The Sheriff was shown shaking hands, embracing or being embraced, and occasionally both; he was depicted eating pie, catching and eating smelt, giving or receiving various awards, cups and plaques, and crowning, of course, an endless assortment of queens.

"Love, your spell is everywhere," I murmured.

"Hm . . ." the Lieutenant said. "He must own stock in Eastman Kodak."

There were other pictures of the Sheriff, many others, posed smilingly with politicians ranging from notaries to governors, all winners, and others with people whose affiliations, amidst such a glut of good fellowship, I could not immediately make out. Also prominently displayed, of course, were the framed diplomas which the Sheriff had won for the cleanliness of his jail. One diploma that caught my eye I determined I must one day steal, I simply had to have it. Some ironic wag had squashed a cockroach on the outside glass, where it remained, and from whence, embalmed in its own juice, it beckoned the beholder in a sort of macabre good-jailkeeping seal of approval. I sighed and turned to the Lieutenant.

"Before we talk about your case, Lieutenant, suppose we talk a little about you," I said. "Sort of helps a lawyer to get the feel of his case, to sense some of the things that mightn't be in the law books. I believe the psychologists sometimes call this the frame of reference."

"I wouldn't know," Lieutenant Manion said.

"We'll pass that. How old are you?"

"Thirty-six."

"How old is your wife?"

"Forty-one."

"The newspapers said thirty-five."

After a pause: "She's forty-one."

"I see. Is it your first marriage?" The conversation was going fairly like a cablegram.

"No."

"Suppose you tell me the matrimonial score and save time. Like Sergeant Friday, all I want are the facts, man."

"Is all this necessary?"

"Suppose you let me be the judge."

"It's my second."

"How did the first end?"

"Divorce."

"Did you or she get it?"

"She."

"What grounds?"

"Cruelty, eating crackers in bed, that sort of thing." He paused and

24

softly stroked his mustache. "The real grounds were she'd found another man while I was in World War Two. I did not fight the case."

"I see. In the war did you serve in the European or Pacific theaters?"

"Both."

"Action in both?"

"Plenty."

"Decorations?"

"Plenty. Anybody who doesn't cut and run gets those. They're like K-rations."

"Talking about K, how about Korea?"

"I was there."

"Action?"

"Plenty. Got there just in time for the big bugout from the Yalu."

"What's bugout? It sounds faintly lecherous to me."

"It means retreat."

"Well, whadya know?" I said. "Any Korean decorations?"

"Plenty."

Ah, I had a genuine military hero on my hands; one who was not only modest but traditionally reticent as hell, too. And wouldn't he look nice in court all decked out in his ribbons and decorations? I could already see Old Glory fluttering over the jury. "What," I went on, "what brought you 'way up in this forlorn neck of the woods?"

"Well, after the Korean cease-fire I was sent back to the States. Since then I've been shifted around to various outfits as a special instructor. That's why Laura and I got a trailer."

"Who's Laura?"

"My wife."

"And you were a special instructor in what?"

"Anti-aircraft artillery. It seems your big Lake Superior makes a nice safe place to lob shells into."

"Tell me about your wife," I said.

Again the merest flutter of the eyes: "What do you want to know?"

"Oh, things like matrimonial statistics, including present status."

"I'm her second husband. She divorced the other one."

Old Glory sagged a little. "Hm. . . . Did you know your—ah —predecessor?"

"Very well. We once served in the same outfit."

Old Glory sagged still farther. "You mean you and he were buddies?"

There was the slightest pause. "*You* might call it that."

I had received a musket ball through the heart and I saw I'd better brush up on the idiom of the modern fighting man. But to hell with it. "I see," I said. "Now suppose you tell me where your ex-buddy was when you took up with his wife." The ex-D.A. was beginning to enjoy turning the screws on Mister Cool, the anti-aircraft expert who scoffed at decorations.

"Germany. Army of occupation."

"And where were you two?"

"Georgia."

Old Glory hung limp and dead on its staff. "It made a neat arrangement, didn't it?" I said. He did not answer. "Did either of you have any children from your previous marriages?"

"No."

"Or from this one?"

"No."

"Any prospects?"

Mister Cool fell silent.

"Any prospects?" I repeated.

Savagely: "Not unless that dirty bastard Quill knocked her up!"

Here was a sudden revealing step upon dangerous ground, very dangerous ground. In a touchy case like this there were legal land mines lying all over, and I wasn't quite ready to chance exploding them. So I abruptly veered away.

"What kind of a weapon did you use to dispatch Quill?"

The dark eyes gleamed. "A German lüger. War souvenir, World War Two."

"Let's see, that's a semi-automatic pistol, fairly equivalent to our .38?" Having seen one once, I felt something like Hanson Baldwin and I tried to keep the note of pride out of my voice.

His answer practically made us old battle-scarred buddies. "Yes," he replied.

"The cops have it now, of course?"

"Yes. I gave it to the state police."

"Tell me where you got this pistol. Where and how? It may possibly be important."

"Is it necessary?"

"Look, friend," I said, "suppose you tend to your military knitting and I'll tend to the department of legal B.S."

Lieutenant Manion flushed and sat up straight. The dark eyes clouded and gazed even farther away. "Well," he began slowly, "we were advancing in Germany, the spring before the end of the European war. It was dusk and I was leading some men out on night patrol. About twelve of us. The sector had been badly shelled and there was very little cover. Intelligence had told us the Germans were in full retreat, that the way was clear."

"Go on," I said, listening carefully, mentally appraising the possible effect of all this on a civilian jury.

"Field intelligence was wrong," he went on. "Suddenly there was a burst of small-arms fire. Three of my men fell, two of them killed outright, I learned later. The third died back at base."

"Go on," I said.

"All of us hit the ground and stayed there. As it grew darker I took a quick look and saw a fleeting flash of gray, a gray sleeve, disappearing behind a stub of ruined chimney."

"What'd you do?" I said.

"We could have rushed the place, but I didn't know then how many there were. One thing was clear: if this wasn't a lone sniper it was probably either them or us. I couldn't communicate with my men, so I crawled on my belly, making a wide circle, and finally got behind the chimney."

"A wide-end crawl," I observed.

"It was a lone sniper. I crawled closer to get within safe pistol range—and then I let him have it."

"In the back, from behind?" I said, dismayed, thinking of Old Glory, the playing fields of Eton, the Boy Scout oath.

He laughed briefly: his first sign of mirth. "It was either him or me. He'd just shot three of my men. I didn't stop to pose him."

"Go on," I said.

"When I got up to him I found he was an old lieutenant, gray, tattered, and already wounded. He must have been around sixty. His left arm was in a dirty sling. He had a patch over one eye. The other eye glared at me like a wolf in a trap. In fact he looked like a battered old timber wolf. He was still clutching the lüger pistol. He tried to raise it. He'd rigged up a rifle stock to it. He swore at me in German."

"What happened?"

27

"I was going to let him have some more—and then he died. Here was a good soldier. So I took his pistol as a souvenir." Frederic Manion paused and fiddled a bit with the Ming holder. "That's how I got the lüger."

Old Glory was rippling and standing out straight. But I'd seen many duck hunters generate more excitement telling about their misses. "Excuse me," I said, rising. "I'll be back shortly."

"Yes," Mister Cool murmured, solemn as an owl, turning his attention to the Ming holder.

Outside I reflected that whatever else they were or weren't, Lieutenant Manion and the old German sniper shared one thing: they were both good soldiers, dedicated disciples of the philosophy of "Ours is not to reason why. . . ." Yes, somehow, someway, at the trial I'd have to try to get that lovely lüger story in. But how could I do it? And what was I thinking! Polly Biegler was the man, remember, who wasn't going to take this case. Were aging ex-D.A.'s as helpless as old fire horses? Did they begin to snort and prance and paw at their mangers whenever they heard the clang of the fire bell?

I used Sulo's phone to call my office. Sleeping Sulo didn't even stir in his chair. "Maida," I said, "it's kind of looking like we might be in this damned Manion murder case."

"Good, good," Maida said. "But what's he going to pay you with? Purple Hearts? Didn't you know professional soldiers never have a dime? Remember, I was once married to one."

I gulped and swallowed like a kid caught raiding a cooky jar. "I don't know yet. We—we haven't discussed it. All I'm after now are the facts, ma'am. You're so coldly commercial, Maida."

"Well, you'd *better* discuss your fee, you'd better get commercial. I've just been going over your check book."

"Sh. . . . Not over the phone, Maida. I'm supposed to be the successful, well-heeled defense lawyer. I'm loaded, see, and I only take cases out of my sheer love for an oppressed Humanity. My heart bleedeth for the under dog. I'm just an incorrigible old Liberal who toils solely for blind Justice and the battered Bill of Rights."

"You're also damned near broke. Tell me, what'd you do with the fee in the King estate, help salt a uranium mine?"

"I just bought a few necessaries."

"What necessaries?" Maida persisted.

"Only a little booze and a Burberry jacket. My old one's in tatters. And a nice little surprise for your birthday. Look, I called to tell you I won't be back this afternoon and you lecture me how broke we are. Better cancel any appointments. I'll finish up on the mail tomorrow."

"There are no appointments," Maida said. "People are beginning to think you've migrated to the woods. And I'm beginning to think maybe they're right. Parnell McCarthy was in, there's an air-mail special from your mother—and that's all."

"What'd Parn want?"

"He had his usual Monday morning sickness. Probably wanted money—what else does he ever want? Will you be back this afternoon?"

"No, I'll work here and then I'm going fishing tonight."

"Fishing, fishing, fishing," Maida said. "You just had a long weekend of it. Look, Boss, are you mad at the trout?"

"I'm afraid it's a blood feud, Maida. For years I caught them and now they've caught me. I'm getting to hate 'em worse than women. And there'll be damn little time for fishing once I dive into this case—if I take it. If you've nothing better to do but brood over my check book you can leave early."

"Anything to do!" Maida snorted. "I'm on the latest Mickey Spillane."

"Good girl. Always improving the mind, eh, Maida? But I thought you'd waded through the Spillane abattoirs long ago."

"I re-read him every year, faithfully, like some people take a retreat. I find him so consoling."

"Not retreat, Maida," I said. "The magic word is bugout."

"*What did you say?*"

"Bugout," I said softly. "And good-by."

That's the way it is between Maida and me.

I hung up the phone and stole a look at Sulo, who'd begun gently to snore. I speculated that some day some Good Samaritan would tiptoe in and take down the big brass key and empty the jail, stink and all. I also wondered what Lieutenant Manion might be tempted to do if he knew that the only person who stood between him and freedom was fast asleep. I turned to rejoin him and found him standing in the Sheriff's open office door. "Don't worry," he said, smiling slightly. "I'm not going to bolt. It wouldn't help and anyway it might be fun to wait and see what happens."

"Ya, ya, ya," Sulo muttered, rubbing his eyes. "You through already, Polly?"

chapter 4

We were back at the Sheriff's desk. It was time to get down to cases. "Last night after I talked with your wife on the phone I read the newspaper account in your case," I said. "Have you?"

"Yes, naturally."

"Is it substantially correct?"

"Yes."

"Touching only the high spots now, the newspaper states that you walked into Barney Quill's bar at Thunder Bay about forty-five minutes past midnight last Friday night—really early Saturday—and shot him five times; that you drove in your car back to your house trailer in the Thunder Bay tourist park; that you awakened the deputized caretaker of the park and told him you had just shot Quill; that he then left to summon the state police from Iron Bay; and that you waited in your trailer until the officers arrived. Is that correct?"

"Yes."

"The paper further states that the officers then took you into custody and brought you in to this jail; that your wife accompanied you; and that your wife told the officers that earlier that evening Barney Quill had raped her in the woods and then later beat her up at the entrance gate of the tourist park. Correct?"

"Yes."

"That the jail physician was called, who took a vaginal smear; that this smear was later reported by him negative for sperm; that he gave out his opinion that she had not been raped; and that your wife volunteered to take a polygraph or lie-detector test as to the truth of her story; that such a test was given but the results are undisclosed. Right?"

"Yes."

"The newspaper also states that you have refused to amplify your original oral statement to the officers that you shot Barney Quill. Right?"

"Yes."

"You have not made or signed any other statement to the police?"

"No."

"All right. So far so good. Now let's talk about some things that may or may not have been in the newspaper. Did you see Barney Quill rape your wife?"

For the first time Mr. Cool's eyes showed some reaction; they seemed to move lidlessly, swiftly, like a serpent's—more of a quick glittering flutter than a blink. "No," he said softly.

"Did you see him beat her up at the gate?"

"No."

"Or hear her shout, as she claimed?"

"No. . . . Well I did seem to hear shouting, as though in my dreams. Anyway I met her at the trailer door."

The old ex-D.A. was hitting his stride. "So the first time you learned of the attacks on your wife by Barney was when *she* told you about them?"

"Yes."

"What did you do then?" I'd force him to say something more than yes or no.

"I took care of her, of course. She was in terrible shape. One eye was nearly closed, both eyes and her face were badly bruised, also her arms; her skirt was torn, her panties were missing, and—and—" He paused and again there was the glitter of a coiled serpent in his eyes.

"Go on," I said.

"And this—this man left his—his marks on her thighs." This was more hissed than spoken.

"What, if anything, did you do with these—ah—marks?"

"I wiped them off her body and burned the evidence."

"Right then and there?"

"Immediately."

I paused and examined my nails. Still examining them, I said, "Did it not occur to you that this would have been pretty conclusive evidence that the man had had sexual intercourse with her?"

His dark eyes seemed to wall up and cloud over; he sipped his small mustache that I was learning to love so well; and then he went into the ritual of loading his Ming holder.

"Did it?" I repeated.

"Did it what?" he said coolly.

It was no time for evasions. "Did it not occur to you that *you* were destroying the best evidence that Quill had laid her?"

"I never thought of that," he blurted, almost flinging the Ming holder from him. "I—I couldn't stand the sight—I—I couldn't get rid of it fast enough."

"Did this happen before or after you shot Barney Quill?"

"Before."

"Hm. . . . How long did you remain with your wife before you went to the hotel bar?"

"I don't remember."

"I think it is important, and I suggest you try."

After a pause. "Maybe an hour."

"Maybe more?"

"Maybe."

"Maybe less?"

"Maybe."

I paused and lit a cigar. I took my time. I had reached a point where a few wrong answers to a few right questions would leave me with a client—if I took his case—whose cause was legally defenseless. Either I stopped now and begged off and let some other lawyer worry over it or I asked him the few fatal questions and let him hang himself. Or else, like any smart lawyer, I went into the Lecture. I studied my man, who sat as inscrutable as an Arab, delicately fingering his Ming holder, daintily sipping his dark mustache. He apparently did not realize how close I had him to admitting that he was guilty of first degree murder, that is, that he "feloniously, wilfully and of his malice aforethought did kill and murder one Barney Quill." The man was a sitting duck.

It was tempting for me to ask the fatal question, sorely tempting for me to let this cool bastard boil in the oil of his own lardy ego. Why should I barter my years of experience to try to save this Mister Cool? Why, oh why, indeed? It was a nice question and I sat there pondering it. Was it because I saw a chance to beat this case, and at the same time beat Mitch Lodwick? Hm. . . . Or because it was my big chance to win a big tough case and finally knock that garrulous old fraud of an Amos Crocker from his pedestal as the leading criminal defense lawyer of the county, if not the Peninsula? Hm. . . . Was it because I was running for Congress against Mitch and this was my opportunity not only to beat him, but to demonstrate by dramatic contrast our relative capabilities? More dimly, but there: was it because some character had once made a drunken pass at my older sister, Gail, when she was in high school, years before, and my father Oliver had beaten him within an inch of his life and then dared the authorities to arrest him—a dare they didn't take? Or was it because a frustrated 4F could now bask in the reflected glory of defending a genuine military hero, a man who had fought in two bitter wars? Was it because of all of these things? And what did any of this have to do with the guilt or innocence of Frederic Manion? Or this elusive thing called Justice?

At this point Sulo Kangas poked his head in the door. "Noontime," he said. "Lunch he's served." As I sat pondering how Sulo had ever come awake, whether he had set an alarm clock, he gave me a look of dawning inspiration and said: "You like eat with us, Polly?" He beamed, the genial host. "You very welcome."

I recoiled inwardly with horror at the thought. Sheriff Battisfore's food would doubtless sustain life but, I suspected, contribute little or nothing to its sublimity. I glanced at my watch and swiftly arose.

"Sorry, Sulo," I lied stoically. "Got a luncheon date downtown." I glanced at my prospective client and found he was smiling. The man was actually smiling.

"Well done, Counselor," he murmured after Sulo had retired. "Hope you enjoy your lunch."

"Thanks," I said. "Same to you. See you at two."

I drove to the Iron Bay Club and had a leisurely lunch. After lunch I played Billy Webb at cribbage and won over thirteen dollars. I was going hot and skunked him twice. By two I was back at the jail and was pleased to find that Sheriff Battisfore was still away. Perhaps I still wouldn't have to go up in the cell blocks to see my man.

"Do you mind if we use the Sheriff's office again, Sulo?" I inquired sweetly. I was afraid I had offended him by failing to stay for lunch.

"Sure, sure, sure, Polly," Sulo replied, ever good-natured. "Sheriff he still be out on patrol."

I waited for Sulo to fetch Lieutenant Manion down from his cell. I reflected that while sheriffs rolled up more patrol mileage (and consequent mileage fees) than almost all other species of flatfoots and cops put together, that during their wanderings they were, as a class, not unlike the three wise monkeys: they heard no evil, spoke no evil, and resolutely saw no evil. I tried to recall the occasions when any sheriff I had ever known or heard about (but one) had ever regularly made any arrests on his very own. The effort was not fruitful. Though sheriffs and their men relentlessly scoured the highways and byways, day and night, lo! no drunk drivers seemed ever to cross their paths, speeders were totally nonexistent, and nobody, but nobody, ever ran a stop sign or a red light. All the public had to do to abolish crime, apparently, was to ignore it—at least crime seemed to flee underground whenever the sheriff was around. It was little short of miraculous. It was also part of the dreary system; a sheriff couldn't possibly change it if he would—that is, and still stay in office.

Old Parnell McCarthy had hit the nail on the head. "How," he once asked me, "how in the name of the blessed saints can you expect a man to turn around and arrest the very people who elect him and keep him in office? It's contrary to human nature and our rare 'good' sheriffs are political freaks whose lot is swift and total political oblivion. We don't *want* good sheriffs. How could we when the only qualification we ask for in a sheriff is that he be twenty-one?" Parnell had paused and rolled his eyes. "And, merciful Heaven, we get what we ask for, that we richly do—they're invariably twenty-one. . . ."

"Hello, there," my man said. "Did you have a good lunch?"

"Look, Manion," I said, suddenly blowing a small gasket, "my name isn't There—it happens to be Biegler." If I was going to represent this aloof bastard I was certainly not going to have him calling me "There."

Coolly: "Excuse me, Mr. Biegler. Did you have a good lunch this noon?"

"Excellent," I said. "And you, Lieutenant Manion?"

"I was just beginning to forget it." He closed his eyes and wrinkled his nose. "Maybe I shouldn't have mentioned it."

" 'Courage, Camille! This pain, too, must pass away,' " I quoted abstractedly. "Sit down," I went on. "I've been thinking about your case during the noon hour."

"That's good," the Lieutenant said. "What's the verdict?"

"Sit down," I repeated, "and listen carefully. Better break out your Ming holder. This is it."

"Yes, sir," said Lieutenant Manion, obediently sitting down and producing the Ming holder. His lawyer was making ready to deliver the Lecture.

And what is the Lecture?

The Lecture is an ancient device that lawyers use to coach their clients so that the client won't quite know he has been coached and his lawyer can still preserve the face-saving illusion that he hasn't done any coaching. For coaching clients, like robbing them, is not only frowned upon, it is downright unethical and bad, very bad. Hence the Lecture, an artful device as old as the law itself, and one used constantly by some of the nicest and most ethical lawyers in the land. "Who, me? I didn't tell him what to say," the lawyer can later comfort himself. "I merely explained the law, see." It is a good practice to scowl and shrug here and add virtuously: "That's my duty, isn't it?"

Verily, the question, like expert lecturing, is unchallengeable.

I was ready to do my duty by my client and he sat regarding me quietly, watchfully, as I lit a new cigar.

"As I told you," I began, "I've been thinking about your case during the noon hour."

"Yes," he replied. "You mentioned that."

"So I did, so I did," I said. "Now I realize there are many questions still to be asked, facts to be discussed," I went on. "And I am not prejudging your case." I paused to discharge the opening salvo of the Lecture. "But as things presently stand I must advise you that in my opinion you have not yet disclosed to me a *legal* defense to this charge of murder."

I again paused to let this sink in. It is a necessary condition to the successful lecture. My man blinked a little and touched both sides of his mustache lightly with the tip of his tongue. "Could it be you are advising me to plead guilty?" he said, smiling ever so slightly.

"I may eventually," I said, "but I didn't quite say that. I merely want at this time for you to have the trained reaction of a man who—" I paused "—who is not without experience in cases of this kind." I was getting a little overwhelmed by the sheer beauty of my own modesty and I fought the impulse to flutter my eyelashes.

"Yes, but how about that bastard Quill raping my wife?" my man said quietly. "How about the 'unwritten law'?"

I had been waiting for that one. "There is no such thing as the 'unwritten law' in Anglo-American jurisprudence," I said, a little pontifically. "It is merely another one of those dearly hugged folk-myths that people regularly die for, like the notion that raw rhubarb is good for the clap or that all chorus girls lay or that night air is bad. In fact many a man who has depended on the myth of the 'unwritten law' has instead depended from a rope." I paused, rather relishing the phrase, and resolved to remember it.

"But there is no capital punishment in Michigan, is there?" the Lieutenant said. My man had evidently been doing some thinking on his own during the noon recess.

"The rope was a figure of speech," I said. "We lawyers are great fellows for figures of speech. But to answer your question: except for treason—and of that there's been no recorded case—you are correct: there is no capital punishment in Michigan." I paused and went on. "But I would offhand guess, Lieutenant, that if you were convicted of this charge you might prefer that there were."

I had sunk the harpoon pretty far. Lieutenant Manion stared down at his strong delicate hands a moment and then at me. "You've made a pretty shrewd guess," he answered slowly. He looked about the bleak, gray-painted room and, stout man, took a deep breath. "I'd sooner die than spend my days in a place like this," he said.

"It wouldn't be quite like this," I said. "Worse, much worse. This is a mere way station to Hell."

"Yes," he said. "Prison would be worse."

"Have we disposed of the 'unwritten law'?" I said.

"Perhaps," he said. "But unwritten law or no, doesn't a man have a legal right to kill a man who has raped his wife? Isn't that the *written* law, then?"

"No, only to prevent it, or if he has caught him at it, or, finally, to prevent his escape." We were treading dangerous ground again and I spoke rapidly to prevent any interruption. "In fact, Lieutenant, for all the elaborate hemorrhage of words in the law books about the legal defenses to murder there are only about three basic defenses: one, that it didn't happen but was instead a suicide or accident or what not; two, that whether it happened or not you didn't do it, such as alibi, mistaken identity and so forth; and three, that even if it happened and you did it, your action was legally justified or excusable." I paused to see how my student was doing.

The Lieutenant grew thoughtful. "Where do I fit in that rosy picture?" he responded nicely.

"I can tell you better where you don't fit," I went on. "Since a whole barroom full of people saw you shoot down Barney Quill in apparent cold blood, you scarcely fit in the first two classes of defenses. I'm afraid we needn't waste time on those." I paused. "If you fit anywhere it's got to be in the third. So we'd better bear down on that."

"You mean," Lieutenant Manion said, "that my only possible defense in this case is to find some justification or excuse?"

My lecture was proceeding nicely according to schedule. "You're learning rapidly," I said, nodding approvingly. "Merely add *legal* justification or excuse and I'll mark you an A."

"And you say that a man is not justified in killing a man who has just raped and beat up his wife?"

"Morally, perhaps, but not legally. Not after it's all over, as it was here." I paused, wondering why I didn't go to Detroit and lecture in night school. That way, too, I would be close enough to go see all my old school's home football games. "Hail to the victors valiant. . . ." "You see, Lieutenant," I went on, "it's not the *act* of killing a man that makes it murder; it is the circumstances, the time, and the state of mind or purpose which induced the act." I paused, and could almost hear my old Crimes professor, J. B. "Jabby" White, droning this out in law school nearly twenty years before. It was amazing how the old stuff stuck.

The Lieutenant's eyes narrowed and flickered ever so little. "Maybe," he began, and cleared his throat. "On second thought, maybe I *did* catch Quill in the act. I've never precisely told the police one way or the other." His eyes regarded me quietly, steadily. This man, I saw, was not only an apt student of the Lecture; like most people (including lawyers) he indubitably possessed a heart full of larceny. He was also, perhaps instinctively, trying to turn the Lecture on his lawyer. "I've never really told them," he concluded.

A lawyer in the midst of his Lecture is apt to cling to the slenderest reed to bolster his wavering virtue. "But you've told *me*," I said, pausing complacently, swollen with rectitude, grateful for the swift surge of virtue he'd afforded me. "And anyway," I went on, "you would have had to dispatch him then, not, as you've already admitted, an hour or so later. The catching and killing must combine. And that's true even if you'd actually caught him at it—which you didn't. I've just now told you that *time* is one of the factors in determining whether a homicide is a murder or not. Here it's a big one. Don't you see?—in your case *time* is the rub; it's the elapsed *time* between the rape and the killing that permits the People to bear down and argue that your shooting of Barney Quill was a deliberate, malicious and premeditated act. And that, my friend, is no more than they've charged you with."

Stoically: "Are you telling me to plead guilty?"

"Look, we've been over that. When I'm ready to advise you to cop out you'll know it. Right now I want you to realize what you're up against, man."

The Lieutenant blinked his eyes thoughtfully. "I'm busy realizing," he said.

"Try to look at it this way, Lieutenant," I went on, warmed to my lecture. "Just as murder itself is one of the most elemental and primitive of crimes, so also the law of murder is, for all the torrent of words written about it, still pretty elemental and primitive in its basic concepts. The human tribe learned early that indiscriminate killing was not only poor for tribal decorum and well-being but threatened its very survival and was therefore bad in itself. So murder became taboo. Are you still with me?"

"Go on."

"At the same time it was seen that there were occasions when a killing might nevertheless still be justified. Stated most baldly it all pretty much boiled down to this: Thou shalt not kill—except to save yourself, your property, or your loved ones. That simple statement still embraces by far most of the modern defenses to murder. If a man tries to take my life or my wife or my cow I may kill him to prevent it. But if I chase him off or, more like your situation, if he should steal my wife or my cow while I am away fishing (or sleeping in my trailer) I must pursue other tribal remedies when I discover it. I must do so because I did not catch him at it, the damage is done, the danger is past, the culprit may be dealt with later and at leisure.

"You will observe that this catching-him-at-it business involves the important factor of time, of time sequence, that I just mentioned. Even the 'unwritten law' defense you brought up usually involves the notion of a cuckolded husband discovering his wife in the nuptial bed with the iceman. Or perhaps these days it's the deep-freeze man. In any case nearly all of these defense-of-property-and-person murder defenses—'self-help' defenses they may be called—involve the idea of the person who is killed being caught in the act, red-handed, before there is *time* for the killer to call for help or complain to the tribal elders—the police in our times. Is it seeping through?"

The Lieutenant nodded glumly.

"The notion that one might later, after the fact, go kill the cow or wife stealer was rejected by most early tribal men as it is still widely rejected today. It was and is rejected because the 'defending' killer has had time to cool off, the thing is over and done, the emergency no longer exists, the offender can be punished at leisure and in an orderly way, and, finally, probably because such a defense is less susceptible of unbiased confirmation and thus opens the door to being invented. Anyway, one may lawfully kill another to save his wife or his cow or his own life but not to punish the doer after it is all over. Now my anthropology may possibly be a little haywire but not my law. The law says that the business of punishment must be left solely to it, which is the People.

"Applying all this to your own situation, Lieutenant, whatever happened to your wife was over and done when you found it out. You could not save her; she'd had it, her danger was past; and if Barney Quill raped her he could have been dealt with by due process of law. It so happens that rape and murder both carry life sentences in this state, but not death. By your action you usurped the law and imposed the death penalty on Barney Quill. Society, the tribe, now seeks to punish you for breaking one of its most ancient and basic taboos."

We sat silently, the Lieutenant again sipping his mustache. He looked a little morose. "But can't the jury let me go, whatever the damned law is?" he asked.

"Of course it can," I said. "And juries often do. But that's not because of a legal defense but rather despite the lack of one. Juries, in common with women drivers, are apt to do the damnedest things. Gambling on what a jury will do is like playing the horses. The notorious undependability of juries, the chance involved, is one of the absorbing features of the law. That's what makes the practice of law, like prostitution, one of the last of the unpredictable professions —both employ the seductive arts, both try to display their wares to the best advantage, and both must pretend enthusiastically to woo total strangers. And that's why most successful trial lawyers are helpless showmen; that's why they are about nine-tenths ham actor and one-tenth lawyer. But as things now stand in your case, all the *law* would be against you. The judge would be virtually forced to instruct the jury to convict you. Don't you see? A jury would find it tough to let you go; they'd have to really work at it. Legally your situation presents a classic one of premeditated murder."

Quietly: "You don't want to take my case, then?"

"Not quite so fast. I'm not ready to make that decision. Look, in a murder case the jury has only a few narrow choices. Among them, it *might* let you go. It *might* also up and convict you. A judge trying you without a jury would surely have to, as I have said. Now do you want to go into court with the dice loaded? With all the law and instructions stacked against you?" I paused to deliver my clincher. "Well, whether you're willing to do so, I'm not. I will either find a sound and plausible legal defense in your case or else advise you to cop out." I paused thoughtfully. "Then there's one other possible 'or else.'"

"Or else what?"

A chastening hint, a light play on the client's fear that the lawyer of his choice might walk out on him is also sound strategy during the Lecture. It tends to keep the subject both alert and appropriately humble. "Or else, Lieutenant, you can find yourself another lawyer," I said, waiting for him to squirm.

"Like who?" the Lieutenant inquired coolly and without squirming. "Who do you recommend?"

Things weren't proceeding according to plan. But I couldn't back down or display weakness now. If this cool bastard wanted someone like roaring old Crocker he could damn well have him. "Why, we have a splendid old ham-acting lawyer in this county," I replied. "He's all ham—real boneless country-cured ham. He's also the Peninsula's expert on unwritten law." I could have added, but charitably didn't, that this last was largely so because I'd never known him to crack a law book. "I might even intercede for you with him," I said.

"You mean Amos Crocker?" he said calmly.

I lifted my eyebrows in surprise. "Maybe," I parried. "How come you know about Crocker?"

"We tried to get him," Mister Cool replied. "Couldn't because he'd broken his leg."

"Leg?" I said. "Old Crocker broke his leg? I didn't know." I felt a sudden wave of pity for the windy fulminating old fraud. Beside Parnell McCarthy he was about the last of the old-time colorful gallus-snapping practitioners left in the county. The rest of us were getting to be a fine, colorless, soft-shoe breed, something like a cross between a claims adjuster and an ulcerated public accountant. "When did all this happen?"

"The very night I shot Quill," the Lieutenant said. "Fell climbing out of his tub, his housekeeper told my wife over the phone. Is in the hospital with his leg in traction. Won't be up and around for several months." The Lieutenant looked around the room and sniffed slightly. "That's a trifle too long to wait around in this place. If I've got to go to prison I want to get on with it."

"Hm," I said thoughtfully. I felt curiously chastened and deflated. Here was a client, I saw, who possessed a pretty good lecture style of his own. I found myself fretfully hoping that I was at least the *second* choice. The thought gnawed at me. "I hope I was the second choice?" I said.

"You were," the Lieutenant replied quietly. "By the way, what's this 'cop out' mean?"

The Lieutenant had not only delivered a swift little lecture of his own; he'd also adroitly got me back on my own.

"Lieutenant, I'm charmed," I said, carrying on. "Just as bugout means retreat, so cop out means pretty much the same thing: to plead guilty, toss in the sponge, grab at a straw, confess to the cops, or—as the old English judges so quaintly put it—throw oneself upon the country."

It was rather a big mouthful and the Lieutenant thoughtfully chewed on it. "Hm. . . . You mean you simply don't want to take a chance on the 'unwritten law'?"

I stared up at the ceiling, pursing my lips. "You can put it that way if you want. Yes, that's fair enough. I'm a lawyer, not a juggler or a hypnotist nor even a magician or boy orator. When I undertake to defend a man before a jury I want to have a fighting *legal* chance to acquit him. That includes having a decent chance to move for a new trial or successfully appeal. Maybe you were morally entitled to plug Barney Quill. I'll even concede it. But in court I prefer to leave the moral judgments to the angels. I doubtless possess my fair share of ham, like most lawyers, but I do not want to go into court and depend simply upon the charity or stupidity or state of the liver of twelve jurors." I paused. With old Crocker now safely out of the picture I could perhaps afford to bear down even harder. "What's more, I don't intend to," I said. "Have I made myself clear?"

"I'm afraid you have, Counselor."

"And, since you still seem to hug the 'unwritten law,' there's one more thing. There's the important matter of saving face. We complacent palefaces of the West like to think that this business of saving face is a sin, a sort of half-juvenile and half-inscrutable *mystique* confined solely to the Orient." I paused. "That's a lot of —a lot of unmitigated—"

"Horseshit," Lieutenant Manion said, as solemn as an owl.

"Precisely," I said. "Spoken like a true soldier and a gentleman, Lieutenant. And thanks. But getting back to face. . . . All of us, everywhere, all of the time, spend our waking hours saving face. This case itself is riddled with face. After all, one of the mute unspoken reasons you are being prosecuted is to save face, community face. The biggest reason I hesitate to take your case, as things now stand, is my fear of losing it. That is merely a negative form of advance face-saving. Face, face, face. Everybody has to save face, and, whether they have to or not, everyone tries to; it's one of the basic compulsions of men." I paused. "Are you following me?"

"Yes. It's most interesting," he answered gravely. I glanced at him keenly. It was rather hard at times, I saw, to tell when this character was being sarcastic.

"Thanks," I said. "That brings me to my sixty-four-dollar point. Even jurors have to save face. Get this now. The jury in your case might simply be dying to let you go on your own story, or because they have fallen for your wife, or have learned to hate Barney Quill's guts, or all of these things and more. But if the judge—who's got nice big legal face to save, too—must under the law virtually tell the jurors to convict you, as I think he must now surely do, then the only way they can possibly let you go is by flying in the face of the judge's instructions—that is, by losing, not saving face. Don't you see? You and I would be in there asking twelve citizens, twelve total strangers, to publicly lose their precious face to save yours. It's asking a lot and I hope you don't have to risk it."

Lieutenant Manion produced the Ming holder and studied it

carefully, as though for the first time. "What do you recommend then?" he said.

It was a good question. "I don't know yet. So far I've been trying to impress you with the importance, the naked necessity, of our finding a valid legal defense, if one exists, in addition to the 'unwritten law' you so dearly want to cling to. Put it this way: what Barney Quill might have done to your wife before you killed him may present a favorable condition, an equitable climate, to a possible jury acquittal. But alone it simply isn't enough." I paused. "Not enough for Paul Biegler, anyway."

"You mean you want to find a way to give the jurors some decently plausible legal peg to hang their verdict on so that they might let me go—and still save face?"

My man was responding beautifully to the lecture. "Precisely," I said, adding hastily: "Whether you have such a defense of course remains to be seen. But I hope, Lieutenant, I have shown you how vital it is to find one if it exists."

"I think you have, Counselor," he said slowly. "I rather think now you really have." He paused. "Tell me, tell me more about this justification or excuse business. Excuse me," he added, smiling faintly, "I mean *legal* justification or excuse."

"First I got to go phone my office," I said, arising. "That'll also give me a chance for some solitary skull practice. It's been quite a while since I've had to brush up on my murder."

I was back with my man and ready to go. The signs were good: for the first time he was smoking *without* the Ming holder. "We will now explore the absorbing subject of legal justification or excuse," I said.

"You may fire when ready, Gridley," the Lieutenant said.

I looked hopefully at the man. Was it barely possible that he possessed a rudimentary sense of humor? "Well, take self-defense," I began. "That's the classic example of justifiable homicide. On the basis of what I've so far heard and read about your case I do not think we need pause too long over that. Do you?"

"Perhaps not," Lieutenant Manion conceded. "We'll pass it for now."

"Let's," I said dryly. "Then there's the defense of habitation, defense of property, and the defense of relatives or friends. Now there are more ramifications to these defenses than a dog has fleas, but we won't explore them now. I've already told you at length why I don't think you can invoke the possible defense of your wife. When you shot Quill her need for defense had passed. It's as simple as that."

"Go on," Lieutenant Manion said, frowning.

"Then there's the defense of a homicide committed to prevent a felony—say you're being robbed—; to prevent the escape of the felon—suppose he's getting away with your wallet—; or to arrest a felon—you've caught up with him and he's either trying to get away or has actually escaped."

At this point I paused and blinked thoughtfully. An idea no bigger than a pea rattled faintly at the back door of my mind. Let's see. . . . Wouldn't it be true that if Barney Quill actually raped Laura Manion *he* would be a felon at large at the time he was shot? The pea kept faintly rattling. But so what, so what? "Hm. . . ." I said. It would bear pondering.

The Lieutenant's eyes gleamed and bored into mine. "Who—what do you see?" he said. It was becoming increasingly clear that this soldier was no dummy.

"Nothing," I lied glibly. "Not a thing." The student was getting ahead of the lecturer and that would never do. And wherever my idea might drop into the ultimate defense picture, I sensed that now was not the time to try to fit it. "I was just thinking," I concluded.

"Yes," Lieutenant Manion said. "You were just thinking." He

smiled faintly. "Go on, then; what are some of the other legal justifications or excuses?"

"Then there's the tricky and dubious defense of intoxication. Personally I've never seen it succeed. But since you were not drunk when you shot Quill we shall mercifully not dwell on that. Or were you?"

"I was cold sober. Please go on."

"Then finally there's the defense of insanity." I paused and spoke abruptly, airily: "Well, that just about winds it up." I arose as though making ready to leave.

"Tell me more."

"There is no more." I slowly paced up and down the room.

"I mean about this insanity."

"Oh, insanity," I said, elaborately surprised. It was like luring a trained seal with a herring. "Well, insanity, where proven, is a complete defense to murder. It does not legally justify the killing, like self-defense, say, but rather excuses it." The lecturer was hitting his stride. He was also on the home stretch. "Our law requires that a punishable killing—in fact, any crime—must be committed by a sapient human being, one capable, as the law insists, of distinguishing between right and wrong. If a man is insane, legally insane, the act of homicide may still be murder but the law excuses the perpetrator."

Lieutenant Manion was sitting erect now, very still and erect. "I see—and this—this perpetrator, what happens to him if he should—should be excused?"

"Under Michigan law—like that of many other states—if he is acquitted of murder on the grounds of insanity it is provided that he must be sent to a hospital for the criminally insane until he is pronounced sane." I drummed my fingers on the Sheriff's desk and glanced at my watch, the picture of a man eager to be gone.

My man was baying along the scent now. "How long does it take to get him out of there?"

"Out of where?" I asked innocently.

"Out of this insane hospital!"

"Oh, you mean where a man claims he was insane at the time of the offense but is sane at the time of the trial and his possible acquittal?"

"Exactly."

"I don't know," I said, stroking my chin. "Months, maybe a

year. It really takes a bit of doing. Being D.A. so long I've never really had to study that phase of it. I got them in there; it was somebody else's problem to spring them. And I didn't dream this defense might come up in your case."

My naïvete was somewhat excessive; it had been obvious to me from merely reading the newspaper the night before that insanity was the best, if not the only, legal defense the man had. And here I'd just slammed shut every other escape hatch and told him this was the last. Only a cretin could have missed it, and I was rapidly learning that Lieutenant Manion was no cretin.

"Tell me more," Lieutenant Manion said quietly.

"I may add that the law that requires persons acquitted on the grounds of insanity to be sent away is designed to discourage phony pleas of insanity in criminal cases."

"Yes?"

"So the man who successfully invokes the defense of insanity is taking a calculated risk, like the time you took the chance that the old German lieutenant was alone behind his ruined chimney."

I paused and knocked out my pipe. The Lecture was about over. The rest was up to the student. The Lieutenant looked out the window. He studied his Ming holder. I sat very still. Then he looked at me. "Maybe," he said, "maybe I was insane."

Very casually: "Maybe you were insane when?" I said. "When you shot the German lieutenant?"

"You know what I mean. When I shot Barney Quill."

Thoughtfully: "Hm. . . . Why do you say that?"

"Well, I can't really say," he went on slowly. "I—I guess I blacked out. I can't remember a thing after I saw him standing behind the bar that night until I got back to my trailer."

"You mean—you mean you don't remember shooting him?" I shook my head in wonderment.

"Yes, that's what I mean."

"You don't even remember driving home?"

"No."

"You don't even remember threatening Barney's bartender when he followed you outside after the shooting—as the newspaper says you did?" I paused and held my breath. "You don't remember telling him, 'Do you want some, too, Buster?'?"

The smoldering dark eyes flickered ever so little. "No, not a thing."

"My, my," I said, blinking my eyes, contemplating the wonder of it all. "Maybe you've got something there."

The Lecture was over; I had told my man the law; and now he had told me things that might possibly invoke the defense of insanity. It had all been done with mirrors. Or rather with padded hammers. There remained only the loose ends to gather in. I'd try to make it short.

I turned and looked out the sooty window. "Let me think a minute," I said. Then I turned and studied the impaled cockroach. All right, I thought—maybe my man was insane when he shot Barney Quill. Maybe he was nuttier than a fruit cake and maybe he had blacked out and didn't remember a thing. So far so good. But there was one flaw, one small thorn in this insanity business, and one that had to be faced, and fast. And wasn't it far better to face it now, before I got committed in the case, than later on in the harsh glow of the courtroom? I turned back to my man.

"Look, Lieutenant. Hold your hat. I'm about to pitch you a fast ball. . . . Maybe you were insane. Maybe you didn't remember a thing. But you and the newspaper agree on one thing. Both of you tell me that right after you returned to the trailer park, after shooting Barney Quill, you woke up the deputized caretaker and told him: 'I just shot Barney Quill.' Now is that correct?" Again I held my breath.

I rather think he saw what was coming, but he replied steadily enough. "That is right," he answered because he had to, there was no other answer, no escape; he was already committed on that one far past the point of no return.

Slowly, easily: "All right, then, Lieutenant. Now tell me, how come you could tell the caretaker you had just shot Barney Quill if you had really blacked out and didn't remember a thing? *Who told you?*"

"Well," he began. Then he stopped cold and closed his eyes. He was stalled. It was the first time I'd seen him really grope. The silence continued. Was I, I wondered, developing into one of those incurable ex-D.A.'s, the unreconstructed kind who can always find more reasons for convicting their clients than acquitting them?

"Come, come, Lieutenant," I said. "Think!"

Impatiently, the lower lip still projected: "I *am* thinking! I'm try-ing to remember, damn it."

I was thankful a jury wasn't watching him during the process. It also occurred to me that he must have been a charming child. "Come, now, man," I pressed, "what could possibly have led you to tell the caretaker you'd just shot Barney if it is true that you didn't remember it?"

He spoke rapidly, jerkily. "All right. . . . It's coming back. . . . Barney Quill was the last man I saw before I blacked out. . . . In fact his was the only face I saw in the whole damned place. . . . My gun. . . . I knew when I entered the barroom the clip of my lüger was loaded. When I got back to my trailer I saw it was empty. There's a thing that pops up. . . ." He threw out his hands. "Don't you see? I figured I *must* have shot him, that's all. So I went and told the caretaker I had." He paused and looked up at me like a child who'd just recited his Christmas poem. Had he done all right?

It was the only plausible explanation he could have made. "I see," I said thoughtfully. "So that's the way it is?" But, old fire horse that I was, I yearned to be D.A. and be faced with such an answer. It would have been a pleasure to rip and dig at this man. "I see," I repeated. So far, I felt, this was the biggest flaw, the highest hurdle, to a successful plea of insanity. It, too, would take some pondering.

I glanced at my watch and arose. After all I hadn't fished for two whole days. "That's enough for today," I said. "Class is dismissed. I'll see you again tomorrow."

"Are you taking my case?"

"I don't know yet. Among other things, Lieutenant, there's still the little matter of my fee."

"I was afraid of that."

I was at the sheriff's door. "Well, I'll see you tomorrow," I said.

"Just one more question," the Lieutenant said.

"I am your slave—but only for one minute," I said. "Shoot."

"How are we doin'?"

"No more now, Lieutenant," I said, smiling. "We've both had a busy day. I'll venture this: I think maybe we're finding a way to save somebody some face. You see, saving face is one of the most important and least spoken of 'defenses' known to criminal law."

"What I said to the caretaker won't spoil things, will it?"

"I don't know. We can't have everything, chum. I'll add only this: if the jury really wants to find you insane, wants to let you go, all hell won't stop 'em. Now so long. I've got work to do." I turned to leave.

"Good night, Mr. Biegler," the Lieutenant said. "Hope you have good fishing."

I wheeled around. "How in hell did you know that?"

Smiling: "Saw your rod case and gear in your car—from my cell window. I don't think you would have left them bake all day in the sun unless you were going fishing directly from here."

This poor man was crazy; crazy like a fox. "Thanks," I said, smiling sheepishly. The Lecture was over. My smart lieutenant had passed with flying colors. I also suspected that at times my nimble fox might have been several jumps ahead of me.

chapter 7

That night I slept poorly. A lawyer caught in the toils of a murder case is like a man newly fallen in love: his involvement is total. All he can think about, talk about, brood about, dream about, is his case, his lovely lousy goddam case. Whether fishing, shaving, even lying up with a dame, it is always there, the pulsing eternal insistent thump thump of his case. Alas, it is true: the lover in love and the lawyer in murder share equally one of the most exquisite, baffling, delightful, frustrating, exhilarating, fatiguing, intriguing experiences known to man. And it looked like I was rapidly falling in "love."

"Good morning, Mr. Clerk," I said to Sulo. "Is there a Lieutenant Manion still registered here? Or has he checked out?" I had been using the same old gambit on Sulo for ten years and it never failed to convulse him. It didn't fail now. For Sulo was of the old school; old jokes to him were like old cheese: their very mustiness seemed to make him relish them all the more. In fact I had him in stitches; we two were bad enough to be on TV; Sulo was the perfect straight man.

"Dat's a good one, Polly," Sulo gasped, when he had partly recovered. Still convulsed, he reached for his big brass key. "Ho, ho, ho. . . . I—I go get your soldier man. He, he. . . . You can use Sheriff's office you like. He be out road patrol."

It was reassuring to learn that the relentless bloodhound of a sheriff was already abroad stamping out crime. It also gave me a chance to have a quiet chat with Sulo. "Sit down a minute, Sulo," I said. "We haven't had a little visit for a long time." I felt like an insurance solicitor coddling a hot prospect. "Tell me, how's your lumbago?"

"Sure, sure, sure," Sulo said, gratefully sitting down under the portrait of the man coveted by the F.B.I.

"Say, Sulo," I said, before he could launch on the saga of his lumbago, "I don't suppose you were on duty the night they brought Lieutenant Manion in? You're still always on days, aren't you?"

"Sure, you bet, Polly, always on days. Too old now dis night business."

"Hm. . . . Lieutenant Manion wants to hire me for his lawyer, Sulo. But I don't know, I don't know." I pondered the problem with my old friend. "Say, what kind of a woman is his wife?"

Sulo brightened visibly. "Oh, nice lady, nice nice lady." He shook his head appreciatively. "Good looker, too—even with dose black eyes." Sulo winked and brought both arms out and down across his chest in an abrupt half-moon. "Good bumps, too. Boy, oh boy, like dat what-you-call, Maryland Monroe. . . ."

"Why, Sulo, you old goat," I reproved him. "And don't be carried away. Remember what happened to Barney Quill."

I'd lost Sulo, he was off again, drunk with laughter, and while I waited for him to collect himself I reflected what a nice thoughtful democratic guy I was to be passing the time of day with my old former fellow officer. And busy as I was, too. The thought gave me a warm glow. It also occurred to me what a shabby trick it was for me to be sitting there trying to pump this affably innocent old jailer. How crafty and double-crossing could a man get? And all to save the skin of a man who, for simple honor and dignity and the plain virtues, probably wasn't fit to shine Sulo's shoes. But was I doing any of it for Lieutenant Manion? Wasn't it really all for Polly Biegler? In any case the very least I could do was to be frank with my old friend.

Sulo had recovered and was feeling the small of his back, a sure prelude to a blow-by-blow account of his lumbago. "Look, Sulo," I said, heading him off, "I've got to ask you a question, one simple question. If you don't know the answer I wish you'd tell me. If you do know and don't want to tell me, that's all right, too. Is that fair enough?"

"Shoot, Polly," Sulo said soberly.

"Do you know whether Barney Quill raped Laura Manion?"

Sulo surveyed me steadily with his faded blue eyes. He glanced away and back again. "You ask *me*, Polly?" he said, shrugging evasively. "How can I know—I was home in bed. Vy don't you ask dat lady? She was dere."

We sat silently. Sulo now clearly knew I was pumping him, but at least I had leveled with him. I unwrapped a cigar and chewed the end but did not light it. I had to level still more. "Don't tell me if you don't want to, Sulo," I said. "I wouldn't want to hurt or involve you for the world. But I've got to decide whether I'm taking this case—I've got to know today, this morning, in a few minutes. And if I take it I want to win it, it's damned important to me as well as to the Lieutenant. And if I can really know that Barney raped this woman I think maybe I can win it." I paused. "That's the straight dope, Sulo."

Sulo glanced furtively around the room. "I tink maybe he did rape her," he said quietly. The way he said it made the word sound like "rap," which, upon reflection, still did not make me quibble.

"How do you know?"

"Dat lie 'tector test say she tell da trut'," Sulo said.

"Are you *sure*, I mean about the lie-detector results, Sulo?" I pressed. "I've got to be sure."

"State police he tell Sheriff; Sheriff he tell me," Sulo said simply. "Dat's true, Polly. I vould not tell you lie about it."

"Thanks, Sulo," I said, briefly taking his hand. "That's all I want to know. I feel better already, much better. I guess you can fetch down the Lieutenant now."

"Sure, sure, sure," Sulo said, opening and clanking shut his iron door and locking himself in. He paused on the other side and regarded me thoughtfully through the bars. He smiled faintly. "T'ank you, Polly," he said dryly. "My lumbago, t'anks, she's to be much better, much much better." He turned and shuffled away upstairs, chuckling to himself. Good old Sulo, good old lumbago.

Just as a lawyer needn't love his client to adequately represent him, so he doesn't necessarily have to believe in his moral or legal innocence. But sometimes it helps, and it was helping now, and I felt greatly relieved to have had my little chat with Sulo. So the lie-detector test showed she was telling the truth, had it? Was the prosecution going to sit on the results? If they were, how was I going to get them before the jury? Especially since the results of these tests were in any case inadmissible in court? Well, I'd have to face that headache later on. . . .

Sulo had told me more than he realized, much more. This was, in fact, the first big break in the case. For now I not only had confirmation that the lady had been "rapped," important as that was, but also that her entire story was substantially true. I knew from experience that during the polygraph test the thorough state police would have covered every detail of the case with her: the events before the rape, the rape itself, and the scene later at the trailer park gate where Barney had allegedly beaten her up. And that last part would absolve my man from any lingering suspicion that he had himself beaten her up in a fit of jealous rage. It further tended to buttress the truth of Lieutenant Manion's story of his movements after his wife had reached the trailer. Now I not only knew these things were true but I knew that the prosecution also knew them. While all this still did not afford Lieutenant Manion an open-and-shut legal defense, I now knew what the People knew and, perhaps equally important, I further knew that they didn't know I knew. It was all a little complicated and I wasn't sure yet where it led. Perhaps I could lure the prosecution into trying to hide the results. . . . I heard the clank and creak of the iron door.

"Good morning, *Mister* Biegler," the familiar mocking voice said.

"Oh, it's you, Lieutenant. Good morning."

"You seem buried in thought this morning."

I sniffed the air like a beagle. "Merely incipient coma induced by partial asphyxia." I arose and held my hand toward the sheriff's door. "Shall we retire to the lilac room and carry on? I'll rally shortly."

"You first, Counselor, you first," the Lieutenant replied gravely.

"Ah, thank you, Lieutenant."

I had done it again to Sulo, and we left him strangling and wounded in his chair under the wanted felon. "He, he, he . . ." I was touched. Good old Sulo; lumbago and all, he still appreciated his old D.A.

"Lieutenant Manion," I said, facing him, "I've decided to take your case."

"Good, good. How much is your fee?"

"Three grand. Is that fair enough?"

"Fair enough. I rather thought it might be more."

"Maybe I'd better raise it, then. I always want my clients to feel satisfied."

"I'm real satisfied—three thousand is most fair and reasonable."

"Good. When can you pay it?"

"It'll have to be later. Right now I'm broke."

"*What!*"

"I'm broke. At this moment I couldn't pay you three dollars."

"Can you raise it?"

"No."

"How about your trailer?"

"Both it and my car are mortgaged to the hilt."

"How about your relatives? Everybody has a rich uncle."

"I don't have any uncles, rich or poor. Both my parents are dead. My only close relative is a married sister in Dubuque. She and her husband owe *me* money. They have four kids and a mortgage."

"You seem to spring from well-mortgaged stock," I said. "Look, Manion, why did you call me down here if you knew you couldn't pay me? Did you think perhaps I ran a veterans' legal aid bureau?"

"I needed a lawyer and I wanted the best."

"You mean the second best, don't you? Or have you forgotten about that eminent authority on unwritten law, old Crocker?"

The Lieutenant shrugged and regarded me steadily. "Well," he said slowly, "if you won't represent me I suppose I'll have to try someone else."

I stared at him. Was it possible that this man sensed that by now I would almost have paid *him* to stay in the case? "You let me waste a whole goddam day on this case when you knew all along you couldn't pay me," I said, trying hard to work up a pout.

"You didn't ask me," he said.

The man had me there. He couldn't be expected to know that any half-decent attorney could scarcely discuss his fee before he knew whether he wanted to enter a case. At the same time, though, I could well have probed him a little about his general financial condition when I first met him the morning before. And probably should have. Why didn't I face it? Wasn't it the solemn truth that I had suspected all along he didn't have any money, as Maida had warned me, and had deliberately put off asking him until it was too late, until I was hopelessly enmeshed? As for Maida, how would I ever square all this with her and our depleted check book? The thought made me smile.

"Look, Manion," I said. "How much can you pay me and when?"

"I can pay you a hundred and fifty dollars on account next week. It's pay day then."

"You realize, of course, that if I accept that I—that I've enlisted for the duration?"

Coolly: "Yes. That's why I'm offering it."

There was a kind of engaging frankness about this cool pirate. "When could you pay me the balance?"

"I don't know. If I'm acquitted I'll give you a promissory note and I can pay you so much a month."

"Famous last words," I said. "And suppose you're convicted?"

"Then I guess both of us lose. But isn't that just another of those calculated risks—like pleading insanity?"

The needling bastard. . . . I had to put in one more try, for Maida's sake. "Supposing I said I won't take your case till you pay me half my fee?"

Shrugging: "I'd just have to regretfully get someone else, I'm afraid."

"You'd risk that?" I said. "You'd actually risk it?"

Smiling slightly: "I've got my legal defense now, haven't I? I was insane, wasn't I? How can I possibly lose?"

I was now getting the Lecture in reverse. I stared admiringly at the man, at this shrewd, gambling, dead-beat son-of-a-bitch. He had me helplessly coming his way and I was morally certain that he now knew I just had to take on this case. The moment of decision was at hand; I would either go fishing or else go to work. I took a deep breath and held it, pain and all.

"Lieutenant Manion," I said, extending my hand, "you've got yourself a lawyer. And I seem to have a client. Now let's get down to work. We've plenty of it."

He took my hand. "It's a pleasure, Counselor. Where do we start? You'll have to tell me, you know. Remember, I've been ill and I'm just recovering my wits."

"Your wits will do nicely. First let's go out and see Sulo. I want to discuss with him the possibility of our doing our talking outside in my car. The stink of this place is getting me down. Even for three grand on the line I don't think I can stand it much longer." I held the door open for my client. We found Sulo nodding in his chair and I stood debating whether to awaken him.

The outer jail door opened and in stalked a character straight out of *High Noon*. His big mail-order felt hat was pushed back on his perspiring forehead; his exquisitely tailored and stitched gabardine shirt, with its cascades of pearl buttons at the shaped pockets and cuffs, was negligently open at the tanned throat, from which depended two cords held by a dollar-sized round silver clasp engraved not with Justice, not with Liberty, but with a bucking bronco. The richly tailored trousers were tucked carelessly into the tops of dusty hand-stitched laceless boots and all he lacked, I saw, was a Bull Durham tag dangling over his heart.

"Fourscore and seven years ago," I found myself perversely thinking, "there came forth upon this continent an ancient dust storm; whereupon an entire province of old Texas was picked up and hurled aloft and held magically suspended all these years. Lo! today, may God help us, it has been dumped upon the far shores of Lake Superior. Yippee yi yi!"

It was a solemn moment and I restrained an impulse to kneel. Sheriff Max Battisfore was back at last from highway patrol. His keen gray eyes restlessly searched the room. They found mine and lit with gladness; you could see the very glow of gladness in them.

"Well, hello, *Paul*," the Sheriff said. He grasped my hand in both of his and looked me straight in the eye. "If it isn't my favorite ex-D.A. In person not a movie. How's the old boy? Long time no see. Is old Sulo there treating you and the Lieutenant O.K.?" He slapped my shoulder and kept pumping my hand. The Sheriff had come a long way, I saw; he had developed a boisterous and irresistible gift for camaraderie; he made one feel—I groped for words—so terribly *wanted*. We might belong to opposite political parties, his attitude seemed to say, but real friendship was something bigger, finer, than mere party. "How are you, anyway, you old buckaroo?" he ran on, playfully digging me in the ribs.

"I'm fine, thanks, Max," I said, smiling and retreating out of range. "Just fine. How are you?"

"Oh, fine, fine. Any phone calls, Sulo? Oh, on my pad. . . . Yes, Polly, I feel just like a horse's father. If I felt any better Sulo there'd have to lock me up in one of my own cells." He paused as Sulo obediently snorted. Musty cheese, musty jokes. . . . "Tell me, man, how the hell are you, anyway?"

"I'm fine, Max," I repeated soberly, and, since Max's concern over my health had been doubly relieved and certified, I added: "If you've got a minute I'd like to have a chat with you?"

"Sure, sure, Polly. Right this way." He led the way into his office and bent over a memorandum pad on his desk. He called out to Sulo. "Phone the Missus, Sulo, and tell her I got that Community Chest kickoff dinner tonight, after that the Amvets, then bowling. . . . Shut the door, Polly, and sit down. Make yourself at home. Long time no see. Tell me, how the hell—ah—won't you have a cigarette?"

I gestured with the stub of a cigar. "No thanks, Max, I'm still faithfully on these Italian reefers, still smoking the poor man's marijuana."

The Sheriff wagged his head. "Still the same old joker, too, Polly. Lord, it's good to see you, man. How do you feel, I mean, how are you really feeling?"

"Look, Max," I said, taking the plunge, "what were the results of Laura Manion's lie-detector test?" I held my lighter poised at my cold cigar. The flame burnt my finger.

"Oh, that," the Sheriff replied, without a pause. "As a foxy old D.A. like you well knows—remember those good old days, Polly?— the state police made that test. They made the test, they've got the results." He fleetingly laid a confiding hand on my knee. "You remember how jealous they always were of their prerogatives." He nodded sagely. "Well, Polly, they still are. Jealous as all hell. So wouldn't it be better all around for you to go ask them?" He again looked at his desk pad. "Call operator Eleven, Detroit," he murmured absently. He looked up. "Boy, Polly, it's been good to see you. Tell me, man, how the hell are you?"

"I guess maybe you're right, Max," I grudgingly admitted, standing up. "It's their baby, I'd better go ask them." I paused, pondering the problem aloud. "But what's the use of asking them? They probably wouldn't tell me—and anyway the results wouldn't be admissible in court." I too could confide. "I think maybe I'll skip it," I said resolutely. "Yes, I think I may just skip the whole thing. Only complicate matters. To hell with the lie-detector test." I pumped the Sheriff's free hand. He had grabbed up the phone with the other. "Thanks, Max," I said. "Sorry to have troubled you."

"Any time at all, Polly. Long time no see. Boy, it's been good to see you, you old buckaroo. . . . Hello, Operator, this is Sheriff

57

Battisfore. Give me operator Eleven at Detroit. That's right, honey, just about an hour ago. . . . Yes, dearie, for you I'll hold on forever. . . ."

Max stood silhouetted against his wall of framed photographs. For the first time it occurred to me that there were no pictures showing him out pursuing felons or making an arrest, in fact none showing the man in the simple act of being sheriff. . . . I nevertheless found it an impressive scene, as though one had long read about and seen some fabulous personage in the newsreels and on TV and then suddenly been privileged to confront him, relaxed and friendly, in the intimate glow of his own home. One had never realized what a remarkable personality he was.

"There's just one more thing, Max," I said. "I was just going to ask Sulo about it, but perhaps I'd better ask the head man himself. I'm in Manion's case now and he and I are going to have a lot to talk about." I paused diffidently. "There'll be lots to do, too, and the trial's just three weeks away," I explained.

"Naturally," the Sheriff said. "And he's retained one of the best lawyers in the business, Polly. The very best, for my money."

"Thanks, Max," I said. I was finding trouble coming to the point. "Well, the county still won't furnish you a jail conference room and I hate for us to be cluttering up your office and being underfoot all the time. I realize you have your work to do."

"Yes?" the Sheriff said helpfully.

"Well, I was wondering how about the Lieutenant and me occasionally sitting outside in my car, when your office is in use, I mean? That way we could talk without interruption and in private and at the same time not be in your hair." That way, too, I thought wistfully, we could occasionally breathe without pain.

"Hm. . . ." the Sheriff said. He pursed his lips and closed his eyes and nodded his head. "Hm. . . ." He stole a look at me. "There's always his cell, Polly," he said thoughtfully. I remained resolutely silent. "Hm," the Sheriff repeated, squinting again, and it was fun trying to follow his shrewd weighing of the angles, assaying of the factors, yes, counting of the very votes. What was he thinking? Might it not be something like this?—Murder was a nonbailable offense, wasn't it, and Manion certainly had no goddam business outside except in custody, had he? There could be criticism, bad criticism, too, and if the damned fool skipped, made a break, it might be political suicide. But Biegler there was an old hand, an old fox, wasn't he?—and, hm, a fairly big wheel in his party, too—

and he'd certainly warn his Lieutenant his goose would be cooked but good if he tried any funny stuff and took a powder. . . . And Polly wouldn't forget this favor, would he? And the Lieutenant was a combat veteran of two wars, wasn't he, and poor old Barney Quill wasn't, and of course all *that* had nothing to do with the case, but. . . .

"Hm," the Sheriff mused, nodding his head.

"Maybe I'd better skip it, Max," I said. "Maybe people'd say that because you're such an active veteran yourself you were playing favorites with war veterans. Maybe even the veterans would get down on you for taking a chance on a fellow veteran, a man who'd dare lay a finger on a man that had maybe raped and beat up his wife." I had delivered what I hoped was my clincher; I paused and awaited the jury's verdict.

"It's O.K., Polly," the Sheriff said quietly, almost casually. "Take him outside any time you want. He'll be in your custody."

"No cuffs or leg irons?" I said.

"No cuffs or leg irons," the Sheriff replied. "He won't run—and anyway you won't let him—neither of you can afford to."

It was a shrewd analysis. "Thanks, Max," I said. There was something big about the man; the job of being—and remaining—sheriff hadn't quite stamped that out. And I felt elated, elated not only to occasionally escape the jail, delightful a prospect as that was, and further elated because the Sheriff's action tacitly confirmed the results of the lie-detector test, but most of all elated because this most representative citizen, this shrewd walking (or rather patrolling) litmus of community sentiment had virtually told me that to his mind at least the prevailing feeling was running toward my man. I was even surer of it now than if Elmo Roper had conducted a county-wide poll. And after all the jury was nothing more than a group of representative citizens, wasn't it? If Max himself felt this way about my man then why shouldn't they? Yes, this was the second big break in the case. Stocks were picking up. "I won't forget this, Max," I said, opening the door.

"It's nothing at all, Polly," the Sheriff said. He craned his neck. "Hey, there—come on in, Sulo," he shouted out beyond me. "Yes sir, Polly. Any time at all. Lord, it's good to see you looking so fit. You're as tanned as a—as a hound's tooth."

"Fishing pallor," I said.

"You've lost some weight, too, haven't you, Polly? You're as lean as a—as a—"

"Cigar-store Indian," I said. "Any weight I've shed, Max," I continued, ruefully exploring the receding area over my temples, "is solely from losing hair. Time, like crime, marches on."

"You kill me, Polly," the Sheriff said, chuckling, shifting the receiver to his other ear and clicking the phone.

chapter 9

It was pleasant sitting out in the warm sun, smelling the rank August smell of Mrs. Battisfore's flower garden, listening to the distant bumblebee hum of traffic and the drone and clatter of the trusty prisoners (the Sheriff's regular clients, the county's convalescing drunk-and-disorderly set) mowing the big sloping courthouse lawn—idly watching the sea gulls dipping and wheeling and soaring so far out over the glittering big lake. We smoked and watched silently and I reflected with lazy unoriginality that the main trouble with the world was the people in it. Someone had said it more floridly if not better: "Where every prospect pleases, and only man is vile."

"We'll need a psychiatrist," I said.

"Why?"

"To prove your insanity. Insanity, Lieutenant, is a medical question and for us, the defense, to create a legal issue on that score we must present expert testimony that you were insane. Once that is done, however, the issue is created and then the burden of disproving your insanity falls squarely on the People. That is our biggest and most pressing problem."

"I see," my man said. "Then I guess we get a psychiatrist. But if it's a medical question wouldn't a local doctor do equally as well?"

"No, my friend, a local doctor wouldn't do at all. Those boys already have their hands full delivering the population and trying to keep up with the latest miracle drugs without moving into the tangled realm of the mind. What's more, most of them don't know any more about it than you or I."

"You're too modest, Counselor. Have you forgotten it was you who injected insanity into this case?"

"No," I answered carefully. "I merely told you what the possible legal defenses were—it was you who told me facts from which one might conclude you may have been insane." I saw I'd have to chink that crack in my lecture and keep it chinked. "In any case, even if we were able to find any doctor hereabouts foolhardy enough to testify to your insanity, all the People would have to do to blast it would be to throw a real psychiatrist at him and cut him—along with your insanity defense—to ribbons. You see, psychiatrists are simply a different breed of cats. For example, when plain doctors and lawyers and soldiers and similar riffraff go to a burlesque show they go to watch the girls' legs and titties. But not a psychiatrist. When one of those birds stoops to attend a burlesque *he* goes to watch the audience. Hell, man, you can't pit a mere doctor against a monster like that."

"But how would the People get to know?"

"How would they know what?"

"How would they know whether we were going to call a doctor or a psychiatrist—or even that we are going to claim insanity at all? So how could they possibly be prepared to refute it?"

This client of mine was no dummy and I was glad he wasn't lobbing shells at me. "Because the law says that we must serve notice on the prosecution in advance of the trial of our intention to plead insanity, and at the same time give the names of our witnesses, expert or otherwise. We can't keep it a secret. Surprise pleas of insanity are 'no fair,' the law sensibly says. We've got to tip our hand in advance."

"It's a pretty unscientific thing," my man said thoughtfully. "This insanity business is pretty damned unscientific."

"Why do you say that?"

"Well, we can't prove insanity without a medical expert, you tell me. Yet you and I have already decided I was insane, we know that we're going to plead insanity—you tell me it's the only legal defense I've got. And even I can see that now. In other words you a mere lawyer and I a dumb soldier have between us decided that I was medically and legally insane. Having decided that, we must now go out and shop around for a medical expert to confirm *our* settled conclusion. Yet you tell me an ordinary medical doctor won't do." The Lieutenant shook his head. "It all sounds damned unscientific to me."

It irked me unaccountably to hear this Mister Cool so blithely undertake to criticize my profession. It was all right if a member of the family did, but for a perfect stranger . . . "Lieutenant," I said, "the easiest thing in the world is for a layman to poke fun at the law. Lawyers and the law are sitting ducks for ridicule and always have been. The average layman may in all his lifetime collide with but one small branch of the law, which he understands but imperfectly. He usually knows whether he won or lost. He may also remember that Dickens, grumbling through Mr. Bumble, once called the law an ass. So for him all the law is henceforth an ass, and, overnight, he becomes its severest critic."

"But I still don't get it," the Lieutenant said. "On this score at least, the law looks like a prime ass."

"Granted," I said. "But the point I wish to make is that from this people may not safely proceed to damn all law. You of all men should be grateful that the massive structure known as the law really exists. It so happens that it represents your only hope."

"How do you mean?" the Lieutenant said, bristling.

"I'll try to tell you," I said. "Mr. Bumble was only partly right. He was only part right because, for all its lurching and shambling imbe cilities, the law—and only the law—is what keeps our society from bursting apart at the seams, from becoming a snarling jungle. While the law is not perfect, God knows, no other system has yet been found for governing men except violence. The law is society's safety valve, its most painless way to achieve social catharsis; any other way lies anarchy. More precisely, Lieutenant, in your case the law is all that stops Barney Quill's relatives from charging in here and seeking out and shooting up every Manion on sight. It is also what would keep the heavily mortgaged Manions of Dubuque from in turn coming a-gunning for the Quills, in other words what keeps the fix you're now in from fanning out into a sort of Upper Peninsula version of Hatfield-McCoy."

I paused, warming to my unfamiliar role as a defender of law. "The law is the busy fireman that puts out society's brush fires; that gives people a *nonphysical* method to discharge hostile feelings and settle violent differences; that substitutes orderly ritual for the rule of tooth and claw. The very slowness of the law, its massive impersonality, its insistence upon proceeding according to settled and ancient rules—all this tends to cool and bank the fires of passion and violence and replace them with order and reason. That is a tremendous accomplishment in itself, however a particular case may turn out. As someone has well said, 'The difference between an alley-fight and a debate is law.'" I paused. "What's more, all our fine Magna Chartas and constitutions and bills of right and all the rest would be nothing but a lot of archaic and high-flown rhetoric if we could not and did not at all times have the *law* to buttress them, to interpret them, to breathe meaning and force and life into them. Lofty abstractions about individual liberty and justice do not enforce themselves. These things must be reforged in men's hearts every day. And they are reforged by the law, for every jury trial in the land is a small daily miracle of democracy in action."

The Lieutenant stared at me with an amused half-smile as I soared away.

"Why, just look, man—just look at Russia," I went on. "There the law has been replaced by a stoic joyless gang of lumpy characters in round hats and floppy pants and double-breasted overcoats, men who peremptorily crack down on their Lieutenant Manions and everyone, all in the name of the juggernaut state. *They* are the law. There you would have 'confessed' joyfully days ago." I shook my head. "In fact, Heaven help us, just look almost anywhere these days. The midnight knock on the door, the whisking before a firing squad, the guttural barked command—then silence, nothing but anonymous dead silence. . . . No one even dare *ask* what became of you, much less defend you; such proletarian curiosity is apt to prove abruptly fatal."

The Lieutenant was smiling now. "I didn't know you cared," he said. "I only hope you're half as eloquent during my trial."

I hadn't quite known myself how much I cared, and I couldn't help smiling. "Having said all that, Lieutenant, it remains to be added that you're absolutely right on insanity. The present outlook and ritual of the law on legal insanity is almost as primitive and nonsensical as when we manacled and tortured our insane. I agree with you."

The Lieutenant frowned and looked concerned. "I hope you haven't talked yourself out of my defense of insanity. And supposing our chosen psychiatrist, when we find him, says I'm not nuts?"

"In that event we keep shopping around, as you say, till we can live-trap one who does." I shook my head. "So a-shopping we must go. I love that word. I can't wait to tell it to Parnell."

The Lieutenant eyed me sharply. "Who is Parnell?"

"Oh, just an old lawyer friend. My legal whetstone, I call him."

"I see. Where do we—ah—go shopping to find this psychiatrist?"

I thoughtfully lit a cigar. "That may be a real problem," I said. "Either nobody in the Peninsula is insane or else all of us are nuts. In any case psychiatrists seem to shun the place. The only psychiatrists I know about are connected with public institutions of some kind: the veterans' hospital at Iron Mountain, the prison over at Marquette, the insane asylum at Newberry, the various children's clinics, that sort of place. Most are salaried staff men and I'm afraid we can't expect to get any of them. The People are much more likely to pop up with one of those."

"What do we do, then?"

"We go shopping, my friend."

The Lieutenant shrugged. "Well, I suppose if we must we must. Where do we start?"

"Not where, Lieutenant—the burning question is *what with?*

64

I rather suspect that psychiatrists are no more philanthropic than us lawyers. In fact less so than one foolish lawyer I happen to know. They'll expect to be well paid—and on the line."

"You're making it rather difficult. How can I pay a psychiatrist? You know I'm broke. Hell, man, I can't even pay you."

I spoke not unkindly. "You might try helping me, that's all. And stop feeling so goddam sorry for yourself." I paused. "There's one other place we could get a psychiatrist. I was half hoping you might have suggested it."

"Where's that?" the Lieutenant said evenly.

"From the United States Army," I replied.

"I don't know whether the Army would."

"I don't know either, but you might tell me where and who to write. It might also be well to pause here for a little review to impress you with how serious this thing is. One, your only legal defense is insanity. Two, to prove it you must have a psychiatrist. Three, you can't afford a psychiatrist. Four, then we've got to go out and live-trap one some other way. Do you have the picture?"

"I'll give you the name and address of my C.O. before you leave," the Lieutenant replied. "Don't let me forget."

"You better do it now. I'm phoning or writing him tonight. For this, my friend, happens to be the heart of your case."

As my client sat writing out the address, a woman drove up to the side of the courthouse in a black sedan. She got out and a small frisking short-haired terrier followed her, the dog carrying in its mouth a lighted flashlight, of all things. The woman wore dark glasses and as she advanced across the lawn toward us I thought for a moment it was a certain Hollywood tigress: she had the same buoyant step, the same free-swinging stride and came generous blouseful; she had even the same mass of piled-up russet hair, the high color, the full cherry-red lips. But, no, it wasn't my lovely celluloid dream queen. Before she reached my car I knew this was the woman over whom my client had killed Barney Quill.

"Hello, Manny," she said in a low musical voice. "How come you're out here in the sun? Did that nice Sheriff finally decide to let you go?"

"Hi, Laura," my client said. "How are you? How's Rover? Did you get the trailer moved?" By this time we were both out of the car. "This is Paul Biegler, Laura. He's taking my case. He's arranged for us to talk out here."

"How do you do, Mr. Biegler," Laura Manion said, extending her hand. She smiled ruefully. "I do hope you can help Manny out of this terrible mess I've got him in."

"I'll try, Mrs. Manion. If all of us do our part I think there's a fair chance." I sounded, I thought, a little like a professionally pessimistic football coach on the eve of the big game.

There was a small thud of silence. Lieutenant Manion knelt and petted the little dog. The animal was in an ecstasy of yipping joy over seeing him. "Rover hasn't seen Manny since—since that awful night," Laura Manion explained.

"And you?" I asked quietly. "When did you last see your husband?"

"Why, Sunday afternoon. Why do you ask?"

"I just wondered, that's all. Just making talk." I paused. "By the way, when can you and I talk?"

"Why, any time you wish," she said, tilting her head. "I came here today to see you. Now, if you like."

"The sooner the better," I said. "Do you think all of us should talk together?"

There was a perceptible pause. She pursed her moist red lips. "Why, just as you and Manny think best," she said.

The Lieutenant was still kneeling, petting the dog. "What do you think, Lieutenant?" I said.

Lieutenant Manion looked up at me sideways. "Suppose you call the shot, Mr. Biegler? Whatever you think is best." I glanced at his wife and it seemed to me that she shook her head.

"I think we two had better talk alone, at least for now, Lieutenant," I said. "Do you think you can stand going back to the loving care of Sulo? I'd prefer to talk out here in the car." There was another little jolt of silence, almost like that of relief. "There's one other thing," I said. "It seems quite likely that all of us are going to see quite a lot of each other from now on. I'm no particular slave to the modern cult of informality, but may I suggest that we call each other by our first names?"

"O.K., Paul," the Lieutenant said, rising and saluting. "I'll leave you and Laura to talk." He turned to his wife. "I'll see you later, Hon." He started for the jail. "Come on, Rover," he called and the little dog ran joyfully after him. Frederic and Laura Manion, I observed, had not touched each other during this encounter.

I held the car door open for Mrs. Manion. She got in and I closed it and then walked around and sat in the driver's side. "Will you please remove your glasses, Mrs. Manion?" I said.

"The name is Laura," she said. "Remember? If you can stand what you're going to see, I guess I can." She removed her glasses.

"Good Lord!" I said. In my ten years as D.A. I had never seen a pair of more grievously blackened eyes, and professionally I had been exposed to plenty. "Did Barney Quill really do that?"

I caught my breath. Her eyes were large and a sort of luminous aquarium green. Looking into them was like peering into the depths of the sea. I had never seen anything quite like them before and I was beginning, however dimly, to understand a little what it was that might have driven Barney Quill off his rocker. The woman was breathtakingly attractive, disturbingly so, in a sort of vibrant electric way. Her femaleness was blatant to the point of flamboyance; there was something steamily tropical about her; she was, there was no other word for it, shockingly desirable. All this was something of a trick, too, for a woman with two of the loveliest shiners I ever saw. I remembered something Parnell McCarthy had once said. "Some women radiate sex," he had said. "All the others merely trade in it." She raised her long eyelashes and regarded me solemnly, nodding her head. "Yes," she whispered. "Barney Quill did this to me."

"You'd better put on those dark glasses," I said wryly, feeling a little giddy. I fumbled for a cigar. "Do you mind if I smoke?"

"Not at all," she answered in her low voice. "That's if you'll give me a light."

We smoked in silence for a while. "I guess the first thing I'd better find out," I began, "is whether you plan to stay for the trial—to stay, that is, and help?"

The dark glasses abruptly swept around and bored into my eyes; I could almost see the round staring of those greenish depths. "Why how can you ask such a thing, Mr. Biegler?" she said evenly. "Whatever made you think I wouldn't stay?"

"Look, Mrs. Manion," I said, "I ask it because as your husband's lawyer I have to know. You're a key witness in this case, and if you don't plan to stay—stay and help out—I would say your husband's chances for beating this rap are pretty slim. I figure they're only about fifty-fifty as it is. And you still haven't answered my question." I was sorry that I had asked her to cover her eyes. I felt that about now they might be revealing to watch. "The question is, are you with him or against him?"

Laura Manion crushed her newly lit cigarette out in my ash tray. Her hand shook as she found a fresh one and turned toward me for a light. She inhaled the smoke deeply and held it and when she exhaled it seemed to escape her like a sob.

"Steady," I said quietly. "One can never tell how a case like this will turn out." I paused, cautiously feeling my way, following my nebulous but growing hunch that all was not well between this woman and her husband. "One can never bank on the result of a jury trial. A key witness might go away, and a man still get off. Or a key witness might stay, and the man still go to prison. One never knows about these things."

She had listened tensely. "What did Manny tell you?" she said. "I don't mean about the case, but about us, about our lives together, about any plans we may have had for the future?"

Ah, so they'd planned to separate, I thought. "Not a thing, Mrs. Manion; not a hint, not a clue," I said truthfully. "That I swear."

"How could you know then—how can you sense—" She broke off and again rubbed out her cigarette and turned and faced me. "Tell me," she said, speaking swiftly, "how could you doubt but what I'd stay and help? Did it seem so—so obvious to you that there was any question that I mightn't? Tell me, please tell me."

"Why, Mrs. Manion," I said blandly, "I've never doubted for a moment but that you'd stay. It's just routine for us lawyers to try to make sure of our witnesses. I guess perhaps I was a little clumsy and blunt about it. I've been away from this business for a little while."

"Was it because there was no sign of affection when we met just now—was that it?" She removed her glasses and her eyes glistened with tears.

"Are you staying, Laura?" I said.

"Yes," she said slowly, closing her wet eyes. "Yes, I'm staying. That's the least I can do for poor Manny."

"Then I noticed it, yes. You knew I did and I wanted you to know I did. And if you're staying I don't think it will be good if too many other people notice it. This is a small watchful community, doubly alerted by this murder, and, as in all such places, nasty harmful little rumors, often baseless, have a habit of traveling with the speed of light." I opened the car door on my side. "Excuse me, Mrs. Manion, I've got to go speak to the jailer. I'll be back in a moment. We've still lots and lots to talk about."

She leaned swiftly toward me with one hand on the seat. "Not a word to Manny," she said. "Please, not a word."

"I don't know what you're talking about, Laura," I said, smiling. "But whatever it is, nary a word."

chapter 11

As I was leaving the jail I ran smack into the prosecutor, Mitch Lodwick, just leaving the sheriff's office. We greeted each other and shook hands. The young prosecutor was a manly picture in tan: light tan summer suit, a pleated tan shirt and silk polka-dot tie, rich two-toned tan sport oxfords, a smart-looking waffle-colored soft straw hat with a folded tan ribbon. Then there was his tanned smiling face which made his flashing white teeth seem almost ir.decently incongruous. He looked as though he belonged more on the front porch of a country club than prowling Max Battisfore's jail.

"Well, Polly," Mitch said, "Max just tells me you're in the Manion case. So I guess we're going 'round and 'round again. This one looks like a real little daisy."

"It has everything but Technicolor, Mitch," I said. "Murder, rape and even a little dog. Hollywood couldn't have done better."

Mitch smiled. "*Alleged* rape, don't you mean, Polly?"

"I wouldn't know for sure, Mitch. I just got into the case and have barely met the lady."

Mitch grinned evilly. "Barely, Polly? I hear tell in some quarters that the last man who barely met up with her died from lead poisoning." He lowered his voice. "I was hoping I'd run into you."

"Well, here I am, Mitch. What's up?" Was this, I thought, to be the word on the lie-detector test?

"It's about a continuance," Mitch said. "What do you say to our agreeing to continue the case from the September term over until the December term? We've both got this damned Congressional election coming up—remember?—and I can't imagine your wanting to forsake your beloved trout for any mere murder case. And Judge Maitland is still at Mayo Brothers' and quite likely will not be able to sit in September. I assume you'd prefer, as I do, to have him try the case rather than gamble on some unknown grab-bag judge assigned from downstate. What do you say?"

I stood there thinking. I found the offer attractive on all counts, especially the desirability of having my wise old judge with whom I had worked so long, Judge Maitland. The judge in this case, I saw, was going to have to be a real lawyer, not some amiable political mountebank with a black gown and a law degree. And there were still other good reasons, too, that Mitch hadn't mentioned because he wasn't aware of them. If the case was continued over to the December term, wouldn't I also have a much better chance to insist upon, and get, a substantial payment on my fee? The Lord knew that that was plenty important. Then there was the thorny question of lining up a competent psychiatrist and getting my man through his paces, and my growing doubt whether all this could be done—if indeed it could be done at all—in time for the September term of court. There was really only one big objection to a continuance: my client himself.

"What do you say, Polly?" Mitch said. "Do we continue the case? I didn't think there'd be any question."

I shook my head. "No, Mitch, I'm afraid we can't agree to any continuance. I'd like to, I really would, for all the reasons you say and several more. But murder, as you know, is an unbailable offense, and I can't very well ask my man to sit in Max's jail here for an additional three months simply to suit our convenience. And there's no assurance that Judge Maitland will be able to sit even in December. In fact I for one am getting a little afraid he may never sit again. Thanks, anyway, Mitch. I hope you see my point."

"I do see your point," Mitch said, nodding thoughtfully. "Then how about copping your lieutenant out next month on second degree and getting the whole damned thing washed up and over with?"

I shook my head. "No, Mitch, he could still get up to life for that. Too rough, too risky. He wouldn't stand for that and I wouldn't let him. But I have a suggestion. How about your lowering the charge to manslaughter so that I can get my man out on bail? That way you and I will get our cherished continuance, you can go out charming the voters, and I go out alarming the trout—and everybody lives happily ever after. Then before the December term we could seriously explore the possibility of his copping out to manslaughter, providing, of course, that you and Judge Maitland are sufficiently imbued with the spirit of Yuletide charity."

"No, Polly. This deal is murder or it's nothing. You know that. Would you lower to manslaughter if you were still D.A.?" Mitch snapped his fingers. "From life down to a fifteen-year max, just like that? How could I ever square that?"

"A nicely returned ball, Mitch," I said, smiling. "But if I were D.A. and satisfied that Barney Quill had raped the Manion woman I really think I'd seriously consider making a lower charge." I paused. "Especially if I had a nice big fat lie-detector test, say, to back me up—that's if it did back me up." I paused thoughtfully. "But I guess maybe I wouldn't lower the charge if I still thought the rape were 'alleged,' as you just called it."

My reference to the lie-detector test had not been according to plan. But Mitch, who certainly knew the results, had just seen the Sheriff, and Max had doubtless related our recent conversation on the subject. I waited for him to speak.

Mitch blinked thoughtfully and cleared his throat. Then he moved deftly around me, like a shifty halfback, and opened the outside jail door. "Well, Polly, I guess it looks like we go to work soon. You don't go for the continuance and I can't go for lowering to manslaughter." Smiling. "But what are you going to use for a defense? Old box tops? Half the town of Thunder Bay saw your lieutenant plug Barney."

"Don't fret, Mitch, I'll come up with something. And as a last resort there's always that reliable home remedy: Old Doctor Crocker's Special Cure-all for Accused Felons."

"What's that?"

I furrowed my brow into a Patrick Henry frown, clapped one hand across my breast and pointed scornfully at an imaginary jury. "Ladees an' gen'emen!" I thundered. "You cain't guess this man into state's prison! Why, folks, I wouldn't send a yaller dawg to a dawg pound based on this here now evidence!"

"Perfect," Mitch said, laughing. "All you lack is Old Crocker's red wig. Well, so long, Polly."

"So long, Mitch."

The jail door breathed shut on its pneumatic hinge and that, I saw, was that.

Laura Manion was pacing up and down beside my car when I emerged from the jail. When she saw me she stamped out her cigarette and got quickly into the car. I had no sooner joined her than she began to talk, rapidly, breathlessly.

"You've seen Manny. . . . You've told him, I *know* you have . . . and you told me you wouldn't. . . . Oh, why did you do it when you promised you wouldn't?" She was perilously close to breaking down. "I should never—I—I—"

"Mrs. Manion!" I spoke sharply. "Please get hold of yourself. I haven't laid eyes on the man. Here, light a cigarette and calm yourself." I twirled my lighter and held it, waiting until she had taken several deep drags before I spoke. "Am I forgiven?" I said.

"I'm sorry," she said. "But you left so abruptly—and stayed so long. Whatever kept you so long?"

"Did you see that handsome man in tan just leave the jail?"

She nodded. "Yes. Who is he?"

"He's the old devil D.A., Mitchell Lodwick. I've just been talking to him." I briefly recounted my conversation with Mitch. "So that's what old Squealer Biegler's been up to," I concluded. "Am I reinstated in your confidence?"

"I'm sorry, Paul," she repeated, laying her hand impulsively on my arm. "I'm so terribly upset and—and—"

"Afraid?" I suggested. "Is that the word? Are you afraid of your husband, Laura? Is that the cause of the tension?" I paused and went on. "I think I have a right to know what gives between you two. I can't very well do my best if I'm working in the dark."

Again she took off her glasses and looked at me, long and searchingly. I felt as though I were gliding to the bottom of the sea in William Beebe's bathysphere. I fumbled to find a cigar and tore my eyes from hers to light it.

"Yes," she said, in a low voice. "I'll trust you, Paul. And I've simply got to talk to someone or I'll explode. I—I—" She paused and smiled. "I don't know where to begin."

I flicked my cigar at the ash tray. "Suppose you begin with my question," I suggested. "Are you afraid of your husband?"

When she spoke it was as though to herself. "Afraid? Afraid?" She turned toward me. "No, Paul, it isn't fear, precisely, it—it's something at once more subtle and more degrading than that. Have you ever been jealous?"

"You mean over a woman I cared for?"

She quickly nodded her head. "Yes, that's what I mean. Of someone you really loved?"

"Mercifully no," I replied thoughtfully. "Not ever seriously, that is, beyond occasional pangs. And that was long ago. . . . I consider jealousy the most corrosive and destructive of all emotions and I long ago made up my mind that I refused to be jealous of anyone or anything. Life is simply too goddam short. But my views on jealousy won't help your husband beat this murder rap and yours might." I paused and went on. "Is jealousy at the bottom of the tension between Manny and you?" This was an important and possibly serious development and I had to know.

She sat thoughtfully silent. "Yes," she said slowly, "jealousy more nearly covers it than any single word." She closed her eyes for a moment and then continued. "I'll try to tell you," she said. "Manny has always been jealous of me, even before we were married. I should have known how it would be. But then I found it only flattering and protective." She paused. "Afterwards, after we were married, I discovered how—how terrible it could be."

"We're playing truth, now, Laura, so I won't beat around the bush. Did he ever have any possible reason to be jealous?"

Her answer seemed too swift, too certain, for dissembling. "No, no! Never once. And God knows it was not for lack of opportunity." She smiled, and her smile had about it a certain little-girl quality of wistfulness and pathos. "This thing—" she gestured vaguely—"whatever it is I have—has always been . . . difficult." She shook her head. "I don't mean to have you think I don't like gaiety and fun and flattery," she went on. "And men, too, but not in the way that Manny apparently thinks I do. He's jealous of any man I meet in the most casual way. In fact he's probably jealous of you at this very moment."

I gave an involuntary start and for a prickly instant I could visualize a lüger trained on my back. Then it occurred to me that there was always the possibility that she was gilding the lily, that, being emotionally upset and understandably distraught by her recent experience she was somehow trying to expiate her sense of guilt. I remembered suddenly that my client had the day before spotted my fishing gear in my car. My car was parked in the same place. There was one way to find out a few things, a fast and simple way.

"Excuse me," I said abruptly, and I quickly got out of my car and elaborately yawned and stretched, at the same time wheeling and glancing casually up at the jail windows. Despite the dust and soot there was no mistake: I had caught a retreating glimpse of a familiar dark be-mustached face, the merest flash of disappearing Army khaki. Now any poor man had a right, I conceded, to stand and stare out of his cell window; in fact I knew that some of them simply had to, like animals in a cage. But here the quick retreat had done it, had told the story; the jealous Lieutenant stood convicted; I now saw that this woman was probably telling me the truth.

"Are you all right?" she inquired anxiously as I regained my place beside her.

"Leg cramps," I said wryly. "Please go on with your story."

"Well, there isn't much more to tell. I thought when Manny got assigned up here that things would be better. This wasn't his regular outfit, you know."

"Were they?" I said. "Were things any better?"

She shook her head. "No, they were worse, if possible. It just

74

meant a whole new strange crew of men for him to be jealous over."
She paused. "Manny's really a grand person, but he's strangling my
feeling for him. How can you continue to love a man who constantly makes you feel like a—a common street-walker?"

"Go on," I said. I did not propose to digress any further on jealousy
or the male's reactions to it.

"Just two weeks ago we attended an Army cocktail party at the
hotel. Some silly half-drunk young second lieutenant I'd never seen
before kept following me around and calling me Cleopatra. He was
just a boy, I suppose I could have been his mother. Finally he
playfully grabbed and kissed my hand, like an overzealous puppy. It
was just one of those things all Army people experience and understand. But Manny knocked him down. That's the last time I was
out—socially—until that awful night. Why, I think he was even half
jealous of Barney Quill."

I pricked up my ears. "How do you mean?"

"We'd gone to Barney's bar several times. It was about the only
decent place to drink in town. Barney was one of those loquacious
blarney-tongued operators who'd flatter a witch on a broomstick provided only she was wearing a skirt. He paused at our table once or
twice—he did the same at most of the others, too—and ran out his
poor little stock of complimentary banter, the same dreary sort of
thing I've heard in a hundred bars and Army posts, with or without
Manny. But this time Manny went into one of his more elaborate
sulks. So we quit going to Barney's bar."

"Was there any incident—any scene?" I asked, holding my breath.

"No, thank goodness. Manny made me hurry my drink and we
left." She shook her head. "It was so utterly childish. It's all so
childish—and now so tragic. And I feel so guilty."

I spoke casually. "Have you mentioned any of these things we've
just been discussing to the state police?—or to anyone?"

"Heavens no. I told them all about the—the incidents of that
night, of course. I had nothing to hide."

"You are sure of this. Think back now."

"I am positive."

"Did you tell them about the sexual attack by Barney? And all the
rest, both before and after the attack?"

"In great detail."

"Did you tell all this during your lie-detector test?"

"Why, yes, of course," she said impatiently.

"Who first suggested that you take this test?"

"I did. I'd read about them somewhere." She incuriously studied her nails.

"Do you know the results of the test?"

"No, I haven't given it a thought. But if the machine's any good there could only be one result. I told them the simple truth. Heaven knows that was bad enough."

I had not meant to tell either the Lieutenant or Mrs. Manion, at least for the time, that I knew the results of the lie test; this, not only to protect Sulo but for certain reasons of my own. I now saw I would have to change my plans.

"Well, you passed the test," I said. "It showed you were telling the truth."

"Oh," she said, with mild interest. "Did that handsome young prosecutor just tell you?"

"You see well with your dark glasses, madam," I said. "No, the handsome prosecutor didn't tell me. I can't tell you how I know, but I know. There are certain trade symptoms I have learned to recognize." One of them occurred to me as I spoke. Mitch surely knew the results of the test, and if it had been bad for our side he would certainly have told me so to aid his cause when he was making his pitch for a guilty plea to second degree murder. He had no reason then to hide the results of a bad test—bad for our side—and several good selling reasons not to. Why hadn't I thought of it before?

"Does Manny know?" she said.

"Not yet, but I've decided to tell him." For it was now plain to me that I'd have to reassure this troubled man, and fast, or we perhaps might not need to employ a psychiatrist or anyone to tell us he was insane; he actually *would* be. "There's one more thing," I said. "Don't tell a soul you know the result of this lie-detector thing. If people ask you—anyone—simply tell them you don't know. This may be vital. Do you promise?"

"Just as you say, Paul. And you won't tell Manny these things I've just told you."

I shuddered inwardly at the thought. "Heavens no, my good woman. And don't you."

"No, of course not," she said, smiling wanly. "Now we have secrets. And I do hope I have made you see certain things more clearly."

"I'm beginning to see a number of things," I said.

She again quickly placed her hand on my arm. "Please don't think I have said any of this to criticize Manny. Or to be disloyal. He was—he is—so tender and good in so many ways. He'd go through hell and high water for me."

"He might even kill for you?" I said.

She buried her face in her hands and I regretted having spoken. I was afraid she was going to cry. "Steady, Laura," I said. "The man probably can't help himself. I sometimes think that jealousy is a disease—a sort of disease of the personality or of the emotions. I don't know. . . . You want to help him. As his lawyer I want to help him." I paused. "Now I must go. I want to talk to you in the morning. Tonight I must work on this case. I suggest you go put on a little scene of loving reunion with Manny for the benefit of Sulo and the Sheriff. But mostly, I guess, for Manny. I'm getting a little worried about that man."

"Thank you, Paul," she said. She extended her hand and I took it. "You've been very understanding. I feel much better already." She kept her hand in mine.

"We have secrets, now, Laura, so I'll tell you another one. I wouldn't have mentioned it except for what you've told me this afternoon." I looked down at her hand. "Your husband's jail window overlooks my car." She colored and withdrew her hand quickly. I got out of the car and walked around to open her door. I forced myself not to look up at the jail window.

"Good night, Paul," Laura Manion said, smiling.

"Good night, Laura. Keep the chin up—like a good Army wife."

That night I worked late in my office. I looked some law and wrote out a letter for Maida to sign for me and send the Lieutenant's commanding officer, reviewing the case and its problems and putting in an urgent request for an Army psychiatrist. Then I left a note for Maida to tell Parnell McCarthy I wanted to see him at my office late the next night. "After fishing," I added defiantly. Then I fell into my unmade bed.

"Hi, Sulo," I said. "Greetings from the early bird. I want to see the Lieutenant for a minute. How about my skipping up to his cell and saving a lot of commotion?"

"Sure, sure, skip away, Polly," Sulo amiably agreed, taking down his big brass key and admitting me to the inner sanctum, the jail proper. "Three flights up, den turn right, den walk to end—his cell door's unlocked—an' dat's where you Lieutenant live his new address." Sulo chuckled over his little joke.

I managed a wan little smile as I started up the steep iron-shod stairs. "If Mrs. Manion shows up tell her to wait in my car."

As I trudged up the clanking echoing stairs winding through a maze of pipes of all kinds, water pipes, sewer pipes, steam pipes and miscellaneous brackets and girders, all done in battleship gray, I reflected that men could apparently get used to almost anything. Thousands of men, all over the world, lived in places like this and worse.

I thought of the hundreds of uncomplaining iron miners only a few miles away who daily plunged down into the chill and damp of ill-lit holes in the ground where for hours on end they groped their way about as through some vast insecure cheese. I thought, too, of the time I had once inadvertently wandered into the sawyers' room of a flooring mill, while campaigning, and had suddenly been so clutched and frozen by the demented screaming and awful banshee wailing of the dozens and scores of whirling saws—each presided over by a calmly oblivious workman—that it was only with physical effort I had turned and fled the place in terror. Even my usually dogged zeal for votes for Biegler had failed to hold me.

From a distant cell I heard an unseen player strumming softly and expertly on a guitar, accompanying a quavering falsetto voice, a voice plaintively beseeching his sweetheart to meet him on that opposite shore. I stopped and held my breath, suddenly caught and wrenched, helplessly plucked at the heartstrings, unaccountably moved by this wry mingling of sadness and comedy. I resisted an impulse to go seek out this anonymous artist, to take his hand, to behold at last a person who didn't treat this haunting evocative instrument as a species of drum. But there was murder to be unraveled and I must not get sidetracked. I shrugged and moved on, reflecting that I must have been a guitar-playing gardener at some Spanish hacienda during a previous incarnation. Pablo O'Biegler, no doubt.

"*Oh, tell me you'll leave me no more*," the quavering voice pursued me. "*When we meet on that opposite shore. . . .*"

"Hello, Polly!" someone called from one of the nearer cells, and I recognized the wreckage of one of Chippewa's more persistently dedicated drunkards. This gaunt alcoholic specter was gaily waving at me, as though it was I who was caught in jail and he instead a mere passing visitor. I waved back, not very gaily, and as I toiled my way up the last flight of stairs I heard him explaining in an extravagantly loud voice to his cell neighbor just who I was and what a hell of a hard-boiled prosecutor I had been. "But good, though. Boy! Why, that Polly there even once sent *me* to prison on t'ird-offense drunk and disorderly. . . ." It was nice, I thought, to have such a grateful and satisfied customer.

"Good morning, Lieutenant," I said.

My client was sitting on his unmade cot reading a newspaper, clad in old fatigue trousers and a white T-shirt, his dark hair rumpled and uncombed and his face unshaven. Except for the smudge of mustache he reminded me of a photograph I'd once seen of Lawrence of Arabia.

"Oh, good morning, good morning," he said, quickly rising and pointing to the lone stool next to the gaping seatless toilet. "Please sit down. I—I didn't expect you quite so early or I'd have been ready." He gestured at his cell. "Forgive the appearance of this—this—"

"Sty," I said helpfully, sitting down. I had forgotten how oppressively squalid the cells really were. Nor had I realized that the man had carefully groomed and dressed himself for his daily sessions with me. "Here," I said, handing him a thick book, "this may help take your mind off your surroundings." It was Thomas Wolfe's *Look Homeward, Angel.* "I hope you haven't already read it."

"Oh, thanks. Thank you very much." He examined the thick book gingerly. "No—no I haven't read it," he said. He leaned over his cot and carefully shoved the book under his pillow, patting the pillow to hide it. "Haven't ever heard of it, in fact." He laughed briefly. "I'm just a typical army type, I guess, interested only in three things: in wine, women, and war, or as I once heard a soldier say in Pusan, in beer, broads, and battle. Is it any good?"

"Good?" I said. "Good?" I repeated. "It was written by a ravaged whale of a man—written with his own threshing flukes dipped in his own raging blood. . . . But I didn't climb 'way up here to talk of Wolfe." I lowered my voice. "I came to tell you that your wife passed her lie-detector test. She was telling the truth."

The Lieutenant sat staring at me in tense coiled silence. He stared searchingly, almost uncomprehendingly. The dark eyes fluttered. Then: "How do you know this?" he said, his voice suddenly gone husky with emotion. His eyes, too, had grown narrow and slitted with craft. My hunch, I felt, had not been wrong: he had suspected her all along.

"I can't tell you, Lieutenant," I replied steadily. "But I know it is true." I paused. "There is now not the slightest doubt in my mind that your wife's story is true in every important particular—including the rape." The lieutenant had closed his eyes and sat, tight-lipped, shaking his head quickly from side to side. "The poor bastard," I thought. "The poor tormented bastard." The canker of doubt had still been gnawing at him whether it had really been rape, whether *she* mightn't have encouraged or even solicited Barney Quill.

"There's one more thing," I said, rising to leave. "We must not let anyone know that we know what we know. That makes a nice cryptic sentence, doesn't it? I mean the result of this test." I turned to go.

"I understand," the Lieutenant said. "You're leaving so soon? Oh, I suppose you prefer to wait for me below." He smiled and glanced about his cell. "I wouldn't much blame you. I won't be long." He arose and walked to the cell door.

"I won't be seeing you until some time this afternoon, Lieutenant," I said. "Oh, by the way, I wrote the Army last night about furnishing us a psychiatrist. I held out the tin cup and piled it on. Right now I'm going to talk with your wife. I expect we'll have a rather heavy session this morning." I paused. "I would prefer that you weren't there."

The Lieutenant stood frozen in his tracks. "But you talked with her yesterday," he suddenly blurted. "You talked for—for over two hours. Why—I—" He had paused, fallen silent, and stood nervously chewing his lower lip.

"Yes, Lieutenant?" I said, turning and facing him. "Have you said all you wanted to say? Are you done?"

The man's face was a brick-like crimson. "I—I was just thinking," he said.

I stood watching the man, wavering between scorn and pity. "Lieutenant," I said softly, "I don't think I'd like to know what you're thinking. I don't think I'd really like it. You've already revealed quite enough." I paused. "And if I may say so, it seems to me that you are in enough trouble already without dreaming up any more. Now come off of it, Lieutenant. Please. We've got to fight a real danger—this damned murder case."

I held out my hand. He still stood there frozen, still flushed and frowning, his eyes unblinking, his lower lip caught in his teeth. There was a perceptible pause and then he took my hand. "Yes, sir!" he said, and the phrase escaped him like a pent jet of steam. I turned and quickly left.

As I clattered down the ringing jail stairs I whipped out my handkerchief and patted my forehead. The guitar had fallen silent. It seemed that I still had a client. I discovered that I was running and I slowed to a walk. Reaching the bottom I rattled the big main door like a man fleeing from nightmare. "For Christ's sake let me out of here, Sulo!" I shouted. "I need air. I—I'm suffocating."

"Don't get your bowels in a uproar," Sulo said, hurrying to release me from—from precisely what I did not know. . . .

I stood outside the jail door, breathing deeply. God, it was good to be alive and—and free from witnessing an open cancer of jealousy. When I reached the car Laura Manion and her little dog were awaiting me.

"Did you tell Manny?" she asked eagerly before I fairly got seated. "How did he take it?"

"Did I tell him what?" I said sharply, knowing what she meant and feeling an unaccountable prick of irritation. What kind of a pair of emotional juveniles was I getting mixed up with?

"Why, the results of the lie-detector test, of course. I could scarcely wait to ask you."

"Oh, that," I said almost gaily, fighting back the dark mood I seemed to be in. "Yes, I told him," I said airily. "Everything was fine, fine. I also told him to keep mum." I paused, feeling not unlike a sort of badgered and teetering diplomatic referee, like someone trying to promote sweetness and light, say, between the Soviets and the U.S.A. "Everything's under control," I went on. "He's getting himself and his bachelor quarters tidied up and I plan to see him after lunch. In the meantime I'd like to hear your story. I want it from A to Z. Would you care to light up?"

"Do you want me to tell it just as I told it to the state police?"

"I want it just as you told it to the state police, plus," I said.

"Plus what?"

I smiled. "Plus, my dear, what you *didn't* tell the state police. Come now, Laura, you're a smart woman and you're doubtless several light years ahead of me. I want all the story—plus all of the angles, good or bad. Don't you see, if you don't tell your lawyer what he may have to face and fight—"

"Where shall I begin?" she said, smiling.

"Suppose," I said, "suppose you begin at A."

"I had ironed most of the afternoon," Laura Manion said, beginning on a nice domestic note. "Manny had got home from the firing point a little later than usual, about six o'clock—I mean the night of the shooting." She was wearing slacks and a tight sweater—I saw I'd have to speak to her about that—and had drawn her legs up under her, sitting cross-legged, Indian fashion. "I think he'd stopped off at Barney's bar with some other officers and had a round or two of drinks—he was sleepy and hungry."

"Was he drunk?" I said.

"Oh, no, just so-so—just relaxed, merely a pleasant glow."

"I see," I said. "Did you tell the police about that?—I mean about his sleepiness, about the pleasant glow?"

"I didn't tell them and they didn't ask me."

"Very well," I said. "Go on. I'll try not to interrupt unless I have to."

Laura Manion went on with her story. Manny had taken a brief nap before dinner; then he had eaten; then he had taken another nap. Later he had awakened and asked for a highball, but there was no whisky in the trailer; then he had wanted some beer, but there was no beer. Laura Manion had suggested that they go visit Barney's bar but Manny had grunted and turned his face to the wall.

"And what were you doing all this time?" I said.

"Being frightfully bored," she replied. "I hadn't been out of that damned trailer in over a week, except to shop. It was beginning to feel like a cell."

"Cleopatra," I thought. "Imprisoned Cleopatra chained to the ironing board of a mortgaged trailer." There was something faintly incongruous in the picture. "Go on," I said.

Manny had again fallen asleep. A full moon had swum up out of Lake Superior, sifting through the pines surrounding the trailer. It was a gorgeous summer night and for a time she had sat watching the shimmering lake. Laura had finally awakened Manny and told him she planned going to the bar at the hotel to get some beer. Would he like to go along? Manny had yawned and thought no, but said he might join her later. Then he had fallen asleep again. This time he had begun to snore. He had sounded, she thought, "like a missing outboard motor."

Laura had listened to his snoring as long as she could and then she had called her little dog Rover and taken her flashlight and walked up to Barney's hotel bar, taking the path through the woods. That was her regular route to town, much shorter than going by the road. She thought it had been shortly before nine o'clock, she couldn't exactly remember, anyway it was getting dusk. She must have got there in about ten minutes.

Barney's hotel bar was almost deserted, there were only a few customers, and those mostly locals. No, there were no Army people. There might have been a tourist or two. Oh, yes, the tourist park where the Manions stayed was quite full; it was that time of the year. "Tourists to the right of us; tourists to the left of us. . . ." The only others in the bar were the bartender, whose name was Paquette, she thought, and a blonde waitress called Fern something or other, she wasn't quite sure of her last name, perhaps Malmquist or Youngquist, something like that. We certainly had some rather odd names up in this neck of the woods, didn't we?

"Yes," I admitted. "Up here Smith is an odder name, however. And where was Barney Quill? Wasn't he there when you arrived?"

"No, he didn't appear until later. I ordered a highball—my regular drink, a bourbon and tall water—and then I went over and played the pinball machine."

"*Pinball!*" I said, recoiling in horror. Somehow or other I couldn't quite visualize this beautiful creature and pinball. "You played pinball?" I asked her incredulously.

She smiled, defiant in her waywardness. "I love to play pinball," she said. "I guess I'm funny that way."

"You share your neurosis with millions," I said, shaking my head sadly. "Why there are even some people who love to square-dance—square-dance to hill-billy music sung through the left nostril. I have beheld it with these tired old eyes."

"An Army wife has to find some way to pass her time—and still stay an Army wife," she said. "Anyway, I love it."

"Go on," I said wearily.

She had gone on playing pinball; there was no escape from it; more lights had lit, more bells had rung, still more colors and numbers had flashed and cascaded, the machine was wracked with more tremors and seizures—and she had gone on playing pinball. Then Barney Quill had appeared quietly at her side and challenged her to a game for a drink. She had accepted his challenge and they had played and she had won the first game. Yes, Fern had served them their drinks over at the machine.

"This Barney—what shape was he in?" I said. "How did he act?

Did he seem to be drunk? Did he—did he make any kind of a play for you?"

"He appeared sober to me. And I must say he acted like a gentleman. In the place, that is. There was no suggestion of any play"— she paused and smiled—"and from long experience I think I've grown fairly sensitive to all the signs."

"Yes, I suppose. Did the police ask you about this, too?"

"Yes. And I gave them the same answer, because it was true. He was friendly and courteous, no less and no more."

"Go on," I said. "When did you finally wrench yourself away from the hypnosis of pinball?"

She and Barney had played several more games. They had had some of their drinks at the bar. During the evening she had had three or four highballs; she was quite sure it was not more than four. No, she was not intoxicated, just feeling relaxed and enjoying herself, perhaps about like Manny had felt when he had come home for supper. Then she had noticed it was nearing eleven so she ordered her six-pack of beer and made ready to leave. It was then that Barney suggested that he drive her back to the trailer. Yes, he was still courteous but she had thanked him and declined, saying that with her flashlight and dog Rover she would make it all right walking.

Barney had then warned her that there were a lot of strange characters floating about the town at that time of the year and that he felt it was his duty to see the Lieutenant's wife safely home. And then he had mentioned the bears.

"Bears!" I said. First there was pinball, now there were bears. Little Laura and the three bears. "What bears?" I said.

"It seems that nearly every evening the black bears move in to scavenge the village and trailer-park garbage dumps. I remembered that Manny had mentioned seeing a bear one night while driving along the main road. Then I recalled that one of our soldiers had wounded one only the week before."

"What did you do?"

"Well, by that time I was of half a mind to ride with him but I knew that Manny didn't like Barney—or any man that was nice to me, for that matter—so I again declined and thanked him for the pleasant evening. I then went back to the rest room, back beyond the pinball machine, to tidy up so that when I was ready to leave I could slip out the side door of the bar without further notice."

"I understand," I said.

Laura Manion had lighted her flashlight when she emerged from the rest room and given it to Rover—he carried it in his mouth like a bone, it was his little trick—and she and Rover had slipped out of the side door as she had planned.

"What happened then?" I said.

Someone standing in the shadows had said "Psst!" and come forward. It was Barney. He had the motor of his car running and he again asked her to let him drive her home; once more he expressed his concern over the anonymous characters and the bears.

"What did you do?" I said.

"Well, it seemed frightfully dark outside after the brightly lit barroom. And, foolishly as it turned out, I was growing more afraid of possible strange bears than of any strange men. It also struck me as ungracious and rather insulting for me to continue to refuse him. It seemed much easier to let him drive me home—it was so close. So I consented and Rover and I got in his car, Rover sitting between us with his flashlight."

"Go on," I said.

"Well, Barney drove down the main road to the regular car entrance to the trailer park. It's only a short way beyond the footpath I had taken earlier while coming to the hotel. When he turned in toward the tourist park I remember feeling a little silly for having refused a ride so long—for there he was, driving me straight home, just as he had promised."

"Proceed," I said.

"There is a little stretch of heavily wooded road just before you get to the boundary of the tourist park, the main entrance. When we got there I saw a gate closed squarely across the road. I had never seen it before."

"What happened then?"

"As I started to open the car door and thank him for driving me home he laid his hand on my hand or arm—not forcibly, just lightly —and told me that he had forgotten that the caretaker locked the gate at night; that he knew of another little road into the park that had no gate and would not be closed; and there was no use in my getting all dusty going through the fence and walking the sandy road, he'd gladly take me the other way. With that he backed the car swiftly out to the main road and shot it into forward gear and drove away down the road—in a direction still farther away from the hotel bar."

"Up to that time had you felt any particular sense of alarm?"

"No, none whatever."

"All right. Then what happened?"

"He drove rapidly down the road and then turned abruptly off the main road onto a strange narrow two-rut road to the right and away from the tourist park. That was the first time I had any feeling that things were not right. I said, 'Barney, where are you going?' Instead of answering me he grabbed my arm, tightly this time, and kept driving furiously. I don't know how far we drove. Suddenly he stopped the bouncing car and turned out the lights. By that time I was thoroughly alarmed and I opened the door and tried to get out, but he dragged me back in. He was terribly strong. Then Rover the dog started to whine and Barney opened his door and threw him out. All the while he hadn't spoken a word. I couldn't see a thing, but I could hear Rover whimpering outside."

"Go on," I said.

"Then Barney got close up against me, very close, and said in a hoarse wild voice I could scarcely recognize that he was going to rape me."

"He used that word?"

"That's the very word he used. Then he said I'd better come across—that was also his expression—or I'd never get out of the car alive. All the while he was pawing away at me, trying to get at me, and I was trying to fight him off."

"Up to this time had you screamed?"

"No. I guess I sensed it was no use; it seemed like we were miles from anywhere; it was like being marooned in the middle of a jungle. And I was growing terribly afraid now that he might kill me, as he had threatened."

"Go on."

"All the while he kept clawing at me and beating me on the knees with his fists, a regular tattoo. I had my knees clamped together. I felt myself growing weaker. Finally I said: 'If you do this to me my husband will kill you.'"

"You told him *that?*" I said, wincing my eyes shut.

"Yes, I was getting desperate and I thought by saying that I might scare him off and bring him to his senses. And furthermore I meant it."

This opened up certain glum vistas; vistas, I saw, that should mightily please an alert prosecutor. But now was no time to get into that. "What happened then?" I said.

"My saying that only seemed to make him worse, if anything. He laughed, if you could call it that—it was a horrible cackling sound—

and said Manny wouldn't have the guts to kill him; that he, Barney, was one of the best pistol shots in Michigan, in the Midwest, anywhere; that he was a whiz at Judo and I don't remember what all, and that he could take on a dozen Army guys like Manny with one arm tied behind his back. He ranted on like a madman. It seemed he was just about the best there was at anything."

"Hm," I said. "Interesting, very, very interesting. Go on."

"I again said that if he did that to me Manny would kill him—we were struggling all the time, remember—and with that he suddenly crouched away from me and hit me with his fist. Hard. He swore at me. 'Take that, you goddam Army slut!' is one of the things I remember he said. I almost lost consciousness. I felt something ripping as he tore off my panties. About all I can remember after that is that he kept clawing and beating away at my knees like a maniac. I was practically out. I could hear the dog whimpering and crying outside, scratching at the door."

I was watching her closely during this recital. She did not sigh or weep or hesitate; rather she told her story as though she were trying faithfully to recount some bad dream. "And then what?" I said.

"Well, finally I knew he was—well, he had succeeded, he was getting his way."

"You're sure of that?"

"A woman does not mistake these things, Paul. I still ache from the man; I did not want him; I was. . . . Surely you understand all this. . . ."

"Go on," I said, nodding.

"He was like a raging beast. I did not fight any more. In the first place I couldn't any longer; anyway it seemed better to have this awful nightmare over with. I lost all track of time. All I recall is that suddenly he wasn't at me, that Rover was back beside me, that the car was moving once again. I must have partly fainted. All I wanted then was to get away from this madman. It seemed as though he wanted to rend something; to tear it apart."

"Did either of you speak? More than you have recounted, I mean?"

"No, no other words were spoken. Barney was breathing deeply, almost like a dying man, a hideous guttural noise between a sob and a moan. It was the eeriest sound I have ever heard and was in a way—this may sound terribly odd to you—one of the worst parts of my experience. It was as though he was about to cry, to break down. . . ." She shook her head. "I still hear it at night."

"Go on," I said.

"Finally we were out on the main road. Then I saw we were again nearing the locked gate. I grabbed for the door and got it partly open at the same time that Barney grabbed for me. I couldn't get out. He wanted to take off my sweater. . . . Then he wanted me to totally undress. We'd try it that way, he said. He was like a madman, all the time plucking away trying to rip off my sweater. By this time the car had to stop or it would have hit the gate. I somehow again opened the car door and Rover leapt out. His flashlight was still burning. Barney still had hold of me. 'He's going to kill me,' I thought. I suddenly gathered myself and somehow wrenched away from him and ran. I could see Rover with his light running furiously back and forth between an opening in the fence. I ran towards him, towards the light."

"Did you get through the fence?"

"I don't really know. Barney was suddenly upon me. He tripped me and kicked me and then fell on me. Then he started hitting me with his fists, hard, all over my face and body, repeatedly. I swear he was trying to kill me. I felt myself fainting, I was nearly out. That was when I screamed. I screamed two or three times with all my might. Suddenly I discovered that I was alone, running, following Rover and his light, running towards our trailer. I tripped and fell and got up again—I don't know how many times—but always I kept running toward the light."

"You saw no more of Barney?"

She closed her eyes and shook her head. "No. I never laid eyes on him again—alive or dead."

"Go on," I said.

"As I got to the door of our trailer Manny was just coming out. He seemed only half awake. He told me later he'd dreamed I was screaming and woke up. I fell into his arms."

I looked at my watch. "Do you want a rest?" I said. "Maybe to smoke or walk the dog?" If she didn't, I did.

"No, no," she said, and then she smiled. "But perhaps you do."

"I think I'll take a five," I said. "In the meantime you can collect your thoughts."

"If you do this to me Manny will kill you," Laura Manion had said. And she had been right; she had known her Manny and Barney hadn't. Barney had "done that" and Manny had had the guts, all right; he had marched out and killed Barney. The reaction had been as starkly primitive and elemental—yes, and as inevitable—as holding one's hand over an open fire: perforce the hand would be burned. If Manny had been insane that night then Barney himself must have been stark raving mad. In fact the certainty that something bad would happen to him if he raped Laura Manion cast the biggest doubt on her story. What in hell did Barney Quill *think* would happen to him if he did but half of what she claimed? Had the man been trying deliberately to destroy himself? Who was this guy Barney Quill? What was *his* trouble? I saw I still had lots and lots of work to do; that there were still many baffling questions in this weird case.

"Manny will kill you," she had said. The fateful phrase buzzed like a gnat in my ears. And as the defense lawyer I didn't pretend to like it. But my hands were tied; there was nothing I could do about it; the fatal words had been uttered. I shook my head. Lawyers were something like actors, I reflected: their range was limited by the play; they had to take the script as they found it; they dared not change the words or tinker with the dialogue. When they did they became either ham actors, on the one hand, or else shysters. What Laura Manion had said was natural enough, Heaven knows, but I was sure that if I had been writing the script I would not have let her say what she had said. For one thing, in one breath didn't it take a lot of wind out of the sails of our insanity plea? Didn't this revealing warning she had given Barney tend rather to stamp the act as a deliberate killing done in a fit of murderous retribution and revenge, just as she had predicted? And had she told the police what she had told Barney? Perhaps even more important, had she told *Manny* what she had told Barney? Had she in effect suggested to her husband that he go out and dispatch the doomed and waiting Barney? Well, I would find out very soon.

"Laura," I said, beside her in the car once again, "did you tell the police about warning Barney that Manny would kill him if—if he 'molested' you, as our family newspapers love to call rape?"

"Yes, yes, of course. I told the police everything that happened, everything I could recall that was said and done. Wasn't that all right?"

"Yes, of course." I proceeded calmly. There was no use in my uselessly scaring her. "And did you also tell Manny what you'd told Barney?" I held my breath as I awaited her answer.

"Yes, he was the first one I told," she replied.

My heart sank. This could be a serious development in the case, not only marring the effectiveness before a jury of our claim of insanity but possibly the even more important question of whether a reputable psychiatrist would now ever find insanity at all, in view of it. Well, I had better get all the bad news at once.

"And did you also tell the police that you had already told Manny?" I asked.

"Yes," she replied, and my spirits sank even lower. "I told Manny about it on the way driving in to the jail. The officers undoubtedly heard me and anyway I told them again later."

My spirits soared and I could almost—but not quite—have hugged her. "You mean," I said, "that the *first* time you told Manny was *after* the shooting?—not before?"

My mounting concern and sudden relief had been totally lost on Laura. "Why, yes. I never thought of telling him before," she replied easily. "I guess I was afraid, too, that Manny would do just what he did do. I knew the man. . . . Anyway, things happened so fast. . . ."

"What were you wearing that night?" I said, veering abruptly away from this troublesome subject. "Were you dressed as you are now?" Looking again, I was somehow hopeful she wasn't. But then, hadn't she already mentioned wearing a sweater?

"Well," she said thoughtfully, "I had on a sweater, one very much like this"—I winced inwardly—"and a skirt and a slip and panties."

"Any girdle?" I inquired hopefully.

"Heaven's no," she said. "I never wear the things."

"These . . . panties that Barney tore off—who has them now? The police?"

"I've never seen them since. We gave the ripped skirt to the police. The next day the police drove me and Rover in to the spot—they apparently determined it by some fresh tire burns nearby on the grass where Barney had evidently turned around, and also by the way poor Rover whined and carried on at that place" (she reached over and affectionately patted the dog as she spoke), "but they never found my panties though they scoured the woods all around the place. All they found were my glasses—still intact, thank goodness."

"Glasses?" I said. "You mean to tell me you were wearing glasses through all this?"

"No, not wearing but carrying them in their case. I'd been holding them in my hand and in the struggle with Barney when I first tried to get out of the car I must have dropped them."

"Why aren't you wearing them now?" I said.

"Well, right now I'm afraid I still need my dark glasses." She laughed her rich chuckling laugh. "Anyway I only use them for reading or anything close up. I had used them to play pinball that night." She again laughed. "I'm surely glad they found them—I can't even read a headline without my glasses."

"Glasses!" I mused. Another small score for our side. It was going to be hard at best, I saw, to tone down this concupiscent-looking creature, but I would have to make the try. However she might despise wearing a girdle she was damned well going to have to wear one at the trial. I'd have to remember to tell her.

"I seem to recall that you or your husband mentioned something about moving your trailer," I said. "What was all that about?"

"I've moved our trailer from the tourist park in Thunder Bay down to a small private trailer lot in Iron Bay," she said. "First of all, I wanted to get away from that—that place"—she paused—"and also get away from the tourists and curiosity seekers. Ever since that night they have surrounded the place, almost day and night, it seemed, as though I were some kind of two-headed monster. I was in a state of siege. Every time I dared go out the door, there they were, owlishly staring at me or boldly asking that Rover and I pose for their cameras. Some were even bold enough to want to discuss the details of the case with me. I've never seen such an exhibition of morbid prying curiosity." She shook her head.

"The price of fame, madam," I said. "But you haven't seen anything yet. Just wait till the trial. You will discover that morbid curiosity is not confined solely to tourists. It's the nature of the human beast, I'm afraid."

"You—you think the trial will be crowded?" she inquired anxiously.

"Solidly," I said. "The case has everything. Rape, murder. Even a little dog." But I saw the look of "courtroom fright" overtaking her again so I swiftly changed the subject. "Did you tell the police substantially the same story you have told me, up to now?"

She nodded. "Yes, practically the same." She shrugged and laughed. "I had to. That's the way it was."

"Well," I said. "You have told it very well, well and effectively. It has the ring of truth. I only hope you can do as well in court."

"Thank you, Paul," she said. "I'll certainly try."

"There's one more thing—an important thing."

"What's that?" she said.

"You understand of course that when we're in court during the trial the prosecutor will get to question you when I am done?"

"Yes, I supposed that he would. They always do in the movies, don't they? Wagging their fingers and all?"

"Well, he may try to shake your story, or confuse you, or try to bring out things that we might not ourselves particularly like to bring out. I cannot now predict what they might be. But do you follow me?"

She nodded.

"What I want to impress upon you," I continued, "is to at all times tell the truth. I think that so far you have been, but Mitch— I mean the prosecutor—may try to draw things from you, possibly new things, that in your natural confusion or desire to help you may feel are better to hide or soft-pedal—or even to lie about." I paused. "Don't do it. When in doubt tell the truth. It's the best little confounder of clever cross-examination in the business. I know whereof I speak. Now I'll try to keep Mitch from roaming too far afield, but the latitude allowed in cross-examination can be deadly and Mitch may nevertheless try to give you a bad time."

Laura shook her head. "Why should he try to do that to me? And he looks so open and frank—so nice and kindly, too."

"He may try it to shake or cast doubt on your story of the rape. The brutal fact of this rape is his big problem in this case and he will know it. Don't you see, Laura, if he can keep pecking away at you and lower your guard and get you to tell some silly little untruth on some minor point, and then later in rebuttal or in some other way demonstrate that little lie of yours to the jury—if he can do that, then maybe he can cast a doubt on our big truth—the bitter and otherwise unescapable truth of the rape. Don't you see? It's one of the oldest tricks in the law."

"Yes, I see, Paul. But why should he try to shake my story on the rape? He already knows that I told the truth—he has his own lie-detector test to tell him that."

I laughed, a little cynically, I'm afraid. "Dear woman," I said, "a lawyer in court trying to win a big case is like a newspaper man sitting on top of a big scoop—he's not to be trusted. Never. At such times a lawyer would betray his own grandmother. So help me, I've done it myself. In fact I used to be quite a little bearcat at the business."

She shook her head. "How utterly sordid," she said. "I—I thought the law was above that. . . . How can a lawyer possibly try to twist and pervert what he already knows to be the truth?"

"We lawyers quickly develop a protective scar tissue to take care of that," I said. "It's all rather simple. It is our lofty conviction, hugged so dearly to our hearts, that our cause is basically just and right and that those on the other side are just a pack of lying and guilty knaves." I shook my head. "It's merely the same old dilemma of man in a new guise: that supposed noble ends can ever justify shabby means. Mitch will tell himself—and with considerable force —that even if Barney *did* rape you, it gave Manny no legal justification to kill him. So the man must be guilty. From there it's only a small jump, a mere breeze, to convincing himself that the ultimate truth or falsity of the rape doesn't really matter. Don't you see?"

"I'm afraid I do," Laura Manion said, nevertheless shaking her head dubiously.

I was growing afraid that I had told her too much too early and had maybe built up in her what lawyers call "court fright," the legal version of mike fright or camera jitters in the amiable world of radio and television. But it had to be done; it would be no easier if I sprung it on her just before the trial; and this way she could perhaps at least have time to ponder and learn to live with her burden.

"Don't let the prospect get you down, Laura," I said. "All you have to do is open those big eyes of yours wide and tell the truth. I can see that comes naturally to you anyway, and here we must make sure that nobody tells any small untruths so that we can protect our big truth. I hope I can cuff the prosecution all over the lot with *that.* So let's not weaken our rape story to gain any small temporary triumphs." It was refreshing, I reflected, that legal strategy and the truth could occasionally walk gaily hand in hand.

"Thank you, Paul," she said, touching my arm briefly. "I'll open my eyes real wide and just let the truth flow out." She paused and smiled. "You really want to win this case, don't you?"

"Didn't you know, madam," I said, laughing, "that I too am convinced of the justice and right of our cause? The prosecution is nothing but a pack of lying scoundrels. You see, it's an occupational disease of us lawyers." I glanced at my watch. It was nearing the lunch hour. And I could see Mister Cool padding restlessly up and down his cell, peering anxiously out of his sooty window, drilling my back with his smoldering dark eyes.

"Speaking of your big wide eyes," I continued, "I want you to go find a photographer today and have your black eyes photographed in all their glory. And all your bruises, too. They've faded out some even since yesterday. To make sure have him take at least two shots of each pose. When this thing's all over, I'll give you a set to place among your souvenirs. Better go to Tom Bennett; I'll phone him first. I don't want him playing up your bruises—they scarcely need that—but I also don't want him to go artistic on us and play them down. As a class these picture men have a weakness that way; they seem to want to make everyone come out looking like week-old albino rabbits. I'm a Mathew Brady man myself. And don't you go and try to look glamorous." I got out of the car. "Then come back over here when you're done. I want to hear the rest of your story."

"It shall be done, Paul," Laura Manion said, laughing. "And I promise to look like a perfect witch."

"That, madam," I said gallantly, "will take a bit of doing."

chapter 15

If clients and witnesses sometimes suffer from courtroom jitters, lawyers themselves occasionally come down with what might more clumsily be called "preparation-of-the-case" jitters. That noon while I ate lunch at the Iron Bay Club I thought I detected some preliminary twinges in myself. The symptoms are subtle and rather hard to pin down; I seemed suddenly gripped by a feeling of unreality about the case and its possible outcome, a wry sensation of inadequacy and doubt, a notion that I was somehow missing the boat; an anxious feeling that I had got so close to this damned case that I couldn't see the forest for the trees.

I also discovered that I was holding an uneaten sandwich poised in mid-air. I abruptly took a big bite into it and one or two of my fellow diners glanced quickly in my direction, as one does when a creep is abroad. "Wrong order," I muttered in a sandwich-muffled voice. "Place goin' plumb to hell."

Tentative trial strategies which seemed inspired from on high were now crowding in and colliding head on with still other but inconsistent strategies which had seemed no less brilliant at birth. It was high time, I reflected, that I get to hell away from the turbulent Manions and their tangled emotional problems and turn my searchlight on the raw case itself. From there on it was only a breeze for me to decide to go fishing. I sighed and pushed my unfinished sandwich away and went upstairs and phoned the county jail.

"Is this you, Sulo?" I asked, as though there was anyone else in the whole wide world who could say "Iron 'Liffs County Yail speaking" with half the Old World charm of Sulo. "This is Polly Biegler," I went on. "Look, Sulo, please tell the Manions that I've been unavoidably detained and won't be able to see them this afternoon."

"You been *wat?*" Sulo shouted, and it came back to me that he had always shouted over the phone; he was one of those resolute diehards who would never quite believe that such gadgets were here to stay.

"Look, Sulo, tell my Army man I won't be there today. Yes . . . I mean no . . . I won't be there." I too was shouting. "Have you got it? *I won't be there!* I'm sick, I'm going fishing, I'm drunk! I won't be there!"

"Sewer, sewer, sewer, Polly," Sulo said mildly. "Vy don't you tell me dat in da first 'lace? You von't be over here today."

"Good-by, Sulo," I said. "I love you madly."

"Vat you say?" Sulo shouted.

"*I won't be there!*" I shouted back, closing my eyes and resting the receiver gently on its cradle.

Yes, it was about time to go fishing.

But it was still too early and far too bright for good fishing so I ordered a bottle of beer and picked up an outdoor magazine and idly thumbed the pages. The mosquito-infested crisp-bacon world of outdoor sportsmen, I saw, was this season fast going to hell in an outboard motor. Tucked away between the jungle of ads I found an article on a new way of plug casting for bass. I read it, as one sometimes macaberly reads the obituaries of complete strangers. The incongruity of my reading about bass or bass fishing, which I loathed, reminded me of the time my friend Raymond and I had once, on a fishing trip, visited the shack of old Dan McGinnis, the king of Oxbow Lake. Danny lived by himself—"batched" in the U.P. idiom—in one of the wildest and remotest areas of the county. One had to walk the last several miles to get there; not even the best jeep could quite negotiate that bush country. We had found old Danny sitting by his window, patched elbows propped on his checkered oilcloth-covered kitchen table, poring over a tattered old pulp magazine. His lips were moving silently as though he were reciting a litany. So absorbed was he in his reading that he barely looked up when we stomped in and dumped our packsacks and fishing gear on his floor.

"What are you reading, Danny?" Raymond had politely asked.

"Oh, who me?" Danny replied, annoyedly looking up. "Why, I'm readin' a story about a kind of a hermit fella what lives 'way up in the north woods—all by hisself. He's slowly goin' crazy, it says here. Livin' all alone all year 'round. Can you imagine the likes of a pore crazy bastard doin' that? Unnatural, I calls it. Yep, yep, yep. Damned int'restin', though!"

And there I now sat, in the heart of some of the finest trout fishing in the country, reading an article designed to teach poor trapped city guys and Indiana farmers how they might catch more wormy *bass*, a fish that I personally regarded as scarcely a cut above a chain-store lobster. I slammed shut the magazine and stalked out of the place and down the street to Doc Trembath's office.

The Doctor's office was crowded as usual, and as usual mostly with glowering and stoically pregnant women, who were his specialty; but Doc's receptionist was an understanding woman who seemed to sense that my own pregnancy was more advanced, and in a few minutes I was seated beside the doctor himself, an enormous big hulking field marshal of a man with the gentle long-suffering mien of an overworked angel.

"I'm defending the Manion murder case," I said, shaking his big paw, "and believe it or not I need some advice on the mechanics of sex. How the mighty are fallen. Please try to give it to me straight —not in the pig Latin you doctors ordinarily use."

"Fire away," Doctor Trembath said, sighing wearily and lighting a cigarette.

"You've doubtless read about the case in the papers, including the fact that Manion's wife claims that Barney Quill had raped her," I said.

"Yes," the Doctor said. He was a quiet sort of man, and he rarely wasted words. The women adored him; a sheer case of the attraction of opposites.

"Well, the lady in the case, Laura Manion, is a fireball of a woman. She's now living with her second husband. Could a doctor tell by examining her whether she had been raped?"

The Doctor slowly shook his head no.

"Or that she had recently had intercourse?"

"Only if a smear showed spermatozoa."

"The Manions tell me that old Doc Dompierre tilted her up over at the jail the other night, at their request, and took a smear with a swab stick. He has since reported it was negative for male sperm."

"Did he first dilate the—vaginal opening?" Doc asked, mindful of my warning against medical Latin.

"The Manions say no. But is the way he did it kosher?"

"That is not the way I would have done it," the Doctor said.

"But is it one medically accepted way?" I persisted.

"No," he said. "I would say it is definitely not."

"If it appeared that the lady was excessively tender and sore— might not that be some evidence that she had been forcibly had?"

The Doctor looked up at the ceiling and blinked thoughtfully. "I would rather put it this way," he said, speaking carefully. "The symptoms you speak of are purely subjective, so a physician could not himself testify as to her pain and soreness. There would thus be no direct physical evidence of a rape or indeed of any act of intercourse that he could testify to. But if the woman's claim as to such soreness were true and also her claim that it was the result of an unwelcome act of intercourse—if her story was believed, in other words—a careful physician could testify that this was some evidence that the intercourse had been against her will." He paused and smiled faintly. "I suppose I don't have to tell you that a normal woman has to be receptive to the act—she has to be ready. I further understand that among you lawyers the woman's unwillingness is an important element of legal rape."

"Right, Doctor," I said. "But would you so testify if you were asked in court—that her sensitivity could have been the result of intercourse against her will?"

He thought for a moment. "I would want to examine her first," he said.

The good Doctor had led with his chin. "Good," I said. "When can you look her over?"

The Doctor grunted and gestured wearily at the roomful of waiting females. "Another one more or less won't make much difference, I guess." He sighed. "Sometimes I wish I had taken up steamfitting —some trade where I could just throw down my wrench and walk away when the whistle blew."

"Perhaps, Doctor," I said, "perhaps your world view is growing a trifle too confined."

He smiled wanly. "When do you want to send her in?"

"How about this afternoon?"

"I suppose. Yes, send her along."

"Will you also check her for any possible bruises and lacerations, there or elsewhere, and please make notes of your findings?"

"Yes, yes. Send her along."

"Thank you, Doctor. Now just one more question: Is there any way that an autopsy on Barney Quill could have shown that *he* had had intercourse shortly before his death and reached a climax?"

"There is."

"How?"

"By possible stains on his body or clothing, and better yet by examination of the seminal vesicles, which would naturally be depleted—that is, if he had recently reached a sexual climax. Here, I'll show you." He reached over and selected a thick medical book and flipped the pages and showed me and explained a picture of the complicated things that happen to the human male as he embarks on love's last embrace.

"Ah, nature, it's wonderful," I said, when he was done. "But I think that henceforth I'll stick exclusively to fishing."

"May I ask if an autopsy was performed on the deceased?" the Doctor said.

"I assume so," I said. "That's the only sure way the People can prove the cause of death—which is part of what we lawyers call the *corpus delicti*, you know, if you'll excuse my foreign accent."

"Was an examination made of the body and clothing for the things we've just discussed?"

"That's exactly what I don't know, Doc. That's one of the reasons I came to see you." I had come to the hard part, and I paused. "Would you have any objection, Doctor, to testifying for the defense on these things—if it should become necessary?" I said. "In fairness I should add that it probably will become necessary."

The Doctor sat pondering and puffing his cigarette. Here was a grievously busy man, one of the busiest and best in the county. Yet could I much blame him if he shied away from getting mixed up in such a malodorous and flamboyant murder case? "Doctor Orion Trembath, prominent Iron Bay physician and surgeon, today testified for the defense!" the newspapers would proclaim. And he would naturally anticipate all that.

"Doc," I said softly, rising, "this Lieutenant of mine—'way up here among strangers—he's a pretty goddam lonely man. And he's stony broke, too. I'll try to find someone else if—if you'd rather not help."

The Doctor crushed out his cigarette and arose and extended his hand. Tall as I am he towered over me. "If the going gets too rough," he said, "you can count on me."

"Thank you, Doctor," I said. "I hope no one's popped out there while we've been talking."

The stoically pregnant women seemed to glower harder than ever as I, the interloping male, one of the hateful carefree breed responsible for their plight, stole through their swollen ranks and clattered down the stairs. Ah, but they didn't realize all the fine mechanical secrets I now knew about their husbands and lovers. And anyway I had got my doctor, the one I had wanted, one whose opinions were not for sale to the highest bidder. Outside I found that the sun had clouded over. I glanced up at the weather tower. A gentle wind was blowing out of the west. "And when the wind is from the west, that's when fishing is the best." My nostrils began to dilate.

I walked back up to the club and called the jail again and asked Sulo to please get the Lieutenant on the phone. The Lieutenant, it appeared, was still sitting there waiting for me. Sulo would put him on. "You lawyer man vants you!" he shouted.

"I won't be over this afternoon, Lieutenant," I said.

"Yes, Sulo just told me a while ago. I'm waiting for Laura. Is everything all right?"

"Just getting a little punchy, is all, and I'm going fishing. I want to be alone to roll some spitballs for Mr. Lodwick."

The Lieutenant laughed, and I briefly told him of the arrangements I had made for an examination of his wife later that afternoon by Doctor Trembath. "Please see that she gets there," I added.

"But she already has a doctor," the Lieutenant countered in that aggrieved voice I was getting to know so well.

"Yes, I know," I said.

"Then isn't he enough? Do we need *two?*"

I mentally counted to ten. "I don't want to seem picky, Lieutenant, but I happen to consider your particular doctor professionally on a par with Amos Crocker. In fact he must have recommended him." I paused. "Listen, Lieutenant, I'm getting a little weary of having to threaten to pull out of this goddam case every time I want your consent to any recommendation I make. But I should warn you—if you insist upon having that doctor I think you'd better also plan to stick around and wait for old Crocker's leg to mend. They'd make such a charming pair; they both improvise so well. Do I make myself clear?"

"You do."

"Now are you sending your wife over to the new doctor?" There was a long pause, and I could picture the quick angry flush, the sipping of the tiny mustache, the biting of the lower lip. "I've been counting ten, Lieutenant, and I'm almost there."

"Yes, damn it! I'll send her."

"Ah, that's better. Now I can away to my fishing with a carefree heart."

"I hope you fall in."

"What's that!"

"I said, damn it, I hope you have good luck."

"That's the old fight, Lieutenant. I heard you the first time. Now you're talking my language."

"Will you be down tomorrow?"

I hadn't thought of it before, at least consciously, and my answer came out of a clear sky. "No, Lieutenant, I won't be down tomorrow. I've just decided it's time for me to visit the scene of this business. Tomorrow I'm going to Thunder Bay."

"When will I see you, then?"

"Probably the next day. But don't pin me down. I'll see you when I see you. Right now I'm going fishing."

So I went fishing and my heart was carefree and gay. At dusk I snapped my leader on two trout of voting age and finally, just at dark, latched on to grandpa and the fight was on. "Come, come, sweet lover darlin'," I coaxed and wheedled. "Come to daddy, come to daddy." Twenty minutes later I went into the familiar daisy hoop and slipped the net under him. "Ah. . . ." It was my biggest brook trout of the season. It looked like a dappled and dripping slice of sunset in the wavering light of my flashlight. But best of all, for twenty whole minutes I had managed to forget all about the Manion case.

chapter 16

When I got home from fishing I found old Parnell McCarthy dozing on the bench that the chiropractor across the hall had thoughtfully provided for the lame and halt who sought his services.

Parnell sat with his chubby hands locked across the front of his colorful Tattersall vest. I had picked the vest up for him, much to Maida's dismay, on one of my Canadian fishing trips; it was among his proudest possessions, perhaps something like a barber and his Cadillac; and it occurred to me that I'd never once seen him button his coat across this flaming garment since I'd presented it to him the year before. I secretly longed to wear such a vest myself, but, craven soul, somehow lacked the nerve.

Parnell rocked gently as he slumbered. "Whistler's delinquent little brother," I thought wryly. The old man's series of chins rested gently on his chest and when he exhaled his puttering lips sounded faintly like a far-off motorboat. Well, not so far off, I thought judiciously; rather more like the blubbery trumpeting sounds that my father Oliver's horses used to make with their lips after I had watered them down for the night when I was a kid. I hadn't heard that sound in years. Parnell sighed and trumpeted away.

I stood looking down at my old friend. I leaned forward and smelled his breath. "Ah, apparently sober," I concluded with relief. I sniffed again to make sure. Just then Parnell opened one eye and caught me at it.

"Ought to be ashamed of yourself, boy," he rumbled, "sniffin' an' spyin' on an old gentleman just after taking his evenin' catnap—not *catnip!*" He lurched heavily to his feet. "Where in hell was you at? I nearly gave you up. Ah, fishin', I see by your outlandish and evil-smelling costume. What fetid malarial bog did you wallow through today? And must you get yourself up to look and smell like a beachcomber to catch a mere fish? You see, I can sniff, too, my fine laddie buck. . . . C'mon, let's get going, boy. There's work to be done. Come now—tell me the whole story, from B to bunghole. I'm fairly dyin' to hear it."

I unlocked my office and brought in my fresh laundry which was resting against the door. I waved Parnell to a comfortable chair, put my fish on ice, got into my pajamas and an old bathrobe, lit a fire which thoughtful Maida had laid in the Franklin stove and turned out the lights. Then I sat and told Parnell the whole story, the good and the bad, my plans and hopes, all my fears and anxieties.

He sat quietly through the whole recital, for the most part silent and unblinking, at times looking variously, in the flickering firelight, like a statue of Judgment, an aging satyr, a seedy race-track tout, the Buddha himself, the late W. C. Fields, a bust of Socrates—and even that lovely old ad for Lash's Bitters. But mostly, thank goodness, he looked like good old shrewd old kindly old Parnell McCarthy.

Parnell interrupted me rarely and then only briefly, in such a way that I knew that his alert mind was racing, racing faster than the numbers and lights on a runaway pinball machine. It felt good just to have him there, and already some of the confusion and uncertainty that had oppressed me earlier in the day seemed magically to disappear in the simple act of telling.

Down across the deserted square the cracked bell of the clock in the city hall tower sounded one. I loved its wavering clangor. The bell had been cracked since November 11, 1918, and any city father that suggested replacing it courted swift political oblivion. The sound was more of a jarring thud than a knell; a prolonged metallic shudder, as though some giant armed with a sledge had struck a broken rail. At length the dissonant echo faded and died away.

"Well, Parnell," I said, "what does the prosecuting attorney say? Does the defense have a Chinaman's chance? Don't spare my feelings. Give me both barrels, my friend."

"I'm thinkin'," he said, closing his eyes and tugging at the grizzled slack of his throat.

This was our little game. During most of my time as prosecutor Parnell had acted as a sort of volunteer attorney for the defense. We had "tried" all my big tough cases in advance, sitting by the Franklin stove or across the top of Grandma Biegler's old dining-room table. Thus had Parnell hammered and tested—and frequently revised—the theory and strategy of my cases on the stout anvil of his mind. He was, as I had told Mister Cool, my legal whetstone.

This sagacious old man was in fact probably the biggest single reason I had run up, as D.A., the record of convictions of which he seemed so much prouder than I. I often wondered why he bothered and I sometimes sensed vaguely, as I sensed now, that to him I was a sort of what-might-have-been.

"Do I have a chance?" I repeated.

"Of course you've got a chance," he began gruffly. He cleared his throat. "Don't talk that way, boy. Don't sell yourself short. It's poor psychology and, worse yet, in your case false modesty, too. It doesn't become you, boy. Let us please dispense with the chat of the bull.

You're good and you damn well know it." He shook his head. "Quite a case, boy, quite a case indeed," he said musingly. "I—I only wish I were in it." He sighed. "It's been many a year since I've wished that about any case."

This was the opening I had been waiting for. "You're going to be in it, Parnell," I said quietly. "Right up to the hilt. All you got to do is say yes. What do you say?"

It grew silent. Parnell sat very still and I thought for a moment he had dozed off again. I leaned closer and saw that his eyes were open, wide open. In the dying fire glow I thought they glistened suspiciously, but I may have been mistaken. "You mean that, boy?" he said, barely above a whisper. "You really want me in your big murder case?"

"You heard me, Parn. I want you, I need you, and I mean it. I'm not being magnanimous, either. I simply and selfishly need your goddam help. You know what winning this case means to me, I don't have to tell you."

"I—I'll do it, Paul," he said, "but on one condition."

"What's that, Parn?"

"That Parnell McCarthy stays behind the scenes, strictly in the background. You understand? Not even your client must know. Nobody but us—and Miss Maida, of course. There must be no leak."

"Why, Parn?" I said. "Tell me why?" This was an interesting development.

Parnell snorted. "The sight of this bloated whisky-drinkin' red-nosed old man settin' at a counsel table would be enough to queer any case," he went on. "Lord knows you got hurdles enough to get over without addin' me. And if anything went wrong—the ever unpredictable jury you know, boy—I wouldn't want that on my conscience or on yours. I—it's better that I do my sittin' beside you in spirit. I'll be close by in any case." He paused. "And there's one other reason, boy."

"Tell me, Parn?"

"When you win this case I want it to be solely *your* victory. You're already on the right track, boy, you know that, and you don't really need me. You won lots of your big cases before we ever became friends. I'll try to help in my own fumblin' way, of course, but it's enough for an old party like me to see *you* make the grade. Do you understand what I'm sayin?" He paused and, almost angrily, cleared his throat. "I—I—Oh, hell, give me one of those awful Eyetalian cigars. I'll smoke it out of self-defense—that abominable stinker of yours is makin' me eyes smart. Lord help me, it smells like a Bermuda onion. Is it really an onion now, boy?"

"I understand, Parn," I said, passing him a cigar. "I'll accept your terms on one condition."

"Ah, what's that, now? You'd think we was after discussin' the terms of a goddam ninety-nine-year chain-store lease. Whatever is your fine condition now?"

"That we share whatever fee I get straight across the board," I said. "I told you what it was and—and the chance I'm probably taking in ever getting it."

Parnell blinked his eyes. "What you aimin' to do, Paul? Make an old man bawl? Is that what you're after tryin' to do?"

"I mean it, Parn, just like I meant asking you into the case," I said gruffly. "We share the fee or no partnership in the case. That's only fair."

"Bless you, boy, I'll do it. I'll do it to help you and humor your generous whim. Having said that it may be ungracious and commercial-soundin' of me to add that if you don't get paid before the trial you probably never will after, win or lose." He laughed briefly. "I have to say that now so you won't think it's money I'm after, which God knows I ain't and never been. But you aren't either, Paul, you're a lawyer, too, not a misdirected shopkeeper who'd mistakenly gone to law school. I'm pleased and mighty proud that you would undertake to defend this lonely man with—without—"

"Look, Parn," I broke in, "you know goddam well that the plight of Lieutenant Manion has got little or nothing to do with my taking this case. Don't give me that blarney. Please, Parn, please—don't try to build me up into a bleeding liberal. Now please lay off."

"The role fits you more than you think, boy, more than you think," Parnell went on. "Now you listen to me. You didn't consent to continue your man's case when that young Mitch fellow gave you the golden chance, did you? No you didn't. Now you could have sold that continuance to your client and you know damn well you could, still keepin' your hand in the case for all your other reasons, and still givin' yourself more time to pry some money out of him. And more time for your fishin'. All this you could have done. I say I'm proud of you, damn it. You wouldn't let the poor bastard lay in jail for another three or four months. Now let's hear no more bulldozin' about it. Poke up that fire and fetch me a bottle of beer." He grimaced. "I'd just as lief drink mare's water but there's work to be done—and let's get down to business."

I drew myself up proudly. "I'll have you understand, Mr. McCarthy, that I pay over five bucks a case for my beer. Every bottle is tested by virgins in rubber gloves. No finger touch. I've even seen Heinie the brewmaster on TV. Charming articulate fellow who talks through a permanent mist of sauerkraut, like my great-uncle Otto. 'Mine goot friendts, dis malt, dese hops—da pest vat money can puy, *ya!*' Authentic, see, very Old World, and all done purely for love, like mother's bread. Perhaps you'd prefer some nice tepid tap water instead."

"Get on wid you," Parnell said, grinning and holding a match to his cigar, then archly cocking his head. "And who, pray tell—who tests them there virgins?"

Parnell took a sip of his beer. He swallowed, looked thoughtful, and then made a wry face, like a small boy distastefully eating his spinach. "The original diagnosis was correct," he said. "Better you sue your goot friendt Heinie, *ya!*"

"Very well, Mr. Prosecutor," I said. "Quit slandering my hospitality. Let's have your reasons why my man should be convicted. It's getting late."

He stared at me vacantly for a moment and then leaned forward, speaking earnestly. "If I were prosecutor, boy," he began, "I would hammer relentlessly at this one big question: If the defendant Manion did not take a gun and go to Barney Quill's bar *solely* to kill him, why in hell else did he go there? 'Members of the jury,' I would say, 'here is a man who deliberately takes a loaded pistol, secretes it on his person, unerringly seeks out the man who had just raped his wife—and pumps him full of lead. Why, why, why—if it was not solely to kill the man, which is promptly what he did?' " Parnell paused, his gray eyes glowing and alight. "Does defense counsel concede any merit in this argument? How, my resourceful friend, do you propose to get around that?"

"Go on, Parn," I said. "There's more, much more. Hit me with all of it and then I'll try to fight back."

"Yes, there's more to it," Parnell continued thoughtfully. "In connection with this same line of argument, and also to dispute your claim of insanity, I would keep harping on the fact that, immediately after the shooting, the defendant apparently threatened to shoot the bartender, who followed him from the place, and then returned to his trailer and gave himself up to the deputized caretaker of the trailer camp with these significant words: 'I just shot Barney Quill.' In other words: 'Take me in, Mister Policeman, my mission is accomplished; I went there to *get* Barney and by God I *got* him.' Are these the actions of a crazy man, of a man who didn't know what he was doing? Why, even his wife, who knew his jealous nature, predicted he would kill Barney—and I'm damned if that's what he didn't."

"Objection, Parn," I said. "No fair on that jealousy business. That's inside information I hope the prosecution doesn't and won't have. But otherwise you've been hitting me where it really hurts."

"Objection overruled," Parnell continued coolly. "This young Lodwick fellow is inexperienced and all, and perhaps no great heavyweight as a prosecutor, at least yet, but he'll simply *smell* jealousy from her statement that your man would kill Barney *if*. . . . And if he doesn't smell it the jury probably will anyway."

"I don't pretend to like that statement of hers, Parn," I said. "You know it's got me worried. But I would argue back that here was a woman in a desperate plight—about to be raped—who seized at a straw, a last desperate deterrent stratagem, the threat of physical retaliation and punishment if Barney should rape her. What else could the poor woman do or say? And after all, how in hell could she know what her husband might do? Just how many other men can the People show he had killed for raping her? And think of how much worse it would be if *before* the shooting she'd told Manion what she'd told Barney."

"Good boy, Polly," Parnell said, nodding. "Yes, a fairly good answer, young man. Did you just think of it?"

"I guess I've been brooding about it all the time I was fishing today." I shook my head gloomily. "But there's still a lot of work to be done. I've barely scratched the surface. For one thing, I've an enormous lot of law to look. I simply haven't had time to get at it. Anyway, I'd like to get all the facts first. All we want are the facts, ma'am."

"*We've* got a lot of work to do," Parnell said reprovingly. "*We've* got a lot of law to look. Remember, I'm in this case now, too, young man."

"I sit corrected," I said, smiling. "But right now you're the prosecutor. Proceed with your indictment, Mr. D.A."

After that Parnell and I kicked the case around, planned strategies, rejected them, substituted others, pondered how we might get in evidence of the rape, how the prosecution might block it, how we might try to bring out at least the fact of Laura's lie-detector test . . . Parnell finally hauled out his silver watch.

"Lord help us, I haven't been up so late since Terence Cronin's wake. This is enough for tonight, lad. Now get along with you to bed. We've both got to keep our wits about us in this here case; it just reeks with lovely points of law. By the way, Judge Maitland will be sitting, I do hope."

I shook my head. "No, Parn, I'm afraid not. He's still over at Mayo's and his condition isn't good."

"Who then?"

"I haven't the foggiest notion. And if Mitch knows he isn't saying. I hope it isn't one of those dreary downstate political hacks—we're going to need a real lawyer on this one. By the way, I'm driving up to Thunder Bay tomorrow to have a look around. Want to come along?"

"Bless you, of course I do. I been standin' here waitin' for you to ask me. And Maida, too?"

"Maida?" I said. "Why in hell Maida? She's just a dame that types letters and reads Mickey Spillane."

"Maida," Parn replied firmly. "There's detective work to be done. If there's some nice ripe skulduggery up there in Thunder Bay, a smart woman will nose it out. Maida is smart and she goes along. That's an order from senior counsel, young man."

"Yes, sir, Mr. McCarthy," I said meekly. "Please, sir, when do we leave?"

"Sharp at eight from your office."

"But Maida doesn't get here till nine. And I haven't the heart to phone her at this ungodly hour. My God, it's after two."

As Parnell walked to the door there seemed to be a sprightliness in his bearing I hadn't seen in years. "Set your clock and call her at seven, boy. Old Thomas Edison thrived for years on four hours rest. Does a young man like you want to rot in bed?" He waved his hand airily. "There's work to be done and we must up and away. We're leavin' here at eight."

"Yes, sir," I said. "Anything more, sir? And many thanks, Parn. You—you've already given me lots of food for ulcers."

Parnell hooked his thumb through the armhole of his tattersall vest and grinned his irresistible melting Irish grin. "Good night, Polly, and God bless you. Tonight you've made me feel more like a real lawyer than I have in years and years." He paused. "Now I—I must hurry away before I really break down and bawl. Good night, goddam it."

"Good night, Parn," I called softly after his plodding retreating figure.

I went to the phonograph and put on a recording of Debussy's haunting "The Blessed Damozel." Then I sat in the darkness staring into the fire. Little unseen bellows seemed occasionally to fitfully fan the dying embers, making them glow and fade like tethered fireflies. I contemplated the eternal fascination and mystery of fire. . . . I sighed; I was tired, tired bodily and mentally. "So now, Biegler," I mused, "you're about to become a private eye." It was a new role for me and I wondered if I would do half as well as Parnell had in his new role as prosecutor.

The phonograph took over, the women's voices now murmurously joining the orchestra, swelling, fading, soaring into ecstasies of moving and melancholy sound. I sat there covered with gooseflesh until the last strains had died away. The fire was out. I shivered and tottered my way to my bedroom, set the alarm clock, yawned prodigiously and flung my pajama bottoms in a corner—and fell on the bed, asleep instantly. I dreamt a dream, an interminable dream about a monster brook trout that seemed bent upon pulling me into the water. For a while it was touch and go. All that finally saved me from a watery grave was the hideous clatter of my alarm. I squinted one eye open; it was broad daylight; Detective Biegler must be up and at the keyhole.

So sinless and devoted to the pastoral virtues is the Upper Peninsula that trained private investigators are virtually nonexistent. As everywhere, of course, there are the usual proportion of yearning adolescents and occasional eccentrics who have won a tin star and a fingerprint outfit from one of the mail-order diploma mills, the kind that turn out detectives in twelve easy lessons. But these groping souls would do us no good; they generally wound up with a black eye or in reporting on dead beats for credit bureaus at two dollars a head. More often they wound up with the black eye anyway, after which they tended to enroll in courses on advanced refrigeration.

Peninsula lawyers or clients or anyone requiring the services of a real private detective had perforce either to import one or do it themselves. Since my client couldn't even pay me or his psychiatrist, let alone a detective, hiring one was clearly out of the question; we would have to play detective ourselves.

Thunder Bay was a former logging and commercial fishing village on Lake Superior that had quietly swooned and expired when the white pine was cut and the fish were caught. After sleeping through a generation or more of genteel Rip Van Winkle poverty it had been rediscovered and miraculously resuscitated by the advent of those curious seasonal wanderers, that modern American gypsy known as the Summer Tourist. As the care and feeding of tourists had more and more absorbed the attentions of the townsfolk, more and more had I avoided the place; as a class tourists had a tendency unduly to grieve me; and it came as something of a shock to recall that I had not been near the picturesque old town in a dozen-odd years. Barney Quill, a comparative newcomer, was nothing more to me than a name; I seemed to have read about him once or twice in the newspapers; he had shot a bear or caught a big fish or some such thing. . . .

As Maida and Parnell and I drove along the lake shore, all of us squeezed in the front seat of my coupe, I saw that I had forgotten how beautiful the drive to Thunder Bay was; the towering sighing groves of fragrant Norway pines, the broad expanses of clean white sand, the sea gulls, always the endlessly wheeling sea gulls; an occasional bald eagle seeming bent on soaring straight up to Heaven; tne intermittent craggy and pine-clad granite or sandstone hills, sometimes rising gauntly to the dignity of small mountains, then again sudden stretches of sand or more maiestic Norway pines—and always, of course, the vast glittering heaving lake, the world's largest inland sea, as treacherous and deceitful as a spurned woman, either caressing or raging at the shore, more often turbulent than not, but today on its best company manners, presenting the falsely placid aspect of a mill pond.

"I've been thinkin'," Parnell McCarthy began.

"Please, Parn," I begged. "Please, not about the damned case, not now." I gestured toward the lake. "All this incredible beauty. Sometimes I think I fish too much."

"I've been thinkin'," Parnell solemnly went on, "that it's been well over a quarter-century since I've troubled to come along this way. That last time my Nora and I were in a buckboard drawn by a team of bay mares. . . . I've been thinking of what fools indeed we mortals be, letting all this beauty languish unseen while we, like suicidal lemmings, hurry on our way to our obscure graves, chasing dollars, chasing women, chasing trout, chasing the dubious pleasures of the bottle." He sighed and took a deep breath. "The waste, the hideous waste of living—it's enough to make one weep. Boy, I must indeed mend me ways."

"Stop, Parn, stop," Maida said, giggling like a schoolgirl. "You sound more and more like Cyrano. If you keep on like this I swear I'll fall in love."

I glanced at Maida. "When did you exchange Spillane for Rostand?" I inquired silkily. "If I may say so, I think we'd better flee this lovely lake shore before all of us start cracking up."

The car toiled up a steep granite bluff, the roadway hacked out between towering walls of solid rock, and then began the long descent. There, spread out before us, was the village of Thunder Bay, as neat and ordered as though viewed from an airplane, clustered tightly among the tall pines along the edge of the glittering and now peaceful bay that had given the town its name.

"And now to the wars," I said, clamping a fresh cigar in my teeth and stepping on the gas.

I speculated a little on what it was that drew the tourists to this remote place. It lacked the reek of ancient lore possessed by St. Ignace, with its great new bridge and "authentic" Indian chieftains in full regalia solemnly selling the lamblike tourists equally authentic hundred-year-old tomahawks made the winter before in Gaylord; it did not have the endlessly photogenic locks of Sault Ste. Marie, which could boast, and endlessly did, that its locks annually handled more tonnage than any in the world; its shoreline was not adorned with the tinted and dramatic Pictured Rocks of Munising; it lacked Marquette's imposing iron ore loading docks, each dwarfing in height and length even the *Queen Mary*.

No, the town did not possess any of these alluring tourist properties; it had no golf courses or crumbling fortresses; it had no tall roaring waterfalls from the top of which a monotonous procession of legendary Indian maidens had leapt for love and love alone; it lacked any medicinal springs to throw orange peels and coke bottles into or any copper or iron mines or towering ski jumps or Indian burial mounds or places to dig for agates or ancient arrowheads; nor had it any displays of two-headed calves or trained bears or wolves or even any mangy coyotes. Nor, final ignominy, had any of its hamburger stands or lunch counters, so far as I knew, been blessed by Duncan Hines. Perhaps, I reflected, perhaps it possessed the simple but incomparable attributes of rural quiet, fresh sea-washed air which blew the mosquitoes away—and great natural beauty, a beauty as yet unmarred by man. And, as I presently saw, it certainly had the tourists; the place was teeming with them; and I slowed down abruptly to avoid collecting a representative specimen on my fender, a prospective trophy more revolting for me to contemplate than the head of a bull moose.

"Look where you're driving, Mac!" my near specimen shouted.

"Excuse me," I apologized contritely, "I should have taken the sidewalk."

We drove slowly up the main street of the town, past the tourist park on our right, nestled in among a tall grove of pines on the lake shore, past the usual cluster of gas stations, a grocery store, the post office, then two churches and, as though to achieve proportion and balance, an abrupt rash of neon-lit taverns, the inevitable souvenir shop, a beauty parlor, and all the rest. Near the end of the long street, on our right and overlooking the lake, stood a large white and attractive three-story frame structure. A screened-in veranda ran along the entire front and half the side nearest the lake. This was the Thunder Bay Inn, in the barroom of which the proprietor Barney Quill had met his death such a short time before. The last time I had seen the Inn it had been boarded up and now, freshly painted, it was a mecca for school marms and summer tourists. A short distance past the Inn I stopped the car and turned off the key.

"Well, Parn," I said, "what's the strategy?"

"Polly," Parnell said, "I suggest you drop me off at one of the smaller taverns—no fear, I'm not going to drink—and then drop

Maida at the beauty shop for a manicure or something. Both strike me as being likely spots to begin our search. Then you hie yourself directly to the Inn. The word will fan out soon enough that you're in town and they'll be expecting you. So you might as well go there first and be done with it. Then I suggest we all meet back at the hotel around noon and have lunch and possibly compare notes. What do you think?"

I nodded. "Sounds fine to me, Parn."

"But I don't *need* a manicure," Maida pouted. "Anyway, I do my own nails."

Parnell bowed gallantly. "I will grant that any attention from these sordid entrepreneurs of beauty to your comely person, dear lady, would be carrying coals to Newcastle," he said, "but I'm equally sure that your great wit, matched only by your ravishing beauty, will suggest to you a plausible reason for visiting their malodorous precincts."

"I've warned you, Parnell," Maida laughed. "If you keep running on this way you're going to have an infatuated female on your hands."

"Ah, my dear, I shall impatiently await and welcome that eventuality," Parnell replied, again gravely bowing with his air of impishness and antique courtliness. He held up a pudgy hand, his gray eyes dancing. "But please, Madam, please, I beg of you—do not ever suggest matrimony," he continued gravely. "Men have contrived fewer devices more deadly to romance than marriage itself." He fluttered his fingers lightly through the air. "Gay wings," he murmured, blowing Maida a kiss. "Ah lass, let us stoutly resolve ever to remain gay and unfettered."

"Ah, Parnell, Parnell. . . ." Maida murmured, wistfully shaking her head.

"Ah, Cyrano, Cyrano," I muttered, stirring restlessly. Parnell must have been quite a boy in his day, I reflected, quite a boy. . . . "Rubbish!" I said petulantly, wheeling the car around in an abrupt U-turn. Enough of this romantic buffoonery.

chapter 19

With some trepidation I deposited Parnell at the first tavern we came to and then Maida at the beauty parlor, wishing them good luck. Then I drove back to the hotel, parked my car near the street entrance to the taproom—the same door Lieutenant Manion had come and left by when he had shot Barney—and lit up a cigar, took a deep breath, and pushed against the door.

It did not yield. I rattled and wrenched at the knob; the door was locked. A small typewritten sign on the glass informed me that the place would not be open for business until noon. I peered through the window; the place was dim and there was no sign of activity. I shrugged and walked around front to the main entrance of the hotel; perhaps I could at least get a peek at the bar. Since the hotel stood on a steep sandy hill, the front accordingly rose considerably higher above the street level than in the rear, where the building in fact ran a few feet into the hill. I mounted the steps to the screened-in porch.

I had been wrong; Mr. Duncan Hines had been there before me, as his discreetly beckoning little tin sign now reassured me. Thunder Bay had at last made the grade; one could now dine in the certified knowledge that Duncan approved. I could visualize this ubiquitous little man—his bib full of gravy stains, his pockets full of pills, his soul full of hope—gnawing his way across a continent, leaving diplomas of approval in his wake like a sort of gastronomic Kilroy. I sighed and moved into the hotel. "Peptic ulcers can now be gaily faced," I thought. "Duncan has et here."

The lobby was deserted except for a knot of numbed and somnambulistic-looking tourists gathered about a flaming large stone fireplace. It was only 72 degrees outside. . . . I glanced quickly around and found a sign on a door saying "Cocktail Lounge." I tried the door and found it unlocked and went quickly down the stairs. "Biegler," I thought, "your career as a detective has officially begun."

The stale beery morning smell of an unaired barroom smote my nostrils. I paused at the bottom to become accustomed to the dim light. I seemed to be alone. The room was large and filled with tables and stacked chairs except for a small roped-off dance space in the center. I spotted Laura Manion's pinball machine in the corner, to my left, standing between an upright piano and a garishly colored jukebox. Adjoining this and nearer me were the wash rooms. I advanced slowly into the room. To my right about thirty feet from the street door I had just tried to enter, was the bar itself. I gave a start. Standing motionless behind the bar, holding a towel and glass in his hands and intently regarding me, was a small dark man, a wiry, foxy-looking little man in a white apron.

"Hello," I said, advancing. "I'm Paul Biegler from Chippewa, Lieutenant Manion's lawyer."

"Yes, I know," he replied, averting his eyes, busily polishing his glass. "What can I do for you, Mr. Biegler? I'm Paquette the bartender."

"Well," I said, smiling, "after you've served me a bottle of pop—your choice—you might tell me if you were present during the shooting."

The soft drink and a glass were placed before me with deft dispatch; the money rung up; and then he was back polishing another glass. "I was present," he said evenly. "Just like it said in the newspapers."

"Maybe we could talk a little about what happened," I said.

"Maybe," he said, inspecting his glass in the light. "And then again, maybe we could not."

This sort of sparring could go on for days, I saw, an enterprise for which I lacked both the time and taste; I preferred seeing my little foxes in the woods. I swiftly decided to level with my cozy friend. Either he would talk or he wouldn't; the sooner I found it out the better. Even his failure to talk might prove something or other.

"Look, Mr. Paquette," I said, "whether you choose to clam up or talk is a matter of considerable indifference to me. I'll have my crack at you in court—where you'll bloody well have to talk and plenty. But maybe all of us would save a lot of time and turmoil if you'd help me to find out what I came here to find out and which I promise you I will find out."

The polishing had stopped. "Like what?" he said.

I shrugged. "Oh, for a starter, like where Barney and Manny—I mean Lieutenant Manion—were standing when the shots were fired."

"I didn't see any shots fired."

This had not been clear from the newspaper reports. "Where were you?" I said.

"I was standing out on the floor talking with some customers at a table. We'd had an unusually busy night and Mr. Quill had relieved me so that I could have a rest. He was always thoughtful that way. The crowd was thinning out."

"The ever-thoughtful *Mister* Quill," I thought, and then a little bell tinkled in my mind. The tired bartender had said he was standing out on the floor. Here was a poor fatigued bartender, who had been relieved by his thoughtful boss so that he could rest, *standing* out on the floor talking to his customers. I went baying along the scent. "Who were these customers?" I asked casually.

"Fellow called Pedersen and his wife and a friend from Iron Bay. They'd been out for a drive."

I made a mental note to remember the name. "Where was the Pedersen table located?" I went on.

"Out on the floor."

"Naturally," I said. "But *where* on the floor? Over by the pinball machine? The stairs? The piano?" I paused, pointing, suddenly sure it was by none of these. "Or was their table over by the outside door there?"

"Yes," he murmured.

Anyone standing by the window near the door, I guessed, could have commanded an unobstructed view of any patron approaching the door from the outside. Even a patron, say, like Lieutenant Manion. But better I lay off that now, I decided; no use clamming up this sly character at the outset. Well, maybe I should explore it just a bit, to worry him, to let him guess a little what I really suspected.

"How come, Mr. Paquette?" I continued easily. "How come you didn't sit down when you chatted with the Pedersens? Aren't there usually four chairs at a table?"

He shot me a quick look, but he answered readily enough. "They had a package on the other chair," he said. From the quick little gleam of triumph in his eyes I guessed he was telling the truth. But his triumph was short-lived; I could not let him off the hook so easily.

"Couldn't this poor tired bartender have sat and held their package in his lap? Don't tell me it was an anvil. Or couldn't he have drawn up another chair?" I held up a warning hand. "Now don't tell me there weren't any spare chairs—the crowd was thinning out, remember?"

This time I had really tagged him. He scowled and compressed his lips and glanced apprehensively in the direction of the stairway.

"Or perhaps," I went on, "you're like the postman who climbs mountains on his vacation—you simply love to stand on your own two feet."

Like most people, Mr. Paquette could stand almost anything but ridicule. "What you driving at?" he demanded angrily. "Sitting or standing—what goddam difference does it make?"

"Little Standing Bull," I thought. But I wasn't ready to spell out my thoughts, at least not quite yet, and anyway I was sure now that he knew that I knew. Perhaps it would give him a little more respect for the truth.

"Don't race your motor," I said. "In any case Barney Quill was alone behind the bar when Lieutenant Manion came in?"

"I've already told you he was."

"Sitting or standing?"

"Standing. He always stood when he was at the bar."

I pondered my next question. "How long had he been relieving you, standing there alone behind the bar?"

"Oh, for upwards of an hour I'd say."

Little Standing Bull had kept the weary vigil by the door for nearly a whole hour! "And *when* had he relieved you?"

"Around midnight, I should say."

"And what time was the shooting?"

"At twelve forty-six exactly."

"How would you know that?"

"At the first shot I wheeled around and looked at the clock."

Had he been surprised, I wondered, to see the wrong man down? The clock was on the wall behind the bar. "Then you must have seen some of the other shots fired, didn't you, Mr. Paquette?"

He lit a cigarette and I thought his hand trembled ever so little. "I saw Lieutenant Manion standing up on the bar rail, leaning over and pointing at something down behind the bar."

I had long ago learned that this nice air of meticulous fairness in a witness was often a sure sign that he was hostile or lying. "Come now, that something was of course Barney Quill, wasn't it?"

"Well, yes. It turned out to be."

"And where at the bar was the Lieutenant standing?"

He pointed. "Near the middle, there, right between those two service rails. It was the only place open; the bar itself was crowded, all with men. Barney had just bought another round of drinks. He was generous that way. The Lieutenant turned and left almost as soon as I'd turned around. I ran out the door after him—the door you just tried to enter."

"Oh, so you saw me out there. What happened then?"

"When I got outside he wheeled around and faced me and said: 'Do you want some, too, Buster?' "

I winced over that one, but continued bravely.

"What did you do?"

"I said, 'No, sir' and hurried back inside."

This was even worse for our side than the newspaper had reported it; this grim fighting talk from my Lieutenant was more than a little inconsistent with our proposed picture of a man whose wits had departed him from shock and excessive grief. But the show must go on. . . . "And Buster isn't your name, of course?" I went on.

"No, Alphonse is my first name. People generally call me Al or Phonse."

Yes, people continue to be as original as all hell, I thought. "Was Barney still alive?"

"No; he'd apparently died instantly. Five out of the six shots got to him. The man didn't have a chance."

"You mean a chance to fire a shot himself?"

Quickly: "I mean a chance to live."

"To your knowledge did either man speak?"

"I personally heard nothing but later I heard that Barney had said 'Good evening, Lieutenant.' "

"What about Manion—had anyone heard him speak?"

"No. Apparently he did not utter a word although several persons later claimed they had spoken to him, including one of our waitresses."

"What's her name?"

"Fern Rundquist."

This was fairly good news; see, my poor addled client couldn't see or hear anything. The defense was up, down, then in a neutral corner. . . . "Did you go look at Barney?" I said.

"Yes."

"Did you examine his body?"

"Yes, but not closely until after I'd cleared the bar and locked the place."

"What time was that?"

"About one o'clock. Nobody had to be urged to leave; most of them fled the joint right after the shooting."

"So that finally you were left all alone with the dead body?"

"Well, yes. Somebody had to wait for the police."

"Who called them?"

"I did."

"When?"

He hesitated for an instant. "It will all be a matter of record, you know," I said. "*They'll* tell me if you don't."

"I was just thinking," he said. "About one-fifteen, I should say."

"My, my. How come you waited so long to notify the police, Mr. Paquette?"

"Oh, the excitement and all—I—I guess I just forgot."

"Hm, your boss is shot to death at twelve forty-six—in all the excitement you don't forget to note *that*—and then you remember a half hour later that maybe the police should be notified. It simply hadn't occurred to you before, is that it?"

"Right," he snapped.

I sipped my drink and lit a fresh cigar. Alphonse Paquette had resumed polishing a glass. I noted that it was the same one he had already polished at length. This man, I concluded, probably knew much more than he had told anyone, or perhaps ever intended to tell anyone, but certain probabilities had already emerged despite his reluctance. I was now convinced that Barney Quill had been waiting for the Lieutenant; that he had deliberately relieved his bartender not only to get him out of the way of the anticipated show down but also to in turn warn Barney and further so that he, Barney could get behind the bar himself. It had been his fortress. Then by buying drinks he had further surrounded himself with an unwitting protective human cordon—all but at the waitresses' service station, which customers were everywhere supposed not to occupy. That this one open spot had proved to be Barney's Achilles' heel was a nice ironic touch. I was now equally sure that he must have been armed —else why should he have waited around at all? I decided to play my hunch.

"When did the police arrive?"

"It was shortly after two—the distance and winding roads, you know."

"Yes, I know." I paused. "So you were alone with the body for over an hour?"

"Why, yes, that's correct. Somebody had to take the rap and wait." He was still preoccupied with the same glass, polishing it intently, and I was growing afraid he would wear it out.

"You just told me that," I said and again I paused. "Would you mind greatly putting down that glass, Mr. Paquette? You've been working on it for the last half-hour. Anyway, I like to look at the people I'm talking with, it's an old-fashioned notion I have."

He had put down the glass and stood facing me with an air of defiant and unfeigned hostility. "I'm looking, Mister," he said. "Fire away."

"Good," I said. "Now was it during this lonely hour-long vigil that you removed the firearms from behind the bar and got rid of them?"

His eyes bored steadily into mine. But the look of angry hostility now seemed mingled with a sudden gleam of fear. "What pistols?" he said evenly, trying to control himself. "I don't know what you're talking about. Who said anything about pistols? If you've come up here to set smart lawyer traps for me, you'd better be on your way, Mister. I've got work to do."

"You seem already to have fallen into one of those 'lawyer traps,' my friend. I said 'firearms' not 'pistols.' What did you do with the pistols?"

He had grown suddenly tense and pale. "Well, it—it would scarcely have been a rifle," he countered.

"I wouldn't know," I said. "But *you* called them pistols—I didn't. You'd better remember that for the trial. Don't fall into that trap again."

"Is that all?" he said coldly. "Is that all you wanted to ask me?"

"Scarcely," I said. "But perhaps we'd better move on to—to something less sensitive. Had Barney left the place during the evening?"

Sullenly: "Yes."

"When?"

"Around eleven, shortly before Mrs. Manion left."

"When did you next see him?"

"Around midnight, shortly before he relieved me."

"Which way did he enter—from the street or the hotel stairs?" I paused. "Remember, others will know."

Uneasily: "He came down from the hotel."

So far so good; that would give Barney the time and opportunity to change and clean up and—ah, yes—get rid of Laura Manion's missing underpants.

"Had he changed his clothes?" I asked. There was no answer and I repeated the question. He still remained silent. "Must I continue to remind you with every question that I can find out from others if you won't talk?"

"Why don't you go and ask the others, then?" he demanded hotly. "Why do you keep firing away at me?"

"One talks to but one witness at a time," I said. "Right now your number is up." I shrugged. "But if you want it that way. . . ." I turned as though to leave. "Perhaps you'd prefer to have me bring out in court that you wouldn't answer that simple little question?"

He almost spat his reply. "He'd changed from a white shirt to a sweat shirt. He—he often did. It was a hot night. What other clothes he'd changed I wouldn't know. I was the man's bartender, not his valet."

"Perhaps the sweat shirt gave him more freedom to lift a glass, say —or even a gun?" I said gently. "Weren't you surprised when you wheeled around and saw the Lieutenant still standing and not Barney? And when you wheeled could it have been that you were checking the time so you could testify later—for Barney?"

He smiled frostily and I swiftly concluded I would rather take him scowling. "Suppose," he said slowly, "suppose you try checking that one with the others."

His dart was well aimed, I saw, and I saw further that as far as he was concerned I would get little or nothing out of him that could not be confirmed by others. "At any rate," I said, "Barney comes down in his sweat shirt and immediately relieves you from behind the bar."

"That's correct. Everybody saw that." He seemed almost to be apologizing to me—or perhaps to himself—for admitting anything that might help the defense. It was an interesting development; both interesting and challenging. And it could be serious. *Why* was this little man so evasive and hostile?

"Was it Barney's regular practice to relieve you behind the bar?" I said.

His eyes flickered. "Occasionally."

"How often had he relieved you, say, during the last two weeks before the shooting? All this can be checked, too, remember. Now I'll promise cross my heart to quit saying that if you'll just promise to re- member it."

"Well, he just didn't happen to relieve me during that time. Lots of other times, though."

"During the entire last month then?" I said.

"I don't remember."

"I don't think a jury would like that answer. They might even sus- pect you of being evasive or something, and for such a frank and open person that would indeed be a pity. Suppose you try again."

"He didn't relieve me."

Despite some glaring gaps, some of the pieces were now falling into place. "Ah, now we're getting somewhere," I said. "Barney just *happened* to relieve you the very night he also just *happened* to have raped and beat up Laura Manion." It was time to level. "Look, chum, didn't he really tell you to get to hell away from the bar so you wouldn't get hurt? And on his orders weren't you standing by that window for nearly an hour so you could spot the Lieutenant coming and warn Barney?"

"Who said Barney raped her?" he demanded.

"You doubt it?" I said.

"I wasn't there."

"I know you weren't there, comrade. But I just asked you if you doubted that he'd raped her." He had a cute little habit of turning my question to other channels.

Defiantly: "Yes, I doubt it. If he laid her at all, which I also doubt, it was with her willing consent. Anybody can see she's a floozie."

There was going to be great fun with this winning character in court, I saw. "I see," I said. "You couldn't tell me just now whether he raped her, because you weren't there, but now, still not having been there, you have all the answers as to what happened. Is that it?" I paused, pondering whether to risk drying up this man by further antagonizing him or to push on, doggedly getting as much as I could by a softer approach. I decided to take the risk and speak a few homely truths.

"Mr. Paquette," I said, "you don't like my asking you all these embarrassing questions, I suppose, and I really can't blame you. Nobody likes the hot seat. In fact you obviously bitterly resent my asking them. But that's the penalty for having a ringside seat at a murder, and it so happens that a man's freedom and whole future rides on this case. And you happen to have some of the answers. Now I intend to get those answers, my friend, but you are not coming clean with me, not even halfway clean. And if I can see that you aren't, I promise you I'll make a jury see it. What you've had from me so far, unpleasant as you may find it, will be nothing to the going over I'll give you in court unless you come off this cozy routine. I'll make a damn fool or liar out of you or both. I—I'll burn your ass to a crisp."

He flushed with hot anger and took a quick step back. "Is that a threat?" For a moment I thought he might try to hit me. The moment passed.

"No, not a threat," I said, "but a promise. I'd rather call it a little preview of what lies in store for you if you don't try telling the truth. And fast. The truth is so easy, Mr. Paquette; nothing to make up, no evasions, no traps, no entanglements, no inconsistent statements

124

to try to explain away. Just the simple truth. I recommend you try it sometime. Why not now?"

"You think everything I've told you is a pack of lies?" he demanded.

"Of course not. But you're holding back, you're not telling the *whole* truth. Do you think I'm a goddam dummy, man? I've been bulldozed by experts. While you're good and will doubtless improve, you still don't quite pitch in that league."

"What do you mean?" he said.

"You're leveling with me only on the things you know I already know or that others will testify to anyway, or things you know I can check you up on. And you're evasive, evasive as hell. A little while ago I asked you if it wasn't true that instead of relieving you Barney sent you away from the bar so you'd be out of range when the fireworks started and also to warn him. You didn't attempt to answer me. Did you think I'd forget that question or that it'd just go away?"

Alphonse Paquette blinked his eyes thoughtfully. I had apparently given him food for thought; he seemed to be weighing something, considering the pros and cons of some situation I knew not of. I wondered what his angle was. I was convinced now that he was holding back, but why was he? Why this loyalty, this desire to shield something or someone? Had the thoughtful and relieving Mister Barney meant so much to him? And, if so, what was there in it for him? Who'd put the "silencer" on him and why?

"You still haven't answered me," I said.

He sighed and shook his head. "He didn't *send* me away," he said almost doggedly. "He relieved me, just like I told you. I wasn't watching for Lieutenant Manion or anyone."

I sensed that I'd almost had him. "Very well, my friend. You want it that way; you've chosen your course. But don't forget I warned you. And I don't mind telling you you're lying by the clock. Even a child can see that."

"It's the truth, I tell you," he said sullenly, almost resignedly. The anger and defiance were gone now—gone or hidden—; all he wanted was for me to go away.

I decided to gratify his desire up to a point; I would leave temporarily to go visit the wash room. "Excuse me," I said. "I'm going to the can and I'll expect to see you here when I come back."

I was mildly surprised to find him there upon my return and I wasted no time in boring in. "How long did you work for Barney?" I began. "Cheer up. See, that's another question you can afford to answer truthfully. I can check it and it surely can't hurt anything anyway."

Tonelessly: "Eighteen months."

"Had you known him before that?"

"No. I just blew in. He needed a bartender and I got the job."

"Who are you working for now?"

After a pause, "I'm not sure."

"Come, come, man. Surely somebody is in charge of this joint. Who is he? Or are you the new boss man?"

"It's a woman."

I felt a small inward jolt of recognition. Of course, a woman—there simply had to be a dame. Why hadn't I thought of *that* before? Well, a man couldn't think of everything—and during trout season women were the farthest thing from my mind. Well, almost the farthest. . . . "This woman," I said, "who is she?"

"Mary Pilant. You'll find her upstairs. She's running things up there. She—she was Barney's hostess."

He had hesitated ever so little over the word "hostess." It opened up new vistas. "Is she—is she going to own the place now?"

"I wouldn't know," he said. "I'm just a dumb bartender, you know. I just work here. Why don't you try asking her?"

"Not so dumb," I said. "But we'll pass that; I can find that out easily enough elsewhere."

"You can?" he said, looking surprised. "How?"

"By checking the files in probate court or the records in the register of deeds office down in Iron Bay. Or else by wiring the Liquor Control Commission in Lansing regarding any pending application for the transfer of your liquor license. And there are other ways. We live in an age of papers and records, you know; one can't even properly die these days without some notary or other clamping his official seal on the corpse. But it seems a shame, doesn't it, to put me to all that needless bother?" I paused. "Come, Alphonse, does she own the joint? Don't mar our budding new friendship by making me suspect you're holding out on me."

"Barney left a will," he said resignedly. "I guess he left the works to Mary—Miss Pilant. In fact I know he did. It's still got to go through probate court and all, but I guess she'll eventually get everything." He spread out his thin supple hands as though to embrace the place. "*Everything.*"

"Was this Mary person present during the shooting?"

"No."

"Hm. . . . Where was she?"

He dropped his eyes. "I really wouldn't know," he replied, and I made a mental note to check on that one.

I had a sudden hunch. "This will, Alphonse," I said, "were you one of the witnesses to it?"

He looked startled. "How do you know that?"

I laughed. "I have lived, Alphonse, I have lived. And when did Barney make out this will that you witnessed, Alphonse? Or would you prefer me to check up on that myself?"

"About three weeks before—before he was killed."

"Was Barney married?"

"Married and divorced. Long ago. Down in Wisconsin."

"Any parents?"

"Both dead."

"Any children?"

He smiled fleetingly, and I put the smile away in cold storage. So Barney had been that way. . . . "I think there was a daughter," he said.

"Did he leave any other relatives and did any of them show up for the funeral?"

"He was buried down in Wisconsin."

"Very well, but my question had two horns," I said. "How about the relatives?"

He glanced nervously in the direction of the stairway. "Besides the divorced wife and daughter there may have been a married sister. I don't know nothing about that." He stirred uneasily; oddly enough, this new subject seemed to bother him more than the shooting itself.

I paused and lit another Italian cigar, pondering this swift change in the picture. The plot, like homemade French pea soup, was getting thicker and thicker. If Barney had not left any will his daughter would get everything; that was plainly the law; she would be his sole heir. If he left no wife, and willed everything to a stranger, then the stranger would get everything and the daughter nothing; that was equally the law. But if a relative or guardian or someone contested

127

and could somehow successfully block the will—because of coercion, undue influence, fraud, drunkenness, mental incapacity and the like —then the will would fall and the daughter take all. And the stakes were certainly high enough—a prosperous and well kept summer hotel located on the main tourist beat. In any will contest, too, the witnesses to the will would hold important—and *valuable* trumps. A light was beginning to dawn.

"Who was the other witness to the will?" I said.

"The night clerk upstairs."

It was almost too neat; this left Mary Pilant and her loyal employees solely in the driver's seat. I decided to test my growing hunch of the cause—or one of the causes—of all this reticence. Could it be from fear of someone upsetting the will?

"How about Barney's drinking?" I said.

He threw out his hands. "He drank some. Most people in this business almost have to."

"Yes, I suppose. Like the well-known fact that proprietors of candy-stores hang around all day eating candy," I said. "But on the day of the shooting—how about his drinking then?"

"He drank about the same as usual. In fact he drank about the same amount every day."

"Look, friend, one could truthfully say that about a quart-a-day-man, or even a hopeless drunk. The question is: how *much* was he drinking?"

"If you mean he was drunk, he wasn't. He'd had his regular quota."

Patiently: "And how much was that?"

"Oh, a few shots more or less."

"Hell, man, don't give me that stuff—he drank more than that with Laura Manion alone. What in hell was he doing behind the bar for an hour buying house drinks and all—swiggling soda pop? But we'll pass that for now and take up this interesting Mary person— what was she to Barney?"

He smiled a tight knowing little smile. "Why don't you go ask her? She's very friendly. I've already told you she was his hostess." He glanced quickly at the clock over the bar. "Excuse me, I've got to go unlock the street door." He sighed. "It's about time for the tourist gang to show up."

It was 11:30 and the sign on the door had said 12:00. Did my nervous friend want to let the tourist herd in simply so that he might be interrupted? I decided to let it pass.

Instead of unlocking the outside door Alphonse Paquette had quickly scampered up the stairs to the hotel, doubtless to warn the heiress apparent, Mary Pilant, that the villainous and nosy Biegler was abroad. I was left alone in the big empty barroom, whereupon all the malty frustrated yearnings and boozy instincts implanted in me by generations of sturdy distillers and brewers and saloonkeepers by the name of Biegler swept suddenly over me; I found myself gliding behind the bar as though drawn by a magnet. "Hm. . . ." I said, and paused.

On the floor in the middle of the bar was a large dark blotch. That would be the spot where Barney had fallen. I carefully studied the bar at this point. Then I knelt and surveyed the situation from that position. "Hm. . . ." About six inches below the surface of the bar itself, near the bar service station and out of sight of anyone standing in front, I found a narrow wooden shelf about four feet long. I whistled softly and leaned closer. It was made of wood inferior to that of the bar itself and had been added later, crudely added, I saw, as though the job had been done by an amateur. And to what purpose? Right now it held a forlorn collection of assorted salt and pepper shakers and mustard jars. But it could also, I plainly saw, have held a small arsenal of firearms, yes, even a sawed-off shotgun or short rifle in a pinch. It could even have held a brace of pistols.

I turned my back on the bar, facing the bar mirror and bottle shelf. The mirror seemed intact. I craned over the rows of bottles, on my tiptoes. There was a neat small splintered hole near the base of the mirror, about the height—yes—of a man's heart. If this had been caused by one of my man's shots, then at least one of the bottles should have been broken. As I walked out from behind the bar I felt like Sherlock Holmes and longed for a curved bulldog pipe and one of those fore-and-aft-peaked deer-stalker's caps. Yes, damn it, and a checkered tattersall vest. Someone was rattling at the locked street door. I could hear him swearing softly and I visualized him standing out there, sagging with thirst, eyes glazed and tongue parched and dangling. I longed to slip a pair of frilled elastic garters over my shirt sleeves and let him in and then scamper back behind the bar, palms down and elbows out. "What's yores, pardner?" I would say as he advanced. I shook my head. "Down, Grandpa, down," I thought; this was no time to be playing at saloonkeeper.

It struck me that the bartender and his new boss must be having quite a huddle. And the need must have been pressing for them to leave me alone with all this wealth of booze. I felt touched and honored by this subtle testimonial to my honesty and sobriety. The thirsting door-rattler had given up and gone away, but I took solace in the knowledge that he had but a short way to go to find another oasis.

I walked over towards the door and stood by the table and window where the bartender had said he stood "resting." An awning outside somewhat obstructed my view and I stooped to what I judged to be the height of the shorter Paquette. Ah, the view was now fine—I could see outside and, turning slightly, also see the bar, a perfect place for a warning lookout. I glanced around. On the wall adjoining the door on the other side, closer to the bar, was a large bulletin board which appeared to be covered with various anouncements, scores, newspaper clippings, snapshots and the like. I quickly moved over that way and put on my glasses.

I found myself shortly thinking of Max Battisfore, the Sheriff. For this bulletin board, I discovered, was a shrine apparently dedicated by Barney Quill to Barney Quill about Barney Quill; it was devoted almost solely to celebrating his exploits as a fisherman, hunter, expert marksman and, to a lesser extent, as a bowler, downhill skier, and racer of outboard motor-boats. And there had been many exploits; there were dozens and scores of snapshots and photos and newspaper clippings, old and new, all attesting his prowess in all of these things and more: Barney Quill had won the turkey shoot the previous fall, he'd won a skeet shoot, he'd placed first in another pistol shoot; he'd skied the Iron Bay course in 1:53. Over here Barney had shot the biggest buck at over two hundred yards; Barney had caught the largest brook trout last season, and on a mere 5-X leader, too (I read this particular item with an envious pang); Barney and his outboard had won—

"He was really quite a guy, wasn't he?" a voice behind me said. Startled, I wheeled around. Alphonse Paquette, the bartender, had returned.

"What nice soft shoes you wear, Grandma," I said.

He smiled faintly. "Have to wear 'em for my bunions. Standing all hours at that goddam bar, you know."

"And standing and enjoying the view from this goddam window when you're not," I said. "Did you have a nice little chat about me with Mary Pilant?" I said, smiling.

"Most satisfactory and to the point. She told me to keep my trap shut. No more questions and no more answers. Those were the lady's orders—and she's the boss."

Well, Mary Pilant might have been just a trifle late, I thought. I wondered what kind of witch she would be. Probably a pearl-laden dame with gold teeth and a baritone voice who shaved twice a week; the kind who, after five minutes, started calling total strangers "darling" and "honey" and who wore long loopy earrings from which small boys could depend while performing gymnastics. The picture was not good; maybe I could shove her off on Parnell.

"Well," I said, "since you can't or won't talk I guess I might as well up and leave. It's time for lunch, anyway. When a journeyman lawyer can't talk he's in a bad way; he can't very well open his mouth without asking questions."

"So I've noticed."

Something on the bulletin board had caught my eye. Caught and perplexed me. "But I have just one more question, an easy harmless little one," I said. "And it demands no more cerebration than those certified questions on TV where people constantly win life annuities and round trips to Jamaica for guessing President Lincoln's first name. Just one little question."

"Will you promise to lay off and go, then? I've got my work to do."

"On my honor as an Eagle Scout," I said. "But I won't promise I won't be back."

He shook his head and sighed. "Shoot your damned question. You lawyers are boring in all the time."

"That's the prettiest compliment I've had since I retired from public life," I said. "Thank you, Al." I pointed at a large glossy un-framed photograph on the bulletin board. It showed a couple standing on a sandy beach. The man, who had wavy hair which was graying at the temples—and who was clearly Barney, I judged from the other pictures—was smiling down at the woman, a stunning-look-ing brunette who was gravely regarding the camera. They were a striking, handsome-looking couple and I would have guessed they were married or in love except for one thing—the considerable dis-parity in their years; I guessed that the man, in a pinch, was old enough to be her father. Could it be possible that this fragile and well-bred-appearing young woman was the scheming Mary Pilant?

"Is that Barney and Mary?" I said.

"That's Barney and Mary," he said. "I've a good-looking boss, don't you think?"

"Very," I said, trying to hide my confusion over this sudden new development. The pea soup was getting thicker. "Now I go," I said, "like I promised," and like a good Eagle Scout I marched resolutely to the stairway. I paused on the first step and looked around. "One friendly tip," I said, "not a question."

"What's that?" he said, with an elaborate show of patience.

"Don't remove the gun shelf from behind the bar. It's too late—I've already seen it and it'll only look worse if you take it out now. You should've done that before the police came—at the same time you got rid of the pistols."

"Next murder I'll remember to rehearse it," he said. "You wouldn't want to play the part of the dead body, would you? It would be a real pleasure to have you."

"Only over *your* dead body, Buster," I said, turning and trudging slowly up the stairs. Here was really quite an amiable character. Certainly not dumb either; perhaps only a little nervous. I wondered how much his cut would be if everything turned out all right. Well I certainly did not wish either him or the charming Mary Pilant any harm. Live and let live was my motto. No, no harm at all—just so long as they did not foul up the defense of my murder case. But when they moved into that area there would really be war, charm or no charm. And it was beginning to look like war.

I had told Mitch that this case had everything but Technicolor. It had been the prize understatement of the year. For Technicolor had now been added and its name was Mary Pilant. I quickened my step on the stair.

Hotels that aspire to look cozy and homelike generally succeed about as dismally as chain-bakeries fool anyone by calling their lumps of pumped-up dough Grandma Higgins' homemade bread; but insofar as any hotel can perhaps be made to look homelike, someone had almost succeeded with the Thunder Bay Inn. The place was actually attractive. Even with all the milling tourists there was an atmosphere of uncontrived hominess and cheer about it, especially about the lobby, that defied analysis.

Perhaps it was the handsome stone fireplace or the superb heads of three white-tailed deer over it (Barney would undoubtedly have shot those), or the colorful and yet restful drapes at the large picture windows overlooking the blue expanse of lake, or the attractively paneled walls of unfinished red cedar that glowed and shone like burnished copper, or the carefully selected prints and photographs—and even a few interesting water colors—all of which depicted scenes indigenous to the Peninsula rather than the usual tourist art showing fairy dream castles in Wales. Whatever the reason the room possessed undeniable charm. Would the enigmatic Mary Pilant have had a hand in all this, I wondered.

The lobby was crowded with people, including Maida, who was sitting by the fireplace oblivious to the clatter and turmoil around her, her nose buried in one of her inevitable mystery thrillers. Mystery thriller indeed, I thought. Here she was, working on a case that had more real mystery about it than a dozen contrived thrillers, a case as bristling with mystery as a porcupine with quills—and she sat reading a damned mystery thriller. I thought of my old hermit Danny McGinnis incredulously glued to his story about his fellow hermit.

True, in our case there was little mystery about what had actually taken place—that was becoming all too brutally apparent. But these facts, however melodramatic, skimmed but the surface, were in themselves merely the tip of the iceberg at sea; it was the "inner facts," the heart of the case itself, that teemed with the stuff of real mystery, the deepening tangle of dark impulses and mixed motives of real men and women.

I glanced about. There was a milling group of vacantly staring people wandering aimlessly up and down, most of whom appeared to be carrying boxes of cleansing tissue. But where was all the Army brass? What had happened to the Army? I went over to the lobby desk.

The bespectacled clerk appeared to be playing a losing game of solitaire with a pack of registration cards. His rapt concentration plainly brooked no interruption. "Ah, cheating!" I thought, as he finally dealt a card from the bottom. After an indecent interval he sighed and reshuffled the deck and looked up. "Yes?" he inquired, with that fine mixture of condescension, boredom and inner pain that seems to be the trademark of hotel clerks the world over.

"What happened to the Army?" I said. "I don't see any glittering brass. Has there been a new war?"

"The Army has retreated," he answered solemnly. "They cleared out yesterday, bag and baggage, thank goodness." He rolled his eyes up, obviously a sorely put-upon man. "Nobody knows the troubles I've had," he seemed to be saying.

"Was the retreat according to plan or because of the shooting of—of Dangerous Dan McGrew?" I said. "I thought the Army was supposed to stay here on maneuvers or something through September."

"The Army has not officially informed me of its reasons for departure," he replied with enviable sarcasm. "All I know is that they have mercifully departed."

"By the way," I asked casually, "were you on duty the night Barney was shot?"

He glanced sharply at me. "What's that to you?" he said coolly.

"I'm Lieutenant Manion's lawyer," I said. "Paul Biegler from Chippewa."

"Oh," he said, shrugging. "I thought you might be another of those prying tourists."

"Smile when you say that, pardner," I said, wincing. "But were you on duty?"

"Yes, I was 'on nights' last week."

"Ah, a break at last," I thought as I pressed rapidly on. "Do you remember when Barney came in? How he was dressed? His general appearance?"

He nodded his head. "I certainly do," he said emphatically. "Barney came running in the front entrance at just about—"

At this juncture a large soft blimp of a woman bustled herself squarely between us and pelted the clerk with a flurry of questions. "Yes, madam, we will serve lunch until one-thirty," he explained patiently. "No, madam, we do not pack lunches for the road. No, madam, the check-out hour is four not five. Yes, madam, downstairs is the place where the 'poor defenseless man' was shot." The clerk turned wearily back to me. "You see how it is?" he murmured. "They're driving me *simply* insane."

"You were just saying. . . ." I began. At that moment a waitress hurried up to the desk, all but running, and spoke earnestly to the clerk. "Miss Pilant wants to see you in the dining room—*immediately!*" she said.

"Yes, yes, of course," he said, innocently trotting away to have his gag applied. So Mary Pilant wanted to play it that way, did she? I turned ruefully, bitterly, upon the still-waiting lady tourist.

"Excuse me for intruding," I said coldly, thinking of how satisfying it would be to hoist her a nice slow kick in the blubber. I stalked away.

So the Army had taken a powder, had it?—gone away, retreated before the superior fire power of Lieutenant Manion? We were certainly getting all the breaks. I had arrived a day late and now couldn't find out what if anything the Army knew. And now even Mary Pilant was getting in my hair. And how was this sudden flight of the Army going to affect our chances for getting one of their damned psychiatrists?

As I stood there morosely Parnell came charging into the lobby, wheezing and puffing like an old wood-burning locomotive, his broad face perspiring and red as a beet. I felt alarmed for him until I saw the look of wild triumph in his eye; the old boy must have come up with something, all right; he looked as proud and pleased as an old dog with a new bone. He brushed blindly past me and joined Maida at the fireplace, flopping down in a chair like a winded whale, but not quite so overcome, I noted, that he forgot to display the tattersall vest for the bedazzled tourists.

As I threaded my way glumly through the milling crowd to join Parnell and Maida I found my way blocked by the same lady tourist who had just interrupted the clerk and me. She was intently studying a large road map affixed to the wall, leaning over and thoughtfully scratching her fanny. The target was magnificent and I stood itchily weighing the possibilities for making a successful drop kick. . . . She was hoydenishly clad in Bermuda shorts large enough to sail the *Kon-Tiki*. She wore a bandana top and a girlish head scarf and on the incredibly tiny feet of her lumpy piano legs she wore some sort of gay open-toed sandals. She was, I saw, of the common or sun-worshiper variety of tourist, looking as though she had been but recently dipped, and held, in a boiling lobster pot. As Mencken once said, she was the sort of female that made a man want to burn every bed in the world.

"Merciful God," I thought, studying this prize specimen of *homo tourosis.*

"How do you like my new hair-do, Boss?" Maida chirped amiably as I joined them.

"Fine," I conceded, "if looking like a curly blonde Zulu is an effective disguise for the undercover work you're doing. But the jackpot question is: are the results worth all the sacrifice? Who are you trying to look like, Mata Hari on a drunk?"

She appealed to Parnell. "See, Parn, see," she pouted. "Now you can see why I'm so starved for a kind word."

I stole a look at the still-scratching lady tourist. "On second thought, Maida," I said, "you look positively ravishing. Pardon my outburst—I've just been through a harrowing experience. Let's go eat and I'll tell you."

As we entered the dining room a young woman came forward to meet us. I caught my breath. It was Mary Pilant. She was much lovelier in person than her photograph, small and poised, with wide intelligent dark eyes.

"Three?" she inquired politely.

"Please," I said. "And please, too—far away from the tourists."

"Perhaps you would prefer to dine on the veranda," she suggested. "We keep a few overflow tables set up out there. And there you will not only escape the tourists"—she paused and smiled slightly—"but be alone to talk."

"Thank you," I said, smiling back. "That's very thoughtful of you. By all means take us to the veranda."

As she led the way through the multitude of noisily feeding tourists I watched her with the kind of avid and rueful admiration that balding middle-aged males bestow upon hopelessly unattainable young loveliness. I noted the poise and slender grace of her walk, the trim modeling of her legs and ankles, the small ears and small well-shaped head with the tendrils of dark hair curling up from the nape of her neck, the sort of pent and brooding intelligence of her face. Yes, poise and grace and intelligence was the verdict for Mary Pilant.

And how, I wondered, how had a character like Barney Quill ever . . . ? Why, he was even older than I. I sighed and recalled Justice Holmes's classic comment to Justice Brandeis. The two had been out for a Washington stroll. A pert little stenographer had overtaken and gone tripping past them, her bouncing little hams and partridge breasts all contributing their part. "Ah, Louis, Louis," the great Holmes had sighed, shaking his leonine head regretfully. "Ah, to be seventy again. . . ." Right now I would have gladly settled for forty.

"Here we are," Mary Pilant said, pausing at a tastefully laid table which commanded a breathless view of the lake.

"Thank you, young lady," I said. "What a lovely outlook. I see I must come here more often."

"By all means, Mr. Biegler," she said, smiling. "We have many points of interest in our little town."

"So I've observed," I said. "I've already been investigating some of them, as you may have heard. But I'm sure there are many more—that is if my view should not be too much obstructed."

She held my eyes for an instant as I watched her faintly mocking smile. It was like a game of chess. "I'll send you a waitress in a minute," she said, turning away.

"Who's that?" Maida said as soon as she had left. "Who is that adorable creature? And what kind of verbal sparring were you two up to? It sounded like Esperanto to me."

"That's Mary Pilant," I said. "She used to be Barney Quill's hostess. I'll get to the sparring part later."

Parnell had grown rather quiet. "Lovely, lovely," he muttered, turning and gazing pensively out over the lake.

Maida's eyes had widened with wonder and envy. "So *that's* the woman in the case," she murmured. "I—I guess I had half expected a two-headed female monster, some sort of scheming witch."

"I know what you mean," I said. "Tell me," I went on, "tell me what you learned about her? There's something here that doesn't add up."

Maida had learned plenty. She had to wait over half an hour for her turn at the beauty parlor. The place was crowded with beauty-starved females, both tourists and locals, besides the half-dozen-odd employees. "The place was like a steambath." And all of them were buzzing about the shooting of Barney Quill; it was just about all they had talked about.

"What was the burden of their chatter, Maida?" I said. "We can cover the details later."

"Well," Maida began, "according to some stories this Mary person was supposed to have been Barney's mistress—although there seems to be considerable doubt on that score."

Parnell spoke up. "When any group of females clacking in a beauty parlor in any degree ever spares one of their sisters," he observed dryly, "they have created, I should say, a tremendous doubt on that score."

I glanced quickly at Parnell. Had he fallen for Mary? If so, that would make two of us. . . . "Who is she, Maida, where is she from?" I went on.

"It seems that she came to Thunder Bay several summers ago with a group of vacationing schoolteachers," Maida continued. "She must be a livin' doll, because Barney fell for her like a ton of bricks—so the word goes—and made her boss lady of the place and of all the college-girl waitresses—at twice her schoolteacher pay. When her own gang of schoolteachers went back to their brats she remained behind as Barney's hostess, just like that."

"Well, I can't much blame him," Parnell said thoughtfully. He sighed heavily and again his gaze wandered out over the glittering lake. "She—she reminds me of someone I once knew," he said slowly, "—over a million years ago. . . ."

I again glanced quickly at Parnell. Was he referring to his own lost Nora? If so perhaps I could now understand and view his checkered career in a new light.

"But if Barney cared so much for Mary Pilant," I said, "how come he did this terrible thing to Laura Manion? What's the story on that?"

"Well," Maida said, "there're half a dozen stories on that: one, that Barney was half-crazed with drink, again that Laura Manion had led him on that night and even before, then again that this rape routine was just an old trick of Barney's with summer tourists. Then there's the school of scandal in reverse that claims he didn't even rape or touch Laura Manion at all—although all agree that he was a ravening wolf." Maida paused. "On this wolf business I even suspect that the girl who worked on me knew personally whereof she spoke. I seemed to detect a note of wistfulness."

"Will the Voice of Experience please proceed?" I said.

"The most persistent story I heard was that Barney had simply blown his stack over the thought of losing Mary Pilant—that she somehow, in some way, triggered the whole explosion." Maida paused and lowered her voice. "Here comes the waitress!" she hissed, as artfully as Mata Hari herself.

I waited impatiently for the waitress to take our order and depart.

"What do you mean—about Barney losing her, about her triggering any explosion?"

"The story is that Mary Pilant had recently taken up with some young Army officer with Lieutenant Manion's outfit—a second-louie called Loftus, Sonny Loftus they called him—and that Barney had tried to break it off. One version is that Barney had offered to marry her, another to also give her this hotel—but that she had refused to stop seeing the young officer and was even about to leave or had threatened to do so. It's all gossip, of course, but I guess in these real small towns you can't even yawn in decent privacy. And here I thought Chippewa was bad enough." She paused and smiled slyly. "And I do manage to yawn there occasionally. . . ."

"Go on," I said. "Leave us not pause now to hear the diverting story of your secret love life. Remember, the trial is next month."

"You make a point, Boss," Maida amiably agreed. "All the stories seem to agree that Barney had lately started to drink heavily—it seems the man could always carry a tremendous load—right up until the night Laura Manion had wandered into the bar to play pinball."

"But why—why did he do this?" I said, more to myself than to Maida. "How does he keep—or win back—the lovely Mary by doing such a spectacularly evil thing?"

"That's the burning mystery," Maida said. "That's what's got everybody baffled." She shook her head. "It beats me, Boss."

"Perhaps Barney was really the one that needed a psychiatrist," I said, half to myself.

Parnell spoke slowly, "In a way it seems—it almost seems as though the Manions wandered onto the stage of a Greek drama in which they had no part, indeed a drama upon which the curtain had already nearly fallen."

Shrewd old Parnell, I thought. "Well said, Parn," I agreed, as he beamed with pleasure. "It looks more and more like the Manions may have been mere innocently casual pawns in some bigger, more mysterious game. It's up to us to try to find out about the game. It may hold the solution."

Yet I wondered what all this had to do with the defense to this murder charge. Assuming we learned all, so what? And why was Mary Pilant so apparently bent on shielding Barney? Or *was* it to shield Barney? Was it rather to make sure that the will was not upset, that she would ultimately get all the swag for herself? I shook my head dubiously. Such avid and calculated avarice somehow didn't seem to fit this lovely feminine creature, it simply didn't signify. But there was much in this case that didn't signify. Why had she even been working for such a man? "Watch out, Biegler," I thought. "Don't go seeing shimmering brunette mirages, don't go getting soft over a passing vision of dark velvet loveliness. Remember, comrade, 'A rag, a bone . . .' And whatever the lady's motives may be, your sole motive now is to get at the truth!"

"*Jiggers!*" Maida warned.

The waitress appeared and took our dessert orders while Maida chattered disarmingly on about the lovely pines, the gorgeous weather, the priceless view, her eyes glowing and dancing with the excitement of her new role. "*Magnifique!*" I said, when the waitress had departed. "By all means we must send you to Moscow to spy on the Moujiks."

"To think," Maida said, "just to think that I have been pounding a typewriter all these years when—when there's work like this to be done. Work my eye, absorbing play—

"Dusting a typewriter, you mean," I said, "at least since I got in this damned case. And as for this being fun, I'll still take the hay. And remember, lawyers don't often get bizarre cases like this to work on. Most criminal cases are duller than contract bridge. In fact, during my hundred and ten years as prosecutor there were few I can offhand remember that could even hold a candle to it."

Parnell turned to me. "Suppose you bring us up to date, Polly."

"Yes," Maida breathed, "I can't wait. This is like working on a Chinese puzzle. Even Mickey Spillane has nothing on this—and we've only got *one* murder." She shook her head in wonder. "It doesn't seem possible—*only one murder!*"

The dessert had been served and we were on our third cup of coffee before I described how I had discovered the gun shelf under the bar. And I hit only the high spots. I told them my theory about the bartender serving as lookout, about the bulletin board, about the lovable bartender finally clamming up, about the abrupt summons of the desk clerk to the dining room to have his gag adjusted. It was well after two o'clock when I was done.

"You mean," Maida said wonderingly, spreading her hands, "you mean Mary Pilant gets all this loot anyway—even when she was stepping out with another man? Wouldn't you know. And I can't get one lone male to take me out to dinner—even when I pay."

"At least you've got two tottering old badgers taking you out to

140

lunch," I comforted her. "You got to play it cool, Maida, play it cool." I turned to the silent Parnell. "Well, Parn, I guess it's your turn. You not only look like a cat that has just swallowed a mouse, but even like a mouse that has just swallowed a cat. Purge yourself, my friend."

chapter 22

Parnell had had a busy morning; in fact, as he unfolded the story of his activities that forenoon I marveled that such an arthritic and ailing old man could have accomplished even half so much in so short a time. Few professional detectives could have covered so much ground, I felt, and none, I was certain, could have done so to better purpose. The old boy was a born detective: shrewd, resourceful, and always keeping his eye on the main chance, and as he talked on I stared at him with increasing admiration.

He had got off to a slow start; the only people in the first tavern had been a "stupendously drunken" Indian and the proprietor—"a great purple-nosed bladder-faced individual with the eyes of a cod, to which he was obviously related, and who, with equal obviousness, had joyously dedicated his life to the consumption of his own wares." The moment Parnell had brought up the subject of the fatal shooting this charming man· had clammed up and fled to the back room.

"It was plain that this numbed and sodden intellectual pygmy was not being evasive or cute," Parnell explained. "I swear rather that in his addled alcoholic mind he had worked out the notion that, since his tavern was the closest to Barney's, he was next on the list to be shot and I had come to shoot him." Parnell shook his head. " 'Killer' McCarthy," he said. "The Lord save us, an' me not knowin' which end of a gun to shoot."

Parnell had covered every tavern in town—there were seven—and had doggedly consumed at least one bottle of pop in each. "I never drank so much of the vile stuff since I left law school," he explained. Fortunately in all the other taverns—which were patronized largely by locals or by truck drivers or pulp cutters from the surrounding logging camps—they were all either already talking about the shooting or were more than willing to resume their favorite topic. He had learned a lot about the life and times of the late Barney Quill, hunter and fisherman and expert shot who had failed only once. . . .

"I shall not pause now and recount just where and from whom I learned what I learned," Parnell went on, "but by the time I got to the last tavern several things had clearly emerged regarding the character and reputation of the deceased."

"Let's have 'em, Parn," I said.

"First and foremost he was perhaps the most thoroughly disliked person in town," Parnell said. "The general air of rejoicing over his demise was as shocking as it was obvious. To borrow one of your inelegant but colorful phrases, Paul, most people simply 'hated his guts,' his insufferable affectation of superior virtue, his apparently illy disguised cock-of-the-walk attitude that he was a sort of superman who could outshoot, outfight, outlove, out-anything any three men in town."

"There is some evidence, you know, Parn, that he may not have been too far wrong," I said.

"I had not proceeded far before I discovered that this vast dislike was also mingled with fear," Parnell went on, "and a fear that appeared pretty well grounded." He paused. "It seems that the reports were pretty much all the truth: he *could* outhunt, outshoot, outfight and out all the rest just about any one man, if not three, in all of Thunder Bay. Not to mention the sylvan environs, which I shall presently get to. Apparently the man not only *thought* he was good, he *was* good. He wanted to be Mr. Big of Thunder Bay and Mastodon Township and by God he was. And in his pursuit of this dubious distinction he seems to have known no personal fear. A truly amazin' character, that he was."

"Can you give us an example?" I said. "It might be important, you know."

"Well," Parnell went on, tolerantly overlooking my interruption, "take the time he almost kilt the husky young truck driver who came to beat him up." Parnell paused thoughtfully and pursed his lips. "Yes, that's a moderately good illustration. There are many others."

"Oh, lovely, lovely," Maida said, leaning forward.

"It seems that before this Mary Pilant young lady came to work for Barney—" Parnell's eyes seemed to soften at her name—"Barney's hotel and bar, particularly the bar, had been pretty much a rendezvous for roistering lumberjacks and truck drivers and the various seedy and besotted local gentry, slaves all to strong drink. But when Miss Mary came on the scene all that abruptly changed; she evidently sold Barney on the notion that he was wastin' his time and talents; that the real money was to be made from the tourists. But the local characters would first have to be sent on their way. Anyway, and whatever happened, the welcome mat was suddenly removed— the local characters were one day told by Barney to get the hell out and stay out."

"You mean there wasn't any fight after all?" Maida said, seeming on the verge of tears. "They went like sheep?"

"Patience, my dove," Parnell said. "There were fights indeed, fisticuffs and eye-gougings and broken heads beyond the wildest dreams of even your literary hero. The local gentry resented bitterly losing their happy drinking home to the tourists; they had been there first; and so they still insisted on coming back to Barney's." Parnell paused. "Alas, the results were inevitable."

"How do you mean?" Maida breathlessly put in.

"As fast as they came in the door Barney threw them out, with a sort of monotonous abstracted regularity, like a bored Keystone cop flailing his constituents with his night stick. It got so the tourists would gather, particularly on Saturday nights, to watch the mighty evacuation. For a time it became a sort of tourist feature of Thunder Bay, like watching the bears at the garbage dump—Barney was again house-cleanin' his bar."

"Lovely," Maida murmured, blinking her eyes.

"If the interlopers wanted to box, Barney boxed 'em; if they wanted to wrassle, he wrassled 'em; and if they wanted to play dirty, he cheerfully obliged 'em. It seems that among his many other attainments he excelled in the dark arts of Judo or jujitsu or whatever it's called. Really an amazin' fellow he was, a sort of Ben Franklin of the world of physical attainment and violence. Why, one night three 'jacks rushed Barney—all of them younger than he—and when the smoke cleared away one was knocked cold on the floor and had to be assisted away, the other had fled into the night, and the third was moaning and holding a broken wrist. Nobody is yet quite sure how it happened. In any event it was a clear case of an irresistible force colliding with *three* highly removable objects."

"Lieutenant Manion should have been awarded the Congressional Medal for daring to face him," I said. "And here they want to send the poor man to prison."

"Don't forget the husky young truck driver," Maida reminded Parnell, her appetite whetted. "Remember, you promised."

"Presently, my dear, presently," Parnell said, smiling benevolently. "After that last fracas things understandably calmed down, and for an interval the tourists inherited the Thunder Bay Inn undisturbed —that is, until this husky young truck driver came to town, or rather to one of the nearby lumber camps."

"Who was he, where was he from?" Maida begged.

"No matter, but it appears that he was not only nearly twice the size of Barney, who was evidently not an unusually large man, but also less than half his age. Moreover he had been an amateur pugilist of no mean attainments and had, it seemed, reached the semi-finals in those—those Diamond Glove contests sponsored by that shyly self-admitted world's greatest newspaper, the Chicago *Tribune*."

"*Golden* Gloves you mean, Parn," I said, hoping to keep him off *that* subject. "It's the annual Golden Gloves Tournaments."

"Ah yes, golden," Parn said. "But no matter, no matter, golden or tin—the fight's the thing."

"Aye, the fight, the fight—let's have the fight!" the avid Maida chimed in.

"When the men at this young boxer's camp learned of his prowess in fisticuffs, the very next Saturday night they came to town and marched in a body into Barney's, with this stout young gladiator at their head, and demanded drinks for the house from Barney."

"What happened?" I said.

"Don't interrupt!" Maida said, plucking my sleeve.

"Well, Barney and the young man fought, of course. They fought their fight with their fists. They fought by the bar, they fought behind the bar, they fought on the dance floor, they fought on the stairs, they once fought out in the street. They fought for an hour and seven minutes by the clock—the men who told me were there and saw it—until—until this Barney, himself like his adversary all tattered and bloody and nearly done in, suddenly executed a quick feint with his left"—in his excitement Parnell had arisen and now flailed out with his pudgy arms—"and brought over a sizzling right—*wham!* —and the youthful pride of the lumberjacks toppled and crashed like a tall Norway pine."

"*Timber!*" Maida yelped with delight. "You—you mean Barney knocked him cold?"

"Rather extensively," Parnell replied dryly. "Barney stowed him away in a deep freeze. The fight was over. His comrades shouldered their fallen hero and silently took him away. One of the men who told me the story said it was so bad that he had to drive the young boxer's truck back to camp. The next morning the vanquished young gladiator hobbled to the paymaster and drew his time and quit the camp." Parnell paused and sighed, as though reluctant to be done with his yarn. "And that was the last visitation of the local lumberjacks and unwanted barflies upon the hallowed premises of the Thunder Bay Inn."

"Good God, Parn," I said, horrified at the thought. "All this must have happened while I was still prosecutor. Where were the police? the Sheriff? I never heard a whisper about any of this. It seems incredible."

"Perhaps the gendarmes thought Barney was himself a sufficient if unwitting force for law and order. Or perhaps it was a case of discretion being the better part of valor. The only deputy sheriff in town was the kindly little old man who is the caretaker of the trailer park—the same man that our Lieutenant gave himself up to the night he shot Barney."

"Better raise the ante to *two* Congressional Medals, Boss," Maida put in. "My God, I should have known this Barney person. What a man, what a man. . . ."

A waitress appeared and hovered expectantly over our still littered table. I glanced at my watch. "It's getting late," I said. "Let's get out of here and finish our talk in the car."

"I can't wait," Maida said, busily putting her face together.

As I settled for our bill in the main dining room Mary Pilant was no-where to be seen. "Thank you, young lady," I said to the waitress. "We enjoyed our luncheon immensely—the service, the view, the delicious lake trout—all were superb. I'm sorry we kept you waiting so long and please tell Miss Pilant that we'll surely be back. Don't forget now."

"Thank you," the waitress murmured, gliding away to retrieve her tip.

"Hark! the candidate for Congress bestows his first snow job," Maida jibed sarcastically. "Charm to burn for everyone but his downtrodden steno. Henceforth I'm voting straight Federalist."

"Ah, the truth emerges," I fought back. "I've suspected you of ballot-box treachery all along."

"Aren't you going to try to see her?" Parnell said as we moved out to the lobby. "Mary Pilant, I mean?"

I shook my head. "No use, Parn. Certainly not now at least, while she's playing us this glacial chill. If and when I ever do see her I want to have all the story, or as much of it as we're ever likely to get. I haven't even heard all your story yet, but from the Cheshire cat grin on your face I know you've still got something up your sleeve." I paused and lowered my voice. "Stand by and watch, now, while I go try to speak to the clerk. You'll see how much use it is to talk with her."

I moved over to the desk. "Pardon me," I said. "When we were interrupted this noon . . ." I began. The clerk looked up and regarded me stonily. "Is there any use?" I said. "Is the gag really on that tight?"

To his credit the little man looked embarrassed as he shook his head. "No use," he said. "I'm sorry. . . . I need the job."

"But you'll have to tell me eventually," I pressed him quietly. "I'll get it out of you in court anyway."

He stared at me blankly for a moment and then glanced toward the dining room. "Will you?" he said, and turned away. I wheeled around and, yes, Mary Pilant was standing motionless in the door-way. She smiled and nodded agreeably at me and moved out of sight into the dining room.

"Sad, sad," Parnell murmured as we left, shaking his head dolefully. "It—it's hard to believe she could stoop to such deception and intrigue. She signaled him, all right, I saw her shake her head, I *saw* her. Ah me, ah me, what a dreary complicated old world. . . ."

"This really looks like war, Parn," I said, setting my jaw and doubtless adding three new wrinkles to my already knotted forehead. One thing was plain: whatever her motives, Mary Pilant in her quiet way was every bit the relentless fighter that her late boss had been, the fabulous and unbelievable Barney Quill. "You see, Parn," I said, "this little lady happens to be suppressing the truth— and truth that we happen to need badly."

Parnell sighed and shook his head. It grieved him mightily that his sweet Nora-Mary should carry on this way.

Before leaving town we drove into the tourist park to get the lay of the land, pausing at the now open gate and the smaller adjoining opening in the fence through which Laura Manion's little dog had lighted her way the night Barney had raped and beaten her. Maida was in a seventh heaven of pleasure just to be present at the scene of so much delicious violence. "And it looks so placid and innocent now," she breathed. "Brr. . . ."

The road wound through the park and around under the Norway pines toward the lake and then circled northerly and inland again back to the caretaker's cottage, near which the Manion trailer had been parked, as we guessed from the area of yellowed grass. Parnell asked me to note that the trailer had stood considerably north of the gate, that is, closer to the town and Barney's than the entrance gate itself. I put my hand on the door to get out. "Where you goin'?" Parnell politely inquired.

"I thought I'd go see the caretaker," I said. "Want to come along?"

"Spare yourself," Parnell said loftily. "I've seen him already. I didn't waste my mornin' like some I know, standin' around in the town's fanciest bar."

"Was it worth it?"

"I'll tell you when we get rollin'—the sight of all these tourists an' trailers is giving me hay fever. Let us away. A-*kerchoo*. . . ."

On the way out of town I paused by a rather obscure two-rut dirt road turning off the main road and running into the woods westerly, away from the tourist park. I pointed. "That would be the road that Barney drove Laura in on when he raped her," I said.

In his morning wanderings Parnell had heard that one of Lieutenant Manion's shots had not only broken the bar mirror but also a bottle of bonded whisky; that Barney had been an expert shot with all manner of small arms, including rifles, shotguns and pistols, particularly pistols; that he possessed a considerable collection of all types of firearms, again particularly including pistols; that he was reputed to have kept firearms stashed somewhere behind the bar; that he had also kept on the back bar a velvet-covered plaque on which was displayed, for the awe of the tourists, the many medals and ribbons he had won for his shooting prowess.

"I didn't see any medals, Parn," I said, "and I looked around pretty carefully."

"Maybe they were buried with the man," Maida helpfully suggested. "I read somewhere last winter where they'd buried ski wax and goggles and all with a skier who'd broken his neck."

"The ski wax was probably used to fill the empty brain cavity," I said.

"The medals were there as late as the night of the shooting," Parnell said. "One of my local informants had seen them earlier in the evening."

"I thought Barney didn't allow any of the local peasantry in his place," Maida said.

"Only a select and fumigated few who regularly behaved—and bathed—up to the new high standards," Parnell replied. "And presumably only those who were properly awed by the great Barney himself."

"What about the caretaker, Parn?" I said. "Did you learn anything new?"

"Ah, yes, the caretaker," Parnell said with relish. "Fine little old man by the name of Lemon. He happened to be in one of the last taverns I hit, merely buying a package of Peerless, he isn't a drinking man he told me. One of the patrons pointed him out and I simply went up and introduced myself and asked me questions. He had no hesitation in answering. Fine, frank little old man—and nimble for his years, too."

"What'd you find out?" I said. "Beyond the fact that he was nimble?"

"Well, first of all I inquired and learned from him there was no other automobile road leading into or from the park; in other words that Barney lied by the clock when he told Laura Manion he could drive her home another way."

"Good, Parn, good; we must remember that."

"I also learned that the caretaker liked the Manions, particularly the wife, and that, to again borrow your coarse idiom, he hated Barney's guts. He called him a bully and a braggart and said that while officially he frowned upon violence and murder that the town was well rid of him."

"Fine, fine, Parn. Go on."

"He also likes Mary Pilant and thinks she's a perfect lady and can't understand why she would ever have worked for such a rogue as Barney much less have been his mistress, which he thoroughlv doubted." Parnell paused. "Yes, a fine observant truthful little old man," he said, obviously pleased to have dredged up a strong pro-Mary fan in his travels.

"What else, Parn? All this is good, but what else? I can tell you're holding out. Let's have it."

I was not wrong; with his instinctive Irish sense of drama, Parnell had indeed saved the best for the last. He hemmed and hawed and trumpeted, clearing his throat, and finally spoke.

"Now I'm coming to the good part," he said. "You see, Polly, at the trial we must be prepared to meet a claim or at least an inference by the prosecution that Barney did not rape our lady in the woods, but rather that the affair was a mutual party, an easy lay, as you might say, and further that it was not Barney who beat her up at the gate but rather her angry and jealous husband up at the trailer, *after* she came home. Do you follow me?"

"That I do, Parn," I said soberly. "And the possibility has bothered me a lot, as you know."

"Well, I now think we may have medicine to block any such claim." Parnell paused, nursing his scoop like a mother her first-born. "Real medicine," he added mysteriously.

"Speak, man, speak!" Maida broke in. "You're killing me dead."

"Have patience, my fragile doll," Parnell gently reproved her. "Well, two tourists who had been staying here for nearly a month— an old couple from Akron—checked out with their trailer early this morning, this here now very identical morning. They had just said good-by to Mr. Lemon and were turning away to depart when the woman remarked, just casual like, passin' the time of day, that she hoped now her nightmares would go away and she could at last get a good night's sleep."

"What happened?" Maida panted.

"Well," Parnell went placidly on, "Mr. Lemon naturally asked her what she meant about her nightmares. And she up and told him she still woke up at night hearing the screams of that poor woman at the gate—"

"Are you sure she said *at the gate*, Parn?" I broke in. "Are you sure? This is vital, you know."

"At the gate," Parnell answered firmly. "And at precisely eleven fifty-nine, she looked at her clock. I asked the caretaker several times whether she said at the gate and he said he was sure. Then he pointed out to me that this Ohio couple's trailer had been, of all the trailers in the park, the closest one to the gate, and that anyway the shouts *had* to be at or near the gate and not up at the trailer because this Ohio woman was a little deaf and both she and her husband had been awakened by the screams, while he, Mr. Lemon, a light sleeper with good hearing whose cottage is right near the Manions' trailer, heard nary a sound."

"Lord, Parn," I said, "this is a wonderful break, wonderful. Did you get their names?"

Parnell patted his breast pocket. "I've got their names and addresses written down in my notebook here. They already told their stories to the state police. And that should surely blast any attempt by the prosecution to move the beating up to the trailer."

"What else did you find out?" I demanded. "I can see you still got something up your sleeve."

Parnell frowned and grew serious. "You're right, Paul," he said. "There's more." Parnell sighed. "What I'm about to tell you may hold the key to the whole perplexing *why* of this case. I refer to Mary Pilant."

"Then why so glum, Parn?" Maida said. "Out with it, man."

"When I rushed into the hotel this noon I was just bursting to tell about it." Parnell paused and sighed heavily. "After I *saw* Mary Pilant my little triumph turned to ashes—and then I didn't want to tell, and I still don't."

"Nora, again," I thought. "Whatever you think best, Parn," I began—

"But I've got to tell it, it's too important to the case. I don't know precisely how we can use it, if at all, but like much else we have learned today that we probably can't use, this is important to an even bigger thing—it should help us to see and understand our case." Parnell sighed. "When a lawyer once really *understands* his case, half the battle is won."

"All right, Parn," I said quietly.

"I had reached the seventh and last tavern," Parnell began, "when I ran into a nice-looking young soldier boy who had come in and was having a bottle of pop. I had already heard that the

Army had pulled out so, nosey me, I barged over and asked him if perchance he was with Lieutenant Manion's outfit. He was, and on a quick hunch I introduced myself and said I was there helping Lieutenant Manion's lawyer investigate the fatal shooting and did he know of anything that might help us. It was a shot in the dark."

"Go on, Parn," I said, wondering what all this had to do with Mary Pilant.

"Well, with that he looked around and pulled me into a back booth and told me that he did have something on his mind that might help us, he wasn't sure, but anyway he'd better tell me as he was just leaving town."

"What did he say, Parn?"

"He said that the night before the shooting his bunkmate had been out on late pass and, the night being moonlit and warm and himself a little full of beer, the bunkmate had decided to walk down the beach a way and take a swim in the raw. Well, he was walking along the beach, quietly minding his own business and all, when suddenly he stumbled. He flashed on his flashlight and saw one of his junior officers lying on the sand and, standing some paces away behind a pile of driftwood, a woman whom he recognized only as the good-looking hostess at the Thunder Bay Inn, not even knowing her name. He still don't, as a matter of fact."

"My, my," I said. "And then what happened?"

"He ran like a deer," Parnell said and then fell silent, glumly examining his cold cigar. During the telling he had become more and more morose and I thought it was time to cheer him up. But I still couldn't see how all this was important to our case.

"Well, there's no law against a young couple being on the beach, Parn," I said. "Not yet, at least. Maida told us over lunch, remember, that she'd heard this Mary gal was going with some young officer. What's all this big build-up about?"

"It wasn't their being on the beach," Parnell doggedly went on. "It was their attire, their vestments—or rather the lack." He rolled his eyes at us. "They didn't appear to have on too many clothes."

Maida and I glanced quickly at each other, at loss for words, as glum Parnell stared straight ahead. I felt almost sorry he had found out about the incident. For what possible use could such a thing, however spicy, be to the defense of our case? Surely honorable old Parnell was not suggesting, even obliquely, that we somehow blackmail Mary Pilant into co-operating with the defense? Or was he?

"Maybe this was just Army gossip, Parn," I said. "After all you got the story in a public tavern from a man who wasn't even there."

Parnell shook his head. "No, Polly. I checked on that. I asked this young soldier who he'd heard the story from and he said he had got it directly from this bunkmate who had seen it. Then I asked him when and *where* he had heard it from this bunkmate, and he said his buddy had told him the story over a beer in Barney's bar the next night, that is, the very night of the shooting—early that evening, shortly before Laura Manion had showed up to play pinball. Then I asked him if anyone else knew about this story—now get this, Paul—and he said that no one else knew it, that his buddy had purposely clammed up so that he wouldn't get in a jam with this young officer. I pressed him on this, asking him who was at the bar, and he said no one but the bartender. I asked him if the bartender could possibly have overheard it, and he finally agreed it was possible, because, as he now remembered, the bartender had suddenly left the bar and disappeared upstairs, leaving them alone."

"Technicolor, popcorn buttered generously with old crankcase oil, and a screen a block long," I said, shaking my head. "I swear this case has a h'ant on it."

"You mean," excited Maida said, "you mean, Parn, that the bartender ran and told Barney and then—and then the feathers hit the fan?"

"I—I don't know what I mean," Parnell said bleakly. "I'm telling you what I heard. Then I asked this young soldier where his buddy was and he said he was back at camp loading the last truck preparatory to taking off. I said, 'Take me to him,' and in half an hour—after my first harrowing ride in a jeep—I had the story straight from the young man himself. It checked in every particular."

I longed to have a picture of Parnell and his tattersall riding in a jeep. Even the very waves must have risen in salute. "Where are the young soldiers now, Parn?" I said.

"They're on their way to a camp down in Georgia. They left before noon, already several hours late. I have their names and addresses in my notebook." He shrugged morosely. "And that's my big scoop."

"But if Barney did learn from his bartender of Mary's—ah—indiscretion with this young officer," Maida said, "then why didn't he go a-gunning for the young officer?—or even Mary? Why should he pick on the poor innocent Manions?"

Parnell threw out his hands. "I don't know," he said slowly. "The more I learn about this case the less I know. I don't even know for sure that Barney did know about Mary—ah—being on the beach the night before with the young officer. But it seems common knowledge that he did know she was dating this young fellow and also that he was trying desperately to break it up." Parnell paused. "I guess it would take a whole panel of psychiatrists to unwind the mind of that one. . . . Perhaps he was mad at the whole Army—because of it he was no longer the big frog in Thunder Bay, and finally, to heap insult on injury, it was stealing his girl. Then when Army wife Laura Manion wandered into his web he concentrated all of his accumulated venom and frustration on her." He shook his head. "I don't know—I'm only an old whisky-drinkin' lawyer myself—and also, I'm afraid, a sentimental old fool."

After that we drove along in silence, each lost in his own thoughts, perhaps lost, as I was, in the spell of the magnificent lake, heaving gently with such deceptive tranquillity below us, washed in the glow of the dying sun, each wheeling sea gull seeming nailed in the sky.

On the way home we braved the tourists and stopped off at the Halfway House for our supper, preceded by some well-earned drinks—"just two," we solemnly resolved—and there found a new small Negro combo, with a pixilated piano man who so seared our hearts, or at least mine, that all our resolutions were forgotten. We were so far carried away, in fact, that along about closing time Maida even asked Parnell to dance with her, a calamitous enterprise which I believe the old goat would have undertaken except that he was mercifully stricken with a cramp in his bad leg and had to beg off. Instead all of us wove our way homeward and, fortunately, did not run across any patrolling sheriffs.

Parnell appeared at my office the next morning, even before Maida, and joined me in my second "eye-opener" cup of coffee. "I've been thinking, boy," he said. "I didn't sleep very well last night."

"I've been thinking, too, Parn," I said, indicating an open letter on my desk. "Found that little present at my mail slot last night. Letter from the Army officer I wrote at Thunder Bay giving us the brush-off on an Army psychiatrist. Writes that since Lieutenant Manion didn't belong to his outfit—was just there on loan—we'd better write the Lieutenant's own outfit. Sent me the address." I shook my head. "So we're back to scratch—no psychiatrist and the trial date appproaching on wings."

"That's one of the things I've been mulling over, Paul," Parnell said. "You know, of course, that under the statute we must serve timely notice on the prosecution of our intention to claim the defense of insanity and at least four days before the trial. When do you propose to serve that notice, boy? Time's a-flyin'."

"That problem's been bothering me most all night, Parn—ever since I read that damned letter. Up to now I've been putting off serving the notice for several reasons: till I saw we could actually get a psychiatrist; then with the vague idea of not tipping our hand to the other side any sooner than we had to; and also to possibly prevent or delay the People from sicking their own rebuttal psychiatrists on our man." I paused. "I'm glad you raised the subject because I've just about made up my mind that we should serve the notice now—today—and let the chips fall where they may. What do you think?"

"But won't that do just what you're trying to avoid?" Parnell said thoughtfully. "Tip off our defense and give the other side a longer psychiatric crack at him, as it were? Mind, now, I'm not objectin', boy; I'm merely tryin' to test your thinkin'—our little game, you know. I'm listenin'."

So Parnell and I were away again, endlessly debating the pros and cons of our strategy for the fast approaching trial. I pointed out that if we delayed the serving of our notice this might in itself give the People their grounds for a continuance since Mitch could then argue that he needed additional time in which to obtain a decent rebuttal psychiatric examination. Parnell agreed and then raised the question of whether the People could ever get to examine our man.

"It's a little brainstorm I had during the night," he added.

"What do you mean?" I said. "Surely you're familiar with the procedure that permits a prosecutor in felony cases to file a petition with the Court suggesting insanity and asking for a psychiatric examination and sanity hearing? The moment we file our notice of insanity Mitch can petition the court—on the sole ground that we've thereby furnished him—that the defendant *may* have been insane (he needn't admit it), and hence get to paw over our man."

Parnell grinned evilly. "I'm aware of that procedure, boy," he said. "I have it fully in mind. If and when such a petition is filed we'll simply tell our man to clam up and tell the People's psychiatrist to go fly a kite. He simply won't play."

I fidgeted uneasily. "You mean, Parn, we'd tell Lieutenant Manion not to let the People's psychiatrist have at him?"

"Not only tell him not to let them examine him—but not even talk with them," he said. "I mean our man will tell 'em all to go plumb to hell."

"But how can you expect to get away with it, Parn? That procedure's on the law books, man, and has been for years. Won't I risk being jailed for contempt or something?"

"We'll chance it," Parnell replied. "There are a lot of rusty old things in the law and on the law books, boy, that couldn't stand up for five minutes if their constitutionality were seriously challenged. Nearly every new supreme court report that comes out has at least one shining example. The Legislature's forever getting some unconstitutional bug in its britches, and I think this old law is one of them. I've had my droopy eye on this statute for years and in my opinion it isn't worth the paper it's written on. Constitutionally, I mean."

"I'm beginning to see," I murmured. "I'm beginning to see. . . ."

"Don't you see," Parnell went on, warming to his subject, "one of the basic provisions of both the State and Federal constitutions is that no man shall be compelled to testify against himself in any criminal case. That's of course the Fifth Amendment—the very one that's getting to be such a dirty word these days in certain sturdy flag-waving quarters. . . ."

"Let's not get on that now, Parn," I said, rolling up my eyes.

Parnell had awakened during the night with the whole argument laid out cold. "I must have put a nickel in me subconscious." If any statute or procedure purported to *force* a person charged with crime to submit to a hostile psychiatric examination, wasn't it thereby unconstitutional and bad?

"Hm," I mused, over the bold soundness of the old man's vision. "But supposing the good judge overrules all our fine constitutional arguments? Either we appeal—which is tantamount to a People's continuance—or the other side still gets its examination."

Parnell grinned and shook his head. "No, boy. No such thing. If the judge rules against us our man still tells 'em all to go to hell. And if he tells them that what're they going to do? The Judge, Mitch, the Doctor, anyone? If our man simply won't talk *who's* going to make him talk? They can't threaten to jail *him* for contempt, the poor bastard's already there. And you're in the clear, Polly. You co-operated. And what kind of a psychiatric examination would they have if he wouldn't play ball? The whole procedure of psychoanalysis, to be effective, presumes ardent co-operation from the subject; hence the overstuffed couch."

A key rattled in the outside door and Maida burst in with her usual boisterous calm and only twenty minutes late.

"What you two doing?" she demanded. "Telling dirty stories?"

"I wish to God we were," I said. "We've been exploring the dismal legal swamps of insanity."

"Well," Maida sniffed, "I must say each of you has excellent laboratory material to work on."

"Bring your book, young lady," I said. "Enough of this insubordination. Please respect our years if not our brains. You can't play detective every day. See, Parn, one day out and she's more sassy and spoiled than ever."

Maida went to her room and presently reappeared with her book and bristling battery of pencils. "Back to the salt mines," she sighed, twisting and squaring herself around for her dictation, as all stenographers seem bound to do, like the circling of a dog bedding down for the night.

"Ready?" I said, when the squirmings and maneuvers had ceased.

"Ready."

"I've got a combined notice and proof of service and three letters. Make the notice an original and three—no, four, we need a set for Parn—with one blue cover for filing. Got it?"

"Got it."

I turned to the form of notice of insanity in Judge Gillespie's work on Michigan criminal law and started dictating.

I dictated the notice of insanity and a letter of transmittal to Mitch of his copy and one to the county clerk for the original. "Add a post-script to the county clerk's letter: 'I trust that by pure chance, as usual, you will contrive to get at least one good-looking babe on the jury to ease our pain.'"

Maida sniffed and glanced at Parnell. "Murder or no murder, the boss must always make his little joke."

"Now fix up a letter to a Colonel Mugfur at the address on this letter," I said, handing her the rejection letter from the Army officer at Thunder Bay. "Send him the same letter I wrote the Thunder Bay brass asking for an Army psychiatrist, fixing it where needed to make sense. Send it airmail special delivery. Times a-fleetin'. Have you got it?"

"Got it."

"Good girl. Now type all that up as fast as you can. House Detectives McCarthy and Biegler must clamp on their false mustaches and be off."

"And leave poor little me here all alone?" Maida said plaintively.

"See, Parn, there's no quicker way to ruin a good house-broken stenographer than to let her play detective for a day."

"Almost as bad as queen for a day," Parnell observed with admirable neutrality as Maida plodded out to her salt mine.

I leaned back and lit one of my Neapolitan stink weeds. "Parn, all this stuff we've been discussing is simply further evidence of the crazy state of the law on the defense of insanity in criminal cases," I said. "Take this notice to Mitch. Isn't it a precious example of what I mean? Here we notify Mitch of our intention to claim and prove insanity and at the same time boldly admit that we haven't got—and therefore certainly haven't yet consulted—any psychiatrist. Our man is nuts simply because I say he's nuts. A man is shot down in cold blood. I say his killer should go free because Dr. Biegler has appointed himself sole court psychiatrist. Quick, Watson, my black leather sofa! What a business."

"Don't you exaggerate the situation? After all, it isn't you who determines that the man is insane—you'll still have to go find a psychiatrist to back up your guess."

"We'll find one. You know that, Parn. If we had the money we'd probably have a half a dozen on ice right now."

"Aren't you being a little harsh on the profession of psychiatry, Paul? Do you claim all of them are quacks and charlatans?"

"No, I didn't mean that, Parn. I don't mean that at all. What I guess I mean is—" I paused, "—is that, as Lieutenant Manion said, this whole insanity procedure is so goddam unscientific. I—I guess it grieves me that our profession can prolong such a primitive rickety state of affairs."

"Perhaps, Paul," Parnell said, "and then again perhaps the law is wiser than you think. Perhaps this is just further evidence of the wonderful elasticity of the law, of its broad accommodation, of the room it gives a jury to move around in to reach a just result." Parnell paused thoughtfully. "Justice, you know, lad, cannot be measured with calipers. And surely you do not mean to infer that it would be an unjust verdict if Lieutenant Manion were acquitted on the ground of temporary insanity? Or does your zeal for abstract justice extend even that far?"

Shrewd Parnell was driving me into a corner and both of us knew it. "Well," I said lamely, "no . . . I don't mean exactly that. It—it's just—"

"No, of course you don't mean that, Paul," Parnell dryly cut in. "So what are you belly-aching about? How would you solve the problem, if you think the present system is so bad? What's the new and improved Biegler Plan? Would you like to have some judge appoint a panel of State-paid psychiatrists to say your man was sane when he shot Barney? Would that make you feel better and more scientific? Suppose a panel of bearded 'nonpartisan' psychiatrists paid by the State pawed over our man—as you seem so badly to want—to determine his state of sanity when he shot Barney? What do you think they'd find? I give you three guesses. And what would you do when they emerged from their huddle and found him sane? Why, you'd scream like a wounded horse and race out to find three more psychiatrists who'd swear he was nuts. Probably four. Then maybe the State would raise you two, like a couple of night cooks playing stud poker in the kitchen. Well, at least the way things are you're spared that expensive mockery. It at least won't be a battle of which side can produce the most psychiatrists."

"You're hurtin', Parn," I said, smiling ruefully.

"I think it's time I'm hurtin', boy. What you forget, Polly, is that criminal trials are from their very nature intensely partisan affairs —primitive, knock-down, every-man-for-himself combats—the very opposite of detached scientific determinations. You of all men should know this. In fact I believe that's one of the reasons why—in this wonderful laboratory age when everything we touch or buy is pumped full of science and little else—people are so drawn to the hurly-burly of a criminal trial. They're *starved* for real drama and raw emotion, for the purging catharsis of knowing the chips are really down; they recognize that a criminal trial is the real McCoy." Parnell shook his head. "No, Paul, the law may be wiser than you think. Let us hear no more of its being unscientific."

Parnell had pressed me pretty hard. "Well, Parn, you may be right on there being no easy alternatives to the present procedure," I said. "In fact I rather think you are. But if you're correct in the constitutional analysis you just gave the People will not only not have an equal crack at our defendant but no crack at all. And is that right and just? Damn it, I almost hope Mitch tries to file a petition to examine our man. If you're right under present procedures they *can't* examine him if we won't let them. And I still say that's a primitive, haywire, and goddam unscientific legal arrangement. So suppose we call the argument a draw?"

"Discussion, boy, not argument," Parnell said. "Yes, let's call it a draw. And now that we've neatly drawn and quartered the law of insanity, what else are we doing today?"

"Well, Parn, I think I'd better go visit my people. For one thing I'd better go see if they're still living together—which, God knows, I can't be sure of from day to day. And I must go over some things with them in the light of yesterday's expedition. Like to go along?"

Parnell nodded his head. "That I would, Polly. I've got a little plan of my own. And I guess I'll have to ride with you or go on the bus." He paused and grinned at me. "You know, I haven't done much driving of late years—alas, since that careless Dolly Madison folded my Maxwell around a tree." He blinked his pale blue eyes. "Now I wonder if I *could* still drive? Hm. . . ."

"I don't know what you're talking about, Parn, but I'll drive you," I said, grinning. "What're you up to now, you crafty old fox?"

"Don't be asking, boy. All in good time, all in good time. I've got me a wee plan."

Maida came in with the finished letters which I signed and she stashed away in their envelopes. "Where to today, boys?" she beamed. "I'm rarin' to go."

I sighed and shook my head. "All right, all right," I said. "Put a sign on the door and come tag along. We'll mail this stuff on the way."

"The die is cast," I said soberly, emerging from the Chippewa post office. "For the lieutenant's sake I hope we've guessed right."

For the most part we were silent on the drive to Iron Bay. Maida came to life briefly when we drove past the Halfway House. "Wouldn't you two like to stop off and recapture your lost youth?" she quipped. "Ah, to be young and carefree and gay again—at four-bits a shot."

"Humph," Parnell said, morosely smacking his parched lips. "One day I'm just up an' goin' to quit drinkin' that vile stuff."

"When the moon turns to blue cheese," Maida sniffed.

"Green, my dear," Parnell corrected her. "Yessir, someday soon I'm just gonna up an' quit. . . ."

I let Maida and Parnell off at the side door of the courthouse. "Polly," Parnell said earnestly, "after you get the Lieutenant up to date on yesterday's doings, there's something, one question, I want you to ask him."

"What's that, Parn?"

"Ask him simply this: 'If you didn't intend to kill Barney when you went to the bar with a loaded gun, just what *did* you intend to do?' Ask him that, Paul, and *make* him answer—it could be important."

"O.K., Parn," I said, shrugging. "Is this part of your mysterious wee plan?"

"Could be, could be," Parn said, smiling enigmatically. "Come, Maida, let us away. Your unimaginative boss is getting inquisitive again."

"Hm. . . ." I said, pondering what the sly old goat was up to now.

chapter 26

The Lieutenant and I were sitting in the sun on the rear steps of the courthouse directly across the driveway separating it from the jail. "And so, Lieutenant," I said, "that pretty well brings you up to date on my trip to Thunder Bay."

"Looks like you had a busy day, Counselor," the Lieutenant said.

"Faint praise from the master," I thought. "Middling," I said, thinking that he did not know the half of it, that there was much that I had merely hinted at to him, and still much else that I did not tell him at all, including the reluctance of the people around the Thunder Bay Inn to tell us what they knew. Telling him that—at least now—would only worry and upset him more than he already was; after all I needed him insane only at the time of the shooting, not at the trial as well.

Nor did I tell him what we had learned about Mary Pilant and her midnight tryst on the beach with the young Army officer; however true, this still smacked too much of dreary small-town gossip, and beyond that I had a growing feeling, however vague, that whatever value this tidbit might possess for the defense lay in its *not* becoming common knowledge. If everybody knew, then . . . "Surely, Biegler," I thought, "surely you wouldn't be contemplating a sort of genteel blackmail, would you?" But blackmail was never genteel; however one dressed it up it was an ugly word; perhaps it was prettier to say that I was dimly appraising the possibility—somehow, someway—of exchanging with Mary Pilant a continued discreet silence for, say, a little helpful truth. Yes, that sounded much better. I turned back to my lieutenant.

"Were you aware before that night, Lieutenant, that Barney Quill was an expert shot, especially with pistols?"

"Yes, I'd heard about it and seen his medals on the bar and heard some of the other officers commenting on it—the man apparently made no secret that he was good. But personally I never shot against him."

"Only the one time, you mean—when he lost," I reminded him. "Did you know or ever hear that he owned a lot of guns and pistols and was reputed to keep some behind the bar?"

"It was common talk around the village that he owned quite a collection of guns, including side arms, and that he kept some behind the bar."

"Good. What else?"

"Now that you speak of it I recall that one of our officers told me that this Barney and a group of our boys were discussing small arms one day in his bar and this—this Barney reached down behind the bar and produced a semi-automatic."

"Good. Very good. And you knew about that, then, the night of the shooting?"

"Naturally I knew before the shooting—I've been in the jug ever since."

"True," I said. "But the officer could have come and told you after the shooting. Still I prefer it your way. You never saw any of these guns yourself, then?"

"No, I didn't cotton to this Barney character and avoided both him and his place as much as I could. We were never chummy."

I tried to imagine this aloof client of mine being really chummy with anyone, but gave it up. "And this officer that saw Barney produce the pistol—where is he now?" I said.

"Doubtless on his way to Georgia if the Army pulled out, as you say."

"Hm. . . ." I said. "Did you also know or had you heard that Barney was good at personal combat, that is, with his dukes and Judo and all?"

The Lieutenant shrugged. "Well, I'd heard all about that—this Barney was not one to hide his light, you know—; about how he'd cleaned the lumberjacks out of his place and had done in some husky young boxer. Then Laura confirmed all that when she told me how he'd carried on with her that night bragging about how good he was at Judo and all the rest."

My heart sank. "You mean, she told you this before the shooting?"

"No, later—either here at the jail or on the way."

My heart rose again or whatever it is that hearts do after they stop sinking. "I see," I said, "but at any rate that night you knew when you went to the tavern that you were about to face a tough customer, a man who was widely reputed to be pretty well able to take care of himself against all comers?"

The Lieutenant seemed reluctant to concede that there was anything good about Barney Quill, in any department. "Yes," he grudgingly admitted, "yes, I'd heard that the man was pretty good."

"And nevertheless you had the guts, the raw courage to walk in on him?" I said wonderingly.

He looked at me sharply. "All hell could not have stopped me," he said in a low intense voice.

We were getting on dangerous ground and my impulse was to veer away, and then I thought of the question that Parnell had asked me to ask him. Should I risk asking such a loaded question? But if I didn't, wouldn't the People do so later? Wasn't it better to face up to it now?

"Lieutenant," I said quietly, "I'm going to ask you a question and I want an honest answer. All I ask is that your answer be honest and that you consider well before you answer."

"Shoot," the Lieutenant said.

"If you didn't intend to kill Barney Quill that night when you went to his bar with a loaded gun, just what *did* you intend to do?"

"To—to grab him," the Lieutenant answered quickly. "To—to get my hands on him and hold him—to stop him."

A dim light was beginning to dawn. Had shrewd old Parnell won again? "What do you mean—grab him and hold him?" I said.

"I—I don't exactly know. Just what I said, I guess. . . . If this—this man had done what Laura had said he'd done, what I believed he'd done, then I knew he shouldn't be at large." The Lieutenant paused and spoke rapidly. "Don't you see . . . I couldn't rest with this—this animal still at large. . . . It was all so crazy. . . . If he could have done that how could I know that he wasn't still lurking out there, or that he might come back again or try to skip or that he might even come for me if—if I didn't go grab him and hold him?"

"Grab him and hold him for whom?" I asked, scarcely above a whisper. The brilliance, the audacity of Parnell's shrewd gamble was slowly coming to me.

"For the cops, I guess. All I knew is that I had a feeling I had to go get him before he skipped or somehow got me. I simply *had* to."

"To kill him?" I said.

"No, no—not to kill him—to stop him." The Lieutenant's eyes darkened. "But I'll be honest—I would have killed him if he'd made a false move."

"Did he?" I said. "Did he make a false move?"

"I—I really can't say." The Lieutenant brushed the heel of his thumb across his eyebrows. "It's all so kind of blurred."

"Suppose you try to tell me what you remember," I said. "Think hard."

The Lieutenant blinked his eyes. "When I got near the side of the hotel I parked my car and stood by the side of it for a moment to adjust myself to the light," he began. "Then I went quickly into the bar. This—this Barney was behind the bar facing the rear mirror, his back to me." The Lieutenant spoke jerkily now, as though it were all happening as he spoke. "I see him and he sees me. We watch each other . . . I see nothing else—the bar may have been deserted for all I know . . . the scene is frozen, like in a picture. . . . I move forward, we're still watching each other . . . then when I'm about halfway, perhaps more, between the door and the bar he turns around—whirls, more like—and drops his left forearm across the bar, in front of him, like this. His right arm is down out of sight . . . his lips are curled and moving. . . ." The Lieutenant paused and sighed. "Then I guess I let him have it . . . It's all cloudy after that."

I lit a cigar and puffed away in silence. An inmate of the jail came out and quickly knelt and retrieved one of my cigar butts. I stood up and silently handed him a fresh one and ground the butt under my heel. He mumbled and squeezed past us with his pail and a mop. 'Excuse it, please.' The Lieutenant mopped the sweat off his face. This was the first time I had heard the actual story of the shooting. What carelessness or intuition had ever made me wait till now? I recalled the pea that had rattled vaguely in the back of my mind the day I had pondered the possible significance of the fact that a Barney Quill at large after the rape was an unarrested felon. The pea was sounding like castanets now. Shrewd old Parnell. But there were still some loose ends to gather up. . . .

"If you felt this man had to be 'grabbed,' as you say, didn't it occur to you to go wake up the deputized old caretaker to arrest Barney?" I said. "You knew he was deputized, didn't you?"

Lieutenant Manion laughed briefly and without mirth. "Yes, I guess I knew the old man was a deputy. But I never thought of it or him. Even if I had I wouldn't have bothered him." He turned and looked at me. "If—if this thing had happened to you, Counselor, would *you* have sent your aged father?"

I puffed my cigar and stared at the intricate stonework of the barred jail across the way. "I guess that's the complete answer, Lieutenant," I said. Mitch could do with that what he would. "Yes, I guess we'll leave it rest right there."

I sat and thought, a dead cigar in my mouth. Good old Parnell had at last possibly solved one of our biggest headaches: *Why* had this man gone to the bar? The pieces were beginning to fall into place. I wanted to go find him right away and break the big news. "Hm. . . ." I said.

"I wish I had my camera," a woman's voice said. "You two look as though you were planning a fishing trip." It was Laura Manion and her little dog. Laura quickly kissed the Lieutenant, glancing at me, and then shook my hand and joined us sitting on the sun-lit steps. She was dressed in a becoming dark linen suit and wore sheer stockings and high-heeled shoes and a little straw hat with a short veil that fell over her eyes. This was the first time I had seen her dressed up and I calculated that with glasses and a few yards of hawser to lash her in that, yes, I might risk showing her before a jury.

"I'm glad you came, Laura," I said. "Manny'll tell you about my Thunder Bay trip later but there are some questions." I laughed. "With a lawyer there are always more questions."

The Lieutenant arose as though to leave. "Sit down, Lieutenant," I said. "I don't think there's anything we can't all discuss together. If there is I'll send you back to Sulo. In fact I want both of you to help if you can." I turned to Laura. "Did you remember to have the pictures taken and go visit the doctor?"

"Yes, Paul, I've been photographed and pawed over and peered at like a Hollywood starlet. The pictures will be ready tomorrow."

"Good. Now take this Mary Pilant gal—had both of you met her?"

"Yes," Laura said. "And isn't she charming?"

"Yes," I agreed, remembering a succinct earthy phrase that old Danny McGinnis had for all attractive women: "She'd make a dog break his chain." "Yes, she's certainly charming. Can either of you tell me anything more about her? She worked for Barney, you know." I not only wanted to learn how much Laura and Manny knew but also how little they knew.

"Well," Laura said, "there were stories about her and Barney." She paused. "But as far as I knew she was a perfect lady. One of our young officers was rather sweet on her, too."

"Who was that?"

"I don't remember—Manny might."

I turned toward the Lieutenant. "Sonny Loftus—second lieutenant," he said briefly.

"Were they—was this serious?" I said.

Laura and Manny looked at each other and shrugged. "Lord, I don't know, Paul," she said, smiling at Manny. "These devilish Army men, you know. . . . All work and no play. . . ." She held up her hands. "Serious? A summer flirtation? Who knows?"

"And you, Manny?" I said.

He shook his head. "I wouldn't know," he said, forever helpful.

"How about the bartender, Paquette?" I said.

"He made the best old-fashioneds in town," Manny said. "It was a drink, not a fruit salad."

"He was always courteous to me," Laura said. "I guess he was just an alert smart bartender, a good man for the house. And he was thoughtful to us after the shooting."

I sat up. "How do you mean?" I asked.

"Well, he came and offered to drive me down to the jail to see Manny that first Sunday—I was in no shape to drive—and he brought Manny a carton of his favorite cigarettes."

I pricked up my ears. "Anything else?" I said.

"On the way driving down he told me how sorry he was for Manny and me and said—how did he put it now?—he said he could have told me that Barney was a wolf."

I stared at her. One of the endless fascinations—as well as frustrations—of the law are the constant surprises—both good and bad—that its practitioners get from their clients and witnesses. "You mean," I said, hot on the scent and in full cry now, "you mean Barney's bartender said that he could have warned you that he, Barney, was a wolf? He used that word? He said 'wolf'?"

"Why, yes, Paul. I thought I'd told you that before. He also said Barney had been drinking hard lately and that it was too bad we had come to Thunder Bay when we had. Is—is that good?"

"Clients are clients and lawyers are lawyers—and never the twain shall meet," I thought. "It might help," I agreed. "Anything else?"

"Well, he brought Manny those cigarettes, as I say. He was real nice and thoughtful."

I turned inquiringly toward the Lieutenant. "When he gave me the cigarettes," the Lieutenant said, "he told me how sorry he was for my trouble and said that he wanted me to know that for his part the only thing he held against me was that when I shot Barney I broke a bottle of bonded white-vest bourbon rather than some cheap pilerun cooking whisky."

"He used those terms?"

"Yes. He visited awhile and then he left. Said some friends would drive him back to Thunder Bay. Laura stayed over that night—we were trying to reach you all day. And she also had to go visit your—" he paused and smiled "—your favorite horse doctor."

I restrained the impulse to leap and shout and go seek out Parnell and give him the word. "Have either of you seen him since?" I said. "The bartender, I mean?"

Laura shook her head. "I saw him once on the street in Thunder Bay—naturally I have not been back to the bar—and he paused briefly and inquired for Manny and hurried on his way. That's the last either of us have seen or heard of him."

"Was there any more talk about Barney—when you met him on the street?"

"No. Just as I've told you." Laura paused and reflected. "Now that you speak of it, it does seem he was sort of restrained and reticent. And in a hurry. About all he did was say hello, ask how Manny was —and he was gone."

Again I saw the fine silky hand of Mary Pilant at work. What was the gimmick? What had happened? Here was a man who'd gone out of his way to be nice to the Manions, who'd called his dead boss a wolf—and then, by the time I'd talked to him, had grown shifty and evasive and had referred to Mrs. Manion as a "floozie" and an "easy lay." What was the score? I shook my head.

I then told the Manions of the brush-off on the psychiatrist; that I had now written his own outfit; and that they must begin to learn to live with the grim prospect that we might not be able to get a psychiatrist in time for the trial. "It's only about two and a half weeks away. But I haven't given up yet. I'll pry a psychiatrist out of this Army of yours, Lieutenant, if I have to make a sign and go picket the Pentagon. 'Army unfair to Lieutenant.'" I arose. "Right now I must leave you. Tomorrow is Saturday and I won't be down. Next week I must put on my black sateen sleevelets and hit the law books in earnest. I'll be in touch with you. Good-bye for now." I turned away.

"Happy fishing this weekend, Paul," Laura called after me. I turned and she and the Lieutenant stood smiling, arm in arm, a picture of wedded compatibility and connubial bliss. It was a pity, I thought, that the ubiquitous newspaper photographers were never around when they were really needed.

chapter 27

I went in the sun-blistered back door of the courthouse in search of
Parnell and Maida. Gaining the tall main marble hallway I turned
and climbed the wide marble stairs leading to the courtroom on
the second floor, thinking I might find them in the adjoining law
library. My steps rang hollowly along the deserted upper corridors,
and it occurred to me that there were fewer places in the world
lonelier and emptier than the precincts of a country courtroom between terms of court. For company I'd any day take a lone beaver
dam at dusk. . . .

Making my way to the tangle of corridors in back of the courtroom I found the law library deserted and musty-smelling and hot
as a Finnish *sauna* in the bottled summer heat. Packets of unopened
and dusty law books and advance sheets and pocket-parts cluttered
the tables and chairs. I left this oven and glanced into the jury conference room, where so many fates were decided, and found it empty
except for the long table and the traditional twelve chairs.

The attorneys' conference room was as empty as a morgue except for a pegless cribbage board on a table. The door of the
prosecuting attorney's office—my old one and Mitch's new one—
stood open; the office was also empty except for the dusty desk and
chairs. A fly about the size of a Russian Mig buzzed crazily up and
down one of the sooty windowpanes, with its goal of Lake Superior
gleaming far beyond. The court stenographer's office was empty;
the heavy door to the judge's chambers was closed but unlocked and
I entered. I walked through the dusty book-lined judge's office and
down a short corridor and tried a heavy mahogany door. It breathed
open and shut behind me and I found myself standing alone in the
dim and empty courtroom.

Way back in 1905 the supervisors of Iron Cliffs County outdid
themselves when they built the new county courthouse. Conceiving
the structure as an undying monument to their statesmanship and
proceeding on the theory that if one architectural scheme or motif
could be impressive, a combination of styles would presumably daz-
zle all the more, they had succeeded beyond their wildest dreams.
Few structures in the Peninsula presented a more startling pile of
stone and slate and marble and mortar, vestiges of Roman, Norman
and Gothic architecture vying mightily with each other for pre-

dominance, with authentic nineteenth-century St. Louis Brewery perhaps winning by a nose.

The interior of the courthouse was as lined and overlaid with mahogany and marble as a heavily frosted chocolate cake. Whole quarries and forests must have been gouged and toppled in the sacrifice. The tall marble corridors were large enough to play football in—including the kicking of high punts—while much of the actual business of the courthouse was transacted in cubbyholes. The place was a monument to Thorstein Veblen's theory of "conspicuous waste." At the dedication ceremonies (my mother Belle had told me) loggers and farmers and miners had driven in from all over the county, picnicking on the big lawn, listening to the speeches of the rural statesmen, uneasily beholding this remarkable reason for the sharp increase in the county's bonded indebtedness.

The whole vast structure was topped by a great oval dome, like a sort of inspired Byzantine architectural afterthought, as though a Turkish mosque had flown over during the night and inadvertently dropped a pup. This rounded dome was visible for miles around Iron Bay, and mariners far out on Lake Superior were said regularly to chart their courses by it. But it was also utilitarian, serving as the skylight of the courtroom (for once a nice thrifty note), and I stood gazing up thoughtfully at its stained-glass windows—stained by the pigeons, that is—wondering what happy accident had conspired to make this courtroom not only one of great dignity, but also the one place in the entire courthouse where one did not have to shout like a stevedore to be heard.

The judge's bench, a massive mahogany affair, stood like a lone judicial island on the end of the room nearest me, the mahogany-enclosed sheriff's chair and desk at its right nearer me, the witness stand on the left, and the clerk's railed cubicle running across the front, the ensemble looking faintly like a truncated battleship with suspended mahogany lifeboats. Glancing guiltily around I ascended to the judge's bench and sat myself gingerly in the tall leather swivel chair and tilted it—"Ah"—and nearly fell backwards. "Oops!" I glared around looking for someone to commit for contempt. The glowering oil portraits of three bearded deceased judges seemed to frown down even more fiercely from the wall. . . .

The empty jury box loomed to my left; the two wide leather-topped counsel tables stood out in front, the People's (and plaintiff's) table to my left, the defense table to my right, with tall old-fashioned hourglass brass cuspidors standing like tethered watchdogs at either corner. Immediately beyond the two tables stood the lawyers' chairs, running nearly across the width of the courtroom, then the mahogany rail with the gates at either end, and beyond that the double rows of uncomfortable square mahogany benches for the extra jurors and waiting litigants and witnesses and spectators and curious rubbernecks and sensation-seekers and all the rest. In just over two weeks they would all be there, craning and whispering and sighing and hiccupping and dozing and endlessly shuffling in and out. I lit a cigar and gazed sightlessly toward the rear of the deep chamber and cleared my throat, gutturally and pompously.

"Quiet back there," I growled, "or I'll have to ask the bailiff to remove you! This is my final warning."

Part of my words echoed hollowly back—"final warning . . . warning . . . ing . . . ing . . ." and I repeated the words, enchanted by the sepulchral effect. Had a psychiatrist seen me at that moment he would have sighed and clapped me in the booby hatch. Were all of us secretly a little crazy? I slid from the judge's chair and leapt down off the bench and hurriedly left the courtroom to continue my search for Parnell and Maida. Enough of this summer fantasy. . . . I finally found them in the steel-floored filing vault of the probate court, downstairs, Parnell holding a recorded paper under his glasses and dictating stealthily to Maida.

"*Jiggers!*" I hissed from the doorway.

Parnell started and looked over his steel-rimmed spectacles. "Give us five more minutes and we'll have it," he said, almost in a whisper. "Now beat it before someone comes and discovers us. We're not ready for that."

"Excuse it, please," I said, and I shrugged and went out and paid rather ponderous court to the lovely Etta, the probate registrar, a maiden lady who possessed more warmth and charm at sixty than most women manage to acquire in a lifetime. Had she been a little younger or I a little older I would certainly have considered making a play for her. . . .

"Oh, Polly," Etta blushed, "you say the silliest things, really you do. . . ."

Parnell plodded out of the vault with his battered briefcase, Maida following him like a faithful gun-bearer, the two brushing past me and out into the main corridor.

" 'Parting is such sweet sorrow,' " I told Etta, and left her blushing prettily, overtaking Parnell and Maida near the far end of the long marble corridor. "What's the pitch?" I demanded. "I took a bath last week and I regularly anoint myself with Aladdin Salve—from the large economy jar. What'd you discover in there? Oil or a batch of Confederate twenties?"

"Oil," Parnell said curtly, out of the side of his mouth, like a bookie confiding a tip on the fifth at Pimlico. "Wait till we're alone, damn it. This stuff is hot."

"Yes, sir," I said, meekly clamping my cigar in my mouth and following them dutifully out to the car, like little Rover with his faithful flashlight.

Parnell had put on the rush act, he explained, because the lawyer for the estate was expected momentarily in probate court and the old man didn't want to be discovered "raiding" the Barney Quill file. "I'm not ready for him yet," he added cryptically.

He and Maida were radiant; they had dug out the probate records in the new file: *Estate of Barney Quill, Deceased*. The estate had been started the Monday following the shooting, the day I got in the case. Mary Pilant had filed the petition for probate of the will, listing, as required by law, a daughter, Bernadine Quill, age sixteen, as the sole heir at law, with residence at Three Willows, Wisconsin. The will left everything to Mary Pilant, and was dated—as the bartender had said—about three weeks before the shooting. The next important paper had been an appearance and notice of will contest filed by a Green Bay lawyer on behalf of a Janice Quill, individually and as guardian of the daughter, Bernadine, attacking the will on just about all the classic grounds a will can be attacked on, including undue influence and lack of testamentary capacity on the part of Barney Quill due to his excessive drinking and alcoholism.

"Janice Quill?" I said. "That would be the child's mother—and Barney's divorced wife."

"Correct," Parnell said dryly, "except that the lady does not concede to be the *divorced* wife; she has filed a notice and a flock of supporting affidavits claiming that the Wisconsin divorce between her and Barney was void because she had never been served with process or received adequate notice of Barney's divorce action against her."

"More Technicolor," I said. "What's her angle?" I went on. "Surely after all these years the dame must have known she was divorced. Why in hell should she be trying to undivorce herself now?"

172

"Money," Parnell answered, hunching his shoulders and rubbing his dry palms together. "Just the same old dreary love story—money, money, money. . . . As a fine broth of a former Irish mayor of Chicago once told the graduating school children: 'Boys and girls,' he said, 'remember when you go out into the world that *money* won't buy happiness, *money* won't buy respect, *money* won't buy honor. Confederate money, that is.' " Parnell shook his head. "Don't you see, Paul?—if this woman can dump this old divorce *and* the will, she will come in for her wife's share of Barney's property, the daughter getting the other share. If she can dump the divorce alone, even if the will *is* sustained, she'll come in for her statutory widow's third and certain other loot, come hell or high water, even if the daughter is left out in the cold. It's as neat as bar whisky. And her Wisconsin lawyer's no slouch either—I checked him already in Martindale's."

"Yes," I said, "but how can she expect to come into a Michigan probate court and attempt to make a collateral attack on a foreign decree of divorce? That's *verboten*, isn't it, under the 'full faith and credit' clause of the Constitution?"

"Generally, Polly," Parnell conceded. "But she also alleges that she is initiating action down there to set aside the Wisconsin divorce. Furthermore, if she claims to be Barney's wife, it seems to me that it might be up to Mary Pilant to disprove it."

"Yes, Parn. Now it looks like we've not only got Lieutenant Manion's murder case to defend but Barney Quill's will and divorce as well."

Parnell smiled. "How do you mean, boy?" he said. "What's that to us?"

"Because this will contest and divorce business are plainly affecting our man's chances to win this case. That's why Mary Pilant and the rest of the Thunder Bay Inn crowd have clammed up so. Can't you see? It's to protect the goddam will, not primarily to hurt us. If they can protect their precious will, Mary Pilant will still get roughly two thirds of the swag, come what may, even if the former wife dumps the divorce—and the charming Pilant will get everything if she can sustain both the will and the divorce. So that's why they can't allow Barney to be a boozer and a rounder who was so addled and crazed by drink that he couldn't draw a will and would do this thing to Laura Manion."

"That's just what I figured, too," Parnell said, smiling dryly. "But I scarcely expected a mere criminal lawyer to see the point."

"That's why the bartender suddenly clammed up with the Manions," I ran on, ignoring the shaft. "That's why he's now willing to make a bag out of Laura. That's why Mary Pilant is willing to let our man possibly hang rather than let us get at the truth. It's a fine kettle of fish—and I mean bass, damn it, not trout."

"But what do we care about all this?" Maida said. "How can all this possibly affect our Lieutenant?"

"Because, my dear," I said, "this rape—if I may use such an inelegant word in your sheltered presence—is the golden key to our defense. Anything that sheds any doubt on that brutal fact hurts our case."

"I still don't get it."

"Look, one of the biggest areas of possible doubt in this whole case is that a sober man in his right mind would do what Barney did. To the extent that these lovely people—whatever their motives —successfully picture Barney as a sober, God-fearing, un-pistol-packing Boy Scout, and try to pull down Laura Manion in the process, to that extent they cast doubt on our story—at the same time building up sympathy for the late departed. This sword has several edges, don't you see? What's more, it happens not to be the truth."

"I see," Maida said, frowning. "I think I'll go tear that Mary Pilant's hair."

"I'd just like to walk barefoot in it—and show her the paths of truth," I said wistfully.

"What do you mean when you just said the bartender had clammed up with the Manions?" Parnell demanded. "When was the little man ever unclammed?"

"I'll tell you," I said. "Things are breaking so fast I haven't had time to tell you." I told Parnell and Maida what I had just learned from the Manions about the bartender's expression of sympathy the day after the shooting, and all the rest—this followed by his sudden aloofness. "It's all tying in, now," I continued. "He's Mary's star witness and her key man to sustain the will. The Lord knows what his slice of the boodle will be. Probably a cut out of the bar." I paused.

"Let's sell the plot to the movies," Maida said, "and all take a trip on the proceeds."

"A trip to the monkey house," I said morosely. "Plot these days is anti-intellectual and verboten, the mark of the Philistine, the huckster with a pen. There mustn't be too much story and that should be fog-bound and shrouded in heavy symbolism, including the phallic, like a sort of convoluted literary charade. Symbolism now carries the day, it's the one true ladder to literary heaven."

Parnell grinned and shook his head. "Ah, the woe of it, the impenetrable mystery. And, since the region is reputed to be somewhat murkier than most, it is better that what little action there is should take place in the womb."

"Whatever are you two talking about?" Maida pouted, "I'm sorry I ever mentioned plot. The deal's off."

Parnell was smiling from ear to ear. "And what are you grinning about, you overweight old satyr?" I said. "I'm almost getting sorry I got mixed up in this incredible mess. If—if I didn't see it I wouldn't believe it."

"The records show that old Martin Melstrand of town here is Mary Pilant's lawyer," Parnell said. "As you know, Martin's a shrewd old probate and estate lawyer, but lazy as tropical sin. He won't brief his case till he has to—and unfortunately our trial will be over and done before this will contest is heard. That's still another good reason why our murder case should be continued—by then the will contest and all would be over and done, win or lose, and the heat would be off."

"Hell, Parn," I said morosely, "there'll doubtless be an appeal from probate whichever way it goes—so a continuance in our case is no answer. God, what a maddening case."

"But just think of the law, Polly, the law," Parnell breathed ecstatically. "Think of all the sweet lovely law we've got to search for. I can scarcely wait to get at it. Shall we go home and start now?" He was like a boy uncrating his first bicycle.

"Starting tonight I'm going fishing all weekend, Parn," I said. "I'm going to hole up out at the South camp. I've simply got to crawl off somewhere by myself and submit this case to a jury of my peers —the trout. And, it's probably my last crack at fishing. Monday we've got to start turning over the law books in earnest." I shrugged. "But if you can't wait I won't object to your getting a head start." Parnell's face fell and I recalled with a pang that he had long since drunk up most of his dwindling law library. "Just to play safe I'll give you an extra key to my office," I said, handing him the key. "Any time of the day or night, Counselor," I said. "Remember, we're partners now. If during your nocturnal research any strange dames come prowling around the place they'll be my nieces. Invariably they're my nieces. Send them firmly away."

"Thanks, Polly," Parnell said, soberly pocketing the key. "Thank you, my friend, I'll use it tonight."

"And there's one interesting subject you might start brushing up on right off the bat," I said. "The law of the right of a private person to make an arrest without a warrant for a felony committed out of his presence. Thanks to you, that subject is now right smack in the middle of our case."

Parnell's eyes lit up with quick eagerness. "You remembered to ask him?" he said gleefully. "You really asked him my question? Tell me what he said? That's another one I dreamed up last night in my sleepless bed, Polly. Don't you see?—it—it opens up vistas." He paused and blinked his eyes and shook his head. "Beautiful rolling vistas of lovely law and instructions. Boy oh boy!"

At that moment Parnell looked almost indecently happy; like a man about to cast a fly over the steadily rising granddaddy of all trout. I envied him, for here was one of those rare and lucky mortals whose main hobby, at least next to whisky, happened also to be his profession: the jealous mistress of the law.

Trial

Trial

chapter 1

"Hear ye, hear ye, hear ye!" Sheriff Max Battisfore sang out in his clear baritone voice, holding poised the gavel he had just used to rouse the courtroom to its feet. "The Circuit Court for the county of Iron Cliffs is now in session." He lowered his gavel along with his voice. "Please be seated."

It was ten o'clock on Monday, the first morning of the September term. Most of the lawyers of the county were present and awaiting the call of the court calendar, seated in the reserved chairs which ran along the inside of the long mahogany railing. Parnell sat next to me. His hair had been freshly trimmed and he was wearing a brand-new suit of hounds-tooth gray that he had purchased out of his share of the retainer fee the Lieutenant had paid me. This was the garment's maiden flight, and I observed rather wistfully that the tattersall vest had been banished. And where had he got that rich-looking maroon knit tie? The old boy looked really distinguished and, leaning over and whispering, I told him so.

"G'wan wid ya!" he whispered back hoarsely, beaming with pleasure.

"We will now take up the call of the criminal docket," Judge Weaver announced quietly, consulting his printed calendar. He cleared his throat. "People versus Clarence Madigan," he said. "Breaking and entering in the nighttime."

The criminal defendants who had not posted bail and had perforce waited in jail sat arrayed in the jury box under the watchful eye of Sulo Kangas. Sulo now extravagantly motioned the defendant Madigan to go take his place before the judge's bench. I smiled and winked at Lieutenant Manion, who was sitting next to the hapless Madigan. The Lieutenant frowned as Madigan stumbled and nearly fell stepping down out of the jury box. Madigan and I were old professional acquaintances from my days as D.A., and he grinned at me as he turned to face the Judge. "Poor old Smoky," I thought. "He's gone and done it again."

Mitch Lodwick stood by the court reporter's desk with his mound of pending criminal files. He fished into the first one and found the criminal information and, clearing his throat, began reading.

"State of Michigan, County of Iron Cliffs," Mitch read. "I, Mitchell Lodwick, prosecuting attorney in and for the county of Iron Cliffs, for and in behalf of the People of the State of Michigan, come into said court in the September term thereof and give the court to understand and be informed, that Clarence Madigan, alias 'One-Shot' Madigan, alias 'Smoky' Madigan, late of the City of Iron Bay, in said county and state aforesaid, heretofore, to-wit, on the 4th day of July, last, at the city of Iron Bay in the county aforesaid, in the nighttime of said day, with force and arms, feloniously did break and enter the dwelling house of one Casper Kratz, there situate, with intent to commit a felony therein, to-wit: with intent to commit the crime of larceny, contrary to the form of the statute in such case made and provided and against the peace and dignity of the People of the State of Michigan. Signed: Mitchell Lodwick, Prosecuting Attorney in and for the County of Iron Cliffs, Michigan."

Mitch handed the information up to the judge, returned to his place, and stood examining his nails as Judge Weaver took over. This was the way the law charged Smoky Madigan with running amuck on the Fourth of July and stealing a case of whisky from the basement of the home of a saloonkeeper called Kratz and then going on a blast that made even Smoky's valiant past efforts pale into a sort of uneasy sobriety.

"Mr. Madigan, have you consulted an attorney?" the Judge inquired.

"Nope," Smoky answered airily. "No money. A man's gotta have money to ask 'em the time of day." There was a quick squall of laughter from the lawyers' chairs.

"Do you understand that you have a right to counsel—that is, an attorney—and that if you are financially unable to employ counsel that the court may, if requested, appoint counsel for you at public expense?"

"Yup, I've had 'em before." Smoky had been around and he had also evidently heard that Judge Weaver was from downstate; he wanted no doubt on that score.

"Do you want counsel now or an opportunity to consult with counsel?"

Smoky grinned amiably. "Nope. I went in Casper's place an' stole the whisky, all right. I was sober then an' I remember so I guess I don't need no lawyer to tell me what I did." Smoky paused thoughtfully. "Later, though, I guess I'd of needed all the lawyers here today to help me keep track."

I could vaguely visualize Smoky's meteoric course once he had got his hot hands on Casper's whisky. There was a ripple of subdued laughter and the Judge frowned stonily and the laughter quickly died. "Now, Mr. Madigan," the Judge pushed on, proceeding patiently through the prescribed ritual, though he and every lawyer in the courtroom now knew that Smoky was dying to cop a plea of guilty and get it over with, "do you understand that you have a constitutional right to a trial by jury?"

Smoky nodded his head yes, and Grover Gleason, the court reporter who was busily taking all this down, looked up and frowningly demanded that the defendant answer yes or no.

"The reporter must record all that we say," the Judge explained. "He can't very well hear a nod, you see."

"Yup," Smoky obediently said, glancing rather proudly at the reporter as though to confirm that anyone might be recording for a deathless and panting posterity anything that old Smoky Madigan ever had to say. "I unnerstan' the Constitution says I kin have a jury."

"Do you wish to have a trial by jury?" the Judge quietly persisted.

Smoky shook his head no and then glanced guiltily at the court reporter and added "Nope" in a loud voice. He plainly appreciated the Constitution's efforts on his behalf, but, no thanks, he'd pass this time.

"Now you are charged in the information filed against you, and which you have just heard read, that you broke into a man's house after dark with intent to steal. Do you understand the nature of the offense charged against you?"

"Sure, sure," Smoky replied airily. "Except I didn't actually *break* into no house—I got into old Kratz's cellar through the coal chute. I simply slid in an'—*bomp!*—there I was, practic'ly inside Casper's furnace. An' I not only intended to steal somethin', Judge Your Honor, I really did steal it"—Smoky's voice took on a note of wistful nostalgia—"a hull case of booze." He shook his head over the treasured memory.

Judge Weaver smiled slightly and pushed on. "I must remind you that a basement is part of the dwelling and that if you did steal something while there the law indulges a mild presumption that you probably also intended to steal it. As for the 'breaking' part it is not necessary that one break or smash anything to gain entry; to constitute a 'breaking' in law it is sufficient if one merely lifts a latch—or even the lid of a coal chute. Do you understand that?"

Smoky was getting bored with all this laboring of the obvious. After all, wasn't this his fifth B. & E. rap?—the fifth that he had got caught at, that is? "Sure, sure," he answered. "Speakin' technical, I guess I busted in, Judge, like you say."

"Then you fully understand the charge against you?"

Smoky sighed. "I sure do, Judge. I got nailed fair and square. If I'd a stood sober, though, they'd never of catch me. The shape I was in I was a sittin' duck."

"Then what is your plea—guilty or not guilty?"

"Guilty, of course," Smoky said, turning away to leave.

"Just a minute, Mr. Madigan," the Judge continued patiently. "Before I can accept your plea of guilty there are a few more questions I must ask you. This duty is imposed upon me by law for the protection of the public and of you and men like you, so please bear with me a little longer."

"Shoot," Smoky said indulgently, shrugging his shoulders as though to say, "If this talky old beaver wants to prolong the agony old Smoky ain't going to spoil his fun. . . ."

The Judge aimed and shot: "I ask you, Mr. Madigan, if this plea of guilty you have entered to this information is freely, understandingly and voluntarily made?"

"You bet. I got caught an' I might's so well face it."

"Has there been any undue influence, compulsion or duress on the part of the prosecuting attorney, the officers of this court or any other person to induce you to enter a plea of guilty?"

"I don't understand all them words, Judge, but nobody bulldozed me into coppin' out, if that's what you mean. I've thunk it all out—since the night of July sixth across de alley dere." He hooked a thumb over his shoulder at the jail. "That's when they catch me."

"Very well. Did you enter your plea of guilty because of any threats, inducements or promises made to you by the prosecuting attorney, any officers of this court or any other person? Did anyone promise to go easy on you?"

"Nope. Dey knew dey had me—dey caught me good dis time." Earnestly: "You see, Judge, da coppers never promise a man nuttin' when dey got you dead to rights."

A quiet ripple of laughter ran along the row of waiting lawyers, most of whom were boredly awaiting the call of the civil calendar. The Judge frowned and stared hard and Parnell and I glanced significantly at each other. Whatever else this judge might or might not be, he was plainly going to run his court, there'd be no fooling.

"Do you plead guilty to this charge, then, Mr. Madigan, because you are guilty, because you did the things charged against you by the People in their information?"

"Yup, Your Honor."

"And are you fully aware that you may be punished for your crime?"

Smoky's voice was like a benediction. "I sure am, Judge. I'm kinda like da June bride—it ain't a matter of if but when. All I hope is you send me any udder place but Marquette prison. Any place a-tall but dat crummy joint."

Nobody tittered this time. "I will accept your plea of guilty," the Judge said gravely. "You will be sentenced later, Mr. Madigan. You may now return to your place."

Smoky shrugged and resignedly rolled his eyes up at me as he turned away to resume his seat next to Lieutenant Manion in the jury box. I swallowed a lump in my throat. "The poor dumb likeable kindly bastard," I thought. There but for the Grace of God—

The Judge consulted his calendar. "People versus Clyde Tate," he called out. "Forgery." Sulo waved the luckless Mr. Tate to his feet and he advanced blinking and stood before the Judge, where the whole dreary ritual would again be repeated. I must have witnessed it a thousand times. . . .

Smoky's was the first case on the criminal docket and the Lieutenant's was number twenty-three, numbered democratically on the basis of first come, first served. I whispered to Parnell that I was going out to have a smoke. I left the courtroom and made my way out to the empty jury room—the jury was not due to report for two days—and stood staring out across Lake Superior, watching the long undulant smoke plume of an invisible boat, probably an ore boat, thinking how glad I was that I was no longer prosecuting attorney of Iron Cliffs County—that and reviewing the swift and tangled events of the past two weeks.

We had finally pried a psychiatrist out of the Army, but not before I had all but picketed the Pentagon, not before Parnell and I were ourselves practically candidates for a psychiatrist's couch. In retrospect there was an unreal Alice-In-Wonderland quality about the whole thing, an air of shimmering fantasy, as though we had partaken in some grotesque and unsmiling comedy waveringly enacted at the bottom of the sea. There had been a reverberating silence to my second Army letter; I had waited nearly a week and gotten frantically on the phone; an aide had said that the officer I had written had been in sick bay; the matter would be looked into; I would be duly notified. 'But . . .' I argued. More days had dragged by and I had reopened fire over the phone; the matter was still being looked into; the request was very unusual and had to be studied. . . . This time I had sworn, the Army had sworn, and someone had hung up. . . .

Then I had launched an alarming series of communications: letters, phone calls, telegrams. For a spell I even wildly contemplated launching guided missiles. I had got the Lieutenant and Laura to join me; we had pulled out all the organ stops; we had pelted the Army with words. Then at last I had received a phone call; the matter had crept up the ladder of brass—it had at last come to the attention of the General himself; it was in turn being referred to that patron saint of all Army snafus, the Judge Advocate; it was hoped that I understood that the situation was most unusual; also very ticklish; I must realize that things like this could start a bad precedent; the Army traditionally never liked to interfere with the affairs of the civil courts and certainly didn't want to appear to do so now. Finally, one did not want to predict the ruling in Washington ("smart boy," I thought) but we shouldn't be too disappointed if . . . "What!" I had shouted and then I had sworn, the Army had sworn and someone had hung up. . . .

There the matter uneasily rested. Early the Tuesday morning before court opened—less than a week to go—I tottered out of bed after a sleepless night and fired a telegram at the General himself. Perhaps my wire possessed the eloquence of desperation. I reminded him that our request for a psychiatrist had been pending nearly three weeks; that now it was far too late to turn elsewhere; that surely this was not the first time since Valley Forge that an Army man had run afoul of the civil law and had needed and requested medical or similar aid from the service; that we didn't want to bother them any more than they apparently relished being bothered, but that my man was stony broke, there was no choice, there was simply no other way; that to turn down the Lieutenant's request now was not only to sentence him to three more months in jail—the case having thus to be continued—but possibly for life, since insanity was the heart of our defense. I pointed out that all we requested now was an examination; and I dangled the bait that the Army psychiatrist might still find him sane on the fatal night, in which case we would quietly fold our tents. . . .

I wound up by stating that it would be a plain act of Christian charity to take their man off the spot and that if I didn't get an answer in twenty-four hours my client and I would reluctantly assume that the Army, for which he had fought in two wars, had now deserted him, that the answer was finally no. Then I sat back and waited for a couple of nine-foot M.P.'s to come and take me away.

In the meantime Parnell and I had been looking law and writing legal memorandums and preparing our hypothetical question for a mythical psychiatrist and drafting requests for instructions—all this practically day and night. Then we had gone over the jury list with a fine-comb—phoning, driving, searching, checking, nosing, inquiring—and had prepared little graded dossiers on each prospective juror. Parnell had not taken a drink since the night we had stopped off at the Halfway House, all of which added to the growing sense of fantasy. Only Maida and I had valiantly kept our office from resembling an Upper Peninsula branch of the W.C.T.U.

Parnell had done yeoman service on the law books, coming up with dozens of obscure but pointed old cases I had never heard of. In his green eye-shade he looked like a cashier for a syndicate of bookies and even at times like the master engraver of a ring of counterfeiters. He was in a seventh heaven of delight, planning, digging, writing, dictating. "Take this, dear Maida, if you please. . . ."

"But what's the use?" I wailed. "What's the use of looking all this law if we can't lasso a goddam psychiatrist? And here I've gone and wasted all this fishin'. . . ."

Late that Tuesday night the Army had phoned. Parnell and I had jumped a foot, and I knew it was the Army before I answered. Colonel Somebody-or-other was on the line. My wire had been received and the General had just issued an order. Wait, he would get the order. . . . I strained to catch the sound of marching fifes and rumbling caissons. Ah, yes, here was the order. . . . If the lieutenant would present himself Thursday morning at eight o'clock at the Bellevue Army Hospital in lower Michigan an Army psychiatrist would be assigned to examine him; this order would be confirmed later in writing. In the meantime the Colonel would please kindly like to read me the General's order. The order, in occupationally limpid military prose, read as follows:

> "There will be no objection should the civil authorities
> deliver the accused to an appropriate military facility for
> the purpose of having a psychiatric examination conducted,
> with a view to utilizing the determination at a civil trial.
> Bellevue Army Hospital in Michigan is designated as the
> appropriate medical facility."

"You mean," I said incredulously, "we have to deliver our man to an Army hospital near Detroit before we can have our examination?"

"That is correct, sir."

"But damn it, Colonel," I said, "Lieutenant Manion is in the county jail way up here in the brambles on a charge of first degree murder. Murder is an unbailable offense—he can't get out for love or money. Not even, believe it or not, for the United States Army. Tell me—how do we get to spirit the Lieutenant out of jail and down to lower Michigan for an examination or anything else?"

The Colonel was adamant. "That, sir, is your problem. The General's orders are as I have just read them to you; that is our final word; these orders will be confirmed in writing." Then I had sworn, the Army had sworn—and this time I had hung up and rantingly told Parnell about it.

"I've a damn good notion to go out and get drunk," I said, staring morosely at the telephone. Parnell grabbed up his hat.

"Where you going, old man?" I said. "Keeping me company? Good. We'll pitch us a dandy."

"We're going to the county jail and prevail on the Sheriff to have himself or a deputy drive our man to lower Michigan," Parnell said. "We'll pay the freight and that way he'll technically still be in civil custody. Everybody saves face. It's the only way, Polly. I think it was Napoleon who said, 'If you can't beat an army head on then go 'round it.' C'mon, boy—it's gettin' late."

"Me too," Maida said, grabbing her pad and pencils. "Better take the files, too. Can't ever tell what'll happen next in this haunted case."

We luckily caught Sheriff Battisfore home from highway patrol; in fact I held my audience with him in his bedroom. It was surprising and a little disillusioning to note how prosaically Midwestern he looked out of his cowboy gear and in a rumpled cotton nightshirt. Well at least he was bow-legged. . . . I swiftly explained my adventures with the Army, and then the dilemma posed by the General's order. I remembered that the sheriff was an old Navy hand and I morosely regretted that the Lieutenant had not been in the Navy—I'd bet the *Navy'd* have cut out all this toe dancing and delaying red tape; *they'd* never have let one of their men down. . . .

"What to do? What to do?" I murmured, trying to look half as disconsolate as I felt.

"It's easy, Polly," the Sheriff quietly said. "I'll have my undersheriff Carl Vosper drive him there tomorrow. Carl's a steady head and a good fast driver. You'll have to pay the shot, of course—gas, mileage and Carl's per diem—so nobody gets criticized. . . . Now better you get home and catch some sleep, Polly—you look like you've been pulled through a knothole."

"Sheriff, you're a genius," I said, and we had solemnly clasped hands. From now on for my part Max Battisfore could patrol day and night, dressed even as an Indian chief—he was my man. But instead of going home to bed, Maida and Parnell and I had taken over the Sheriff's office, down in the jail, finishing up our tricky hypothetical question and whipping up a background letter to a psychiatrist we'd never heard of and whose name we still didn't even know.

"Please give this to Sulo to give to Lieutenant Manion in the morning," I told the night turnkey, handing him the fat envelope.

"The Sheriff's typewriter," Maida said, after it was all over, rubbing her numbed fingers, "—it should lie in state in the Smithsonian Institute. It's surely the same machine they used to draft the terms of Cornwallis' surrender."

The birds were twittering and scolding as we drove home. I noted morosely that the leaves were beginning definitely to turn, a bleak reminder that fishing was mostly over and done. . . . Back at the office Parnell almost joined Maida and me in a drink—almost, but not quite.

"Here's to Napoleon, Max Battisfore and Parnell J. McCarthy," I toasted. "My three favorite foxes."

"And here's to Maida," Maida said, toasting herself. "She remembered to fetch the files along. Good old unsung unpaid Maida. . . ."

"You too, my dear," I said, dipping my glass.

Maida grinned amiably. "I am reminded of that defiant alcoholic lay by an anonymous household poet," she said, going into a contralto chant. " 'All animals are strictly dry, they sinless live and swiftly die, but sinful, ginful, rum-soaked men, survive for threescore years and ten.' "

"Amen," I incanted, rolling up my eyes. "Praise the Lord and pass the bourbon, brethren."

"Rumpots," Parnell sniffed. "Nothing but a pair of addled boozing rumpots."

Early the next morning, Wednesday, the Lieutenant and Undersheriff Carl Vosper had taken off for lower Michigan and the Army hospital, armed with our letter. Nothing more had been heard from them until they arrived home just before midnight on Sunday, the night before court opened. The lieutenant had phoned me at once as I had instructed him. I was alone, staring into the glowing Franklin stove.

"Well, Lieutenant, were you crazy?"

"Nuttier than the proverbial fruit cake," the Lieutenant said.

"What'd he call it?"

"Oh, Lord, I can't begin to tell you. But he's even got me convinced now."

"Weren't you convinced before, Lieutenant?" I said softly.

"Oh, yes—yes, of course—but he sort of laid it out for me. It's hard to explain. You'll see."

"But I told you, man, to ask him to give you the thing in a nutshell."

"These guys never speak in nutshells, Counselor. I don't think they know how. Let's see . . . he said that when I shot Barney I was suffering from dissociative reaction, whatever that is—something sometimes known as—hm—as irresistible impulse."

I shut my eyes. "Oh, Lord . . . no, no—*he didn't say that!*"

"That's what the man said. Isn't that good?"

"What's his name?" I continued, wearily evasive. "I'll need it for court in the morning."

"Dr. Matthew Smith. He's also a captain."

"Smith?" I echoed. "Just plain Smith? Are you sure, Lieutenant, you didn't at least say Schmidt? I always thought all psychiatrists simply had to have long foreign names of no less than four syllables in order to get their diplomas—and that all of their first names were Wolfgang."

"Matthew Smith . . . ," the Lieutenant repeated stoically. "Say, have you been drinking, Counselor? Are you sure you're all right?"

"Never felt better since Antietam, Lieutenant. I'll see you in court tomorrow. Now you go to bed and sleep—this is it, my friend."

So irresistible impulse was the verdict. Here Parnell and I had been knocking ourselves out for weeks boning up on the law of traditional "right and wrong" insanity (that is, if a man knew the difference, he was deemed legally sane), the only kind of insanity accepted as a criminal defense in all American courts. And now fate and a reluctant general had dealt us a psychiatrist called Smith, of all things, who said it was irresistible impulse—that is, regardless of whether the Lieutenant could tell the difference between right or wrong when he had shot Barney, he could not help it. . . .

All I knew about the doctrine of irresistible impulse as a defense to crime I had learned years before in Freshman Crimes in law school. The disturbing residue that had clung was that it was coldly and flatly rejected as a defense by the vast majority of the courts in the land. And I knew that the chances were dismally excellent, almost inevitable, that the cautious and traditionally moderate Michigan supreme court would be among them.

I debated phoning Parnell and breaking the bad news. At least I'd have company in my misery. But no, it was too late; the die was cast; we'd gambled and lost. Poor Parnell might as well get a good night's sleep; the grand old boy needed it; no use in both of us. . . . I dragged myself to my tumbled bed and fell on it and lay staring up at the ceiling most of the night, the same ceiling built by my beer-brewing grandfather a million years ago. . . . Now take brewing; there was a simple and sensible trade—you made the beer and millions of people daily succumbed to an irresistible impulse and drank it; by and by they succumbed to another impulse and got rid of it; then they bought some salted peanuts or potato chips and drank still more beer—there was never any monkey business with any supreme court, your own capacity was your only guide. . . . By and by I fell into a sort of fitful doze. "Hear ye, hear ye, hear ye. . . ." rang in my ears until the alarm buzzed.

chapter 2

"People versus Frederic Manion," Judge Weaver said. "The charge: murder."

I stood up and nodded at the Lieutenant and waited until he stood facing the judge—precisely erect and very military-looking in his freshly pressed uniform—where I joined him on his left. Mitch stood on the right, holding the information, looking over at me expectantly. Would I insist upon his wading through the reading of the long information?

"Appearances?" the Judge said.

"Paul Biegler for the defendant," I said. "My formal appearance is already on file, Your Honor."

"Very well," he said, turning toward Mitch. "You may proceed with the reading of the information, Mr. Prosecutor."

"Your Honor," I spoke up, "the defendant waives the reading of the information and stands mute."

"A plea of 'not guilty' will accordingly be entered by the court," the Judge said briskly. "Are both sides ready for trial?"

"The defense is ready," I said, and the Judge turned to Mitch, who stood frowning, with his lower lip jutted out. The Judge cleared his throat.

"We may have to move for a continuance, Your Honor," Mitch said.

The Judge looked inquiringly at me. "The defense is ready," I said. "We have received no formal notice of any motion for a continuance and will be obliged to resist one if made. My client is of course without bail."

"It's back to you, Mr. Prosecutor," the Judge said.

"The other side has filed a notice of the defense of insanity," Mitch said, "but it still hasn't furnished us the name of the psychiatrist witness as required by law."

The Judge looked over his glasses at me. "Mr. Biegler?"

"A copy of the notice of insanity was served on the prosecutor nearly three weeks ago—eighteen days ago to be exact. The original is on file with the clerk. It contained the names of the witnesses then known to us bearing on the issue of insanity. Mr. Lodwick's copy was accompanied by a letter explaining that I could not then give him the name of our psychiatrist for the simple reason that I did not know it, and that I would do so as soon as I did. With leave of the court I am now prepared to do so—I first learned his name only late last night."

The Judge lifted his eyebrows. "Leave is granted," he said, whereupon I stepped forward and handed up to the Judge the original of a supplemental notice containing the name and address of Dr. Matthew Smith. I then gave Mitch a copy. The Judge looked at Mitch. "Do the People still press?" he said.

"I still think we're entitled to a continuance," Mitch said. "Now on the additional ground of surprise."

The Judge spoke quietly. "Do the People after nearly three weeks' notice of the defense of insanity now claim to be surprised that the defense retained *any* psychiatrist to support their claim?" He paused and smiled slightly. "Or rather do you urge, Mr. Lodwick, that this particular defense psychiatrist whose name you've just learned is so eminent in his field and so devastating in his authority that you must have further time to retain still other psychiatrists to possibly confound and refute him?"

The going was getting a little rough and Mitch flushed but stuck doggedly with his guns. "No, Your Honor," he said, "we urge no such thing, nor do we concede it. We believe the psychiatrist we have already retained is fully able to refute the defense's. It—it's simply that the defense hasn't followed the statute."

"Mr. Biegler?" the Judge said.

"Please excuse me a moment, Your Honor," I said, and the Judge nodding, I went to the brief case by my vacant chair and hauled out a volume of the Michigan annotated statues. Parnell sat with his hand over his eyes. I quickly returned to the bench. "Permit me to refer to section 28.1043 of our annotated statutes," I said. The Judge nodded and I continued. "The statute requires that when it is filed and served the notice of insanity shall contain the names of the defendant's witnesses, and I quote, 'known to him at that time.' That the law contemplates the frequent existence of the very situation of which Mr. Lodwick now complains is, we submit, shown clearly by that quotation and by the very next sentence, which reads: 'Names of other witnesses may be filed and served before or during the trial by leave of court. . . .' Your Honor, we have just obtained such leave and the name of the 'other' witness has now been served. We would have had to get Mr. Lodwick out of bed to serve him any sooner. I submit we have fully complied with both the letter and intent of the law."

"I am quite familiar with your statute, Mr. Biegler," the Judge said. He stared out into the courtroom. "It is frequently surprising the things we lawyers sometimes discover in our statutes when we trouble to read them. It's also surprising the amount of time that could also thus be saved." He sighed and turned back to Mitch, who was now as red as the unproverbial brick schoolhouse. "Do the People still press?"

"I have stated my position, Your Honor," Mitch replied doggedly, refusing to back down.

"From what you have said, Mr. Lodwick," the Judge went on, "I gather that the People have also retained a rebuttal psychiatrist?"

"We have, Your Honor."

"And have you yet told Mr. Biegler who he is?"

"No, Your Honor. His name is endorsed on the information along with the other witnesses. Opposing counsel will get his copy directly."

The Judge put the tips of his fingers together and rocked in his chair. He seemed to be studying the clock on the far wall. "Hm. . . ." he said. "The defense doesn't know the name of the People's doctor and the People have just learned the name of the defense's doctor. That makes things pretty even, doesn't it, Mr. Lodwick? Perhaps, at this moment, even slightly in your favor?"

"Yes, Your Honor," Mitch conceded.

The Judge smiled not unkindly. "Then I think perhaps we'll just leave it that way. To the extent that the People have made a motion for a continuance it is denied. How much time will the trial take? I'll also entertain the suggestions of counsel as to when we might get underway."

"I estimate the trial will take two to three days," Mitch said. "I'd like to start Wednesday, the first jury day."

The Judge turned to me.

"Counsel has just handed me a copy of the information," I said. "I have already counted over thirty People's witnesses. I would guess that four days to a week might be closer. Starting Wednesday morning is agreeable with us, however."

"In quite a few years of experience on the bench," the Judge said, "I have found it a pretty safe practice to at least double the estimates of counsel." He smiled. "Lawyers are far too modest; they do not seem adequately to realize their enormous talents for consuming if not wasting time. . . . In any event we will mark this case number one on the trial docket and hope it will end by Christ-

.nas. I like to visit my grandchildren at that season. The trial will commence at nine A.M. this Wednesday." He dropped his voice. "Counsel will please confer with me in chambers after the call of the calendar." The Judge consulted his calendar and then looked up. "People versus Peter Findlay and Lois Green—lewd and lascivious cohabitation."

As Peter and Lois shuffled forward to stand before the Judge the quaint words of Crabbe came back to me: 'Next at our altar stood a luckless pair, brought by strong passions and a warrant there . . .'

I gave the Lieutenant a little push and he marched back to his seat in the jury box. He hadn't opened his mouth; there had been no occasion. I hurried to my seat, stashing my trusty law book away.

"Round number one," Parnell whispered as I sat down. "Good boy."

"We got a judge, Parn," I whispered back. "My God, I think maybe we got a real judge."

The call of the calendar was at last over and done and Judge Weaver and Mitch and I were sitting in the Judge's chambers. "Have a smoke, gentlemen, and relax," he said, smiling. "I've already devoured my attorney for the day. Of late years I'm allowed only one—doctor's strict orders." He sat at his desk carefully filling a large beat-up hod of a briar pipe with a tobacco called Peerless, a pungent working-man's delight which I suspected was salvaged from the ticking of old mattresses—in turn salvaged from orphanages. Mitch and I lit up, both of us silently appraising this unknown downstate judge with whom we had to learn to live for upwards of a week.

"Lovely fall day," Mitch tentatively ventured, glancing at his watch.

"Hm. . . ." the Judge said, finishing his chore and ignoring our alertly proffered lighters, fishing in his pocket for a large wooden match. "Ah," he said, finally blowing out a rolling cloud of smoke. Mitch wrinkled his nose and winked at me.

Judge Harlan Weaver was a big, slow, ponderous-looking man in his mid-fifties, I judged; slow-spoken, slow-acting, and I guessed, far from slow-thinking. He had big hands and large broad fingers. A droopy sandy-gray cowlick, which he kept patiently brushing out of his eyes, lent him a curiously boyish look. I could almost picture him as a barefoot boy at the old swimming-hole in the rich farming community of lower Michigan where he now regularly sat as judge.

He was one of those men who had not changed much in physical appearance, I guessed, since his teens. He regarded us thoughtfully with his calm blue eyes.

"I am, as you gentlemen may have noticed, something of a bear in the courtroom." His voice had a sort of low resonant rumble. "I find that it lends both dignity and dispatch to the work at hand." He puffed thoughtfully. "I also find that lawyers and the public are both apt to construe too much indulgence in a judge as a sign of weakness." He paused. "Now, is there anything on your chests? Anything that might help us facilitate the job that lies ahead?"

"Well," Mitch said, "I'd like to put on our pathologist first, if I may. It's somewhat out of order, I know, but he's a busy man and the Lord knows how long he or we may have to wait if we stick to the strict order of proof." The Judge looked at me.

"Agreed," I said. "A sensible suggestion, Mitch. Let's get Barney killed right off."

"Anything else, gentlemen?" the Judge said.

"I'd also like some seats set aside for the People's witnesses," Mitch said. "There's quite a flock of them, as Paul here observed, and if they don't have reserved seats the crowd may freeze 'em out and—"

"How many do you need?"

"I estimate three benches will do it," Mitch said. "At least for the first day or two."

"It will be ordered"—the Judge glanced at me—"unless the defense contemplates making a motion to segregate." I shook my head no. "Anything else? How about my ordering a fourteen-man jury? It would be a pity to try this case and then have some poor juror come down with the glanders or beri-beri just at the end and we have to try the case all over. How about it, gentlemen? I can order one, anyway, and probably would, but I like to work with counsel when they indicate any disposition to work with me."

"I had planned to make the motion myself if you hadn't raised it," I said.

"Excellent idea," Mitch agreed. "It would be too bad to have to wade through this little daisy twice." He smiled and glanced at me. "And Polly and I have some unfinished political business we want to get to before the snow flies."

"So I've heard," the Judge said. "Very well, I shall enter a journal order for a fourteen-man jury. Anything else?"

"Charts," Mitch said. "We've made a chart of the tavern and also of the defendant's trailer and trailer park and environs with relation to the tavern. Maybe we could save time if. . . ."

The Judge looked at me. "Who measured and made them, Mitch?" I asked.

"Julian Durgo and his state police boys took the measurements and all," Mitch answered. "Anderson and Ives the architects drew the actual charts from their data."

Handsome Detective-Sergeant Julian Durgo of the state police had been one of my old cops when I was D.A. and was one of the best in the business. If Julian said a door was fifteen feet three inches from a certain bar stool or pinball machine, by God, *that* was it—it wasn't fourteen or sixteen. "We won't have any trouble over the charts, Mitch," I said. "In fact, I was hoping you'd furnish some. We can probably stipulate."

"Anything else, gentlemen?" the Judge rumbled on. "I am a firm believer in the proposition that moderately civilized men can agree on much more than they generally do if they would only first trouble to pause and appraise their own vital interests." He smiled. "I say 'moderately civilized' because I've never quite yet met a totally civilized man. I keep looking and hoping, however, incorrigible optimist that I am. Anything else?"

Mitch laughed uncertainly. "That's about all I can think of now, Your Honor," he said. I glanced quickly at the Judge, thinking that if it weren't for this damned murder case we could sit with some tall clinking glasses before my Franklin stove and maybe find out more what made each other tick. Did I detect a strong and possibly kindred vein of wry cynicism in his make-up?

"And you, Mr. Biegler?" the Judge said. "You haven't said very much. Surely a battered old ex-D.A. like you must be loaded for bear with all sorts of suave deviltry. I was one myself once, you know. Any suggestions to ease the pain of our approaching ordeal?"

"Yes, in front of the Franklin," I thought, laughing and drawing a line with my finger across my forehead. "I'm loaded right up to here, Judge," I said. "But wouldn't it be a pity, too, if all of us gave away our little surprises beforehand?"

The Judge swung his chair, his blue eyes looking thoughtfully out over Lake Superior. "A good point, Counselor," he said slowly. "But only up to a point." He looked sideways at me. "When a lawyer keeps his strategy and theory too long to himself," he said, "he sometimes lures the court into error and thus often deceives only himself. And

I say to both of you men that anything you may feel you can legitimately confide to me, to expedite the *correct* resolution of this case, will be treated in confidence. Now I don't mean that either of you should come running to me the moment the other's back is turned—I don't propose to try this case in the hallways or in chambers. Remember, I said 'legitimately confide.' " He paused. "Anything else, Mr. Biegler?"

I had wished for a shrewd and perceptive judge and it looked like I was getting him. And a frank one. I smiled. "Instructions," I said. "If either side should have any requests for instructions, might the court allow counsel to submit them to him before the end of the trial?" The theory of our defense was wrapped up in the requests for instructions that Parnell and I had polished and toiled over for so long; I had not intended showing our hand on them until we had to, but here was a judge plainly asking us to give him a clue, telling us that he could be trusted. Why keep him in the dark, indeed?

"Not only will I entertain your requests for instructions, I want them," the Judge said. "When lawyers sit on their law and strategy as long as they can—perhaps to confound and mystify their opponents—they may compliment the judge's erudition and clairvoyance, perhaps, but they just as often risk mystifying him as well. I don't claim to be a mind reader. Nor do I claim to know all the law. Do you have any requests to submit now?"

"Not quite yet, Your Honor," I lied whitely, glancing at Mitch. I did not want Mitch to know, if I could help it, that I planned to request *any* instructions. "But perhaps, who knows, we'll have one or two later on. If so would we have a chance to amend or supplement our requests in the light of developments at the trial? I suppose counsel should not be held to pre-trial clairvoyance, either."

The Judge smiled and nodded; he had seen my quick glance at Mitch. "Certainly you can amend and supplement your instructions when the time comes. Or start over from scratch, though I wouldn't recommend it. I would treat any preliminary requests more in the nature of a confidential trial memorandum for the sole assistance of the court. So any time at all, Mr. Biegler—and the sooner the better."

"Speaking of trial memos," I said, "they would also of course be treated as confidential?"

"Certainly, Mr. Biegler, unless counsel choose to exchange. And all this of course goes for you, Mr. Prosecutor. The court plays no favorites—except occasionally—and incognito—at distant race tracks."

"Yum," Mitch murmured absently, glancing at his wrist watch, as he had done several times during the Judge's and my exchange. I felt sorry for the poor guy, and could imagine the sweat he was in, faced with his first big murder trial, with thirty-odd subpoenas waiting to get dated and served, with his phone doubtless clanging and cops and lawyers running in and out of his office—on this and all his other cases—and the *people* endlessly clamoring to get at him. "Please, Mr. Lodwick, this will only take a minute." It always took only a minute, and from bitter experience I knew that just about everyone and his idiot brother felt some dark inexplicable compulsion to lie in wait for the D.A. on the very first day of court. No other time would seem to do. . . .

"Very well, gentlemen," the Judge said, rising. "I think our little meeting may have already proved mutually profitable. And I thought it well that we should get to know each other a little better if we must grin and bear with each other in the busy days that lie ahead."

"Thanks, Judge," Mitch said, edging toward the door. "Real nice meeting. . . . Well, I think I better get going. Lots to do—"

The Judge broke in and waved us out the door. "Good day, gentlemen, good day—it so happens I've got a few little odds and ends to take care of myself."

"Nice old guy," Mitch said, as we left the chambers together. "And as full of riddles and old jokes as Joe Miller."

"He'll do, Mitch," I said. "He'll give both sides a fair shake." "Yes," I thought, "this judge will do—he happens also to be a real lawyer." I hurried out to the car to join Parnell. We two would now have to face the uncertain and fateful battle of "irresistible impulse."

chapter 3

I visited briefly with the Lieutenant to hear the story of his adventures with Doctor Smith. He had really been taken over the jumps—examined, questioned, measured, tested, cuffed, rolled, calibrated and jabbed by a corps of various technicians, followed by three long and intensive sessions with the good Doctor himself. And, there was no mistake, it had all added up to "irresistible impulse."

"You told him," I said, "about your blacking out and all after you saw Barney whirl and drop his left forearm on the bar, with his right arm hidden?"

"I told him everything I have told you—possibly even more. He really drilled away at me."

"You of course gave him my letter with our draft of the hypothetical question?"

"Yes. He said they were helpful to him in making his diagnosis and asked me to thank you."

We gathered up some loose ends and, like an anxious father seeing his daughter off to the city, I again warned him not to talk or traffic with any strange strolling doctors or psychiatrists. I also reminded him to remind Laura to be sure and wear her glasses and her new girdle during the trial. And above all no sweaters. "I must go now, Lieutenant," I said. "There's still a little law I must look up."

"This 'irresistible impulse' thing is bothering you, isn't it?" he said.

"Perish the thought," I said, smiling bravely, feeling like a sort of rural Pagliacci. "Keep your chin up, Lieutenant. If I can't see you tomorrow I'll phone you. Wednesday's the big day."

Parnell and I took a long back-road route home to Chippewa through the rolling Finnish farming country. We drove silently for miles drinking in the wild beauty of the scene. I observed with a pang that the stricken summer had indeed waned into colorful northern autumn, like a beautiful woman flushed and waxen with the fevers of approaching death. "O lost and by the wind grieved. . . ."

I told Parnell of my session in chambers with the Judge and Mitch; of my growing conviction that we might possibly have won in the uncertain lottery of strange judges assigned from downstate—I had occasionally worked before some little daisies, curious exhibitionists and bench-thumpers I would not personally have trusted to notarize a quit-claim deed; and that at least we might not have looked all our law in vain; that I was coming to rather like the man.

Parnell was inclined to agree. "I liked the patient way he explained to each criminal defendant his constitutional and other rights before accepting his plea of guilty. It not only shows care and thoroughness but an abiding respect for our traditional constitutional processes— the present-day zeal for which can scarcely be said to be reaching epidemic proportions. . . ." Parnell shook his head and continued. "Yes, Polly, I liked the way he tried to steer that young Mitch fellow away from his ill-informed continuance business, and then the nice way he let the young man down easy when he still wouldn't be steered. That shows kindness and a lack of intellectual arrogance —many judges would have flashed their erudition like a pawnbroker's diamond." Parnell chuckled. "Although I loved the oblique way he properly gave the young fellow a jab or two—though I'm not sure he even felt it."

"It looks like I'm not going to have a chance to raise your pet constitutional question that we recently argued—I mean discussed. As you saw, Mitch still didn't say a word about wanting any sanity examination. It looks like he clean missed the boat. Even up to today I thought he might have something up his sleeve—but his hand came out empty. I almost felt sorry for him."

"'Pride goeth before a fall,'" Parnell intoned. "Anyway, he may have unwittingly scored on this irresistible impulse business. C'mon, boy, drive faster. The spectacle of these autumn leaves is breaking my sentimental old heart, but I can't wait to get at the law books. They hold our answer."

As we sped on our way Parnell went over the list of the People's witnesses endorsed on our copy of the information. "There are thirty-seven," he said. "Alas, Mary Pilant's name is not among them." He sighed. "I won't get to see her, I guess."

I narrowly missed a truck loaded with pulp logs. "The little lady seems to have put herself nicely in the clear," I said. "What's the psychiatrist's name? I clean forgot to look. Please, Lord, make it Wolfgang—don't destroy all my boyish illusions."

"Hm, we'll see," Parn said, again poring over the long list of names. We passed an iron mine on the outskirts of town, and the distant moving dump cars on top of the mountainous stock piles of liver-red ore looked like toys on top of children's sand piles. "There are three doctors listed," Parnell said. "Dr. Raschid—that would be

the pathologist at St. Francis' who did the post on the late Mr. Quill
—and a Dr. Dompierre—"

"That's the county jail physician who took the smear from our
lady," I said, "—or rather, tried to."

"—and a Doctor Gregory—W. Harcourt Gregory, no less."

"That must be their psychiatrist, Parn," I said. "I never heard of
him. Maybe they flew him clean in from Menninger's. And maybe
—leave us pray—maybe the W stands for Wolfgang."

"*Heil! Deutschland über alles,*" Parnell solemnly intoned.

The world of science is said to be full of remarkable examples of
independent researchers, unknown to each other and sometimes
separated by whole continents, coming up with identical answers to
the same puzzling questions at the very same time. At least this was
once true—true before our Soviet cousins rewrote history cozily reminding us that they had invariably got there first. In any case that
night shortly before midnight Parnell and I—separated not by continents but only by Grandma Biegler's old dining-room table—had,
more modestly perhaps, experienced much the same exhilarating
thrill.

We had been chasing the elusive will-o'-the-wisp of irresistible
impulse through the law books most of the afternoon and evening.
I had been concentrating on the Michigan authorities and Parnell,
wearing his green eye-shade and in his shirtsleeves, had been ranging
lovingly through the textbooks and general authorities. I had so far
been unable to find even the mention of the term in the Michigan
sources. Parnell had dug up plenty of fine general statements and
interesting discussions of the doctrine but none that gave us a cross-
reference or clue to our big burning question: the state of the law
on the subject in Michigan. What the law might be in Pennsylvania
or Podunk might prove absorbing to its accused felons and their
lawyers and to detached legal scholars; what it was in Michigan could
prove fatal to a guy called Frederic Manion. Our search possessed
much of the uncertainty and palpitant quality of stalking an elusive
rising trout.

In desperation I had begun doggedly rereading all the old land-
mark cases on insanity in Michigan. Surely, I thought, if Michigan
didn't accept the doctrine of irresistible impulse as a defense to
crime then there must at least be some old case, somewhere, where
the proposition had been urged and turned down. I sighed and went
over and plucked another musty old report out of the stacks and

returned to our littered table. My ears were ringing and my eyes were beginning to blur. I blew the dust off and flipped the pages and was wading through a fine tangle of nineteenth-century judicial prose when suddenly, from out of the parched and yellowed old page of fine print, there had leapt out at me a phrase in block letters two feet high: "If the defendant was not capable of knowing he was doing wrong in the particular act, *or if he had not the power to resist the impulse to do the act* . . . that would be an unsound mind." I swallowed and shut my eyes and shook my head and looked again —lo, the flag was still there. I was mutely sliding the book across the table toward Parnell when he arose and let out a stifled yelp and tossed his green eye-shade into the air.

"Mother Machree!" he shouted, pacing the floor. "Quick, Polly —d-dig out *People versus Durfee,* 62 Michigan 487. I think we're in, I think we're in. . . ."

"It's right in front of you, Counselor," I said. "Read it and weep." Thus had Parnell and I joined the long company of the scientific immortals—we'd found the same answer at the very same time.

Parnell had at last dug up a beautiful annotation on irresistible impulse out of 70 American Law Reports at page 659. It laid it out cold. "Listen to this, Polly," he said, and retrieving his fallen eye-shade he began walking sedately back and forth, like a plump abbot who had just found exquisite confirmation of his long-cherished view of Paradise.

"First, Polly, it traces the history of the leading old English M'Naghten case which, as we know, established the classic test of insanity still prevailing in most states, that is, whether the defendant at the time of doing the act knew the difference between right and wrong. Now listen to this."

"I'm listenin', damn it. Read, man, don't pontificate. I got my LL.B."

"Then it says: 'Since then the "right and wrong" test enunciated by that case, though condemned as being unscientific and based on fallacious principles by the overwhelming weight of medical authority, has nevertheless been tenaciously adhered to by a great many courts.' " Parnell paused and looked owlishly over his glasses at me. "About then, young man, I was ready to quietly turn on the gas. I knew then that the great weight of authority was against us."

"Ah, but did the good old Dodgers come through?" I murmured devoutly.

"Then the annotation reviewed all the old moss-back citations and decisions of our benighted sister states—by this time I'm reading with one eye, lad, waiting for the blow to fall."

"Did our hero win the gal in the end, Parn? Quick—you're killin' me."

Parnell ignored my irreverent comments. "Then I finally come to the part headed 'doctrine recognized.' By then my hands are shakin', boy, as I read that in a *mere handful of states* the rule is that—and listen, now—'. . . the fact that one accused of committing a crime may have been able to comprehend the nature and consequences of his act, and to know that it was wrong, nevertheless if he was forced to its execution by an impulse which he was powerless to control . . . he will be excused.' "

"You should have played Shakespeare, Parn," I said. "In Connecticut barns. You're raisin' goose pimples on me big as trout spawn."

"Then follows the brief list of states," Parnell continued, his eyes glowing. "I go down the list with my finger, squinting down sideways now like a man opening a bottle of two-dollar champagne—Alabama —Arkansas—good old Georgia—Kaintucky, suh—Louisiana—a veritable roll call of dear old Southland—and then—and then good old Copperhead rebel Yankee Michigan! People versus Durfee, bless his soul, way back in 1886, when even old Parnell was but a gleam in Terence McCarthy's eye. In his rather accurate eye I may add— there was eleven of us . . . ! Well, Polly, by then I knew that by the grace of God and our supreme court we had hoisted our Lieutenant over another hurdle. Hail to the addled Durfees!"

"I'm having me a drink," I said, rising. "I'll fetch you a cold orange pop." The old boy had developed quite a tolerance for the stuff.

Parnell was poring lovingly over the old Durfee case when I returned from my forage. "Now how did we ever miss it so long?" he was murmuring. "We both surely must have read this case during the past two weeks—it seems I can even see my own cryptic pencil marks in the margin."

"It's like love or beauty, I guess, Parn," I said. "If a man's not looking for it he'll probably never find it. Well, we weren't looking for irresistible impulse so we didn't find it. And apparently they don't call it that in Michigan anyway. I guess they don't call it nothin'—like Topsy, it just irresistibly growed. Here's mud in your right eye."

But oblivious Parnell was back at his books. " '*Or if he had not the power to resist the impulse to do the act . . .*' " he whispered ecstatically. He shook his head. "What an indescribably lovely line. Ah, what a beautiful instruction it will make."

The cracked clock in the city hall tower boomed twelve. I silently gestured with my glass and drank to the loveliest lawyer I ever knew.

chapter 4

On Wednesday morning at ten minutes to nine—after a quick round of final handshakes—I left Laura and the Lieutenant at the jail office and hurried in the back door of the courthouse and up the broad marble stairs and threaded my way through the crowded and milling corridors back to the Judge's chambers.

"Good morning. . . . Good morning. . . . Good morning. . . ."

The Judge and Mitch and the Sheriff and court reporter, Grover Gleason, were there, the latter sitting in a corner obliviously working one of his inevitable books of crossword puzzles, which he evidently acquired by the five-foot-shelf. Grover lived in a little secret world of words, a mystic faraway world compounded of extinct birds, louse eggs, whole vats of bitter vetch, three-toed sloths, Egyptian sun goddesses, Arabian gulfs and long narrow inlets. . . . A fifth man arose and stood quietly waiting to be introduced. Mitch cleared his throat.

"Polly, this is Claude Dancer of the Attorney General's staff in Lansing—Paul Biegler. Claude's going to kind of sit in with me during the trial."

"How do you do, Biegler," Claude Dancer said in a deep melodious voice, smiling pleasantly, giving me a quick firm handshake. "The boss sent me up to give Mitch here a hand if he needs it. The boy seems nicely on top of his case and I don't think I'll be much in your hair. It's awfully nice to know you."

Claude Dancer was a short, quick-moving, wiry man of about forty; short and bald—much balder than I was, I noted with a kind of wry malice—with fugitive tufts of short hair that looked like patches of fur pasted on either side of his head. This, coupled with his pink complexion and alert, eager and somewhat snub-nosed features, gave him a curiously pixy look, something like a preternaturally wise baby got up like a man—or perhaps an even shrewder man got up to look like a baby, I wasn't quite sure. . . . The big deep voice only compounded my uncertainty. And I would have bet my fly rods against a rusty bait rod that he had taken elocution and declamation and led his debating team in high school.

"Your fame has preceded you, Mr. Dancer," I said. "Permit me to congratulate you on your brilliant handling of that grand jury investigation of graft in Detroit. You really did the rascals in."

Claude Dancer smiled modestly. "Thank you," he said. "I'm sure it will be a pleasure to work with you."

I glanced out the window at the big lake dancing in the sunshine and thoughtfully blinked my eyes. Mitch had finally come up with his little surprise, all right; this time his sleeve had not been empty. Lieutenant Manion was having thrown at him a real ringer, perhaps one of the ablest and shrewdest criminal trial men on the Attorney General's staff. That the Attorney General happened also to be a member of Mitch's political party and that Mitch and I just happened to be running against each other for Congress had nothing to do of course with the case. Perish the thought—such dark thoughts were too cynical and bleak to entertain.

Judge Weaver spoke. "Mr. Dancer was discussing something informally here just before you arrived. Because it concerns you and your client I asked him to wait till you got here. Proceed, Mr. Dancer."

Claude Dancer turned his innocent Kewpie-doll face to me. "Well, Biegler, I did have one little suggestion to make to Mitch after we finally reviewed the case last night."

"What's that?" I said, already quite sure what his suggestion concerned.

Claude Dancer was a fluent and easy talker. He modulated his fine voice like a trained musician, playing on it like a sort of Piatigorsky of the spoken word. "Well, since you've pleaded insanity and got a psychiatrist and the People have likewise retained one," he said, "and since under the statute the People plainly have a right to petition for a mental examination"—he paused—"I assume you're familiar with that procedure, Counselor?"

"Moderately," I said, nodding. "Go on—I'm listening."

"And since it would only unnecessarily delay things to file a formal petition now, it occurred to me that all of us might stipulate informally to adjourn the trial for a day or two so that our doctor can visit a little with your man." He held out his hands. "Merely a time-saving suggestion, is all."

There it was, as simple as rolling off a log; only dullards could fail to grasp the plain wisdom of his course. And so beautifully and plausibly spoken, too. Just a friendly little two- or three-day chat between the People's psychiatrist and Lieutenant Manion. I glanced at the Judge. He sat staring impassively out over the lake, his blue eyes unblinking.

"What you mean, Dancer," I said, "is that you want *me* to agree to let your psychiatrist paw over my man?"

There was a quick outthrust of the supple hands. "Paw? Well, yes, paw, if you like. Merely to save time is all. This will save every-body time."

I turned to Mitch. I wanted to see just how far this suave little man with the big voice was willing to go. "I suppose all your witnesses are subpoenaed and waiting out there, Mitch?" I nodded toward the courtroom. "And the jury panel is all gathered and ready?"

"All set," Mitch said.

I turned back to Claude Dancer. "My answer to your little time-saving suggestion, Mr. Dancer, is regrettably no." I felt nettled that he took me for such a groping backwoods bumpkin. "But I have a little suggestion of my own."

"What's that?" he said, his eager face tilted up at me.

"That we proceed out to the courtroom now so that the People can make on the record their belated motion for leave to file a petition for a mental examination."

"What do you mean?"

It was my turn to hold out my hands. "Why the answer is easy and simple, Mr. Dancer," I said. "So that when the Judge turns you down for daring to come in here at such a late hour and without any excuse, the assembled jurors and newspaper reporters and every-body will nevertheless see the crucial importance the People attach to the necessity of its psychiatrist examining my man." I made an Alphonse-and-Gaston motion with my hand. "Shall we go in now— the court willing?"

Claude Dancer looked at me keenly, like a smart boxer stung in the first round and cagily reappraising the character of his opposition. I glanced at the Judge, who was still preoccupied with the lake, though it did seem there were now little creases and wrinkles gath-ered at the corners of his eyes. "There is no need for any such examination," Claude Dancer announced coldly in that fine deep voice. "Nor do the People concede any such need. It was merely a little time-saving suggestion, was all."

"And money-saving, too," I said, smiling, and I could not resist adding: "Think of all the *money* the public would also be saved by sending home thirty-odd witnesses and a whole regiment of jurors, all of whom would nevertheless have to be paid from the public till. Your concern touches me." Claude Dancer flushed and I saw that I had scored with a sneak right.

"What's a four-letter word describing a woman of ill-repute?" the

206

reporter Grover Gleason said, emerging absently from his puzzle, thoughtfully fluttering his eyes and pursing his lips.

"H-o-r-e," I spelled. "Didn't you know? In the Upper Peninsula, Grover, invariably it's hore."

"Go to hell, Biegler," Grover said.

"My, my, that's a *lewd* word, Grover," I said reprovingly, as Grover looked gratefully at me and sank back to his world of hatching louse eggs.

The Judge spoke evenly, looking at Mitch. "I take it, then, Mr. Prosecutor, that the People do not propose to file a formal petition seeking a psychiatric examination of the respondent?"

I held my breath as Mitch glanced questioningly at Claude Dancer, who quickly shook his head no. The assistant Attorney General's and my glances met and we both smiled. We two had swiftly reached a tacit understanding: this was *our* fight, now, and wasn't it a shame, in a way, that there had to be any third man cluttering up the ring . . . ?

The Judge arose ponderously and shook out his robes, flapping his arms out loosely like a great black bird. "C'mon, gentlemen," he said crisply. "There's an interesting murder case out there waiting to be tried. We won't get it done sparring around in here."

All of us fell back respectfully as the Judge preceded us down the short hallway to the courtroom. He had a sort of bouncing gait, at once deliberate in the planting of each large foot, and yet curiously buoyant, as though he were walking on an invisible trampoline. All of us fell in obediently behind him, like lesser participants in some traditional medieval ritual, as, upon reflection, I guessed indeed we were.

The courtroom was crowded, mostly with women, who in turn were mostly the kind usually found sitting in various states of cataleptic trance under hair dryers in beauty parlors hungrily scanning the latest authentic romances. Every available seat in the back court was taken and the overflow was standing raggedly in the side aisles and along the wall in the rear. The Judge, his black robe swishing, mounted the short steps leading to the bench and stood frowning behind his chair until we had taken our places. A flash-bulb exploded. The Judge, frowning still more, turned and nodded at the waiting Sheriff, who gaveled the assembly to its feet.

"Hear ye, hear ye, hear ye!" Max bawled as though he was out on the open range calling in his lost little dogies. "The Circuit Court for the county of Iron Cliffs is now in session. Please take your seats."

Judge Weaver sat staring stonily out at the milling and whispering crowd. "Ladies and gentlemen," he began in his big flatly resonant voice, "I come here on assignment from lower Michigan to sit in the stead of your own Judge Maitland, who is presently recovering from illness. Now I have no desire to upset the folkways or traditions of this community during murder trials, whatever they may be, but while I am sitting here this is my court and I warn you I am going to run it."

The Judge paused and the spectators discreetly coughed and he went on. "One thing I am going to insist upon is that no spectator who cannot comfortably find a seat be allowed to attend any sessions of the trial of this cause. I had not realized that there were so many among you who were such zealous students of homicide." (I stole a look around for Parnell, but could not find him.) "In any case I must remind you that this is a court of law and not a football game or a prize fight. Our S.R.O. sign is out for repairs. Both the defendant and the People are entitled to a public trial, and they will get one, but I choose to interpret that injunction to mean a *seated* public trial. I am sorry." He turned to the Sheriff. "Mr. Sheriff, please have your men clear the courtroom of all persons who are not seated."

"Yes, sir, Your Honor. Right away, sir." Max bustled forward, shooing out his arms as though he was now herding his little dogies. As the disappointed crowd of standees began slowly to shuffle out of the courtroom, scraping and mumbling, I searched the room for Parnell and found him sitting on the side of the courtroom at my left, in one of the chairs reserved for lawyers, near the tall mahogany door we had just entered. He was staring mystified at Mitch's table—that would be over Claude Dancer—and when he saw me he shrugged and lifted his eyebrows and grinned. "Pride goeth before a fall," I remembered he had said. Pratfall, more like, I thought ruefully.

Mitch's table was impressively littered and nearly hidden with law books and brief cases and a mass of charts and papers and files and exhibits, like a sort of expansive legal smorgasbord. Beyond Mitch's table Bob Birkey, a reporter for the *Gazette*, sat scribbling away at a smaller table. I fished in the brief case at my feet and drew out a thin manila folder of notes and a scratch pad and put them on my bare table, along with a wooden pencil. Parnell and I had Crockerishly planned it this way: the picture of the overpowering well-heeled State arrayed against a poor lonely soldier. . . .

Max Battisfore was back at his place. "Your Honor," he said, "the courtroom is cleared of standees."

"Thank you, Mr. Sheriff," the Judge said. "Now there is one more thing I am going to insist upon. That is that there shall be no photographs taken in this courtroom during this trial. I am both morbid and rabid on this subject. Nor will I permit the publication or circulation of the one that was just taken and I demand that the film be delivered to me. Any violation of these orders will be dealt with summarily by contempt." Smiling faintly he glanced down at the reporter for the *Gazette*. "I have a trained intuition that this word will be conveyed to the offender if he should no longer be present. Mr. Clerk, call the case."

Clovis Pidgeon arose from his mahogany cubicle in front of the Judge's bench and looked up at the guano-stained skylight. For a moment I thought he was going to break into prayer. "People versus Frederic Manion," he called out in his high tenor voice. "The charge: murder."

"Please swear the jurors for examination on the voir dire," the Judge said.

Clovis solemnly faced all the jurors sitting out in back court and raised his right hand. "Please arise and raise your right hands," he announced. His thin eager Gallic face was crowned by a glorious floating thatch of prematurely gray hair, which he wore like a kind of silver beret. "You do solemnly swear," he said, as though intoning a stirring prayer, "that you will true answers make to such questions as may be put to you touching upon your competency to sit as jurors in this cause, so help you God."

The jurors mumbled their "I do's" and sat down. There was a special quaver, a fervor in his voice, that Clovis reserved strictly for occasions like this. He had long since learned the ritual of his job by heart, which left him free to concentrate solely on his delivery, which was matchlessly superb. (These memorable performances also saved passing out a lot of campaign cards.) In fact during court sessions Clovis was not unlike an accomplished bit player who comes dangerously close to stealing the show.

"Please call a jury of fourteen," the Judge prompted Clovis.

Clovis sat down and reached for a square wooden box containing the slips bearing the individual names of each member of the large jury panel. He began ostentatiously shaking the box like a competent bartender mixing a drink, and I remembered wistfully that the man was good in both departments. Then he slid open a panel and, with the flourish of a magician about to extract a rabbit, reached in the box and withdrew a small paper slip.

"Oscar Haverdink!" Clovis intoned.

I wrote this name on my pad and turned and watched an oldish man separate himself from the seated panel in back court and limp his way forward to the empty jury box.

"Doris Flanders!" Clovis called out, and Doris, an undulant lissome young creature with long earrings and much make-up, came gliding up to the box, ostentatiously virginal, flushing self-consciously and carrying her girdled and fragile little treasure of femaleness as though she were guarding a sacred flame. I glanced at Clovis and he found time to give me a knowing small smile of triumph. "Mission accomplished," his glance seemed to say—"see, Polly, we've already drawn our siren for the session."

"John Traski," Clovis called out, and this went on until fourteen hushed and embarrassed jurors—nine men and five women—sat looking expectantly up at the Judge.

"Ladies and gentlemen," the Judge said pleasantly, addressing the fourteen prospective jurors, "this is a criminal case we are about to try and perhaps I can best acquaint you with its precise nature by reading a pertinent portion of the information that the People have filed in this case."

The Judge held up the information. "The People charge in their information that the defendant Frederic Manion, on the 16th day of August, last, and I quote, 'at the Township of Mastodon in the County of Iron Cliffs and State of Michigan, feloniously, wilfully and of his malice aforethought, did kill and murder one Barney Quill.' "

The Judge let the information drop to his desk like a falling leaf and again faced the jury. "That, ladies and gentlemen, charges the offense of first degree murder. Now before we proceed further I want to examine you briefly regarding your qualifications to sit here as jurors. I will expect each of you to speak up even though I may not always address you individually. Please raise your hand if there is any danger I may have overlooked one of you. And please remember that you are under oath. Do you understand?"

There was a nodded rumble of assent from the jury.

The Judge then explained briefly the doctrine of the presumption of innocence and reasonable doubt, and then asked the jurors if they understood and would apply these doctrines to the defendant during the trial. All understood and assented and he then passed on to the statutory qualifications.

"First of all, are all of you citizens? Raise your hand if you are not." Again there was the muttered rumble, like the illy timed response of a congregation in church. No hands were raised. The reporter, who was sitting with his back to the jury, glanced questioningly up at the Judge, who in turn nodded his head affirmatively.

The Judge then went on and asked the usual questions: were any of them deaf or in poor health; were any over seventy and thus wanted to be excused, as they were entitled; did all of them speak and understand English; had any prospective juror served on a jury in circuit court within the last twelve months; were any of them governmental or state or municipal employees and wanted to be excused; were there any justices of the peace or law-enforcement officers among them or were any of them related to any such. . . . All jurors passed with flying colors.

"So much for qualifications," the Judge said. "I shall now examine for cause. Now the prosecuting attorney, Mr. Lodwick, sits at his right of the counsel table nearer you. Now I suppose that some of you jurors are acquainted with him, are you not?"

About half the jurors timidly raised their hands.

"Do any of you know him intimately?"

None responded.

"Do any of you have any pending business with him?" Again none. "Do any of you know any reason or circumstance in your acquaintance with him that would in any manner embarrass you or prevent you from deciding this case freely and squarely on the law and evidence presented here?"

Again a stolid silence.

The Judge then inquired regarding Claude Dancer, "the assistant Attorney General from Lansing," but none knew or had heard of him, they were apparently not up on their grand jury investigations. . . . He then gave me the same treatment he had given Mitch, with substantially the same results, except that practically all of the jurors allowed that they knew me. "Ah, the price of fame," I thought. My ten years of public pettifogging had not yet been entirely forgotten.

"Now take the defendant, Frederic Manion, sitting on Mr. Biegler's left." I could feel the Lieutenant tense and stiffen at my side. "Do any of you know him?"

The jurors sat stolid and unblinking, shaking their heads no and staring curiously at the Lieutenant, who stared straight ahead. So *this* was the soldier who had shot that innkeeper at Thunder Bay?

"Or his wife, Laura Manion? Please rise, Mrs. Manion." Laura was sitting in one of the lawyers' chairs behind us, and she got up, looking very demure and lashed in, and smiled slightly at the jury and sat down, the jurors again shaking their heads.

"Very well," the Judge said. "Now in a general way it is the claim of the People that in the early morning hours of Saturday, September sixteenth—around one A.M. I believe—the Defendant entered the hotel bar of one Barney Quill in the village of Thunder Bay in Mastodon Township in this county and shot him to death. Were any of you acquainted with the deceased?"

A lone juror raised his hand. I consulted my notes; it was Oscar Haverdink, the elderly first juror who had been called. Parnell and I knew he was a retired log scaler in Thunder Bay and that he would be a good juror. We further knew that we could not hope to keep him—that he had hated Barney's guts and didn't care who knew it.

"Mr. Haverdink," the Judge said, "how long had you known the deceased?"

"About nine years, sir—ever since he first came to our town."

"How well did you know him?"

The juror pondered. "Well," he said, "Thunder Bay's a small place. I guess everybody knew of this Barney—Mr. Quill, I mean."

"Have you discussed the case or talked with anyone purporting to know the facts?"

The juror smiled. "I guess that's about all we folks have talked about lately. We don't get much excitement like that up our way. The last killin' was—let's see now—it was near the end of that dry summer—"

"We needn't go into that, Mr. Haverdink," the Judge said kindly. "This case will occupy us nicely. Now don't state it if you have one, but I now ask you if you have formed any impression or opinion on the merits of the case or of the guilt or innocence of the accused?"

The juror looked down at his feet and then at the juror next to him and then back at the Judge. He spoke in a low troubled voice. "You see, Judge, I—I don't like to talk about the dead—"

"*Hold on!*" the Judge broke in rapidly, holding up his hand. "That will be enough." The juror looked around, puzzled, as though he had inadvertently used a dirty word. The Judge motioned counsel up to the bench with his cupped hand and Mitch and I and Claude Dancer, quickly gathered around him like huddled conspirators. "Well, gentlemen," the Judge whispered grimly, leaning forward, "it looks like we struck oil in our first hole."

"Defense oil," Claude Dancer whispered, glaring at me.

"Better ease him off painlessly, Judge," I whispered. "If you don't the People surely will later, anyway, and that'll only delay our case." I smiled at Claude Dancer. "I'll send the banished juror his knighthood later." Mitch whispered briefly with Claude Dancer and then nodded at the Judge, who nodded at us, and we quickly resumed our places at our tables.

"Mr. Haverdink," the Judge went on, "since you live in the same community as the deceased, might you feel better—perhaps less embarrassed—if you were excused from sitting on this case?"

The juror nodded his head eagerly. "Oh, yes, Your Honor, much better. You see, I—"

"That's all. The court will excuse you. You may stand aside now. Any objections from counsel?"

"None, Your Honor," Mitch and I popped up and dutifully replied. I wanted to steal a look at Parnell but didn't dare.

"Mr. Clerk," the Judge said.

The clerk ostentatiously shook up his box and found another name.

"Alexander James Petrie," he announced, and I was positive that never had Mr. Petrie heard his name pronounced with such declamatory fervor and loving care. In fact Clovis' ardor seemed rather excessive, even for him, until I realized that the fall festival of elections was almost upon us, that he was softly heralding the approach of the great biennial Season of Love.

The Lieutenant leaned over and whispered to me. "I don't think that last old fellow cared very much for this Barney person. Too bad we couldn't keep him."

"Not a chance," I whispered. "Anyway, he's already earned his keep. In a sense he was really our first witness, and perhaps one of the best."

The new juror was in his seat. "I must ask all of the jurors to disregard any remarks they may hear from other jurors during this examination," the Judge said. "Nor should any of you draw any inferences from anything you have heard or may hear from each other during this examination. Do you understand that?" The jurors solemnly nodded and I again longed to look at Parnell. The excused juror had driven a first spike for the defense, and the Judge in performing his plain duty had been obliged to hammer it home. Things like this were one of the wry imponderables of jury trials.

The Judge was speaking to the new juror. Had he heard the questions that had been asked the others? Did he . . . had he . . . was he . . . ? No, he didn't know any of us lawyers or the Lieutenant or the dead man. When it was all done the new juror had miraculously survived.

"Now I ask all the jurors if any of you have talked or read about this case?"

All of the jurors raised their hands; any who hadn't would by their failure have virtually convicted themselves of perjury, dumbness, or failing to pay their newspaper delivery boys.

"Have *any* of you formed any impression or opinion as to the guilt or innocence of the accused? Answer simply yes or no or raise your hands."

They had all learned their lessons now; no hands were raised; and fourteen heads shook negatively amidst the mumbled chorus of noes.

"Now I ask if any of you know of any reason whatsoever why you could not enter upon the trial of this case, if you are chosen, with an open mind, bearing in mind that under the law the respondent is presumed to be innocent until his guilt is established beyond a reasonable doubt?"

None did.

"And can each of you render a fair and impartial verdict based solely upon the law and evidence given you here in open court?"

All thought they could. The Judge looked at Mitch. "For cause, gentlemen," he said. "Yours first, Mr. Prosecutor?"

Mitch nodded at the Judge and continued an earnest whispered conversation he was having with Claude Dancer. The Judge opened a law book and began to read to himself. I whispered to my client. "How do they look to you, Lieutenant?" He shrugged. "Your choice, Counselor," he whispered back.

The People had fifteen peremptory challenges and the defense twenty—that is, we could excuse that number of jurors without assigning any cause. A mere airy wave of the hand was enough. "Scat, you divil . . ." as Parnell might say. In addition, we could challenge "for cause" any jurors that our questioning might show to be unqualified or prejudiced or otherwise incompetent. That question would shortly be in my lap.

"The People pass," Mitch finally said. "No questions for cause."

"Up to you, Mr. Biegler," the Judge said.

I swallowed and quickly arose. "The defense passes," I said.

"Peremptory challenges," the Judge said. "Back to you, Mr. Prosecutor."

"Excuse me, Your Honor," Mitch said, and he and Claude Dancer again fell into a whispered huddle and consulted their notes while I drew what I hoped was a leaping trout on my scratch pad. A psychologist would probably have told me I was obsessed with plump mermaids. . . .

"The People will excuse Michael Powers," Mitch finally said.

Juror Powers sat looking as though he had been hit in the face with a wet mop. What had he done? He looked aggrievedly up at the Judge. I was not too displeased at this turn of events: Michael Powers happened also to be one of the jurors on Parnell's and my doubtful list.

"Very well, Mr. Powers, you may stand aside," the Judge said. "You are excused from further service on this case. Thank you. All right, Mr. Clerk."

"Kenneth Medley," Clovis called out lovingly as the late Mr. Powers stalked out of the jury box and into the back court, glaring at Mitch. "One vote for Biegler for Congress," I thought. "The people's pal."

Once again the Judge waded manfully through the whole rigmarole with the new juror; once again the juror somehow made the right answers; once again both sides passed for cause—and at last the big decision was coming up to me. . . . Did I want to boot any of these jurors off on peremptory. "All yours, Mr. Biegler," the Judge said.

"A little time, please, Your Honor," I said, and he nodded and quietly resumed reading his law book. The courtroom grew hushed; this was it. There were still two jurors in the box who were on our doubtful list. The doubts were big and yet not big: Within the year I had defeated the brother of one juror in a rather bitter will contest and once, while prosecutor, I had convicted the husband of a woman juror of drunk driving. Yet smaller things could sway jurors. . . . But, Lord, could a juror be small enough to convict a man of murder because . . . ? Tweedledee, tweedledum. . . .

On the other hand there were several jurors on the panel in back court that I hoped might get to sit. There were also a couple among the fourteen now in the box that I wanted to keep. They weren't ringers or anything like that, but I believed that they would be fair and unbiased jurors with minds of their own. One was an intelligent-looking young Finnish veteran of World War II, an iron miner who lived in one of the farming townships. The other juror I had seen and met casually some years before at a political rally and had been favorably impressed with him. But mightn't a veteran, particularly an intelligent one, be just dying to pay off the Army brass? And mightn't the other one be voting straight Whig by now? And if not, so what? All these and more thoughts came to me. Perhaps it was better to let well enough alone. Perhaps I'd start a spree of challenges if I excused even one. Maybe if I passed on peremptory Mitch might miraculously lay off. After all, there were equally doubtful ones and worse that might still be called.

"What do you think, Lieutenant?" I whispered. I knew what he'd think but I was bound to ask him; one always had to ask them in case anything went wrong. . . . The Lieutenant gave me his expected shrug and I was sobered by his total dependence on me and my judgment. I glanced beyond him at Parnell. He too shrugged almost imperceptibly and I was back with myself. The decision was solely mine, as it had to be. I took a quick breath and arose to my feet.

"Your Honor," I said, "the defense is satisfied with the jury."

"Back to you, Mr. Prosecutor," the Judge said.

Mitch and Claude Dancer fell into a long whispered huddle while I got back to my art and attached a fisherman to the trout I had drawn—a nice balding long-nosed fisherman. In the meantime the jurors, realizing now that they could be banished out of hand, even though they had passed all previous tests, sat trying to look unconcerned, like nervously waiting candidates for membership in a fraternal lodge uneasily wondering whether they would be blackballed.

"Your Honor," Mitch was on his feet, "the People are satisfied."

The miracle had happened; we had selected a jury in a murder case in less than half a day. I had prosecuted criminal cases where the jury selection alone had taken two days, and in one nearly three. And neither side had so much as mentioned insanity or rape, as though both of us were afraid to get into those tangled and controversial subjects before we had to. Lieutenant Manion was a party to another record, too, though he didn't quite know it: this was the first murder case I had ever seen or heard of where the defense had not made a single peremptory challenge. "Jury chosen swiftly in Manion murder case," the *Gazette* would probably say. "Courtroom observers cannot remember greater speed."

"Swear the jury," the Judge quietly said, looking down over his glasses at Clovis.

Clovis popped to his feet and adminstered the final oath to the standing jurors.

"You do solemnly swear," he intoned, "that you shall well and truly try, and true deliverance make, between the People of this state and the prisoner at the bar, whom you shall have in charge, according to the evidence and the laws of this state; so help you God."

This was by all odds Clovis' finest hour; it was a pity, I thought, that he had not done the swearing at the last coronation. No monarch could ever have been more tightly glued to the throne.

The Judge addressed the rest of the waiting petty jurors sitting out in the body of the courtroom. "All other jurors will be excused until next Monday at nine," he said. "If there are any further delays you will be duly notified." He looked at the courtroom clock. "In view of the lateness of the hour I believe we will suspend for the morning." He turned to the Manion jury. "You will be excused until one-thirty. In the meantime please do not talk about the case among yourselves. Or with others, of course. If any persons attempt to discuss the case with you report it to me at once. All right, Mr. Sheriff."

"Hear ye, hear ye, hear ye," Max sang out with deep feeling, seeming inspired by the stellar performance of Clovis. "This honorable court is adjourned until one-thirty."

The Sheriff came up and stood close by at the side of the Lieutenant. After all, here was a man being tried for murder; an alert sheriff certainly wouldn't take any chances. . . . The Lieutenant and I could sit out in my car alone for weeks, of course, but then there was no courtroom full of voters parading by my car. "Nice goin', Sheriff," I murmured. I saw that Mitch and Claude Dancer were engaged in a deep huddle over at their table. "See you," I said to my client and grabbed up my brief case and caught up with and followed the Judge into chambers.

A roll of camera film stood neatly in the middle of the Judge's desk. "When the cat's away the mice do play," the Judge said, dropping the film in his desk drawer. "Yes, Mr. Biegler?"

I hefted the burden I was carrying. "Here's about seven pounds of requests for instructions and also a trial brief, Your Honor," I said, laying a thick manila folder on his desk.

"Oh, fine thank you. I appreciate getting them and will look forward to reading them." Just then the Judge's phone rang and he clamped one big hand over the cradle and grinned sheepishly up at me, blushing like a boy. "Excuse me, Mr. Biegler," he said. "Today's our wedding anniversary—and I think that's Edith now returning my call."

"Congratulations," I murmured, softly closing the big door behind me, wondering that if it was true that every Jack must have his Jill— where and when would I ever find mine?

chapter 6

Parnell and I drove down along the lake shore to an outlying drive-in so that we could eat and talk undisturbed. Most of the tourists had already flown the U.P., winging southward like migratory birds, and I parked so that we could watch the cold glittering lake. We had left Maida home to mind the office and to type up some work or other Parnell had given her—and, I hoped, perhaps take in some money.

"I'm slowly falling in love with that judge," Parnell said. "He seems more and more like our old Judge Maitland—he runs his court like a courtroom, not a popcorn-strewn double feature. And I loved that jab he took at the morbid onlookers." Parnell chuckled. " 'Zealous students of homicide' indeed. Best of all, I think he's all lawyer; I'm sure he'll at least understand if not follow our requested instructions."

I nodded and puffed meditatively on my cheroot.

"You're sure you gave him all the instructions," Parnell went on, "including our newest ones on private arrest and irresistible impulse?"

Parnell had worked up these latest instructions all by himself; they were his pets, his special pride. They were also model statements of terse, understandable and accurate law. "I dumped the whole works on his lap, Parn," I said. "He'll now at least know what we're driving at."

"How do you like Mr. Claude Dancer?" Parnell said archly, looking at me sideways out of the corners of his glasses.

I grunted. "He's going to make us a lot more work," I said. Parnell broke into a smile. "Say, you old goat," I accused him, "I actually believe you're glad Mitch got him in the case."

Parnell's grin broadened. "Well, I like a good fight, boy, and I've got me a fine ringside seat." He continued more soberly. "As a matter of fact, Polly, I'd been a little worried over you and this Mitch."

"What do you mean?"

"Well, this young Mitch fellow is a good boy and will doubtless make a good prosecutor some day if he sticks at it. But as of now you two are so clearly mismatched that I was afraid you'd either not come awake or, if you did, that there might be built up in the jury a sort of unconscious under-dog reaction in favor of Mitch. There's no danger of that now."

"No, Parn," I said, "there's no danger of that now. And I won't likely fall asleep. In fact I've got a hunch—a trained intuition, as the Judge said—that we're in for a real slugging match."

Far out on the gently heaving lake I watched an ore boat slowly hove over the horizon trailing its long tail of smoke like a great floating marine bird, a bird smoking a big cigar. Pretty soon all the boats would be diesels, I thought, and then they would all look like barges on a grimy canal. *They'd* already doomed the old haunting steam whistle, whoever a sinister "they" might be. Wasn't science wonderful? Pretty soon we'd doubtless have mechanical trout. . . .

"Mitch didn't even make a *try* for a psychiatric examination," I said, almost ruefully. "And here we've wasted all that lovely law we looked up on our constitutional question. But I don't like the sly way he smuggled this guy Dancer into the case. He could at least have let me know sooner."

Parnell grinned even more. "I like your keen sense of partisanship, Polly, but don't let it carry you away." I looked at him sharply. "At least you *now* know Claude Dancer's in the case—but neither of them know that I am. Doesn't old Parnell offset Mr. Dancer just a little?" He touched me on the arm. "A little sense of proportion, Polly, and all will be well."

I coudn't help smiling. "You'll do for twelve Claude Dancers, Parn," I said, yawning. "I guess what I need is a decent night's sleep."

"You'll get it," Parnell said, "but not until this case is over." He tugged out his big silver watch. "C'mon, boy, it's time for court. The bell is about ready to ring for round one of the main bout."

The trial began quietly enough. When the crowded court convened I asked the Judge if Laura Manion might sit at our counsel table and he granted my request and Laura joined us. Then the Judge nodded at Mitch's table and Mitch got up and quietly walked up before the jury—"May it please the court and ladies and gentlemen of the jury"—and proceeded to give the People's opening statement. At last we were away. . . . First he introduced Claude Dancer to the jury—"the assistant Attorney General who, at my request, will be associated with me during the trial"—and Claude Dancer got up and made a nice brief friendly bow to the jury and modestly sat down.

Mitch's opening statement was good; it was clear and brief and contained no less than it should. In fact it was so well organized that I suspected that the clever hand of Claude Dancer might have manipulated the strings. I stole a look at Parnell. From the delighted grin on his face I knew he was thinking the same thing. "Why, that nasty old man," I thought, "he's really enjoying seeing me put on the spot." Mitch's statement was as significant in its omissions as it was in what it contained. He made no mention of rape or the taking of any lie-detector tests. It was now plain that the prosecution intended to hew to the line of murder and to block, if it could, any proof of anything else. I clamped my jaw shut and hunched myself forward and stared at Mitch. It had also grown plain that there was no danger of my falling asleep.

"The defense claims that the defendant was temporarily insane at the time the fatal shots were fired," Mitch was saying. "We expect to prove that he was sane and that what he did was done in the heat of passion and anger. We further expect to show that the killing was premeditated and the result of malice aforethought, as the Judge will define those terms. In other words, ladies and gentlemen of the jury, we fully expect to prove and will prove, that the defendant, Frederic Manion, was guilty of the crime of first-degree murder. I thank you."

Mitch returned to his table, where Claude Dancer was silently but rather obviously congratulating him on his opening statement. Rather too obviously, I thought; if my guess was right about the inspiration and source of the statement this byplay smacked a little too much of self-congratulation. And corny deception. If it was true that all good trial lawyers were part actor, then this little man Dancer bid fair to be a little dandy. In any case I found myself growing unaccountably irked with him—and he hadn't yet opened his mouth. He might think he could fool the jury with his behind-the-scenes manipulation of this case, but I resented his thinking he could so easily fool me. But maybe, I thought—maybe he didn't give a damn about fooling me; after all, I didn't have a vote on the jury. I was suffering, I saw, the first vague pangs of a blossoming and abiding love for Mr. Dancer.

"Mr. Biegler," the Judge said. "Do you wish to make your statement now?"

"If Your Honor please," I said, rising, "the defense would like to reserve its statement until later."

"Very well," he said, looking at Mitch's table. "Call your first witness."

"The People will call Dr. Homer Raschid," Mitch announced.

Dr. Raschid, the pathologist at St. Francis' Hospital in Iron Bay, came forward and Clovis Pidgeon popped up dramatically to swear him in, much like a poised tympanist in a hundred-piece orchestra who has waited patiently for a half hour to hit a tiny triangle a single blow. "Clovis the Oath-giver," I thought.

"You do solemnly swear that you will tell the truth, the whole truth, and nothing but the truth, so help you God," Clovis quavered in that lovely far-ranging tenor. There was one thing about Clovis: when he swore a witness that witness stayed sworn. How could any man possibly lie after such a solemn and moving injunction? Yet it was remarkable how many found that they could. . . .

"I do," Dr. Raschid said, and took the witness chair. He was a lean, thin-faced, high-domed sort of individual who looked as though he would be more at home writing sonnets than carving up cadavers. I had never read any of his poetry but I knew him as a highly competent pathologist.

"Your name, please?" Mitch asked.

"Homer Raschid," the doctor replied.

"What is your business or profession?"

"Medical doctor."

"Do you have any specialty, Doctor?"

"Pathologist. St. Francis' Hospital, this city." The doctor spoke rapidly, as though he were anxious to get away for a dental appointment. In a dozen years I had never seen him otherwise, in court or out.

"How long have you practiced medicine, Doctor?"

"Ah. . . ." The doctor blinked his eyes as though he was astonished over the way time flew. "Thirty-one years."

"Where did you obtain your medical education?"

I arose swiftly. "The doctor's eminent qualifications are admitted," I said and Mitch nodded and the doctor looked gratefully over at me, as though I had conferred an honorary degree. I was not trying to butter him up but to get on with the trial and avoid as much needless boredom as possible. Everybody knew that Doc Raschid knew his stuff and that he wouldn't lie to save his own grandmother. On with the butchery. . . .

"Did you have occasion to perform an autopsy on the body of one Barney Quill?" Mitch asked.

"I did."

"When and where?"

"On Sunday night, August seventeenth, in St. Francis' Hospital, this city."

"At whose request?"

"Coroner Leipart's."

"Who was present?"

"The coroner and Detective Sergeant Durgo of the state police and two or three other officers—and of course myself."

"Who identified the body?"

"They did."

"Will you please tell us your findings, Doctor?" Mitch asked.

The doctor reached in a manila folder he was carrying and extracted some sheets of paper. "I made up an autopsy report," he said. "It is fairly long and I will summarize in lay terms if you like."

I arose. "We will agree to such a summary if the People will."

Mitch turned and glanced at Claude Dancer. "The People agree," he said. "Go on, Doctor."

"Well, there were multiple penetrating and perforating wounds of the body such as might be caused by bullets. All in all there were ten such wounds, as though all the bullets had entered and left. One bullet had entered the front of the right shoulder and emerged at the posterior aspect of the right shoulder at the posterior axillary line—pardon me, came out on the other side."

"Go on, Doctor."

"Two bullets entered at the region of the right clavicle and came out at the spine; another went through the heart and right lung and emerged at the right thoracic wall at the level of the ninth rib in the mid axillary line, resulting in massive hemorrhage in both pleural spaces. The fifth bullet perforated the abdomen two inches below the level of the umbilicus and passed through the recti abdominal muscles and emerged about four inches to the left of the mid line. The peritoneum and abdominal cavity were not penetrated."

The wry thought occurred to me that if this was a summary in lay terms, then all of us would have had to take advanced Latin if the good doctor had chosen to give us the full treatment. It also occurred to me that lawyers were slaves to barroom idiom compared with these doctors.

"Were you able to determine the cause of death?" Mitch asked.

"I was."

"Could death have been caused by these wounds you have testified to?"

"They could—it could, I mean."

"In your opinion, Doctor, was death caused by these wounds?"

"It was. In my opinion the wound through the thorax and heart was the immediate and major cause of death. The other wounds of course contributed to death."

"Have you made a typewritten report of your findings?"

"I have. I have it and some copies here."

"May I have them?"

The doctor handed Mitch the copies of the report. "I ask that this original autopsy report be marked People's Exhibit 1 for identification," he said, handing one to the court reporter, who looked up at the clock and then scribbled the People's exhibit number on the paper. Mitch then brought the report over and handed it to me, along with an extra copy. "The People hand the defense the autopsy report for examination," he said.

"A little time, please, Your Honor," I requested, and the Judge blinked and nodded his assent.

The report consisted of five pages of closely typed analysis, tracing in vast detail the course of the bullets and the massive damage done. I was wrong; the doctor's oral summary had been a form of abbreviated slang compared with this. It also reported on other and undamaged areas of the body. Near the end of the report an interesting phrase caught my eye. "Spermatogenesis was occurring in both testes," it said. Had that finding been necessary to determine the cause of death? I read the report to the end and carried it up to Mitch, who stood by the witness. "The defense has no objection," I said.

"The People offer in evidence People's Exhibit 1 for identification as People's Exhibit 1," Mitch said, handing the report to the reporter.

"It may be so received and marked," Judge Weaver said.

"You may examine," Mitch said, and he went back to his table.

I advanced before the witness. "Doctor, did it appear to you that Barney Quill had been shot five times with bullets from a gun?" I asked.

"It did."

"And it appeared that each shot had plowed through him—as a layman might say—and come out on the other side?"

"That is correct."

"A layman might even say that the deceased was well ventilated?"

"Ha. . . . Precisely."

"Then I take it you did not find any bullets?"

"No. I mention that in my report."

"Yes, I noted that. But your conclusion that the wounds were caused by bullets was more or less of a surmise, then, was it not?"

"Well, in a sense yes."

"Based to some extent upon the history of the case and the information given you by the men who requested and were present at the autopsy?"

"Yes."

"You understood when you performed this autopsy that the subject had been shot by the defendant in a barroom?"

"Yes."

"And this and certain other information had been supplied you by the officers?"

"Well, yes. From them and from reading the newspaper, of course."

"But the officers gave you certain background information before you did your post?"

"That is correct."

Someone was walking softly behind me and I turned around. It was Claude Dancer, of all things, now rocking on his heels and staring up innocently at the skylight. I turned back to the witness. "So that to some extent your explorations were suggested by information you had received from them?"

"Yes. But my primary purpose was to determine the cause of death. And I did determine it. I didn't need any information from anybody to do that."

"Of course not, Doctor," I said. "You have made it very plain that the deceased was well drilled." I too wanted to make it perfectly clear to the jury that the defense was not trying to cast any doubt upon the evident fact that the Lieutenant had shot Barney; my design in fact lay quite the other way. But right now I was gunning for different if not bigger game—and the clever Claude Dancer was perhaps smelling a rat. In any case I would soon see. "Tell us then, Doctor," I said slowly, "tell us how come you checked to determine whether spermatogenesis was occurring in the subject's testes?"

"*I object!*" a deep booming voice exploded in my ears, and Claude Dancer had finally flung off the mask of being a mere helper.

"On what grounds, Mr. Dancer?" the Judge inquired mildly.

"On the grounds of incompetency and immateriality," he said. "The People have called this witness to show the cause of death. He has shown it. Cross-examination should be confined to that issue. Surely the question of whether this man was capable of—of spermatogenesis or what not would have no bearing on that issue."

"Mr. Biegler?" the Judge said.

"That is precisely why I asked the question, Your Honor," I said. I turned and picked up the autopsy report from the stenographer's desk. "I now read from that portion of the doctor's report called General Findings on the top of page five, and I quote, 'Spermatogenesis was occurring in both testes.' That is part of the People's autopsy report. That report has now been admitted in evidence in this case and I think I am entitled to inquire into anything that is in their report."

"The objection is overruled," the Judge said. "Take the answer."

"You may answer now, Doctor," I said.

"Answer what?" the understandably bewildered doctor said. "I—I guess I forgot the question."

"Read back the question," the Judge told the reporter.

The reporter scowled and flipped the pages of his notebook, at the same time rapidly moving his lips, whether in reading or profanity I knew not. He found the place and cleared his throat. " 'How come, Doctor, you checked to determine whether spermatogenesis was occurring in the subject's testes?' " he read back in the bored singsong monotone that all court reporters seem occupationally compelled to cultivate.

"You may venture to answer now, Doctor," I suggested. "The coast is clear."

"Because they asked me to," the doctor replied.

"Who asked you to?"

"The officers present."

"I see," I said. "Now did you know when you made that examination that another doctor had taken a vaginal smear from the defendant's wife and had reported it negative for spermatozoa?"

"I did."

"Objection," Claude Dancer boomed. "Based on hearsay, irrelevant. . . . Report of other doctor best evidence."

"You're a little late, Mr. Dancer," the Judge said mildly. "The question seems to have been answered."

"Then I move that the answer be stricken and the jury instructed to disregard both the question and answer."

The Judge's voice seemed to rise a trifle. "The motion is denied. Please proceed, Mr. Biegler."

"Now the primary purpose of this portion of your examination was to determine whether or not the seminal fluid of the deceased contained sperm?" I went on.

"Correct."

"And that inquiry had nothing to do with determining the cause of death?"

"Nothing whatever."

"In determining death you would ordinarily never make such an examination on a body that had so obviously met death from gunshot wounds?"

"Never."

"And you made this particular examination solely because you were asked to do so by the prosecuting officers?"

"I did."

"Now, Doctor, if a question ever arose as to whether a man had had intercourse with a woman who claimed that he had, and her smear for sperm showed negative, whereas the tests on the man were positive for seminal sperm, all that might be some evidence that he had *not* had intercourse, might it not?"

"Objection," Claude Dancer thundered behind me.

"Overruled," the Judge said.

"Yes," the witness answered.

"So that if that question ever arose at some later date—like say at a murder trial—nobody could argue or claim—not even a defense lawyer, for example—that the claimed absence of sperm in the woman *might* have been caused by the absence of sperm in the man?"

I turned around and looked at Claude Dancer, jerking my head sideways, as though ducking a snowball, and the courtroom tittered and Claude Dancer regarded me stonily. I turned back to the witness.

"I suppose that is true," he said. "I assumed then as I do now that that was the main purpose of their request."

"Objection—the witness assumes," Claude Dancer pressed.

"Objection sustained," the Judge ruled.

"Move that the answer be stricken and the jury instructed to disregard."

"The motion is granted. The jury will please disregard the last answer. Proceed, Mr. Biegler."

"Now, Doctor, were you asked to make an examination to determine whether the deceased had recently had intercourse and reached a sexual climax?"

"I was not."

"Did you make any such examination?"

"I did not."

"Could you have done so?"

"I could have."

"Would it have disclosed the answer?"

"It should have."

"But you were not asked to, and you did not?"

"Correct."

"And you did not hear the subject discussed?"

"I did not."

I stole a look at the jury. Some of the jurors were looking at each other and my Finnish ex-soldier was staring straight at me. Did I seem to detect a sort of half-smile on his face?

"Now, Doctor, one or two more questions and I think we'll about be done. Did you make any examination to determine the alcoholic content of the blood of the deceased?"

"I did not."

"Were you asked to?"

"No."

"Could you have made such a determination if requested?"

"Very easily."

"That's all, Doctor. Thank you," I said, and I went back to my table.

"Nice going," the Lieutenant whispered.

"We've at least got our foot in the door," I whispered back.

"Any re-direct, Mr. Prosecutor?" the Judge inquired.

Mitch and his helper conferred. "No further questions," Mitch said, half rising.

The Judge turned to Dr. Raschid. "You may go, Doctor. That is all." As the doctor gratefully sped on his way the Judge looked at the clock. "We will take a fifteen-minute recess," he said gravely. "All right, Mr. Sheriff."

Max hammered the crowded courtroom to its feet. "Hear ye, hear ye, hear ye—this honorable court is recessed for fifteen minutes." There was a collective sigh, like an escaping jet of steam, and most of the crowd scraped and shuffled its way to the exits.

chapter 7

Parnell had disappeared and was nowhere to be found. I hoped that he had not developed a sudden and overpowering thirst. I hurriedly joined the Manions in the conference room, with the Sheriff hovering importantly outside the door—the observant jury had to pass that way—and explained to them the possible significance of some of the testimony that had been developed from the good Dr. Raschid, most of which I was pleased to see they already grasped. Yes, the prosecution now seemed bent on suppressing all mention of the rape, they readily saw. Perhaps if they saw it that way the jury also might, I hoped. Anyway, I could take care of all that later in my argument. I scribbled a quick reminder in my trusty notebook, without which most trial lawyers would fly straight out into space.

But most of all I sought to calm and reassure the Manions; the important thing right now was to keep *them* from flying off into space; most of our real work together had been done. In a tantalizing sense the trial itself was like a well-rehearsed play, a play that was to be played but one night and then carted off forever to storage. But then again, in another and more disturbing sense, it wasn't like a well-rehearsed play at all: inevitably some character would forget his lines or, worse yet, someone might sneak in some surprise new dialogue that might change the whole course of the drama. I was too old and battered an attendant at courtroom "first nights" not to be aware of that ever-gnawing probability. *Something* would surely happen; like poor old Smoky Madigan and his expectant June bride, it was not a question of *whether* but *when*. . . .

"I don't like that Claude Dancer," Laura said, crushing out her cigarette. "He's—he's so cocky and self-assured. And he acts like he hates us."

"Confidentially, Laura," I said, "I'm learning not to love him myself." For one thing, I thought but did not say, he was far too smart and dangerous; moreover he possessed the buzzing persistence of a gnat.

The Lieutenant, sitting on a cold radiator over by the window reading about his then approaching trial in an old *Mining Gazette*, looked up and spoke. "When the Judge overruled Dancer, when you were questioning the doctor, one of the jurors grinned and almost laughed out loud."

"Was it that husky young blond fellow sitting in the first row, on the extreme left end?" I asked.

"That's the one. He seems to be a fan of yours. He watches you like a cat."

I thoughtfully lit a cigar and stared out at the lake. Maybe, I thought, maybe I had better pretty well try my case for this intelligent young juror. (Any fan of Biegler's, of course, was by hypothesis nudging the very portals of genius.) I remembered that when I was D.A. I had almost unconsciously selected and played to a lone juror during my longer trials. Some small sign usually came along, some tiny tacit recognition that you and the juror were talking the same language. And that way one seemed to gain—or at least I seemed to gain—a greater sense of immediacy and impact during one's efforts; that way there seemed to be a tangible goal upon which to concentrate, a discernible target at which to aim whatever arts of conviction and persuasion one possessed. "Hm. . . ." I said absently, holding out my lighter for Laura.

"Thanks, Paul," she said, removing her glasses. "I can't see across the room with these darn things. Can't you also manage to have me knitting bootees?"

I grinned evilly. "Scarcely, my dear," I said. "Scarcely."

Yes, my work was pretty well done with the Manions. If they hadn't learned their roles, if they didn't know their parts, it was far too late to do anything about it now. I remembered the time when, years before, I had taken my bar exams in Lansing, and had gone there several days early, perhaps hoping to soak up some wisdom and a measure of belated inspiration by sheer propinquity alone. Owlish and fear-haunted, I had crept nervously up to the supreme court and called on the clerk, amiable little Jay Metzner, who then also acted as clerk for the bar examiners. He had stopped me at the door.

"Halt!" he commanded. "Not another step, young man! From your ghastly and ravaged appearance I can see you are here bent on taking the bar exams. So you've called on little ol' Jay and you want me to give you an open sesame." He had come over and put both hands on my shoulders. "Well, here's your open sesame, son. Go out and have yourself a few drinks, not too many of course. Then pick yourself up a willing girl if you can. The campus of this old capitol building is fairly heaving with them. Then go out and forget all about your goddam bar examinations." He shook his head. "If after three years of monastic study you don't know your stuff, by God, son, you never will, you never will." And little Jay had been right, bless his soul.

Max Battisfore popped his head in the door. "Five more minutes, Polly," he said. "The Judge wants to see you."

"Thanks. Right away, Max," I said. "I'm getting my grease paint back on. The show must go on."

The Judge and Mitch and Claude Dancer sat chatting in chambers along with the pardoned young photographer from the *Gazette*.

"This young man says his Public, meaning his boss, wants him to take our pictures—out of the courtroom, that is," the Judge smilingly told me. "I thought defense counsel might like to join us."

"Thank you, Judge," I said. "That was thoughtful of you." I had known this subject would come up, sooner or later, and I was ready for it. "But I'm sorry," I lied softly. "Right now I'm up to my ears with my clients. Perhaps later on."

"Very well," the Judge quickly said. "By all means get back to your people."

As I turned away I thought I detected an appreciative gleam in the Judge's eyes. Was he aware of my strategy to build up the all-powerful, much-publicized State against the lone, unsung—and unphotographed—defense? "Over here away from the windows, gentlemen," I heard the photographer saying. I hurried back and told the Manions that under no circumstances should they permit their pictures to be taken. There would be time enough for all that later on, if things went right. I did not even try to explain; just now they had quite enough on their minds.

"Hear ye, hear ye, hear ye. . . ."

The rest of the afternoon session lurched by with a dreary sort of speed. Trials are never fast, except on TV, where drab reality must ever yield to the more pressing reality of peddling the sponsor's nostrums. By stipulation the charts were introduced in evidence and set up before the jury. The next prosecution witness was Coroner Leipart, a rather shy-appearing little man who led a double life—as coroner and undertaker.

Under Mitch's questioning—Claude Dancer seemed to have slipped his mask back on—he told of finding Barney Quill's riddled body lying face down behind the bar. "Lying in a pool of blood." It lay on its right side near the middle of the bar and, yes, the man was quite dead. The bartender had let them in when he had arrived with the state police around 2:00 A.M. What had he done then? Well, after the measurements and "pics" had been taken he'd put the body in the basket and fetched it in to Iron Bay and held it in cold storage until the autopsy on Sunday, which he had attended. Then he had fetched the body back to his place and embalmed it and shipped it off to Wisconsin. As the coroner gave his testimony the thought occurred to me that he might have been talking about the misadventures of a roll of linoleum.

"Your witness," Mitch said.

On cross-examination I brought out that the bartender was alone when he had admitted the coroner and the state police; that this was over an hour from the reported time of the killing; that he, the coroner, had turned the clothing of the deceased over to the state police, who had presumably shipped it to East Lansing to be tested in the crime laboratory. . . .

"For what purpose?" I asked.

"For evidence of sperm or seminal stain," the coroner answered.

I half looked around, waiting for the Lansing "organ" to thunder, but all was pastoral silence. "Do you know the results of those clothing tests, if any?"

"I do not. The state police should."

"Were you present during the autopsy when the officers asked Dr. Raschid to determine the spermatic capacities of the deceased?"

"I was there at all times."

"And?"

"Yes, I was there then."

"And was that done for the purpose of refuting any possible later claim that the deceased might not have possessed those capacities?"

"That was my understanding, yes."

"Was there any discussion among the officers about asking the doctor to determine whether the deceased had recently ejaculated?" I asked. (I wondered how the comely juror, the heavily virginal Doris Flanders, was weathering all this. I sneaked a small look and found that she was bearing up remarkably well, leaning forward on the edge of her seat, in fact.)

"There was some discussion, yes," the coroner said.

"In the presence of the doctor?"

"No."

"And no such examination was made."

"I'm not sure that there could have been."

"Oh? Were you here when Dr. Raschid testified earlier?"

"No, I just got here. I got two cases waiting for me now."

I lifted my eyebrows in surprise. "Two more murdered people?

My, my—I hadn't heard. Seems it never rains but it pours. . . ."

"No, two bodies."

"In your role as coroner or embalmer?"

"Waiting to be embalmed."

"My heartfelt congratulations, Mr. Coroner, but will you please answer my previous question?"

"What question?"

"I asked you whether in fact Dr. Raschid made any examination to find out whether the deceased had"—idiom tugged mightily, but idiom regretfully lost—"had recently reached a sexual climax."

"He did not."

"Or any test for the alcoholic content of the blood?"

"He did not."

"Was that discussed by the officers?"

"I don't know."

"That's all, Mr. Coroner. I think you can get back to your waiting customers now."

Smiling: "They're in no hurry, Mr. Biegler. They rarely complain."

Mitch had no re-direct and he next called a commercial photographer who quickly identified a flock of 6 x 10 glossy photographs he had taken for the prosecution, all of which were by stipulation admitted swiftly in evidence. Barney would have loved them, I thought, because they were all of him: various views of the great Barney lying inert and crumpled behind the bar; Barney lying exposed on the slab, full face, left and right profile, Barney on his back, the ventilation marks showing up splendidly. And showing, too, that beautifully superb and willful body which had been stilled forever all because of one dark and tangled impulse. . . .

"To the defense," Mitch said.

I was about ready to waive cross-examination when Laura Manion leaned over and whispered to me excitedly. "That man! He took some pictures of me that night. I—I just remembered. . . ."

"Good girl," I whispered, and I slowly arose and left my table and walked thoughtfully up toward the witness. Well, here was the first switch in the expected dialogue, I thought; with luck this time perhaps fortunately for our side. But there would be other times, times that would hurt, there always were.

"Mr. Burke," I said pleasantly, indicating the latest exhibits, "were these all the pictures you took for this case?"

He shot a look at Mitch's table. "No, there were some others."

"Perhaps they didn't turn out?" I said.

"No, they all turned out." A note of professional pride crept into his voice. "Most of my pictures turn out."

"Of course, Mr. Burke," I said. "And these you have produced here are splendid examples of your craftmanship." I paused. "Perhaps you forgot to bring the others?" There was no answer and I did not press. "Perhaps the others were needless duplicates?"

"No. They weren't any duplicates of poses."

"Oh," I said surprised. I glanced at the jury and saw that there was growing contagion in my surprise. "Perhaps the other pictures had nothing to do with the case at all?—perhaps they were merely some interesting little side shots? Made to gratify an artistic whim? A gnarled stump you couldn't resist? Perhaps a tree? Or a rummaging bear at the Thunder Bay dump?" I paused. "Perchance even a woman?"

The witness was not happy. "They were photographs of Lieutenant Manion's wife."

I paused and looked around at the clock. The heads of Mitch and his assistant were nodded close in a huddle. I glanced at the jurors who were in turn glancing quickly at each other. My young Finnish juror was looking straight at me and—was it possible?—seemed almost to nod. I turned back to the witness.

"And these pictures of Mrs. Laura Manion—they turned out well?"

"Excellent."

"When did you take them?"

"That very night."

"Then they would show just how Mrs. Manion looked right after the shooting?"

Grimly: "They certainly would."

"How many did you take?"

"Three."

Again I heard the short restless padding footsteps behind me; Mr. Dancer was again stalking my rear.

"Would you mind showing them to me?"

"I don't have them—they're back at my studio."

"What a pity. . . . And I believe you didn't answer me when I asked if you forgot them. How come you didn't bring them along?"

"I was requested not to."

"Hm. . . . Certainly not by anyone connected with this case?"

"Yes, sir."

"Come, Mr. Burke, tell us by whom?"

"*Objection!*" thundered in my ears.

"Overruled," said the Judge, as I ostentatiously ducked and drilled my ear with my little finger—the ear on the jury side. "The witness may answer."

"Mr. Burke," I said softly, "could you have been told not to bring them by anybody presently standing, say, within three city blocks of me?"

"He's standing right behind you. It was Mr. Dunstan there. He merely said it would not be necessary to bring the pictures of Mrs. Manion to court."

"*Dancer!*" Claude Dancer's voice grated in my ear. "The name is Mr. Dancer, not Dunstan."

"See, the man's name is *Mister* Dancer," I reproved the witness. "And the Dunstans might not like any confusion either, you know—they might possibly know Mr. Dancer." (I had to take my fun where I found it; Dancer's turn would inevitably come.)

"I'm sorry," the witness said. "Mr. *Dancer* told me not to."

"Well, if you don't have the pictures you can't very well show them," I said. "But perhaps you can describe for us the picture you saw of Mrs. Manion that night with your own eyes? That might even be better."

"Objection," Mr. Dancer said, less thunderously this time. "Clearly irrelevant and matter of defense, if admissible then, which I doubt."

"I withdraw the question," I said quickly, before the Judge could make his ruling. If little Mr. Dancer thought he was helping his case by keeping this testimony from the jury, which I guessed must be fairly consumed with curiosity about now, he could block away. Most of the disappointment and frustration would be laid at his door. "The witness is back to you," I said, bowing and returning to my table.

"No further questions," Mr. Dancer said, glaring stonily at me. My time will come, I thought. Courage, Camille. . . .

I looked around for Parnell, to bask in his approval, but I could not locate him. "Hell," I thought, "just when I have a fairly good round the old boy would be out puttering around in the locker room." Anyway I hoped he wasn't out there swigging the rubbing alcohol.

"I was having a quiet beer up at the bar," Carl Yates, the game warden, was testifying, the first of a long procession of eyewitnesses. "I had been out earlier patrolling for headlighters. I suspected some of those young soldiers stationed near Thunder Bay were roaring around at night shining deer with their jeeps. In fact I'd already caught several. . . . Well, I'm standing there having my beer, like I said, and suddenly I hear a series of shots, and I turn toward the sound—and there's a man standing up on the rail, leaning far over the bar, clicking an empty gun at something down there below on the other side."

"What did you do?" Mitch asked.

"I got to hell—" the witness glanced quickly up at Judge Weaver. "I'm sorry—I got out of there fast. No place for a game warden."

"Did you know the man who was doing the shooting?"

"Not by name—but I would recognize him."

"Do you see him in the courtroom now?" Mitch asked, and I quickly prodded the Lieutenant to his feet.

"Yes, he's sitting—no, standing—next to Lawyer Biegler there at that other long table—the man with the lieutenant's uniform, with the mustache."

"You are referring and pointing to the defendant in this case, Frederic Manion?"

"I am."

"Your witness," Mitch said.

In my cross-examination I made no attempt to inquire into what movements, if any, Barney may or may not have made just prior to the shooting. I felt that the chances were good to excellent that most of the eyewitnesses, including this one, had not seen any movements simply because just previous to the shooting they were not paying attention, there was no reason to, and that for me to have each witness deny seeing any movements from Barney would be to gratuitously build up the jury's belief that none had occurred. I likewise made no attempt to cast any doubt on the fact that the Lieutenant had fired the fatal shots, in fact my questions assumed quite the contrary. Only Parnell's favorite lawyer, old Amos Crocker, the one and only Willie the Weeper, possessed the bland hardihood to stand before a jury and deny a shooting in one breath and in the next insist that his client was crazy when he did it.

"Mr. Yates," I said, conjuring up a pretty picture, "when Lieutenant Manion shot Barney Quill and the latter slumped and fell and the Lieutenant then stood up on the bar rail and leaned down over the bar and emptied his gun into the fallen man"—I paused—"did the Lieutenant say 'Take that, you s.o.b.' or words to that effect?"

"Not that I heard. My recollection is that at no time did the Lieutenant utter a sound. He came in like a mailman delivering the mail; he delivered his mail and turned around and calmly walked out."

One of the endless fascinations of trying cases, I thought, was the unexpectedly sharp word pictures lay witnesses sometimes painted without even half trying. In fact it was only when they tried that they failed. "Were there any signs of anger on his part?" I pressed on.

"None that I saw. Of course I did not get a good look or stop long after the shooting. I wheeled it for home."

"What time was it? The shooting, I mean?"

"About twelve-forty or twelve-forty-five, as I recall. It was one-one A.M. when I got home, I noted that."

"Now Mr. Yates, this well-earned nightcap of beer you were having—had the deceased treated you to that?"

"Yes. I had put my money on the bar but Barney waved it away. 'On the house, Carl,' he said."

"I see. And was the bar crowded?"

"Yes, practically the whole length. It seemed to me the Lieutenant had got himself in the only place that was left. There's some rails there."

"You are referring to the waitresses' service station?"

"I think so. Anyway, that place where Barney never wanted us to stand."

"And had Barney bought the whole bar a round of drinks?"

"Yes, all of us. I heard tell later it wasn't the first round he bought."

"And was he drinking?"

"Well, he was on the round he bought me."

"Was buying house drinks his usual practice?—if you know?"

"Hm. . . . Let me think." The witness paused. "It was the first time I'd seen him treat the bar since I was stationed at Thunder Bay. That'll be three years come May month."

"And you were a fairly regular customer at Barney's—for your occasional nightly pint of beer, I mean?" I did not want to put this candid hard-working game warden on the spot or appear to make him out a bar fly; for my part any man that protected our U.P. deer and fish—especially the trout for Biegler—was entitled to swill all the beer he could hold, free or not.

He smiled appreciatively. "Yes, a fairly regular customer," he said.

"I see. And where at the bar were you standing and by whom?"

"At the far end, nearest the street, talking to the Mongoose twins." (The Mongoose brothers were two young Indians, both ex-service men, and Parnell's and my pre-trial investigation indicated that any game warden could well afford to relax a bit provided only he could keep the brothers Mongoose forever under his watchful eye.)

I purposely did not get into the anticipated controversial subject of Barney's prowess with firearms and pistols, though this witness undoubtedly would have known. I wanted to get the stage clearly set for the jury in other directions, and not have the picture distorted or forgotten in a flurry of confusing objections from the pouncing Mr. Dancer. The pistols could come later.

"Where was the bartender during all the shooting?" I asked.

"Standing over near the door, I believe. At least I spoke to him there when I came in."

"Was it the usual practice, if you know, for Barney to work alone behind the bar?"

"No, it wasn't. In fact I remarked about it to the Mongoose twins. He often stood at the end or behind the bar, but rarely waited on the trade. His bartender or the barmaids usually attended to that."

"And was it equally unusual for the bartender to be out on the floor—standing by the door?"

The witness looked up thoughtfully at the courtroom skylight. "Well, now that you speak of it, it was. 'Phonse usually stayed behind the bar."

A few more pieces were slipping quietly into the growing mosaic of proof. I glanced around and sure enough Mr. Dancer was again stalking me; the little man seemed to have sensed it too. Well, he'd taken all that trouble to stalk me, and wouldn't it be a shame to keep him standing there so eager and mute? I'd quick have to ask something that would exercise that lovely voice.

"Now, Mr. Yates," I went on, "just before the shooting how did the deceased appear?"

"How do you mean?"

"Did he seem like a man who was nervous or fidgety and expecting something bad to happen"—I paused—"or instead cheerful and calm and at ease?" The question was objectionable on several counts, as

I well knew, but I gambled that my Mr. Dancer was in turn gambler enough and curious enough to want to learn the answer. It looked like I'd won; all was golden silence behind me.

"He appeared perfectly calm and at ease," Carl Yates answered. I could almost hear Claude Dancer purring with contentment behind me, doubtless thinking of what a massive blow our rape story had just taken. How could a man who had just perpetrated such a brutal assault and rape at the same time appear so calm and at ease? I paused to let this impression sink in, and then thought it was time to shatter Claude Dancer's little dream.

I spoke swiftly. "So that if you were not here today testifying in the *murder* case of People versus Frederic Manion, Mr. Yates, you could nevertheless still honestly say the same thing—that Barney Quill was calm and at ease—even if the case being tried here now were instead the trial of People versus Barney Quill for *rape?*"

The witness' unmistakable "yes" and Claude Dancer's booming objection exploded in my ears at the same time. The little man was beside himself, and I wondered how the poor racing reporter could possibly take down the excited flood of words.

"The question is clearly objectionable," the Judge ruled sternly when Claude Dancer finally sputtered into silence, "and both it and the answer will be stricken and the jury asked to totally disregard them." He frowned down at me. "Surely, Mr. Biegler, you must have known how highly improper your question was. In any case I must warn you against a repetition."

"I'm sorry, Your Honor," I apologized contritely. "Please put it down to the excessive zeal of battle," I murmured. "I'll try to mend my ways." I turned to Claude Dancer and the little bristling military brushes of hair on either side of his head seemed to be standing straight out. "The People's witness is back to your assistant, Chief Prosecutor Dancer," I said.

"No questions," Mr. Dancer snapped, and at last any question or pretense of who was assisting whom had flown to the four winds.

As I sat down I saw that Parnell was back in his place, mercifully sober and grinning from ear to ear. We had argued for weeks over the strategy of that last objectionable question, Parnell being for it. His point was that we had to bring out early and dramatically in the trial that if Barney had actually raped Laura he was doing the only thing he could have done, short of running away or surrendering, namely, calmly brazening it out and at the same time building up his defenses to the inevitable charge of rape. Barney *had* to appear calm. I glanced at my favorite juror and found him looking at me. His eyes lit up and I glanced quickly away; it looked like old Parnell had maybe won again. In any case the rape now clearly had its foot in the door. And equally clear to the jury, I hoped, was the People's settled determination to dislodge it and keep it out.

The next eight or ten witnesses, all men, had been standing at the bar and, aside from the minor discrepancies which appear inevitable when different people try to describe the same event, all pretty much agreed that the Lieutenant had walked up to the bar and wordlessly emptied his gun into Barney, that he had stood up on the bar rail after Barney had fallen, and then had as silently turned and left the place. All agreed that the shooting occurred around 12:45. From various of these witnesses, including the inscrutable Mongoose twins, I developed on cross-examination that Barney had bought as high as five rounds of drinks that night; that he himself had apparently taken whisky each time; that all this sudden barroom philanthropy was a noteworthy departure from his previous austerity (the husband of one of the waitresses disagreed with this and, noting the lushness of his large red nose, I did not have the heart to dispute him); that the bartender was standing out on the floor, also a fairly unusual procedure; that Barney seemed to be in good spirits and calm and at ease. From two of the witnesses, I brought out that they had spoken to the Lieutenant as he had approached the bar, just before the shooting, but that the defendant had not returned their greeting or looked at them. These same two witnesses also thought they heard Barney Quill say "Good evening, Lieutenant" or words to that effect as the defendant approached the bar.

Mitch conducted the examination of all of these witnesses, as he did the two waitresses who followed, and I concluded that the Dancer was either trying to recreate the somewhat tarnished impression that Mitch was still running the prosecution or else was saving himself for the more important witnesses ahead, probably both. Neither waitress added much to the story of the shooting, except that one of them also told me on cross-examination that the Lieutenant had failed to return her greeting as he had entered. The other waitress, an amiable plump girl, drew a rumble of laughter when she told Mitch that after the first shot she had "galloped for the ladies' rest room," which in turn drew an admonitory bang from the Judge's gavel and a scowl at the crowd from the Judge.

By then it was going on for five o'clock, and in answer to Mitch's query whether to call any new witnesses, the Judge nodded for him to go ahead, and Mitch had looked at me and shrugged in mute resignation and called Ditlef Pedersen. We not only had a judge who ran his court with an iron hand but one who firmly believed in the full working day foi jurors, lawyers, and witnesses alike. My heart was beginning to go out to Max Battisfore for being so long away from his beloved patrol. Law enforcement out in the brambles was clearly going to pot.

Ditlef Pedersen (I loved the name; it rolled on one's tongue like a lozenge) was the man who had sat at the table near the outside door with his wife and sister-in-law. It was near this table that the bartender, Alphonse Paquette, had stood "resting" after Barney had taken over the bar. Under Mitch's questioning, Mr. Pedersen, a tall blond plasterer from Iron Bay, told how he and his party had stopped off at the bar to have a drink and to pick up some beer to take to their lake-shore cottage for the weekend; how they had chatted for some time with the bartender, who stood by their table; and of how they had suddenly heard a series of shots—"they sounded like giant firecrackers"—and had then seen Lieutenant Manion leaving the place, followed quickly by the bartender.

"Your witness," Mitch said.

"Did the bartender return or remain outside?" I asked.

"He came right back in."

"Did he say anything to you?"

"Yes, he said he recognized it was Lieutenant Manion."

"Anything else?"

"No, he hurried over toward the bar."

"Are you sure he said nothing else?" I pressed, thinking of the "Buster" business.

"Quite positive. We left shortly after. My wife was nervous—she was expecting, you know."

"I hadn't known, Mr. Pedersen. Now how long had the bartender stood by your table?"

"Quite a while—well over half an hour, I believe. Perhaps even more. We were in no hurry—a nice moonlit night and all."

"Yes, of course, Mr. Pedersen. Did the bartender sit down and talk with you?"

"He talked but didn't sit down, though we asked him to several times."

"You *asked* him to sit down?" I said. This was better than I had hoped for—the tired, resting—and watchful—bartender wouldn't even sit down when invited to.

"Yes, but he said he was expecting a friend from out of town and wanted to keep an eye out for him. He kept looking out the window."

I glanced around to the rows of waiting People's witnesses and found the bartender, Alphonse Paquette, sitting with folded arms and staring straight ahead. Mary Pilant was not to be seen; in fact neither Parnell nor I had observed her around the courthouse since the case had opened.

"Did the bartender talk to you and your party?"

"Occasionally. Just small talk—the weather, fishing, the tourists, the soldiers out at the firing point, how Barney had recently won another pistol shoot, casual stuff like that."

I could have gone up and kissed the man. "Casual stuff" indeed. "So the bartender told you that Barney had won another pistol shoot?" I said.

"Yes. We didn't pay much attention; it was an old story; Barney was always winning another pistol shoot—I guess he was one of the best in the business."

I paused thoughtfully. Trial lawyers who sought to polish perfection frequently only managed to cloud it instead. Perhaps I'd better leave well enough alone. I turned around toward Mitch, ignoring Claude Dancer, who was again lurking behind me. "Your witness, Mr. Prosecutor," I said.

Mitch glanced at Claude Dancer as I watched both him and the jury. Ah, there was the little informative shake of the head. "No questions," Mitch hurriedly said.

"Mr. Sheriff," the Judge said, "let's call it a day."

"Hear ye, hear ye . . ." the Sheriff thundered.

chapter 9

Parnell nodded at me and then got up and left for the car. I sat at our table and chatted with Laura and the Lieutenant for a spell while Max stood in an arm-folded "they-shall-not-pass" attitude at a respectable distance from our table. When the murmuring shuffling buzzing crowd of onlookers had finally disappeared, presumably winding their way back to the beauty parlors and damp caves where they dozed between murder trials, Max nodded at me and then jerked his head in the direction of the jail and hurried on his way. His little show was over. . . . My impulse was to let out an exultant whoop. That Max would at this point have left the Lieutenant unattended I took as the best omen so far of the trial; I had been watching carefully for such a sign; I had not the foggiest notion myself how we were progressing.

A lawyer seeking to appraise his case in the midst of a trial is like a deceived husband: he is frequently the last person to suspect the true state of affairs. Max's willingness to let the Lieutenant find his way back to the jail unattended was eloquently telling me that, in his opinion at least, my man was still not in too great danger. And I had developed a wholesome respect for the opinions of Mr. Max Battisfore on matters of mob psychology and the temper of the crowd. After all the man spent most of his waking hours studying it, a veritable Mr. Demos himself. I said nothing of this to the Manions.

"I've got bad news for you, Counselor," the Lieutenant said.

"Good news, bad news, news around the town," I hummed. "How now, Herr Lieutenant? Vass iss da pad noose, ya?"

"Laura picked up the mail earlier today and then forgot to give me a letter from the Army."

"Curses! Don't tell me our psychiatrist has broken a leg?"

"No, not quite that bad. The Army just wrote me they are holding up my pay until this case is over." He shrugged. "I'm sorry—I'd figured on making another payment on your fee."

A lawyer in the midst of trying his case is also apt to be like a visiting oilman running daft and amuck at Las Vegas: money is the farthest thing from his thoughts. "Don't worry about it, Lieutenant," I said airily. "How did you like that left jab I took at our little friend Dancer?"

"Yum," the Lieutenant said vaguely, and Laura reached over and impulsively touched my arm. "Win or lose, Paul, we'll never forget you. You're wonderful."

The talk was veering a little on the moist side and I gave the Manions some suggestions that had occurred to me during the day's take. We finally separated, Laura accompanying her husband out through the main courtroom door toward the jail, and I taking my usual route through the Judge's chambers, a half-conscious hangover from my days as D.A.

Judge Weaver was sitting alone at his desk reading a Michigan law report. A stack of opened and unopened bound law reports were lying around him on his desk. The manila folder containing our thick wedge of requested instructions lay at his elbow. He looked up. "Well, Mr. Biegler, another day, another dollar," he said pleasantly.

"You're a real bearcat for work, Judge," I said. "When do you eat?"

The Judge smiled. "Oh, I don't know. I guess I'm as lazy as the next man. But when counsel load me up with such brain-cracking requests for instructions as you've dumped on me, a man can't help but work. It looks like I'll be burning the midnight oil." He patted the manila folder. "You didn't throw these things together overnight."

"No, Judge," I said, feeling like a monstrous heel that I couldn't tell him that most of the work was Parnell's. "I hope you're finding some food for thought."

The Judge laid both of his big knuckly hands palms down in front of him on his desk. At that moment he reminded me of my dead father, Oliver, about to deliver one of his impromptu after-dinner perorations on the beauties of moderation and keeping early hours. The Judge turned and glanced thoughtfully out the window. "In no sense am I passing on the draft instructions you have given me. They may or may not ultimately be given, in whole or in part." He looked at me. "But you've obviously toiled and thought so hard over these instructions that it is perhaps only an act of mercy to tell you that so far they are checking out. Your authorities do what they should do: they sustain what you cite them for, no more and no less. So far they are among the best instructions on their points I've ever seen." He smiled. "Now let's talk about something else. Sit down and ignite one of your hideous Roman candles—they can't all be duds."

"Thank you, Judge," I murmured, doubly embarrassed because I could not give old Parnell his just due. "That is generous of you—a man gets pretty lonely and uncertain during a trial like this. It—it's like nightmare and ecstasy all stirred up together."

"Yes, I know, I know." The Judge pushed his book away and stuffed his briar pipe. I sat with one leg over the arm of my chair, staring out at the lovely empty lake, longing to be out there, floating along with a loaf of bread, a jug of wine and—and whom? I almost blushed; I had been thinking, of all things, of Mary Pilant.

"You like being a judge, don't you?" I said, forsaking my idle dream.

The Judge glanced at me keenly and smiled. "I have a confession to make, young man," he said, his pipe finally lit. "I am a rabid fan of murder trials, a fan just as hopeless in my way as those hordes of panting and painted harpies out there who are jamming our sessions. I am endlessly fascinated by the raw drama of a murder trial, of the defendant fighting so inarticulately for his freedom—his is the drama of understatement—, of the opposing counsel—those masters of overstatement, flamboyantly fighting for victory, for reputation, for more clients, for political advancement, for God knows what—, of the weathervane jury swaying this way and that, of the judge himself trying his damnedest to guess right and at the same time preserve a measure of decorum." He paused. "Yes, a murder trial is a fascinating pageant."

"Yes, Judge," I agreed soberly. "No play in the world is quite like it. In this kind of drama the show may not only close abruptly but the main actors lose all if they fail."

"It is interesting you should have said that." The Judge reached for a law book. "Listen to this. I found it the other day in Callaghan's work on Michigan procedure and practice—at Section 38.48. The editor who wrote it must be a frustrated philosopher or novelist." He expertly flipped the pages and stopped, murmuring "dum-dum-dum-dum" till he found the place. "Here it is. He is talking about jury trials." The Judge paused and cleared his throat and began reading.

" 'In the course of any jury trial there are likely to be many incidents which will later be raised, by disappointed and astute counsel, as ground for overturning the result,' " the Judge read. " 'This is particularly true in criminal trials, wherein every possible method of influencing the jury one way or the other is customarily resorted to and every conceivable error, in case of appeal, is presented to the reviewing court.' "

The Judge paused and looked up. "Here's the part. Now listen to this. 'The field is a most interesting one. It so far supersedes and renders inconsequential both stage and screen productions, and the best products of the novelists, by sheer force of accumulated actual experience, as to make outpourings of the imagination pale and wilt by factual contrast. . . . Whenever there is a jury trial there is neighborhood interest, reputations at stake, serious liability, and often even future life involved.'"

"Amen," I said. "That man certainly said a mouthful."

The Judge closed his book and slowly shoved it away. "I've presided at murder trials all over the state," he went on. "I actually look for the assignments. Most judges duck 'em and say they can't abide all the ranting and emotional corn. Downstate all the other judges near my bailiwick shake their heads and call me 'First Degree' Weaver." The Judge paused and smiled. "My passion for murder is almost illicit. And for all my concern and reverence for the law I sometimes ruefully suspect that the average murder jury really decides its cases *regardless* of the law." He shrugged and smiled. "That's quite a somber admission from a dedicated old bookworm like me. But I can't help but suspect that you're a student of the same theory yourself—and also of the psychology of the jury."

"Pretty much, Judge," I said. "I've never stopped to figure it out, I guess. But I also guess that men will never devise a better system of determining their clashes with each other and society. At least our jury system, for all its absurdities and imperfections, achieves a sort of rough democracy in action—at least the result is not preordained as it is in some places."

"Ah, yes," the Judge said, looking out over the lake. "Yet we cannot help but dream and grope for perfection. . . ."

"Like a dog baying at the moon," I said.

The Judge nodded his head and lowered his voice. "Man is the only animal that laughs and weeps," he said, "for he is the only animal that is struck by the difference between what things are and what they ought to be."

"That's a powerful observation, Judge," I said. "And spoken beautifully."

The Judge laughed and knocked out his pipe. "I may have said it beautifully, young man, but a fellow called Hazlitt happens to have written it. You better read that man some time if you haven't; he was afflicted terribly with character and brains—two commodities for the possession of which I've observed the ordinary run of men are not excessively notable."

There was a clatter at the outside mahogany door, which opened to introduce a mop handle and a large steaming pail of water and, finally, Smoky Madigan.

"Sorry, gen'emen," Smoky apologized, bowing contritely and noisily backing out. "I figgered the coast was clear." The heavy door clicked closed.

I arose and crushed out my cigar. "Judge," I said slowly, "I like your man Hazlitt's sentiments." I paused and nodded at the closed door. "He encourages me to be bold, in fact. . . ." I again paused, wondering if I dared speak my mind. "If—if I were still prosecutor of this county I'd have dismissed that felony breaking and entering case against that poor bastard and instead charged him with simple larceny and recommended a short rest cure with the Sheriff across the alley, a place where he'd be happy and do some good, not festering down at the branch prison among a lot of hopeless pros. If that man is a criminal then my name is William Hazlitt."

The Judge smiled. "The court is always sensitive to the views of counsel, who are after all officers of the court. We will see, Mr. Biegler, we will see."

"Thank you, Judge, and good night. It was pleasant to chat with you. And happy law-looking."

The Judge looked up from his book to which he had already returned, smiling absently. "Most pleasant, Mr. Biegler, most pleasant. Good day, sir."

I hurried away to tell Parnell the compliment the Judge had paid our instructions and supporting brief. As I clattered down the acres of soiled marble stairs I felt very expansive and virtuous, like a boy scout who had just thrown a rope to a drowning Smoky Madigan. Or had the rope instead been flung from the distant grave of a thoughtful Englishman who had once written "Man is the only animal that laughs and weeps . . ."?

Parnell was not in the car or anywhere around. I peered in the car to see if he had left his brief case. There was no brief case but I found a hurriedly scribbled note on the seat. "Dear Polly," it read, "The old rabbit hound is off on a fresh scent. I can't wait any longer. Don't worry. I'll see you sometime late tomorrow if I'm lucky. And how do I get around? Young man, I've paroled myself and got me a new driver's license and rented a car. You're doing beautifully as I knew you would. Watch out for little Dancer. Now don't worry. Parn."

"Oh, Lord," I said, and I dashed into the jail and brushed past

Sulo into the empty sheriff's office and phoned Maida at her apartment.

"Maida," I said, "where in hell is Parnell? What is he up to?" I read her the cryptic note and explained his disappearance during the day and again now. Maida had not the foggiest notion where he was, honest cross her heart she hadn't.

"Listen, young lady," I said. "You're lying by your grammar school clock. I can always tell when you're lying—after all, I taught you. What're you two up to? What's this sly mysterious work he's been giving you? Come on—talk, damn it."

Instead of talking Maida got her "dandruff" up, as Sulo Kangas might put it. "I won't tell you," she snapped. "I promised not to. Parnell doesn't want you to know or to worry. So don't keep asking me—damn it."

"But I *am* worried," I wailed. "He's a sick overworked old man who hasn't driven a car in over ten years. And that was a hundred-year-old Maxwell that he shifted by prayer and clanking a series of chains. Are you still on the line? Talk, damn it, or—or I'll fire you."

"Fire *me?*" Maida cooed. "First, Buster, you'll have to pay me what you owe me or I'll have the law on your neck. Mitch would be delighted."

That did it. I swore and then Maida swore—backed by her rich heritage from Mickey—and then someone hung up.

"You O.K., Polly?" Sulo inquired anxiously as I emerged from Max's office. "You look little vorried."

"I'm dandy, thanks, Sulo," I said, smiling wanly. "I'm just perfectly dandy. Thanks for using the phone."

So I did the only sensible thing a worried man could do—I stopped off at the Halfway House for one tall drink, just one. By midnight, having bought my way into the jazz combo, that old hepcat Polly Biegler and his borrowed fly-swatters was making crazy with the drums. "Lissen to dat *ma-a-n*. . . ."

chapter 10

When court convened the next morning, Thursday, and my glazed eyes were finally able to focus, I observed that something had been added to Mitch's table—a tall, dark, rather stooped spare man, with a drooping oily-looking old-fashioned black mustache and lean dagger-like face, who made me think of a romantic-looking concert pianist that had visited our town when I was a child. My mother Belle had thought he was handsome beyond words. All of Belle's "handsome" men had a tendency to look all profile, however viewed, like the tall, willowy, and genteelly fatigued characters drawn by Charles Dana Gibson. . . . When the jury had been brought in and that pregnant pre-session hush had fallen upon the courtroom—the time when the Judge would nod to Mitch to reopen hostilities—I arose, my head thumping, and addressed the court.

"Your Honor," I said, "the defense observes that a third person has been added to the prosecution table, and we wonder if the court shares with us our curiosity over his identity and function."

The fourteen pairs of eyes of the equally curious jury bored into the new arrival, who returned their stare with the languid, faintly disdainful nostrilly look of a T. S. Eliot. The Judge nodded at Mitch's table.

"Your Honor," Claude Dancer said, rising, "the gentleman at our table is Dr. W. Harcourt Gregory, the People's psychiatrist in this case. We were about to identify him and ask the court's permission that he sit at the prosecution table as an observer when defense counsel, with characteristic bravado and corn, felt obliged to jump the gun and attempt to make a grandstand play out of it. We now respectfully make the identification and request."

"Mr. Biegler?" the Judge said, rolling his eyes and heaving a sort of heavy here-we-go-again sigh.

I grinned across the room at Claude Dancer, my temples pounding. If this little man felt any irresistible yearning to tilt personalities, I thought, he'd clearly picked himself the wrong day. "The defense regrets boundlessly its bad taste and peasant curiosity in wondering who the strange gentleman might be," I said with suave cantankerousness, "but nevertheless inquires what it is the People want him to observe—perhaps the view from Pompey's Head?"

The Judge frowned and bit his lip to banish his smile. "Mr. Dancer?"

"To observe the defendant, of course," Claude Dancer snapped, "as indefatigably grand-standing counsel very well knows."

Patiently: "Mr. Biegler, the ball is back to you—or should I say stiletto?"

"In that event, Your Honor, the defense has no objection. Not for the world would we impede the course of pure science. In fact I shall move my chair back so that the doctor can get a good look. We express our relief, however, that the new recruit is not, as we fearfully speculated, additional legal reinforcements rushed here from Lansing on behalf of the People."

Dr. Gregory whinnied appreciatively and quickly covered his mouth with his hand. Claude Dancer glared across at me and if, as the saying goes, looks could have killed I was a dead pigeon.

"The People's request is granted," the Judge said drily. He gazed out over the heads of the hushed crowd at the far courtroom clock. "Now that you gentlemen have had your morning setting-up exercises and sufficiently stirred up your bile and vented your spleen, may we dare get on with this trial? Or perhaps you would prefer that the court pause and administer a brisk verbal rubdown?"

Mitch and I popped to our feet. "The People are ready," Mitch said.

"The defense is ready," I croaked, and another day of combat was under way.

Mitch called Ditlef Pedersen's wife and then her pretty blonde sister. Their testimony was substantially the same as that of Ditlef Pedersen. When I had done cross-examining them Mitch got up and spoke to the court.

"Your Honor, there are seven other eyewitnesses to the shooting endorsed on the information, subpoenas for whom have been issued and placed in the hands of the Sheriff for service. The Sheriff has informed me that he is unable to obtain service on any of them for the reason that the witnesses are beyond the confines of the state. For defense counsel's information I may add that three of them were soldiers temporarily stationed near Thunder Bay and now stationed in Georgia, and the other four were tourists who reside out of the state." Mitch then called out the names of the seven missing witnesses.

"Mr. Biegler," the Judge said, "what do you say?"

"The defense inquires of the People whether these witnesses were interviewed before they left and, if so, whether their testimony would be cumulative of testimony which has been or will be offered in the case?" I said.

"All seven witnesses were interviewed and we represent on the record that their testimony would largely be cumulative," Mitch said.

In that event I knew that the court could and doubtless would excuse the People from the necessity of producing these absent witnesses, and that in any case all that the prosecution ever had to do was to make an honest effort to obtain service on the out-state witnesses once the trial date was known, which they had apparently done. A little graciousness now appeared to be in order. "In that case, Your Honor," I said, "the defense waives the production of these seven witnesses and further waives any cross-examination of them. We do this because it must long have been evident to all concerned here that there is not now nor has there ever been any dispute over the fact that the defendant, Frederic Manion, did indeed cause the death of Barney Quill by shooting him. We dispute only that it was murder."

Claude Dancer was on his feet. "There is no need for counsel to make a speech. Either he waives or he doesn't waive—"

"Very well, gentlemen," the Judge broke in. "One good speech doesn't deserve another. Call your next witness, Mr. Prosecutor."

"The People will call Alphonse Paquette," Mitch said, and Clovis Pidgeon arose and dramatically administered his ritual oath and Barney's little bartender, all sleek in a sports outfit and immaculate hair that I suspected had been plastered with goose grease, said "I do" and got up on the witness stand.

"You may sit down," the Judge said.

"Thank you, Your Honor," the witness said.

"State your name, please," Mitch said.

"Alphonse Paquette."

"Where do you live?"

"Thunder Bay, Mich."

"Where do you work?"

"At the Thunder Bay Inn."

"In what capacity?"

"Bartender in the new Lake Superior cocktail lounge and bar." A little tasteful free plug for the home industry was always good, even in court, I thought.

"Were you on duty the night of Friday, August fifteenth, and during the early hours of Saturday, August sixteenth, this year?" Mitch continued.

"I was."

"Did you know the deceased Barney Quill during his lifetime?"

"I did."

"How long?"

"About a year and a half—he was my boss, I worked for him that long."

"Did you know the defendant Frederic Manion prior to that night?"

"I did."

"How long?"

"Approximately three weeks; he was an occasional patron at our bar."

"Can you identify in this courtroom the man you know as Lieutenant Manion?" (I again prodded the Lieutenant, who shot up straight as a ramrod.)

"I can."

"Will you do so?"

"That gentleman in the Army uniform standing next to his lawyer, Mr. Biegler."

"Were you in the bar when the shooting occurred?"

"I was."

"Where were you?"

"I was standing near the table of the Pedersens who last testified here."

"Did you see the actual shooting?"

"No." ("The lying bastard," I thought.)

"Did you hear it?"

"Yes, sir—I heard six shots fired. After about the second shot I looked over and saw a man in an Army fatigue jacket bending down over the bar."

"Then what?"

"Well, then this man raised up and turned and walked out the door near where I stood."

"Did you recognize him?"

"I wasn't sure," the witness answered. (This was, I felt, arrant hogwash; a dozen casual patrons had recognized the Lieutenant at a glance but the hour-long "lookout" hadn't, the cool lying bastard.)

"What did you do then?" Mitch asked. (Ah, here come the "Do you want some, too, Buster?" part, I thought.)

"I rushed out the door after him."

"Were you able to identify him outside?"

"I was. He turned and faced me and I recognized him."

"Who was the man that faced you?"

"Lieutenant Manion."

Mitch turned casually around and glanced at Claude Dancer and again I saw the little telltale nod. "Your witness, Mr. Biegler," Mitch said.

For a moment I sat there stunned. Here was one of the few People's witnesses who possessed vital prosecution information—"Do you want some, too, Buster?"—to help batter down our insanity defense. They had led this witness up to the portal of that damaging information and then quit cold and turned him over to me. What in hell was cooking?

"Reviewing my notes," I lied gently to the Judge, who nodded that I could have more time. I stared sightlessly at the blank pad before me.

If Mitch had been trying the case alone I would not have smelled so strong a rat, but with the little nodding Dancer in there. . . . But what was the rat? Wait! Ah, the strategy was coming to me. . . . Mr. Dancer was by now panting to catch me with my pants down, of course. If they let me blunder ahead with this witness then I, *the defense lawyer*, would doubtless myself bring out the damaging words. That way I would not only mightily please the Dancer by looking like a blundering fool, but, more important, I would at the same time invest the bartender's testimony with greater impact and weight. This is not a witness, the jury could say, who was ready and anxious to spill anything he knew that might hurt the Lieutenant; see, the defense itself had to drag it out of him. It simply must be true. . . . And then if I still escaped the clever trap and failed to ask the magic question, the People could still bring it out on redirect. It was a fine Dancerian spider web. Probably the reason I recognized it was because in the past I had used the same strategy so many times myself.

I arose and walked toward the witness. "Did you speak to the Lieutenant when you 'rushed out the door after him,' as you have just so dramatically described it?"

"Yes. I said, 'Lieutenant Manion.' "

"I see, and this was the same man you have just testified you weren't sure you recognized?"

"Well, yes."

"The lights from the barroom weren't helping you when you correctly called him by name, were they?"

"Well, I guessed it was him."

"My question was, Mr. Paquette, were the lights then helping you?"

"No."

"I see. Now a dozen-odd casual patrons in the bar clearly recognized the Lieutenant but you—who had been standing by the door when he entered and also when he left—you had to guess his identity?"

"That's right."

"The lying bastard," I thought. The phrase was becoming a sort of a litany. "What if anything did the Lieutenant do when you spoke his name?"

"He whirled around."

"And then you were able to confirm your shrewd guess as to who he was?"

"Yes, sir."

The stage was now set and I pressed on. "Did the Lieutenant say anything?"

"Yes."

I glanced over at Claude Dancer, who was staring up at the ceiling, doubtless with glee-crossed fingers. "Will you *please*, Mr. Paquette, tell us what it was he said?" I pressed.

"He said, 'Do you want some, too, Buster?' "

"Ah, and was he pointing his gun at you?"

"I believe he was."

"His *empty* gun?"

"I wouldn't know."

"You heard all the People's witnesses here who testified that the Lieutenant kept clicking his empty gun at Barney, didn't you?"

"Well yes, but I didn't know *then* that it wasn't loaded." (Ah, the clever shifty bastard.)

I glanced around and found Mitch and his assistant with their heads bent together in smiling and busy consultation. "Now, Mr. Paquette," I said, "I assume of course you have told your story of the incidents of that night to the police, have you not?"

"Yes."

"And to Prosecutor Lodwick?"

"Yes."

"And to his part-time helper, Mr. Claude Dancer?"

"Yes."

"And you of course told *all* of them, did you not, what you have just told me, namely, that the Lieutenant wheeled around and said, 'Do you want some, too, Buster?'?"

"Objection!" the Dancer rolled out. "The defense is trying to infer that the prosecution is trying to conceal something. The reason we did not want to bring it out was that it might create error or a mistrial, being possible evidence of the commission of still another criminal offense by the defendant."

I turned and stared across at Claude Dancer. "The defendant is touched by your solicitude for his welfare, Mr. Dancer," I said. "You would only have moved mountains to have brought this out if I hadn't."

"Tut, tut, gentlemen," the Judge reproved us. "I will take the answer."

"Yes, I told all of them about it."

"And when did you tell Mr. Dancer?" I pressed on.

"Last night and again this morning."

"And did he or anyone ever warn you not to tell about this Buster business because it might be error or hurt the Lieutenant's best interests?"

The witness tried to glance around me at the prosecutor's table. "Look at me and answer," I said.

"No, I don't believe that subject was mentioned."

I glanced at my juror and noted that he was following this fairly intricate courtroom waltz. I paused and thought of what this devious character of a bartender had earlier told Laura and the Lieutenant about Barney, about his expression of sympathy and the "wolf" business and all. Perhaps I had better get into that now, I thought, but I would have to do so obliquely; if I came at him cold and asked him straight out he would probably simply deny the whole thing.

"Mr. Paquette," I said, "as a bartender what do you call your cheaper brands of whisky?"

Surprised: "Oh, pilerun or cooking whisky or rat poison—they're just slang names."

"Yes, of course. And your bonded bourbon?"

"Well, simply bonded bourbon or sometimes white-vest stuff."

He apparently still did not see the drift. "I see," I said. "Now what do you call a man who has an insatiable penchant for women —any and all women?"

"What's 'penchant,' sir?"

"Desire, appetite, passion, taste, hunger, yen, my friend."

His eyes flickered and I now saw he'd got the drift. Carefully: "Why, a lady's man, I guess." He glanced at the Judge. "Or maybe simply a damned fool." The courtroom tittered and the Judge glared the onlookers into silence.

"Anything else?"

The Dancer was on his feet. "We don't see the drift of all this, Your Honor. I—"

"You mean, Mr. Dancer, you *do* see the drift," I broke in.

"Proceed, gentlemen, proceed," the Judge said sharply.

"Anything else, Mr. Paquette?" I said.

"Woman chaser," he ventured.

"Hm. . . . Pretty medieval. Please try again."

"Masher."

"Come, now, Mr. Paquette—mashers went out with whalebone corsets and hair nets, but you're getting warmer. Anything else?"

Studiously, thoughtfully, "No, sir, I guess I've run out of terms. You see, sir, I haven't had the educational advantages you've had."

The clever little bastard, I thought. "How about the expression 'wolf'?" I said. "Or perhaps you've led too sheltered a life ever to have heard of that?"

"Naturally I've heard it. It slipped my mind."

"Naturally it would. Clanking around in there with all those rusty old 'mashers' it naturally would. Do you ever use the expression yourself?"

"Nat—" he began, but caught himself. "Of course I have. Everybody does."

"What does it mean?"

"Well, I guess just about what you said—a bear cat for women."

"Have you used the expression lately?"

"I couldn't remember that any more than you could."

"Maybe I can refresh your recollection," I said. "Do you remember driving Mrs. Manion to Iron Bay the Sunday after the shooting?" The witness craned around to look at Claude Dancer. "You needn't look at Mr. Dancer," I said. "I don't believe he was hunting in the U.P. at that time.

Dancer leapt to his feet. "Let the witness answer," he shouted hotly. "Don't try to pretend he's being evasive."

"I wouldn't need to half try," I said.

The Judge spoke wearily; we were wearing him down. "I suggest both of you gentlemen invoke a little silence and let the witness answer. In fact I order you to. Proceed."

"Yes, I remember," the witness answered.

I decided suddenly to veer away from all this and let the witness sizzle a little; a slow broil was sometimes good for the memory. "Now, Mr. Paquette," I said, "you knew the deceased quite intimately, did you not?"

"Yes."

"And did you consider yourself to some extent his confidant?"

"Yes."

"Would it be fair to say that you were as intimate with him as any of his male acquaintances?"

Thoughtfully: "Well, yes."

"And were you able to tell when he was drinking heavily or not?"

"I object," Claude Dancer said. "Nothing in this case involving drinking. Had deceased been dead drunk still no defense to this charge." The little man had an annoying habit of phrasing his objections as though he were dictating a cablegram, a prepaid cablegram. He also possessed an even more annoying habit of coming up with some pretty shrewd objections. "See no connection, Your Honor," he concluded.

"You will, Dancer, you will," I said, recalling in my travail the famous Whistler-Wilde jibe.

"I think possibly the objection may be well taken," the Judge said, "but I will let the witness answer this question."

I nodded at the witness. "I do not believe he was drinking particularly heavily that night," the witness answered.

"I did not ask you if Barney was drinking heavily that night, Mr. Paquette," I said. "I asked you whether you were able to tell *when* he was drinking heavily."

"Yes."

It had to be faced: "And was he drinking heavily that night?"

"No." ("The lying dastard," I thought, varying the formula.)

"Or that day?"

"No."

"And how much did he drink when he was drinking heavily?"

"I object. Witness has said flatly that deceased was not drinking heavily that day, which is the day that concerns us. Anyway, don't see any relevancy or connection."

"Well, you're pushing this pretty far, Mr. Biegler," the Judge said, "but since we're into it I'll take the answer. But I warn you—the limit is near."

I decided to veer from this before I got slapped down. "I'll withdraw the question, Your Honor." I turned back to the witness. "Now I ask you whether from your intimacy with the deceased you knew whether he was an expert pistol shot?"

"Objection. No self-defense in this case. All evidence points to fact defendant was unquestionably the aggressor. Immaterial and irrelevant."

"Mr. Biegler?" the Judge said.

I was in a dilemma. I certainly knew why I wanted to get in the drinking and expert pistol business, Heaven knows, and, since the Judge had all our requests for instructions, he too certainly knew. And the Dancer was shrewd enough to sense that I was up to no good, so he was objecting and, in all candor, I had to admit to myself that, as of now, his objections were probably good. I could have asked the Judge to recess the jury and have argued out all my pet theories in front of God, the jury, and the *Mining Gazette*, but I was not ready to show my hand to the Dancer and thus give him a free road map of my strategy for his future roadblocks. Also my corny sense of drama rebelled at throwing my best curves at this time; I wanted to save a few surprises for the jury. But I couldn't have my cake and eat it, too; I would have to learn to be patient, and being patient with little Mr. Dancer, I was rapidly learning, was an exercise in self-discipline I did not relish.

"We believe this evidence may be material, Your Honor," I said, "and several of the People's witnesses have already indicated—the Pedersens, I believe—that the deceased was such an expert. We believe it has a connection with certain important issues in this case. However, we will of course abide by the court's ruling." It was a lame and reluctant retreat from a tense and touchy courtroom situation.

"I believe that I must sustain the objection," the Judge said slowly. "Until proper issues are raised making such questions relevant I don't think I can permit this line of questions. But I have yet to detect any such issues in the evidence so far in this case. If and when whatever issues you may have in mind should properly be raised here I will allow both sides to go sled length. But not until then. That is the court's ruling."

I glanced at my juror and found him downcast; the only good thing about the Judge's ruling was that it now showed beyond any doubt that my juror cared. Claude Dancer was beaming his satisfaction and approval over such an erudite judge. In the meantime Paul Biegler had long face to save. "Your Honor," I said, "may it be understood, then, that the defense can reserve further cross-examination of this witness until these proper issues should be raised?"

"It may be so understood, and I so rule. This witness and indeed all witnesses are under subpoena here. I will not permanently excuse them and they may not leave the jurisdiction of this court without my permission. If and when the proper issues are raised here to warrant these and similar questions, both sides may have at them to their hearts' content and with the court's blessing."

"Very well, Your Honor," I said. "With that understanding we have no further questions of this witness at this time."

"Any redirect?" the Judge inquired, looking at Mitch.

Claude Dancer thought a moment, his chin resting Napoleonically on his hand. "No, Your Honor," he said. "No further questions."

"There is one more thing, Your Honor," I said. (There was a moving little speech I had been saving for just such an occasion as this.) "I think the time has come for the defense to object to objectional examining tactics of the People. For example, this People's witness, the one now on the stand, started out being examined by the prosecuting attorney, Mr. Lodwick. Then I took over and Mr. Lodwick was retired hastily to the showers and Mr. First Assistant Dancer rolled up his artillery of objections. Then, when it came to redirect, the zealous Mr. Dancer forgets all pretense that this man was ever Mr. Lodwick's witness, and *he* allows that *he* has no further questions to ask him. Mr. Lodwick obediently consults Mr. Dancer but like the Lowells Mr. Dancer evidently consults only God." I paused and glanced at my juror. "Now I am quite willing to take on these two legal giants, any time, any place, but I think in common fairness it should be but one at a time. I don't want both of them in there pitching their fast knuckle balls at me."

It was quite a moving little jury speech, on a par with the best of Amos Crocker's quavering corn, and, sneaking another look, I was relieved to see that my juror had rallied from his slump.

"Your objection is well taken, Mr. Biegler," the Judge said. "I have been waiting for you to raise it. In any case I will lay down a rule on that. Only one counsel on a side will be permitted to examine a given witness. And in view of the number of witnesses in this case I will further rule that that same counsel shall raise any objections to any questions asked that witness." The Judge glanced at the clock. "Mr. Sheriff," he said, "take ten—no, fifteen minutes."

chapter 11

The rest of Thursday morning slipped by on leaden wings. The prosecution seemed bent on cleaning up the odds and ends of its remaining witnesses, saving the best for the last—best for it, that is. Mitch was assigned or had assigned himself this dreary task, and I had dire trouble remaining awake. A whole string of alert good-looking young state police troopers paraded to the stand and, like eager young professors in math, talked endlessly and accurately about the charts and floods of measurements: about where the body lay, how far the bar was from the door, the hotel from the trailer park, the trailer from the caretaker's cottage, measurements ad nauseum. All the while I drank gallons of water and wondered idly where old Parnell had gone and what the old badger was up to.

Mitch had to get the stuff in, he couldn't help it, but I could help some and did by not prolonging the agony. My cross-examination was perfunctory and some witnesses I passed entirely. I did not try to get into Barney's personal life or his habits or his arsenal, which these boys probably didn't know about anyway, and I steered carefully away from all talk of rape and Laura Manion, and above all from the tender question of any lie-detector test. I was determined now not to risk getting seriously slapped down again by the court or to risk tipping off my strategy to the shifty counter-punching Dancer. If the prosecution wanted to play it that way I would wait to get in my licks until the defense took over, indeed even until Christmas. In any case, if the People were going to save their best witnesses for the last, I would also save what I hoped were my best curves for the last. In the meantime I ran out of water and began to see shimmering mirages of lakes of cold tomato juice.

Court mercifully adjourned a little early for the noon recess and I tottered out to my car and groped my way out to Parnell's and my drive-in on Lake Superior. "Closed for the Winter" a sign read. "Ev and Al." Well, happy winter in Florida, Ev and Al, I thought—and may all your troubles continue to be famished tourists. As for you, Biegler, suffer, damn you, suffer. . . . I sat and stared numbly out at the gently heaving lake, at the rolling rhythmically probing waves—"out of the cradle, endlessly rocking"—until at last I had to flee the place to keep from falling asleep.

Parnell's little old caretaker, Mr. Lemon, a gentle wispy little man, was the first People's witness after lunch, with the Dancer in the saddle. With an enviable dispatch and economy of words he adroitly led the witness over the jumps, having him relate how he was indeed a deputy sheriff, that he always wore his deputy badge, and that he was custodian of the trailer park; that his cottage was about thirty feet from the Manion trailer; that he locked the park gate every night at ten and that this was well known to the guests using the park, as he generally told all of them (Dancer was here obliquely veering ahead, in anticipation of our defense story, and I glumly admired the little man's crisp cleverness); and, finally, how he was awakened the night of the shooting.

"And who awoke you?" Mr. Dancer suavely continued.

"Lieutenant Manion," the witness answered.

"For what purpose?"

"He wanted me to take him into custody, sir."

"What if anything did he say?" (Here—now it was coming.)

"He said, 'You better take me, Mr. Lemon—I've just shot Barney Quill.'"

Claude Dancer paused like a good actor to let these pregnant words sink in. "And what time was that?" he continued.

"Just before one A.M."

"What did you do?"

"I told him to go wait in his trailer, that I would go uptown and notify the state police."

"And did he go wait?"

"Yes, sir."

"And the police finally arrived and took over."

"They did. Somebody else notified them first."

Mr. Dancer turned toward me and smiled, he actually smiled, and I swiftly concluded, as I had with Barney's bartender, that if I had to take him at all I much preferred him frowning. He was in a benevolent mood, the day was going nicely, and somehow Biegler was flubbing his shots. . . . "Your witness, Mr. Biegler," he smiled sweetly and padded nimbly back to his assistant boss. I heaved myself to my feet, feeling not a day older than the witness I was about to face.

"How old are you, Mr. Lemon?" I said.

"I'll be sixty-nine in February," he answered.

"And how long have you been custodian of the Thunder Bay tourist and trailer park?"

"Going on nine years, sir."

"And who do you work for—who pays your salary?"

"The township—Mastodon Township."

"And how long have you been a deputy sheriff?"

"Going on three years."

"And who pays your salary for that office?"

Surprised: "Why no one, sir—there just isn't any salary."

"So your sole income—from your work at least—comes from the township of Mastodon as custodian of the tourist and trailer park?"

"Yes, sir."

"Now, as deputy sheriff was it your practice to serve legal papers, roam highways, chase speeders, pinch violators, quell riots, patrol strikes, case the outlying taverns on Saturday nights and pay days—and all the many things that our busy Sheriff here and his loyal deputies are required to do day and night?" (I glanced at the Sheriff. This was Max's pay-off and in his moment of glory he was all flushed and swollen out like a pouter pigeon. At that instant, at least, the Lieutenant could plainly have gotten up and strolled off unhindered to Georgia.)

"Oh, no sir," the witness replied, recoiling in horror at the thought. "I only work at the park."

"As a matter of fact, Mr. Lemon, you've never done any of these things, have you; your deputyship is purely a convenience in connection with your duties in the park; you've never made a dime as deputy; you don't wear a uniform or carry a gun; and you've probably never arrested a man in your life?"

"All that is correct, sir. I don't even own a gun." He hesitated and smiled. "Perhaps I can explain. You—you see, Mr. Biegler, about three years ago some of our town boys began coming around the park at night, singing and disturbing the tourists. Nothing vicious, you know—just being boys. Well, I—I thought if I got to be a deputy sheriff that might scare them a little."

"And did they scare, Mr. Lemon?" I said, smiling.

"Not readily," he said timidly. "It was Mrs. Lemon who finally solved the problem."

"How?"

"Cookies."

"Cookies, Mr. Lemon?"

"Cookies, Mr. Biegler. Isabelle—Mrs. Lemon, I mean—discovered that the best way to silence the town boys at night was to fill them up with homemade cookies." He held out his hands. "We haven't had any trouble since."

What a lovely little man, I thought. I glanced over at Mr. Dancer, who was sunk in profound thought—probably yearning for Isabelle's recipe. "Passing now to the locked gate," I said. "I believe you testified that you close and lock this gate at ten every night, and that this is well known to the patrons of your park?"

"Yes, sir."

"And I assume then that this would be even *better* known to the residents of Thunder Bay?"

"Oh yes, sir—everybody knew that. It's been locked at that hour since the park opened—long before I became caretaker."

"So that if any local resident suggested driving a tourist, say, into the park after that hour, he must surely have known that the gate would be closed and locked?"

"Objection," the Dancer said. "The gate is irrelevant and immaterial."

"Mr. Biegler?" the Judge said.

I was beginning to feel a little benevolent, too. "I'll abide by your ruling, Your Honor."

"The objection is overruled. The People have opened the gate, so to speak, and within reason, the defense may close it. Take the answer."

"Oh, yes sir," Mr. Lemon said. "Everybody knew that."

After that I had myself a time swinging gaily on the creaking park gate, showing that while the caretaker had told the Lieutenant about the gate and given him a key, he hadn't told Laura; that on the few occasions they had stayed out together past ten that he, Mr. Lemon, had left the gate not only unlocked but standing open for them; that there was indeed a foot-stile at the side of the gate but that the tourists rarely, if ever, used it and instead either drove through the gate in cars, or, when walking, used the more northerly short-cut footpath to town which passed near Mr. Lemon's cottage. I also showed that bears were frequently seen in or near the tourist park, especially at night near the garbage dump on the south or entrance end. I finally showed that there was no other automobile road into the park proper except that which passed through the main gate.

"Closing the gate, now, Mr. Lemon," I said, "how did Lieutenant Manion appear when he told you what you say he told you?" Claude Dancer's failure to get into this on direct might be a trap, I sensed, but on the other hand one never knew. . . .

"He was white as a ghost and stood very straight, very erect and soldierly. He—he seemed to have trouble speaking; it seemed like he talked through his teeth. He—he acted like a man in a dream."

"A little caretaker shall lead them," I thought, pausing to let this answer soak in. While it was not entirely inconsistent with cold rage, it was even less inconsistent, I felt, with the picture of a man in the grip of some grave emotional or mental disturbance. I decided to rest the subject there.

"And Mrs. Manion," I said. "Did you see her?"

"Oh yes. I walked over to the trailer with the Lieutenant and she came to the door crying and said, 'Look what Barney did to me.'"

I half crouched, waiting for the booming objection, but no, the Dancer was too smart to nail the point home twice by objecting—the thing had slipped out and maybe it would go away.

"And what was her appearance?" I said, trying to make sure it wouldn't go away.

"She—she was a mess." The witness closed his eyes as though to banish a bad dream.

Everybody in the courtroom and county knew, of course, that Laura Manion had *claimed* that Barney had raped her. But this was the first sliver of actual evidence of the fact. The jury now knew that we were skating on the very edge of the rape. And like the hushed and slack-mouthed women sitting in the courtroom, they were also probably dying to hear about it. But I was damned if I was going to risk getting slapped down again; on the other hand, I had to try to lay the jury's disappointment at some other door. I was beginning to rather like it this way. I looked up at the Judge.

"Your Honor," I said, "we seem to be veering rather close to a keep-off-the-grass subject. I have no desire to annoy the court or to try to circumvent its earlier ruling, and I shall push ahead on the subject or not, as the court will please indicate."

I stood glancing curiously about the room as though it was the first time I had ever seen the place, as unconcerned as any bored and sun-blistered tourist being shown through the place by Sulo. "Hm . . ." said the Judge, leaning back and studying the domed skylight. I had passed him a little poser and we both knew it. But he was equal to the challenge—like a good halfback in trouble he promptly lateraled the ball off to Claude Dancer. "The People, Mr. Dancer?" he said. "What do you say?"

"Absolutely not," the Dancer came faithfully storming through; you could always count on the little man. "The Court has ruled; counsel is aware of it; and there is not a scintilla of evidence of any—" he paused and for once the boy orator was at a loss for words. I was certain he had nearly said "rape."

"Yes, Mr. Dancer?" I leered at him helpfully.

"—of any issue to which this line of questioning would be relevant," he concluded, glaring at me and plumping to his chair.

"Perhaps, Mr. Biegler," the Court suggested, "perhaps in view of the People's attitude you had better push on with something else. You may recall this witness later, of course, as per our earlier understanding."

The entire courtroom sighed a collective sigh, as though someone had punctured a balloon. Nearly everybody seemed to be glaring at somebody else. Most interesting to me, however, was that to a man the jury was now glaring at Claude Dancer. I studied the dusty portraits of the deceased judges until everybody could get thoroughly glared out and then I cleared my throat.

"Now, Mr. Lemon," I said, coming slowly to another delicate subject, "what time did you retire that night?"

"About ten-fifteen, my regular hour, right after closing the gate and listening to the radio newscast."

"And was your rest disturbed between that time and when Lieutenant Manion awoke you around one?"

"No, though I am a light sleeper."

"And your hearing, Mr. Lemon?" I asked softly.

Proudly: "I hear very well. Mrs. Lemon says I can hear a pin drop."

"And your cottage was about how far from the Manion trailer?"

"About thirty feet—just as the chart there says."

"And from your cottage down to the main gate?"

"About three hundred feet like it says."

"And nothing disturbed your slumbers—or at least your rest?"

"No, sir."

Slowly: "No boys sang?"

"No, sir."

"No women screamed?"

"The screams were down by the gate—"

"Objection, objection!" Claude Dancer was fairly breathing on my neck.

There was an edge in the Judge's voice. "Please let the witness complete his answer before you object, Mr. Dancer," he said sharply. He turned toward the witness. "Proceed," he said.

"Those were Mrs. Manion's screams that the Ohio tourists heard down by the gate."

Objection. Hearsay. Tourists best evidence—these were some of the objections that Claude Dancer urged in a torrent upon the Court.

"Your Honor," I said, acting on a sudden hunch. "I withdraw the question. The witness is back to you, Mr. Dancer."

"No questions," he snapped.

"Thank you, Mr. Lemon," I said.

"Call a ten-minute recess, Mr. Sheriff," the Judge said, frowning thoughtfully up at the skylight.

chapter 12

The compassionate Judge must have divined the shape I was in; he excused us a little early that afternoon. Due to some providential mixup two out-county lawyers had wandered into court during the afternoon with their default divorce clients and witnesses, erroneously thinking their cases were scheduled to be heard that day instead of a week later. When, during recess, the Judge learned of their plight he lacked the heart to send them away with their angry and unfreed clients; after all, the profession had to save face. Old drummer-boy Biegler could have kissed all of them, even to the grim-looking clients. By four o'clock Mitch had taken a couple more routine witnesses over the jumps and at last I was free. With a parched tongue and pounding temples I fairly raced out to my car and fled the courthouse and Iron Bay.

It had begun to rain, gently at first and then with a kind of monotonous autumnal savagery. Wounded defense counsel drove home the back way, splashing through colorful dripping tunnels and rolling hillsides of fading leaves, carefully making a wide arc around the beguiling Halfway House, which, I numbly remembered, refused to sell drinks to people over a hundred and one. The day's courtroom hunting had resulted in a mixed bag, some good and some bad. But mostly it had been bad, I morosely concluded, for not only had the bartender and prosecution teamed up to block the defense, but now even the good Judge himself was contributing to the enterprise. And what assurance had I that the little bartender would *ever* open up and tell at least part of the truth, if and when the Judge finally let me really have at him? No, all in all it had not been a good day and the prospects were far from pleasing. And where, dear Lord, where was my wandering Parnell?

On the outskirts of Chippewa I stopped at a little store and, scampering through the rain, picked up a copy of the *Mining Gazette*, which I read avidly, sitting in the steamy rain-pelted car, much as a prizefight fan races from ringside to the nearest newsstand after a big bout as though to confirm what really happened and that, indeed, there had been any fight at all. "Manion murder trial marked by bitter clashes between lawyers," one of the headlines shouted. I read on, unbelieving, held in a fiend's clutch. Was Paul Biegler the quiet trout fisherman really one of the noisy guys mixed up in this unzipped tempest, this snarling courtroom hassle? Were we two really carrying on like "two scorpions in a bottle," as the newspaper said? The young reporter, Bob Birkey, was doing a manful job, and a fair one, too; most of it was there, the good and the bad. But most of the nuances were missing; newspapers rarely ever have time for the nuances. Yet nuances were the heart of this case. "See Murder Trial, p. 8" the newspaper said, and I flipped the pages.

Ah, there were the photographs of the Judge and handsome crewcut Mitch and balding fur-haired Claude Dancer leaping out at me—the Dancer as alert and eager-looking as a well-scrubbed choirboy. Yes, there they all were, bigger than bear-wheat, with row upon gaptoothed row of shelved law books making an impressive backdrop. Little Mr. Dancer was passing a paper to Mitch, the inevitable mysterious document that newspaper photographers somehow feel compelled to trot out—this one doubtless being, I maliciously thought, Mitch's instructions for the day. There was also a good shot of the Judge sitting imperturbable and alone at his desk, then another of Mitch and his man Friday, this time Mitch doubtlessly passing the instructions back. An apt title occurred to me for the last one: "Lieutenant Manion's Wrecking Crew."

Back at my musty office I threw open the windows and phoned in a wire to our psychiatrist that he must arrive not later than Saturday (this was Thursday evening), and then I read my mail. There was a letter from my mother Belle, who would be home in two weeks and hoped her Polly wasn't working too hard and was getting plenty of sleep (at the very thought of sleep I yawned until I feared my jaw was stuck) and who hoped I was regularly watering her geraniums ("Good God," I thought). The rest was bills, bills, bills, tintinnabulations of colorful, autumn-tinted fluttering bills. . . .

I idly tried the television but it was lousy. We were mercifully too far away for good television. I worked for a while on my jury argument; one had always to be prepared for that; trials had a nasty habit of ending abruptly; one suddenly found oneself cut adrift before a jury composed of stony-faced native Buddhas, trying in a fleeting hour or so to carve a modicum of sense out of days of chaos.

"Give jury true picture of tense setup in bar that night," I scribbled away. "Stress Barney knew gate was shut and Laura didn't. Give Dancer hell. Show bartender goddam liar. Take Dancer the prancer apart. . . ." The city hall clock struck nine; darkness fell; I scribbled on and on; the clock boomed ten; my numbed mind simply wasn't tracking; I kept giving Dancer hell; verily, I would incant the little man into oblivion. I yawned and yawned; my head nodded down toward my desk. . . . I must have fallen asleep. . . .

"Polly," someone was saying softly. "Polly, Polly. Wake up, boy. It's me. . . ."

Parnell stood across from me looking like a beardless Father Time; the tired pouches under his fatigue-reddened eyes sagged like those of an old rabbit hound; his new suit was soiled and wrinkled and looked as though it had been rained on. But the old man was smiling and cold sober. He dropped his brief case and sagged into the chair across my desk. "Tire trouble. . . ." he murmured, wagging his head. "I'm not the driver I used to be, boy. What's more, I never was."

"He's home," I thought, "thank God the old man is home." "Where you been at, Parn?" I said wearily, still only partly awake. I hadn't realized until then how much I loved this old man, loved and depended on him.

Parnell sighed and stretched out in his chair like a basking grampus, his plump hands folded across his belly. "First fetch me one of those habit-forming orange pops, Polly boy," he said. He sighed: "Where have I been? Ah, lad, sometimes I don't believe it myself—I feel like I been to the South Pole."

With his pop at his elbow, and part of it in him, Parnell rallied a little and leaned forward. "It happened this way, boy . . ." he began, and away he went on his story of his adventures at the South Pole.

Parnell had been quietly working on the Barney Quill will contest. He and Maida had worked on it for days. He had briefed the whole subject, including the question of the Wisconsin divorce, and had become convinced that legally the opposition didn't have a Chinaman's chance to upset either Barney's will or the divorce. Then he had gone to Mary Pilant's lawyer, Martin Melstrand, and put his cards on the table. He and old Martin were contemporaries; they had taken their bar exams together years before; he knew Martin could be trusted. . . .

"But, Parn," I interrupted, "why—why didn't you tell me? We were partners in this case—remember?"

"I didn't want you to worry, boy. You had enough on your mind tryin' your case. If I failed I—I didn't want. . . ." He paused and held out his soiled hands pleadingly. "Listen me out," he said. "The proof of the pudding—"

"Gathers no moss," I cut in. "Go on," I grumbled dubiously.

Parnell had gone over his brief with Martin Melstrand; he had sold him on the proposition that he was right; Martin Melstrand said that furthermore they had receipts and canceled checks showing that Barney's ex-wife had collected alimony for years; that Barney had indeed been sober when he made the will; that he had been in town for a physical checkup by Doctor Broun; that Martin Melstrand had himself drafted the will and handed it to Barney; that both he and his stenographer and the doctor knew he was then sober; that he had signed it immediately upon returning to Thunder Bay that very day; that in addition to the two witnesses to the will the local justice of the peace had also been present.

Parnell had given a copy of his brief to the grateful Martin Melstrand; he had explained to Martin why we had to get at the truth in our murder case; Martin, a shrewd if lazy lawyer, had clearly understood; Parnell had prevailed on Martin to phone Mary Pilant and reassure her on the will contest and divorce, and at the same time try obliquely (keeping us out of it) to soften her up on the criminal case. Martin had done so in Parnell's presence, but the results had been inconclusive; Mary Pilant had said she was reassured on the will, but she seemed oppressed by the notion that Barney's former wife might still upset the divorce and take anything. She was equally stubborn on conceding anything that might blacken Barney's name or tend to show him guilty of the rape. (As Parnell ran on I kept sinking lower in my chair, as though I was listening in on a bizarre Hollywood story-conference.)

Parnell had then concluded that the only way to remove Mary Pilant's fixation on the Wisconsin divorce business was for him to go there. He had borrowed photostat copies of the alimony receipts and checks from Martin Melstrand. Then he had rented the car and taken off on the hundred-odd mile trek to Green Bay. He had had tire trouble practically all the way and it was daylight when he arrived. He'd snatched a few hours sleep in the car. He was clamoring at the door of the county courthouse when it opened and was soon hard at the files and records in the old divorce case.

The original summons was missing from the file, as he'd expected; he'd next prowled in to the Sheriff's office—"a fine upstandin' broth of a man called Sullivan," and after that the Sullivans and McCarthys had co-operated wonderfully. Parnell had pawed for hours over the sheriff's old records and had finally found an old record showing that a deputy sheriff called Griffin had handled the summons in the old divorce case, the record failing to disclose, however, whether there'd been personal service or not. He'd then learned that old Mike Griffin, the deputy, was retired; yes, he was still living in Green Bay and Sheriff Sullivan would gladly drive Parnell there.

"Wisconsin convention of the Ancient Order of Hibernians," I murmured. "Up Ireland! Down with the blooming redcoats!"

"Convention it was, boy, that it was," Parnell said, pausing to sip his pop and then pressing on. Mike Griffin was a towering, alert, red-wristed Irishman of seventy. Did he remember personally serving a divorce summons on a Mrs. Barney Quill? Janice was her first name. Ah, did he *remember* her? You damn right he remembered that dame with the dyed red hair and livid scar on her right cheek who had sworn at him in everything but Arabian when he'd dared serve a divorce summons on her. Who'd ever forget such a noisy, foul-mouthed harridan? Certainly not old Michael Griffin. . . .

The trio of happy Hibernians had then proceeded back to the sheriff's office, sirens away, and Parnell had dictated a duplicate sheaf of affidavits, to which the affiant Michael Thomas Joseph Griffin had sworn on solemn oath and then laboriously signed his name. Then they had descended in a body upon the Green Bay lawyer of the ex-wife, a large, shrewd, red-headed lawyer.

Parnell paused for breath. "And guess what *his* name was?" he said, his eyes twinkling.

"Grogan," I replied steadily. "Terence O'Toole Grogan, of course."

"You're wrong, boy—it was Patrick Finkelstein!"

"Abie's Irish Rose," I murmured.

Parnell and the lawyer and Mike Griffin had closeted themselves; in due course they had come out and warmly shaken hands all around; the lawyer had thanked Parnell for his information and his brief and had notified him that he was dismissing the Wisconsin proceedings to set aside the divorce and was promptly withdrawing from the Michigan case.

Parnell had then phoned Martin Melstrand the latest developments, and asked him to pass the word on to Mary Pilant, which her grateful lawyer agreed promptly to do. Then he had parted from his Green Bay friends and had started for home in his rented car. He had got caught in a series of thunderstorms, there was more tire trouble. . . .

"I guess, lad, I spent more time *under* that haunted vehicle than in it." He had tried twice to phone the office but couldn't raise me. His last flat was only twenty miles out of Chippewa and he'd had to buy a new tire. "I guess I'll have to buy me the damned trap to protect me invistmint, that I will," he concluded, showing dire signs of his recent Hibernian exposure.

I sat staring at the gallant old man. What were you going to do or say to a whale of a man like that? "Thanks, Parn," I said. "After all the trouble you've gone to, I—I only hope it works."

Parnell shook his head soberly. "That's just the point, boy. It surely won't work if we leave it rest there," he said. "That's only the foundation. Only *you* can now really make it work."

"What do you mean, Parn? Why pick on me? I pay my taxes."

"You must go see Mary Pilant and personally plead your case —you've *got* to, boy. Don't you see? It's your case; it's your man who is in danger; you are the only one who can make her see it." He held out his pudgy hands. "I've passed you the ammunition— now you've got to go fight with it."

"Mary Pilant! Where, when?"

"Now . . . tonight. . . . We can't waste another moment. . . . Time's a fleetin', boy. . . . The trial will maybe be over and done with in another day or so. . . . Don't set there like a droolin' leprechaun—grab up the phone, man."

The clock was striking one as I telephoned the Thunder Bay Hotel and asked the clerk to connect me with Miss Pilant. I half prayed she wouldn't be in, that instead she would be out on the beach playing footsie with some brand-new lover boy.

"Hello," I said. "Is this Miss Pilant? This is Paul Biegler. . . . Yes, Lieutenant Manion's lawyer. I'd like to see you tonight. . . . Yes, I realize it's late, but tomorrow may be *too* late. . . . No, I can't possibly explain over the phone. . . . I can leave at once and with luck be there in an hour. . . . Room two-o-two, you say? Thank you. Good-by."

"Ah, lad, she'll see you," Parnell murmured, and he rolled up his red eyes and his head nodded forward on my desk. In an instant he was asleep and snoring. I hurriedly bundled him into my bedroom and undressed him like a drunkard and put him in my bed and set out his new suit for our maid of all work, Maida, to sponge and press. Then I left a note that I'd see him in court next day and grabbed up my brief case and a toothbrush and a clean shirt and clattered hollowly down the wooden stairs. The rain had stopped, the sky had cleared; it was a beautiful starlit night with the moon coming full. I drove like Paul Revere. On my wild ride I jumped one coyote and nine deer. Good old Parnell was right; he had passed me the ammunition—now it was my turn to get in and fight.

chapter 13

The empty carpeted hallway had that dry, sour, starched, Chinese-laundry smell which seems peculiar to all hotels. The door to room 202 was slightly ajar. I knocked softly and Mary Pilant let me in.

"Good evening, Mr. Biegler," she said, smiling gravely and briefly shaking my hand. She led me in to a sort of darkened sitting room, the most striking feature of which was a large picture window overlooking Lake Superior. Through this window flowed a golden torrent of moonlight. I stopped in my tracks.

"How incredibly beautiful," I murmured, looking out across the vast lake. Whole rivers of liquid moonlight seemed to be coursing and flowing across the broad expanse of glittering lake; the scene was invested with a kind of awesome otherworldly grandeur.

"Beautiful," she said. "I never tire of it." She paused pensively for a moment to watch and then took my hat and rumpled raincoat. "And now," she went on, "what can I bring you to drink? You must surely be ready for one after your long late drive—" she paused "—and your other activities about which I have lately been reading."

"After drinking in this moonlight," I thought, "no man in his right mind should ever want to drink whisky again." "Whisky in a tall glass with lots of ice and water, please," I said gratefully.

As she left to prepare the highball I stood staring out at the lake. I wondered what my strategy would be. Strategy? There was only one possible strategy left now, the purest of all—that of unvarnished truth. This was no time for any lawyers' tricks or sly deceits.

Mary Pilant came in with two drinks. Her dark hair was piled on top of her head and she wore a ruffled peignoir over some sort of silk lounging pajamas which reached high at the throat, Mandarin fashion, along with matching wedge-soled slippers with discreet pompons on the toes. It was hard to equate this poised and beautiful girl with the picture of hard and grasping womanhood she had compelled me to build up in my mind.

"Thank you," I said, taking my drink. "This was very thoughtful of you." I fought back a yawn. "I sure needed it."

She indicated a settee facing the window and herself took a chair nearby, resting her glass on a small table between us, sitting straight as a little girl. I gratefully sat down and then guiltily arose and nodded and took a big swallow of my drink, my first since I had given up being a non-union drummer boy.

"And now, Mr. Biegler," she said coolly, "tell me how you expect me to help your case?"

"You see, Biegler," I said to myself. "How can a mere man expect to outwit a clever dame like this?" I took another gulp of my drink and, with her nodded assent, lit a cigar. Then mentally holding my breath I took the plunge. "I'll try to tell you . . ." I began.

In a rush of words I told her about the problems of my case and the mortal danger I still believed Lieutenant Manion to be in. I told her of my earlier interview with her bartender at Thunder Bay, about which she of course knew, and of my conviction that he was then being evasive and holding back; and, worse yet, how that now in court he was being even more evasive and still holding back. I explained why I considered it so necessary and pressing that we be able to get before the jury the true story of Barney's drinking and possession of pistols and all the rest; I explained how, because of the will contest, I thought I understood why she had been so reluctant to let word of Barney's behavior and drinking get abroad and how I hoped the apparent need for all that had now passed. I told her how old Parnell had worked to brief the subject; how he had gone on alone to Green Bay and broken the case wide open; how he had got home, wet and dog-tired, just before I had phoned her; and how only an hour ago I'd tucked him away in my rumpled bed. I even told her about the coyote and nine deer I had seen on my wild moonlit drive to Thunder Bay.

Mary Pilant sat listening thoughtfully, occasionally sipping her drink. The thought occurred to me that if she was in league with the prosecution and Claude Dancer that surely the stuff was now in the fan; that this could, in fact, be the little man's biggest break of the case. But it was too late for that now, there was no holding back, and I took another drink and pressed on with my story as though I were pleading to a jury of one. I told her how important I considered the proof of the rape to the proper defense of the case; that in my opinion the biggest remaining element of doubt of the rape was that a sober man could have gone out and done what Barney had done.

She got up quietly and, nodding, took my empty glass away while I relit my forgotten cigar and paced up and down in the golden path of streaming moonlight. I felt suddenly old and saddened that I should be here on such a night, bent on such an errand, instead of paying earnest court to this dark and secretive creature. "Steady,

Polly," I thought. "The moonbeams'll get you if you don't watch out."

"Thank you," I said huskily, my hand trembling as she brought me a fresh drink but none for herself. She sat down and lighted a cigarette. Thoughtfully she blew the smoke across the path of moonlight, where it hung in a streaming moted haze of pure gold.

"How," she said quietly, "how can you be so sure that Barney"— she paused—"that he did this thing to this woman?" She looked at me curiously. "Has it never occurred to you that he might not have?"

I looked at her. She sat very still and white in the moonlight, staring out over the lake. Good God, I thought, can it possibly be that this woman still cherishes the notion that he didn't? Or possibly the hope? "Play it true, Polly," I thought. "Play it true." I spoke slowly. "At first I did have my doubts," I said soberly. "And grave ones. I no longer have."

She was looking at me now, studying me. "Why?" she said in a low voice. "Please tell me why?"

Once again I was away. I told her about the caretaker and his story of the Ohio tourists being awakened by hearing a woman's screams at the main gate just before midnight. Then, taking a gulp of my drink, I told her of the lie-detector test Laura Manion had taken and how I was morally certain that it showed she had told the solemn truth about the rape.

Mary Pilant crushed out her cigarette and finished her drink. Did her hand tremble ever so little or was it a trick of the moonlight? "Then," she said evenly, "if you have all this information why should you need anything from me?"

I explained to her that the Ohio tourists were no longer here and that I might have grave trouble getting in the proof of the screams. I also told her that the results of lie-detector tests were not admissible in Michigan or indeed any Anglo-American courts and that I would doubtless encounter even more trouble trying to bring that out. "That's why I had to come to you," I said quietly. "All that I want, all that the Manions want, is but a small measure of truth." I paused. "As for the tourists hearing the screams and the lie-detector test—didn't you know about them?"

She turned toward me and mutely shook her head, and her eyes— there was no mistake of moonlight this time—glistened with tears. "*Mary*—Miss Pilant," I said, awkwardly half rising, "let me get you a drink. I—I—" She shook her head and quickly arose and took my glass and hurried from the room. I went over close to the large window and stood staring out upon the lake. After a time I heard the soft tinkle of ice and Mary Pilant was standing at my side, solemnly handing me my drink. I nodded and we stood there for a long time looking at the lake. She did not speak; I did not speak. I had said my piece—what more was there to say? Finally I said, "I will go now if you prefer it that way."

She laid her hand on my sleeve. "Wait," she whispered. "Please wait. I want to think."

We two stood there until Mary Pilant began quietly to speak. Her voice had the curious quality of a child—a small and lonely child. She told of how she had come to Thunder Bay as a vacationing schoolteacher; of how attracted she had been by the lake and the pines and the wild natural beauty of the place; of how kind and thoughtful Barney had been to her and her friends; of how run-down the hotel was becoming under the reckless and carefree Barney. She told how his dining-room hostess had quit during the height of the tourist rush and of how she had finally consented to fill the breach. She told how Barney had begged her to stay on when the summer was over, promising to raise her salary far above what she could ever earn as a country schoolteacher, promising her a free hand. She dropped her voice. "And he kept his promises."

She again touched my arm lightly and I glanced down at her small white face. "Whatever you may have heard, Paul, and whatever Barney may have been with others, he was a perfect gentleman to me. Always. I regarded him almost as a father."

I nodded and stared out at the flaming lake.

She quietly told me of how hard she had worked building up the hotel; of how well things had gone, despite Barney's occasional erratic behavior and bouts of drinking; of what a witch Barney's ex-wife had been; of how she had finally met Barney's daughter; of how attracted and deeply attached she had become to the shy and troubled child. She paused and was silent for a time. "Perhaps my heart went out to the child because I too came from a broken home."

"I didn't know," I said. "I didn't know any of these things."

"And then this summer the Army came. It seemed to mark the beginning of the end."

I looked at her questioningly and she motioned for us to sit down. I moved from the window and sat and sipped my drink and waited in wondering silence.

She continued to speak in a low voice. She told me that, as she said I doubtless knew, Barney had been the king pin of Thunder Bay until the advent of the Army; that with the coming of the crowd of young, handsome, hard-drinking, hell-for-leather soldiers and officers she had noticed a change come over Barney; that not only had he become increasingly difficult with his drinking and attentions to women, but that what had once passed for camaraderie and fairly excusable braggadocio had that summer taken on alarming overtones of outright neurotic behavior; that finally only he seemed able to reason with Barney, that he seemed to look up to her as his sole loyal champion, his one remaining grasp upon reality. . . .

"I finally persuaded him to go to a doctor in Iron Bay," she went on. "I thought perhaps there was something organically wrong with him. He went, but there was nothing wrong with his body." She paused and shook her head. "What was wrong with Barney lay in his head—there and in his terrible consuming ego. . . . It was then that he took out two large insurance policies for his daughter and me. Perhaps he had a premonition of things to come." Again she paused. "You will have to believe me when I tell you that I knew nothing of the insurance or of his will until—until after that horrible night."

"I believe you," I said.

She smiled sadly. "I suppose you must have thought I was terribly grasping over this estate business. I can't much blame you. But my impulse was to flee the whole thing, especially when Barney's ex-wife started to make trouble. Then I thought of all the work I had done here and of how proud Barney was of the place. So when that really grasping woman started her will contest I determined to stay and fight, for Barney's daughter as much or more than for myself."

"How do you mean?"

She glanced quickly at me. "It is my plan to share the estate with his daughter," she said quietly. "I have already made arrangements for a trust fund that the child's mother can never reach."

Things had been coming pretty fast and I felt clubbed into a sort of mental and emotional coma. I silently held out my glass and she took it and went away. I sighed and leaned back and groped for a cigar and lit the wrong end. I felt for and found another.

"Thank you, thank you," I murmured as she handed me my drink.

"I guess there has also been a feeling of loyalty and gratitude to Barney," she went on, "something that has made me shut my eyes to the possible truth of what he had done. How, I told myself, how could such a kindly, generous man possibly have done such a thing." She paused. "Then I guess there was a sense of guilt. . . ."

"Guilt?" I said softly.

"Guilt that I may have been to blame or partly at least."

"I don't quite understand," I said, feeling glumly afraid that I did.

"Not only did Barney grow jealous of the Army," she went on, "but finally of a young officer I occasionally dated. His—his name was Sonny Loftus."

"Did he have any reason?" I said, my heart pounding, finding myself suddenly interested above and beyond the call of duty. "Did Barney have reason to be jealous?" I held my breath for her answer.

She shook her head. "No. No, Paul. Not any real reason. But in the state he was in it was enough for Barney that I looked at another man. He could not see that Sonny was just a nice gangling boy from Georgia. And a lonely one. We danced mostly, down at Iron Bay, and occasionally picnicked and swam up along the beach. Poor homesick Sonny spent most of his time telling me about his sweetheart back home, whom I gathered was one of the outstanding belles of Atlanta since Scarlett O'Hara."

I tried to keep the note of relieved jubilation out of my voice. "Did Barney know—that this Sonny really meant nothing to you?"

She replied slowly. "I don't know. The more Barney fussed and fumed about my going out with Sonny the more determined I was that I would." She smiled up at me. "Someday, you see, there is always the chance that I might meet a man I really care for. I did not want either to delude Barney or let him feel that I was his prisoner. There is only the one thing that bothers me—that gives me this small feeling of guilt."

"What's that?"

"When this horrible thing happened I wasn't even here. Sonny and I had driven out to the beach to go swimming. There was a full moon. We had been there the night before, too."

"Why should that bother you, Mary?" I barely whispered.

"Well, the night before Barney was killed, while I was changing from my wet swim suit, someone came along the beach and suddenly lit a flashlight. I can't get over the notion that this unknown person might have misunderstood the situation and gone and told Barney." She paused. "In fact, knowing him, at times I've even thought it might have been Barney himself."

"No, no," I said dogmatically, and then hastily recovered. "No," I went on, "I doubt that Barney ever knew of this incident on the beach. It seems to me he would have let you know in some way, either by revoking his will or canceling the insurance or in *some* unmistakable way."

She searched my face in the moonlight. "I hope you're right, Paul," she said. "But he was a devious and endlessly complicated man. Maybe he chose *this* awful way to tell me. Anyway, now you have my secret." She touched my arm. "I hope I can trust you to keep it."

"Honest cross my heart, Mary," I said, setting down my glass and making the sign I had not made since I was a boy. Then I lied gallantly, my first big whopper of the night. "I'm sure Barney knew nothing about your being on the beach. Put it out of your mind, child. I've been digging in this case for weeks and I haven't heard a whisper that you've even known any soldier."

She smiled up at me gratefully. "And then I guess I blinded myself to the truth, mostly for the sake of Barney's daughter. Having such a mother as the child has, I just could not bear the thought that she must now think her father. . . . In fact that still oppresses me more than anything."

"Mary," I said, putting my hand on hers, "please do something for me. In the morning please phone the prosecutor the first thing about the lie-detector test. He'll tell you. Then go see the caretaker, Mr. Lemon, about the tourists who heard the screams. I want you to be sure."

"I will, Paul—but I really know now. I'm afraid it is the truth." She smiled wanly. "You would not have told me if it weren't. I could *see* you were telling the truth. You looked far too desperate and unlawyer-like." She looked down at my hand, still covering hers, and then back at me.

"Thank you, Mary," I said, abruptly rising. "I—I really must be going. I've kept you up way too late. Forgive me for intruding at such an hour."

"Thank you for coming, Paul," Mary Pilant said. "I'm so relieved to be able to talk at last with someone I feel I can trust." She brushed her forehead with the back of her hand. "I—I've been so confused."

"There's only one thing that I must tell you, Mary," I said. "I *must* bring out this rape and the drinking and pistols. It all happened and I must bring it out. You understand that, I hope."

"Yes, I understand," she said ruefully, shaking her head.

"It will be tough on you and the child, I know," I said. "But wouldn't it be much worse for the child to think that her father, cold sober, could have done such a thing? Don't you see, Mary, the truth itself carries a kind of a human if not legal excuse. There was frailty here, too—it was not all pure evil."

She nodded and walked with me to the door. While standing there she looked so utterly alone and helpless that I longed to fold her in my arms and hold her until her troubles went away. Instead I did a most singular thing, at the same time feeling surely as old as George Bernard Shaw, if scarcely as wise: I raised my hand and gingerly patted the top of her head, muttering, "There, there," or some such deathlessly comforting words.

We stood there awkwardly in a shaft of streaming moonlight. Mary Pilant took my hand and clung to it fiercely for a moment with both of hers, staring intently up at me. "You are a good man, Paul Biegler," she whispered, and then *she* did a most singular thing: she grasped both my lapels and pulled me down and her lips barely grazed mine—cool, soft, and tremulous as the wings of a moth. "Good night, Paul," she whispered, turning away and quickly closing the door. I stood alone blinking at the door for a moment and then lurched drunkenly, ecstatically down the silent hallway, restraining a wild impulse to shout and sing and whistle. I was drunk not on whisky but from fatigue and relief for my case and—what else could it be?—a throbbing hope for the future. Her words rang in my ears, over and over. "Someday," she had said, "someday I might meet a man I really care for. . . ." "You are a good man, Paul Biegler. . . ." Surely in my moonlit delirium I must have dreamed the rest.

chapter 14

Sore tempted as I was to get a room and sleep at the Thunder Bay Inn, all things considered I thought I had better not, and instead I drove back to Iron Bay. The trip was a moonlit nightmare, I was so tired, and I snatched a few hours sleep at a hotel near the court-house, leaving a call and rising in time to shave and change my shirt and snatch some breakfast and dash off to court. As I was taking the short cut through the clerk's office the deputy clerk, Mollie, was on the phone. "Here he is now," she said, handing me the phone. Nine o'clock was just striking and I was tempted to ask Mollie to take the number. Then I changed my mind; one never knew. . . .

"Hello," I said. "This is Paul Biegler."

"This is Mary," a low voice said. She told me that she had con-firmed my story of the screams and lie-detector test, and that she had also tried to mollify the bartender, who had evidently learned to love me as much as I him.

"Thank you, Mary. I'll try to handle our little bartender with kid gloves."

"Please, Paul, let me know what happens," she said, "and good luck."

"I'll call you, Mary. . . ." I said. "You know I'll call you."

As I galloped on air up the steel-shod back stairs I could hear the muffled thud of the Sheriff's gavel and I arrived breathless in the courtroom just in time for the "Be seated, please." Well, at last I had direct confirmation on the lie-detector test.

The Judge looked down at my table and then over at Mitch's. "Gentlemen," he said, "normally I insist that counsel arise and re-main standing when addressing the court or examining a witness. But in view of the expanding and uncertain length of this trial and"—he paused and smiled faintly—"and its rather hectic pace, I am henceforth going to let you remain seated if you wish." He smiled. "Do I hear any objections?"

Mitch and Claude Dancer sprang to their feet. "None, Your Honor," they chimed.

"The defense is delighted and grateful, Your Honor," I said, re-maining seated to try out this merciful new dispensation. What a fine, thoughtful judge.

"Call your first witness," the Judge said, nodding at Mitch's table.

"Detective Sergeant Julian Durgo," Claude Dancer announced.

Dark, handsome, curly-haired Julian Durgo took the stand and was sworn. He could have walked on to any movie set without make-up: assured, smart, and taciturn. Despite all this he was a fine officer, both efficient and honest, and I hoped he did not have too much bad news to unfold. I had worked with him my last four or five years as prosecutor and I had never once seen him take an unfair advantage of a criminal defendant, either in court or out. If Jule said a thing was thus or so the chances were pretty good that it was the solemn truth.

Questioned adroitly by Claude Dancer, Julian gave his name and address and briefly recounted his considerable experience as a plain-clothes detective with the state police.

"Did you have occasion to investigate the fatal shooting of Barney Quill?" Claude Dancer asked crisply.

"I did. I headed the investigation," Julian answered quietly.

"Will you tell us what you did?"

Julian Durgo related how he had got the call at the Iron Bay post around 1:15 and immediately proceeded to Thunder Bay with the coroner and Lieutenant Webley and a young state trooper. They had dropped the coroner and spare trooper at the bar to tend to the body and take the measurements and the rest and had gone immediately to the cottage of the caretaker-deputy. Mr. Lemon had pointed out the Manion trailer and the two officers had gone there and identified themselves and been admitted by the Lieutenant and placed him under arrest.

"Did you discuss the shooting then or later with Lieutenant Manion?" Claude Dancer asked.

"I did. Both then and later."

"Will you tell us, Officer, what he said?"

The Judge glanced quickly at me and I shook my head. I could have objected on the grounds that it had not yet been shown that the police had first warned the Lieutenant of his constitutional rights, including his right not to talk. But I did not object because I was morally certain that Julian had indeed warned my man, he always did. Moreover I knew that the jury must be dying to hear the story anyway and if I objected I would betray on our part a lack of candor and an apparent effort to hide the truth. Claude Dancer knew all this, too, and had doubtless set out another of his clever little traps.

"I asked the Lieutenant where the gun was and he pointed at a table and said he would get it, but I said no and instead got it my-

284

self," Julian Durgo replied in his careful, thoughtful way, answering no more than he was asked.

"And is this the gun?" Claude Dancer said, handing the lüger to Julian, who identified it and the gun was quickly admitted in evidence. I wondered whether the dead German lieutenant, from whatever craggy Valhalla he now occupied, could see what was happening to his old gun.

"Were you present later at the bar when an effort was made to recover the bullets?" Claude Dancer asked.

"I was. I conducted the search."

"Were any recovered?"

"Four bullets were found, along with five shell cases. We also discovered that the mirror had been broken along with a bottle of whisky."

"Did you preserve and do you now have the bullets and shell cases?"

"I did and I have," the witness answered, and he produced a tagged cloth sack upon which the court reporter proceeded to mark the People's latest exhibit number. Claude Dancer then reached in the cloth bag and retrieved the bullets.

"And are these the bullets that killed Barney Quill?"

"They are the lead pellets we found in the barroom, sir," Julian Durgo replied evenly, carefully refusing to assume more than he actually knew.

Claude Dancer stood thoughtfully before the jury rolling the bullets lovingly in his fingers, much like Captain Queeg and his famous ball bearings. It was a nice tawdry little show: the lower Michigan criminal lawyer would at once demonstrate to the jury his vast experience in criminal trials and his bored familiarity with the handling of bullets that had snuffed out the lives of murdered men. I stared at him, half in admiration for his cleverness and half in scorn over this glutinous display of courtroom histrionics.

"Pardon me, Your Honor," he said, and he trotted over to my table with his short rumpy canter and, holding his hand high, made as though to dump the bullets in my hand, at the same time saying: "The People now hand defense counsel for inspection the bullets that killed Barney Quill."

"The little bastard," I thought as I quickly folded my arms and leaned back in my chair. "No thanks, Mr. Dancer," I said. "I once saw a bullet. It was removed from the body of a deer hunter"—I squinted appraisingly—"just about your size." I looked up at the Judge. "The defense has no objections, Your Honor."

The courtroom tittered and the Judge frowned and reached for his gavel and then said, when quiet was restored: "The exhibits will be received in evidence. Proceed, Mr. Dancer."

Claude Dancer had glided back before the witness. "Getting back to the defendant at the trailer, what else if anything did he say?"

"He told us that his wife had had some trouble with Barney Quill and that he had gone and shot him. He also asked us whether the man was dead and we said that he was."

"What then?"

"Then we drove him and his wife to the county jail."

"Was there any further talk in the car on the drive down?"

"Yes, on the drive down the Lieutenant said he had thought the whole thing over before going to the bar and had decided that such a man should not live."

Claude Dancer paused to let this sink in and steal a look at me. This was a massive body blow to our insanity defense and both he and I knew it. I glanced at the jury and to a man they were staring intently at the witness. I did not dare stop to ask my man now whether this had happened. Anyway, the dialogue of our drama had now changed sharply against us and I leaned forward as Dancer pressed relentlessly on.

"How did the defendant appear?"

"He was upset and emotional and appeared very angry."

This was probably objectional as an unwarranted inference or conclusion of the witness, but I remained glued to my chair. There was no use underlining how important I considered all this by risking a losing objection. Anyway the jury had heard it now—*they* wouldn't forget. . . .

"What else?" Claude Dancer said, stalking softly.

"He said that he had no regrets over what he'd done, that he'd do it again. Several times more he asked us if the deceased was really dead."

All this was more massive blows to our defense and I sat as still as a mouse. Good God, had the Lieutenant also signed a written confession I didn't know about? Was our defense going straight up the flue?

"Then what?" the Dancer purred.

"Then we arrived at the county jail and I asked the defendant if he cared to make a formal statement and he said no. Then he was booked on murder and locked up and we returned immediately to Thunder Bay to continue the investigation."

Claude Dancer looked over at me with a nodding smile. "Your witness," he said, almost purring.

I glanced over at a white-faced Parnell and then up at the skylight. I had myself a delicate problem. Here was a witness whom I admired and respected both as an officer and a man. I also admired and respected his state police organization. But there was no doubt in my mind that his testimony was being kept under wraps by someone, and that that someone was probably Claude Dancer and not the officer himself. Julian Durgo was the kind of careful and conscientious officer who did not answer more than he was asked, and it was apparent that Dancer had carefully confined his questions only to the parts that were bad. But whatever the reason, Julian's testimony had been sorely damaging to my client—how much I could not yet tell—and I hoped and felt that there must be something that might help. How could I drag all this out without appearing to put this fine officer or his outfit on the spot? Well, drag it out I must. . . .

"Officer Durgo," I said, remaining seated, "on direct examination I believe you testified that the Lieutenant told you that he had shot Barney Quill after he had learned from his wife that she had had 'some trouble' with the deceased, did you not?"

Quietly: "I did, sir."

"Now, officer, were those words 'some trouble' the words Lieutenant Manion used to you or rather are they the words that you have used here in order to briefly describe what it was he actually told you?"

"They were my words, sir. I don't recall that the Lieutenant used that expression."

"All right, Detective," I said, "will you now please tell the court and the jury what the words were that the defendant himself used when he described this trouble his wife had had with the deceased?"

"Yes, sir. He said—"

"*Objection!* Objection, Your Honor," the Dancer boomed. "Court has ruled on all that. Would not be relevant to any issues properly—"

I leapt to my feet. "Lissen, Dancer!" I shouted, suddenly goaded beyond all endurance. "Whaddya tryin' to do—railroad this poor guy to the clink? This is cross-examination in a murder case, not a high-school debate. You and your incessant chatter about relevant issues, issues, issues. . . ." (I could hear the Judge calling my name and pounding his gavel, but the only way he could have stopped me then was to have used it over my head.) "You want to unload all the bad news on my man but none of the good. Issues, issues, issues!" I imitated his voice. " 'Dear Judge, please let's not mention anything as horrid as rape until somebody gets raped! Let's not let Junior go near the water, mother, till he learns how to swim. . . .' Listen, fella—who in—who in the blazes do you think you're foolin'?"

"Mr. Biegler, Mr. Biegler," the Judge kept calling, and I finally turned to him, hot and flushed. He too was deeply flushed with anger. "I must warn you against another such outburst," he said sternly. "You are an experienced lawyer and know better, much better. Henceforth please address your comments on objections solely to the Court. I cannot tolerate another such intemperate display—and I warn you I shall not. The only reason I am overlooking this one is that I realize you men are under such a strain."

"I'm sorry, Your Honor," I said. "I apologize to the court." (In my burst of anger I had not entirely lost sight of the fact that my outburst might obliquely do him some good, too.) "Your Honor," I went on, "I shall now address my remarks on the objections, if I may." The Judge nodded grimly and I went on. "This witness is a key witness for the People. He has investigated this alleged murder. He has given testimony here today which, if unexplained or not further explored, could conceivably be most harmful to this defendant. I think and I insist that we have the right *now*, while the one-sided impact of that testimony is still fresh before the jury, to learn *all* that he knows, everything that the defendant and his wife told him. I think we should have this right in order to bring out the true climate and circumstances in which those admissions, if any, were made. Insanity is an issue in this case; it has been an issue in this case since the start of this trial; and we submit that whatever *trouble* this defendant's wife had had with the deceased must have triggered or at least contributed to that claimed insanity. We now seek to find out what that 'trouble' was."

I paused, my mind racing, feeling that this, at last, was it and that I had better be good. "Among other things this witness has testified that the defendant told him he shot Barney because his wife had had 'some trouble' with the dead man. What kind of trouble? Had Barney called her a bad name? Had he cheated her at pinball? On the face of it it must be apparent even to a child that the defendant said more than that to Officer Durgo if he said anything at all. That he said *something* this witness has already testified. I submit and I urge with the utmost seriousness that we should be entitled to get into that 'something' here and now and not later on after the impression of this adroitly restricted direct testimony has jelled." I dropped my voice; a little genteel warning might not be amiss. "It would be a pity, Your Honor," I said, "to inject grave error into this case now when we are so close to being done." I turned away abruptly and sat down. The fate of the whole case, I felt, now hung in the balance.

The Judge had listened intently and he leaned back in his chair and looked up at the skylight, his fingertips together and his lips thoughtfully pursed. Claude Dancer arose and advanced as though to give argument, but the Judge waved him away. The courtroom grew hushed. I heard the electric click of the clock on the wall behind me and it sounded like a brass gong. The Judge leaned forward and looked at the clock as though to mark the hour of his decision.

"I am going to take the answer," he said.

"The defendant told us that the deceased had raped his wife," Julian Durgo said quietly.

I sighed inwardly and was glad I was seated. "At last," I thought, "at last I got the lady laid!" Never had I had a harder chore, in court or out. . . .

"What else?"

"He said he had taken a nap earlier and that around nine o'clock his wife had gone to the hotel bar to get some beer and that he had planned to join her later. The next thing he knew he heard some screams—and his wife fell in his arms."

"And you saw the wife?"

"Yes, sir."

"What shape was she in?"

"She was semi-hysterical and sobbing and her face and arms were badly bruised."

"And did she tell you her story?"

"She did."

"And what did she say?"

"Objection, Your Honor—this—"

"The objection is overruled. Proceed."

"She said that Barney Quill had raped her and beat her up."

"Without going into detail now, Sergeant, did you ask her and did she tell you that Barney Quill had raped her?"

"I did and she did."

"In great detail?"

"In great detail."

"And did she tell you it was in the woods on the other side of the main road?"

"Yes, sir."

"And about the second attack back at the tourist park gate when she escaped and was caught and further assaulted and screamed and then finally escaped?"

"She did, sir."

"And did she lead you officers to the side road where the first attack was alleged to have occurred?"

"Yes, sir."

"And did you find tire marks and burns and dog tracks in on that road?"

"Yes, sir."

"And looked for her panties but couldn't find them?"

"Correct, sir."

"And was this the 'some trouble' that Lieutenant Manion referred to?"

"It was."

"And was it your notion to come in to this court and call it that?"

Quietly: "It was not, sir."

"Was the suggestion made to you to call it that by someone now in this room?"

The witness looked over at Claude Dancer, as I guessed he would, like a careful officer, to confirm that he was still there. "He is, sir."

I paused and decided to let the subject rest there; I had got Julian Durgo off the hook and rested the blame finally where it belonged.

"There has been testimony here, Officer, that you were given Laura Manion's torn skirt for the purpose of having it tested for sperm or seminal stain. Was it so tested?"

"It was, sir."

"And the results?"

"They were negative."

I had been afraid of that, but I had to make sure on the off-chance that the People's studied silence on the subject had been an attempt to cover up. Claude Dancer had finally sprung one of his little traps on me and he grinned amiably across at me and, wincing, I gravely nodded my congratulations.

"And the clothing worn by the deceased—were they so tested too?"

I pressed doggedly on, like a boxer being helplessly clubbed on the ropes.

"They were."

"And the results?"

"Also negative, sir."

Again a delighted and toothsome Claude Dancer grinned happily over at me. "Would the fact that they were blood-soaked have had any effects on the test?" I went glumly on, taking a shot in the dark.

"It would, sir," the witness answered. "In fact our laboratory man did not see any use in testing them—it seems that excessive blood has a tendency to obliterate or merge evidence of sperm or seminal stain—but he nevertheless did so to complete the tests and quiet any future argument."

Well, I'd softened the blow a little, at least. My next question was aimed more at the jury than at the witness. "There was also present the great possibility that if the deceased *had* raped Mrs. Manion, he would doubtless have changed his clothes before he was shot, was there not?"

Claude Dancer half rose in his chair, as though to object, and then, thinking better, slowly sank back.

"You're reprieved," I prompted the witness. "You may dare to speak now without mortal danger."

"Yes, sir," the witness replied, and at last I was able to leer back at Claude Dancer. It was time, I saw, to forsake the uneasy subject of blood-stained clothing.

"Now, Officer," I said. "I assume you conducted an independent investigation then and later to check on the story of the alleged rape, did you not?"

"I did, sir; an extensive one."

"And did that investigation tend to confirm or refute Mrs. Manion's story of the rape?"

"Confirm it, sir."

"In every particular?"

"In every particular."

"And what were some of these things that confirmed your opinion on that score?"

"Well, sir, the scene of the attack, which I've described." He paused. "The biggest thing was the screams."

"Screams, Detective? What screams?" If I looked surprised I was sure it was not half as much as I felt.

"Mrs. Manion had told us she had screamed several times at the gate. We naturally checked on that—not only to find out if she had screamed but whether the screams might not have instead come from the trailer."

"You mean, Officer, to find out whether it might not have been her husband who beat her up for staying out alley-catting?"

He smiled slightly. "Well, yes, sir, that's about it."

"And what did you learn?"

"That the screams came from the gate, as she had said. We found four tourists whose trailers were closest to the main gate. They all said they were awakened around midnight by a series of screams coming from the gate. One of them also heard a moaning and a dull thud, like something hitting the ground."

"And you have the names and addresses of these witnesses?"

"I have."

"And you had long ago turned this information over to the prosecuting officials?"

"Yes, sir."

I paused and glanced at my juror; I'd been neglecting him lately, but he still looked good. "Now, I ask you, Sergeant, if you are an expert pistol shot?"

Modestly: "Well, Mr. Biegler—yes, sir, I guess I am."

"And you are familiar with pistols and ammunition?"

"I believe I am, sir."

"And have you ever engaged in pistol shoots with persons not in police work?" (This too was a shot in the dark.)

"Occasionally."

"In this county?"

"Yes, sir."

"Was one of them the deceased, Barney Quill?"

"Yes, sir."

"And was he also an expert?"

"Yes, sir. I would say he was among the best I have ever seen."

"We're up, we're down, we're up. . . ." I thought. I reached for the lüger among the exhibits and handed it to the witness. "Are you familiar with this type of weapon?"

"I am, sir. It is a German lüger."

"What happens when it is empty?"

"Well, without getting technical, when it is empty—as it is now, the gun stays open, this gadget goes up, and the trigger clicks loose—like this."

"So that a person familiar with that weapon could tell it was empty simply by looking at it, without opening it?"

"Correct."

I took the gun and returned it to the pile of exhibits. "Returning now, Detective, to your confirmation of Mrs. Manion's story of the rape, was there anything else that tended to convince you of the truth of her story?" (I was at last trying to lead up to the lie-detector test.)

"There was."

"What?"

The witness knew that such tests were inadmissible in court, and he glanced uncertainly at the Judge. "Well," he said, "we questioned her again at length at the state police barracks."

"Who is we?"

"Lieutenant Webley, myself and—" The witness hesitated.

"And who else, Sergeant?"

"Lieutenant Peterhaus, sir."

"What does he do? I don't believe his name is endorsed on the information or was mentioned before in this case?"

"He is our expert on the polygraph."

"And what is the polygraph?"

"It is generally known as the lie detector, sir."

"You mean, Detective, that Mrs. Manion was given a lie-detector test?"

"Objection. Results of polygraphs never admissible in our courts, as counsel well knows."

"Your Honor," I said, "no one is talking about the *results* of any lie-detector test, but whether one was given."

The Judge thoughtfully pursed his lips. "Take the answer," he said.

"She was given such a test, yes."

"And was this test given before or after you had determined on your own whether she was telling the truth?"

"After."

"At whose request?"

"Mrs. Manion's."

"And after the test was given did you change your mind on that score?"

"Your Honor, Your Honor!" Dancer was shouting behind me, nearly beside himself, making little sqealing noises, like a Japanese general fallen on his sword. "This is a sly subterfuge to get around the rule barring such tests. The defense has never asked us for the results. I—I—"

I leered across the room at my excited friend and spoke quietly. "We ask you now, Mr. Dancer."

"Gentlemen, gentlemen," the Judge said, his voice rising. "There has been a question and an objection and I must make a ruling, which I cannot do if you keep up this unholy wrangling. We are skating on thin ice, I realize, but in all conscience I cannot rule that the question is objectionable. Counsel is not asking for the results of any polygraph test but the opinion of the witness based upon certain knowledge possessed by him. Take the answer."

"My mind did not change."

"So that before the polygraph test you believed she was telling the truth?"

"Yes, sir."

"And after?"

"Yes, sir."

"And do you still believe it up to this moment?"

Crisply: "Yes, sir."

"Finally, Officer, wasn't that the real reason you did not ask Dr. Raschid during the autopsy to make any tests for possible recent intercourse or the alcoholic content of the blood?"

Nodding: "Yes, sir."

"It was never with any idea, then or now, that you or your organization wanted to suppress anything here in court?"

"Certainly not."

"But rather because you and your organization were then satisfied beyond all doubt that the rape had in fact taken place and that no further confirmation was necessary?"

"Precisely, sir."

"And at that time, Officer, did you anticipate that any question would ever be raised or issue made over the fact of that rape, least of all by the prosecution?"

The witness shot a look at Claude Dancer's table. "I certainly did not, sir," he said. Julian Durgo, I saw, had not been happy with his role in the trial of this case.

"Thank you, Officer," I said. "Your witness, Mr. Dancer."

Bulldog Dancer was not a man to give up easily. "Officer," he tugged away, "couldn't the screams at the gate have been those of a man?" ("Ah," I thought, "Laura is now raping Barney.")

294

"Possibly, Mr. Dancer," the witness answered crisply. "Except that all the tourists said they were a woman's."

"But did the tourists know it was *this* woman's screams?" he said, pointing at Laura.

"They did not, sir."

"Your witness," Claude Dancer said, looking as triumphant as though he had just uncovered a brand-new batch of Dead Sea scrolls.

"Officer," I said, "during your investigation did you hear of any *other* woman or women who had screamed in the park that night?— at the gate or anywhere?"

Smiling briefly: "I did not, sir."

"You were unable to dig up any evidence of a general epidemic of screaming females that night?"

"Only the one occasion at the gate, sir."

"No further questions," I said.

"The witness is excused," Claude Dancer said.

"Fifteen minutes, Mr. Sheriff," the Judge said

chapter 15

During recess Parnell and I huddled in the conference room where I hastily tried to bring him up to date on my strange moonlit session with Mary Pilant. I told him everything—well, almost everything. His white-faced relief over learning that his Nora-Mary was all the things he'd hoped she might be was touching to behold. "Ah, Polly, Polly, I knew it, lad, I knew it all along. . . ."

I aroused myself from a pensive dream of Mary and shrugged. "Well, Parn," I said, "it now looks as though all our work and worry over the will contest—mostly your work and worry—was all in vain. I guess it doesn't make much difference now whether the bartender comes our way or not."

"Not on your life, Polly," Parnell said. "You've got your rape in, now, yes—and thank goodness for that—but that still is not a *legal* defense to this murder. We've still got that problem to face, and also the big twin problem of *why* the Lieutenant went to the bar that night carrying a concealed weapon. The bartender can help us on all that if he will. Do you think he will, boy?"

"Lord knows, Parn," I said. "I told you what Mary Pilant phoned me. Pretty soon we find out about the slippery bartender. I wish I'd been sweeter to him when I was little. Ah for the days of yesteryear. 'O lost and by the wind—' "

Max Battisfore popped his head in the door. "Second act curtain in two minutes, Polly," he said.

"Thanks, Max," I said, tightening my necktie.

"You know," Parnell said thoughtfully as I snapped shut my swollen brief case, "that Sheriff of ours might have possibilities if he'd only get out of politics. He—he kind of grows on me."

Mitch got up following the recess and addressed the court. "Your Honor, we have now obtained the three photographs of Mrs. Manion taken shortly after the shooting, and we tender them to the defense." He walked over and handed me the three missing photographs. The Lieutenant and Laura and I studied them; Parnell's little old caretaker had described Laura as a "mess," and these pictures richly bore him out; her hair was streaming in her eyes; her face was streaked with dirt and tears; and she possessed two of the loveliest shiners west of Rocky Marciano's former training quarters.

"Thank you, Mr. Prosecutor," I said. "The lost sheep have returned. But I don't want these pictures for my scrapbook: I want them in evidence in this court. Your photographer took them, not mine. I can't get them in. Don't you propose to introduce them in evidence as you have all the others? It will not be necessary to recall the photographer—I'll gladly stipulate."

I had put Mitch on the spot, and he glanced at Claude Dancer for succor, and the little man was shrewd enough to see the red light ahead. He nodded the signal and Mitch murmured "O.K." and the missing pictures were swiftly marked by the reporter and received in evidence as People's exhibits.

I arose by my chair. "Your Honor," I said sweetly, "the defense requests the court's permission to have the jury look at these latest exhibits at this time—that is, if the People raise no objection."

Mitch's hot spots were coming in bunches and he again sought a cue from his assistant and again got the nod—all of which little pantomime the intent jurors carefully absorbed, I noted without dismay. "No objection, Your Honor," he said.

"Very well, Mr. Biegler, the People's photographs of the defendant's wife may be shown to the jury at this time," the Judge said.

I lolled back in my chair, much like a languid tourist with a hamper of beer plunking for bass from a public pier. "I thought maybe Prosecutor Lodwick would graciously hand them to the jury," I said. "He now has them, he's so much closer and so much younger, alas—and he's lately enjoyed such a good rest, too."

Mitch flushed and shot me a dark look, and wordlessly shoved the pictures at the nearest juror. The juror stared at the pictures intently while the others curiously leaned over and craned to see.

"The People will call Dr. Adelord Dompierre," Claude Dancer quickly announced. His strategy was transparent—to get another witness going to distract the jurors from looking at the pictures of the ravished Laura and her elegant black eyes. This became even more clear when he gestured and nodded at Mitch to start examining the witness, who had now reached the stand.

"Your name, please?" Mitch obediently began.

"Your Honor," I said, "may I suggest that the examination of this new witness be held up briefly until the jurors have completed examining the exhibits—that's if Mr. Dancer should not feel compelled to object to an examination of his own exhibits." The withering look the little man shot at me made Mitch's a lingering caress by comparison.

"Of course not, Counselor," Claude Dancer purred suavely, and I grinned back my appreciation of his control and gameness under adverse fire.

The jurors examined the pictures with loving care and finally handed them back to the first juror, who handed them to Mitch, who moved over and dropped them on the mounting pile of People's exhibits as though they were bubbling hot pizzas fresh from the oven.

"The examination may proceed," the Judge said dryly.

Mitch fought his way through the preliminaries—name, address and all—and brought out the doctor's qualifications and then led up to his taking of the slides from Laura the night of the shooting. For this was the county jail physician, an amiable and moderately distracted little man who pattered along in a state of semi-retirement, occupying his time by occasionally delivering a new baby, but mostly in delivering Max's more regular jail tenants from the screaming meanies.

"Did you make a test on the person of Mrs. Laura Manion for the presence of sperm?" Mitch went on.

"Yes."

"When?"

Consulting a notebook: "I was called to the jail about five A.M. on August sixteenth."

"What did you do?"

"Do?" The witness spread his hands. "I take one vaginal slide and I take another deep vaginal slide and I have them tested for sperm."

"What were the results of your test?"

"They were negative, yes."

"Your witness."

I arose and advanced to the People's exhibits and picked up the pictures of Laura and silently handed them to the doctor. "Doctor," I said, "did you notice any bruises or marks on the person of Mrs. Manion when you examined her?" It was like asking a dripping Eskimo in a freshly tipped kayak if the water was cold.

"Oh, sure, sure—she was pretty bad, especially on the face and neck, like it shows."

"Were you instructed to look for and note her welts and bruises?"

"No, no."

"So your remarks about what you observed about her bruises and contusions was merely incidental to the main business of taking your slides?" I said, relieving the witness of the pictures.

"Yes. A man couldn't help but notice."

"And did you ever tell the prosecuting officers about your find-ings concerning any bruises and the like?"

"No."

"And were you ever asked by them about them?"

"No."

"Regarding the smear, how did you take it?"

"Well, I had the woman lie down and I took the smears with an applicator."

"And what's that?"

"A long slender stick with a swab of cotton on the end, so."

"Did you dilate the vaginal orifice?"

"I didn't have to—there was no difficulty, no."

"Did you know when you came to the jail to take the smears that there was some question whether a woman had been raped?"

"Oh, yes."

"Did you know her age—whether she was a mature woman or a virgin of fifteen?"

"No."

"So you took a chance that you might not have to dilate with a speculum?"

"Well, yes." He spread his hands. "I have no speculum."

"But isn't that standard good practice, Doctor, to use a speculum or expander when taking a vaginal slide?"

"Not necessarily. Anyway I had none."

"But aren't there situations where a doctor might *have* to use a speculum to properly take a vaginal slide?"

"Oh, yes."

"Wouldn't it be fair to say, Doctor, that the taking of vaginal slides is not and has never been one of your specialties?"

"Well, yes."

"During the last ten years how many vaginal slides have you taken at the county jail?"

The doctor shrugged. "Oh, maybe four-five. I don't keep track."

"And most of those were for gonorrhea?"

"All of them—except this."

"So that during the last ten years you've taken one set of slides to determine the presence of sperm?—this one?"

"Well, yes."

"And what did you do with these slides?"

"I took them to the laboratory at St. Margaret's Hospital."

"And who worked them up?"

"A technician."

"What kind of technician?"

"Oh, X-ray, like that."

"Is he a doctor or a pathologist or an expert in the field of working up slides to detect the presence of sperm?"

"He is a technician."

"I see—and how old is this technician?"

"Young fellow—thirty or so."

"His main job is to take X-ray pictures of people with broken legs and the like?"

"Yes."

"Doctor, would not the normal or at least the safest procedure have been to take the slides to an expert?"

Shrugging: "Well, the police were in a big hurry and I knew this young fellow came on at seven."

"It was swifter to have the X-ray boy do it if not safer, is that it?"

"Well, yes, I suppose."

"But it would have been safer to bring it to an expert if not so swift?"

"Yes."

"And especially wouldn't this be true, Doctor, if a possible question of rape hung on the results?"

The doctor was getting a little despondent. "Yes," he said.

"Now the local newspaper for the evening of August sixteenth states that you reported you found no sign of rape. Is that a correct report of your findings?"

"No, I didn't say anything like that."

"And you don't know, then, whether or not this woman had been raped?"

"No. It is impossible to tell that on a mature woman."

"And on any question of rape, Doctor, are you for your part willing to accept the word of those who may be in a better position to know?"

Relieved: "Gladly."

"No further questions," I said.

"Back to you, Mr. Prosecutor," the Judge said.

Mitch didn't need a cue from his assistant on this one. "No questions," he hurriedly said.

"Call your next witness."

"Your Honor," Mitch said, "Lieutenant Webley, who accompanied and assisted Detective Sergeant Durgo in the investigation of this case has been stricken with a virus infection since the start of this trial. He is presently in the hospital under a doctor's care. We can produce his doctor if. . . ." Mitch paused and looked over at me.

I arose and addressed the court. I certainly did not want to insist upon another witness coming in and repeating the story of the Lieutenant's damaging admissions on the night of the shooting (during recess the Lieutenant had told me he had no recollection of making them) and I further felt that nobody could have improved on the good things Julian Durgo had had to say.

"The doctor is not necessary, Your Honor," I said. "I have heard of Lieutenant Webley's unfortunate illness and we are satisfied that his testimony is largely cumulative and the defense waives his production here as a witness."

"Very well," Judge Weaver said, "the witness may be excused. Call your next."

"A moment please, Your Honor," Claude Dancer said, and the Judge nodded and Mitch and his assistant fell into a prolonged whispered huddle from which Mitch finally emerged to arise and announce, "Your Honor, the People rest."

A milestone in the trial had been reached—but had it? "Your Honor," I said, "I believe the People inadvertently forgot some unfinished business. I had not completed my cross-examination of the People's witness, Alphonse Paquette, the bartender at the Thunder Bay Inn. I rather think the time is now ripe."

"I believe your point is well taken, Mr. Biegler," the Judge said, looking at Mitch's table. "Gentlemen?"

Claude Dancer half rose from his chair and snapped: "The People recall the witness Paquette."

I carefully watched the sleek little bartender detach himself from the body of the courtroom and hasten to the stand, holding up his hand for the oath.

"You are already sworn," the Judge said kindly. "One oath to a customer. Please be seated."

"The People tender the witness," Claude Dancer said.

"Your witness, Mr. Biegler," the Judge said, and I got up and moved slowly before the witness, who sat facing me tense and very still. It was like approaching a strange beach full of hidden land mines. What would be my opening gambit, my trial balloon? But why beat around the bush?—the little man was either with us or against us.

"The subject, Mr. Paquette, is pistols," I said. "Was Barney Quill an expert pistol shot?"

"Objection, Your Honor," spouted Mr. Dancer, like the Old Faithful geyser in my fifth-grade reader. "The court has already ruled on that. Irrelevant and immaterial. Absolutely beside the point."

"But the People's own witness, Detective Sergeant Durgo, has now made the deceased an expert pistol shot," I said. "We seek only to develop that interesting subject."

The Judge stared out at the clock. "Strictly speaking you may have a point, Mr. Dancer," he said. "But the subject is now in the case, and this witness is now on the stand. Moreover he has been in attendance here at public expense since the start of the trial. And I presume that he, like most of us, has occasionally to work for a living. The witness may answer."

I held my breath for the answer.

"I would say he was an expert, sir," the witness answered.

"Objection, objection. Witness not shown to be qualified to pass expert opinion."

"I'll get to that, Your Honor," I said, "—Mr. Dancer please kindly permitting."

"Proceed, proceed. I'll reserve my ruling," the Judge said.

"Upon what do you base your conclusion, Mr. Paquette, that Barney was an expert pistol shot?" I asked.

This witness was a sensitive soul, I discovered; he was now getting a little annoyed with Claude Dancer, too. "Because I've seen him shoot against the best and beat 'em," he said. "He's won dozens and scores of first prizes at shoots all over the Peninsula. The man was deadly."

"Anything else?"

"I've seen Barney bring down partridge on the wing with a pistol—in fact it's the only way he hunted them."

"Anything else?"

"Barney and I used to go out to the garbage dump with an accumulation of empty bottles from the bar. My job was to toss them up in the air. Barney'd shoot them as fast as I threw them and holler for more. He rarely missed."

"And was Barney's prowess with pistols generally known around Thunder Bay?"

"It was." The witness paused. "Mr. Quill was never one to hide his light under a bushel. He kept his medals on the back-bar."

I looked over at Claude Dancer. "Do the People still press their objection?"

"Ruling, Your Honor," Claude Dancer said, fighting gamely to the end.

"I'm afraid the People's objection is overruled," the Judge said dryly.

I thought I detected a slight smile flit across the face of the witness. "Passing now to any pistols possessed by Mr. Quill," I said. "Did he own any?"

"He has owned many pistols—sometimes as high as fifteen or twenty at a time. I suppose he could have been called an amateur collector. He kept buying and selling and trading them. At the time of the"—the witness paused—"during this past summer he was down to six of his favorites."

"The witness is coming, the witness is coming," I thought. "And where did he keep these pistols?" I pressed exultantly.

The witness hesitated for a moment. "He kept two in his quarters upstairs in the hotel," he said.

"And the other four?" I said, asking the inevitable question.

The witness grew silent and looked up at the skylight. About then I would have given my best fly rod to have been able to peek into his darting mind. The courtroom grew hushed; even the whispering women now seemed to sense that this was a pregnant occasion.

"He kept them down in the barroom," the witness answered in a low voice.

"Loaded?"

"Invariably."

I glanced quickly at Parnell, who sat stoic as a Buddha; then I was back at the witness. "And where in the barroom?" I said.

"Behind the bar."

"And where behind the bar?" I dug away.

"He kept two on a little shelf he'd built in the middle—and one each at either end."

"Were they visible to persons standing in front?"

"They were not."

"And what was the purpose of these pistols?"

The eyes of the witness flickered ever so little and I was afraid I had pressed him too far. "Protection," he said. "Protection against trouble."

"Trouble?" I said.

"Holdups."

This opened up sylvan vistas but I did not follow them; I could not risk drying up this witness now. There was irony here: I had once promised faithfully to clobber this little man; now I sought only ways not to ruffle him. "And were these four pistols behind the bar the night of the shooting?" I asked, trying to keep the glee out of my voice.

"They were not," the witness replied. My heart sank. Was all this a clever trap the witness and Dancer had worked out? And why, oh why, had I asked that one fatal question too much? But if I hadn't Dancer surely would have. . . .

"Where were they?"

"I had locked them up."

"Why?"

"Because of Mr. Quill's drinking and general behavior."

Up, down; up, down. . . . "Did Mr. Quill consent to this?"

"He did not."

I hated to ask the next question, but I had to. If I didn't . . . "Was it these four bar pistols you locked up or all of them?" I asked, and held my breath.

"Only the four. Mr. Quill wouldn't give up the others. We didn't press the point after he promised to keep them up in his rooms."

"We?"

"After he promised Miss Mary Pilant and me. She was the hostess upstairs."

We were getting on delicate territory, and I veered away. I felt like a man walking barefoot on broken glass—with the ghostly Barney on hand shooting up more empty bottles. "Was the fact that you'd locked up these four guns general knowledge?"

"It was known only to Mr. Quill and Miss Pilant and me."

"And can you tell us more about why you felt obliged to lock up the four bar guns?" I said, cautiously feeding out more rope, reluctantly forsaking the role of the probing cross-examiner. I sensed I now had to allow this man room for retreat if I inadvertently pressed too far upon sensitive territory. The position was unique; I'd never before confronted it in a courtroom.

The witness grew thoughtful. "Well," he said slowly, "about two weeks before the shooting Mr. Quill began drinking more than usual. He grew irritable and quarrelsome and difficult—and we decided it was best to remove the guns from the bar."

"When did you lock them up?"

"Just about a week before the shooting."

There were dozens of questions I longed to ask: Had Barney asked for his guns back? Where were they then and now? These and many more questions shuttered crazily across my mind. But no, I couldn't risk it—we didn't need two coats of frosting on our cake.

"Could you venture to tell us the reason why Mr. Quill seemed upset and drank more than usual?" I said. The question was purely rhetorical; I had to ask it because the jury would expect me to. The shrewd witness evidently saw the point.

"No, sir," he said, and he must also have seen my look of relief.

"Could you tell us this, Mr. Paquette?—whatever the reasons, did they appear to have anything to do with the Manions?"

"I would say definitely not, sir. None whatever."

I glanced over at Claude Dancer who sat staring stonily at the far wall, his arms folded like Napoleon at Elba, and I also longed to peek into his darting otter brain.

After that I brought out that Barney Quill had been at the bar earlier that night; that he'd played pinball with Laura, as she claimed; that he'd left about the same time as she had, around 11:00; that he'd returned to the bar shortly after midnight; that he'd relieved the bartender so he could "rest," and pretty much all that the bartender had told me on my earlier visit to Thunder Bay. I carefully avoided the subject of his possibly being a "lookout" (the conversion of hostile witnesses had its disadvantages, too, I saw) and I resolutely stayed away from the subject of Barney's will and the rest. I could always argue the "lookout" business to the jury.

"When Mr. Quill reappeared at the bar," I went on, "did he come in the street door or from upstairs?"

"Upstairs, sir."

"Had he changed his clothing?"

The witness blinked. "My best recollection is that he had," he finally replied. "I recall that he was wearing a loose sweat shirt after, and he'd worn a white shirt before."

"Had it been a warm evening?"

"It was."

"Was it still warm in the bar after midnight?"

"It was. Quite stuffy and warm."

"Ah, truth," I thought, "your spell is irresistible." I paused, and dared not look at Parnell. On a hot night Barney had seen fit to change from a white shirt (dirt, lipstick?) to a hot *loose* sweat shirt (freedom of motion, room to smuggle down his pistols?). "Ladies and gentlemen of the jury . . ." I could almost hear myself saying.

"Mr. Paquette," I said, "the other day when I was questioning you"—I glanced back at Claude Dancer—"and we were so rudely interrupted, we were talking about Barney's drinking. Now was he drinking more than usual that day?"

I crouched waiting for the booming objection, and was almost disappointed when it did not roll forth. Evidently Mr. Dancer was in a pout and was going to stay mad.

"I wouldn't say that day," he replied, and my spirits sank. "I now recall he'd been drinking more than usual for about two weeks." My spirits rose. Up, down, up, down. . . .

"And what was his daily intake during more normal times?"

"Barney could easily drink eight to ten double shots a day."

"And how much was a double shot?"

"Two ounces."

That was eighteen to twenty ounces of whisky a day, I calculated, and I mentally gagged at the thought. "And was that whisky?"

"Yes, bonded 'white-vest' bourbon, as I call it. Mr. Quill drank only the best."

"Now how about during this two weeks before the shooting—how much was he drinking then?"

The witness shook his head. "It must have been easily a fifth. It got so I couldn't keep track."

"That was what you yourself saw?"

"Yes."

"And that didn't take into account what he might take in his rooms or elsewhere?"

"It did not, sir."

Barney had had at least four drinks with Laura and five more at the bar after the rape. That made nine, let's see, eighteen ounces he'd had since 9:00 that night besides whatever else he'd sneaked. It was faintly incredible. Lord, if I kept on at this rate I'd have the man blind drunk, and I didn't want that either.

"Could Barney carry quite a load without showing it?"

"Without showing it to strangers. We who knew him well could tell."

"He was not one to swagger and stagger and talk loud when he was loaded, then?"

"If anything he appeared more gentlemanly than usual. It was a way he had."

The time had come to put on a little more pressure. "About the guns being kept behind the bar against holdups, could you tell us how many holdups you had at the bar of the Thunder Bay Inn this past summer?"

Frowning: "None."

"Any attempts?"

"No."

"Had there been any such attempts during all the time you have worked there?"

"None."

"Have you ever heard of any holdups or attempts made before you came?"

"None."

"But the loaded guns were kept there for holdups?"

Smiling slightly: "For holdups, sir."

I could have gone on to the subject of whether Barney had had his own two guns behind the bar that night, and all the interesting questions that subject suggested, but I dared not. I was afraid to risk it. The jury now plainly knew there were two pistols unaccounted for and the witness might get in a jam with the police if I now made him admit there were guns he had hidden or not told them about. Why drive him to say that there weren't any?

I abruptly abandoned Barney and his guns and drinking. The "white-vest" bourbon had reminded me of something else. I saw I'd have to lower the boom still a little more.

"Did you drive Laura Manion to the jail at Iron Bay to see her husband the Sunday after the shooting?"

The witness stirred uneasily. "I did."

"Did you then give the Lieutenant a carton of cigarettes?"

"I did."

"And did you tell him in substance that the only thing you held against him was that he'd smashed your mirror and shot up a bottle of 'white-vest' bourbon instead of some cheap pilerun whisky?"

His eyes flickered and I saw that our brief honeymoon was about over. "I don't remember precisely what I said." His voice rose. "I was trying to cheer the man up. I may have said something like that for a joke."

"You wouldn't say you hadn't said it?"

"No."

"The fact was that your mirror *was* smashed and you *did* lose a bottle of bonded bourbon?"

"Yes."

"And on the way driving down did you tell Laura Manion that it was too bad she and the Lieutenant had arrived in Thunder Bay when they did?"

"I may have. What I meant was that if they weren't there they couldn't have been in all this trouble."

"Naturally. Maybe you were trying to sympathize?"

"Yes."

I now lowered the boom a little more. "And were you also trying to sympathize when you told Laura Manion you could have warned her that Barney was a wolf?"

I'd tagged him at last and his eyes glittered with sudden anger. "I didn't say I said that," he blurted angrily. "You're trying to trap me with smart lawyer's questions."

Mildly: "I appreciate the testimonial, but I ask you now, Mr. Paquette. Surely that is no trap. Did you say that to Mrs. Manion? Did you refer to Barney as a wolf?"

"I don't recall saying any such thing," he snapped, and candidate Biegler had lost another vote for Congress.

It was my turn to study the skylight. This was the end of the line with this witness; in a sense I had used him and finally betrayed him. But perhaps it was better to close on an angry note before the jury got to thinking that the witness had been reached. I turned to Claude Dancer. "The witness is back to the prosecution."

Claude Dancer had grown grim and white; he looked boiling mad; he'd evidently counted on this witness for big things—the biggest thing probably being negative: a vast pall of silence on the significant disclosures I'd brought out. He arose and walked toward the witness.

"How did Mrs. Manion conduct herself at your barroom that night before the shooting?" he said crisply, as though biting each word.

The question was objectionable on several grounds, including leading one's own witness. It came to me now: this witness prior to his temporary "conversion" had evidently sought, for reasons of his own, to tear down Laura's behavior and character, much as he had to me when he'd called her a "floozie." He'd doubtless gone over all this with Claude Dancer and now the smarting Dancer was trying to bring it all out. I kept stoically silent.

"Well," the witness said, "at times I thought her behavior wasn't quite ladylike." I pricked up my ears.

"Like when?" Claude Dancer snapped.

"Like once when she took off her shoes to play pinball."

"All right. And didn't she do anything else while her shoes were off?"

"I don't recall, sir."

"Didn't she also dance with Hippo Lukes who carried her shoes in his pocket?" (A George Lukes had been one of the People's eye witnesses who had testified earlier to the shooting.)

I still kept silent. The Judge shot a surprised look at me, for this was a grievously objectionable question, leading, suggestive, prejudicial, and just about everything in the book, but I maintained my stolid silence; I was liking it better this way.

"I don't quite recall that, sir," the witness coolly answered.

There was no doubt in my mind now that the witness had told Dancer precisely that; Dancer was a hard and dangerous fighter but I was sure he wouldn't have stooped to make that up.

The color drained from his face, and I almost felt sorry for him—almost but not quite. "Have you been talking with Mr. Biegler since you last appeared in court here the other day?" The inference was plain that I had "reached" the witness, but I kept mum.

"I have, sir," the witness answered, and, startled, I stole a look at Parnell.

"Where and when?" Dancer pressed, beagling away on this scent.

"Why, today—just now, here in court."

Harshly: "I don't mean that. In private?"

"No, sir, I have not had a word with Mr. Biegler since this trial started," he truthfully replied.

"Or with anyone connected with the defense?"

"No sir, not a word," the witness again truthfully answered.

"Did you not tell me in private that, among other things, Mrs. Manion had so danced with Hippo Lukes?"

This was also highly objectionable but I resolutely held my fire. "I don't see how I could have, sir, when I don't recall ever seeing it," the witness answered. "You and I discussed quite a number of things and you may have misunderstood me." He paused. "Possibly you could ask Hippo Lukes himself—he should remember an incident like that."

Hippo Lukes had already been called off, I saw, and this clever lying little bastard of a bartender had doubtless arranged it. Though his testimony was helping us, or at least I hoped it was, I had never felt less gratified or, on the other hand, felt closer to Claude Dancer during the trial than now. The crushed and frustrated little man looked up at the Judge and held out his hands and shrugged. "Your witness," he said, wagging his bristling head.

"I have but one further question," I said. "Was this man Hippo Lukes that Mr. Dancer just referred to the same big red-faced man called George Lukes who testified here as a People's eyewitness the other day and was examined by Mr. Dancer?" I pointed out in the back court. "The same man sitting out there in the front row right now, grinning and with his hands on his knees?"

The witness smiled. "It was. That's our Hippo."

"No further questions," I said, happy to be done with the shifty Alphonse "Call-me-Al" Paquette, a little character who should have been in international counter-espionage rather than wasting his time tending bar.

Claude Dancer nodded his head grimly. "No more," he said. "Enough of this."

"Noon recess," the Judge said, and Max shot up and brought down his gavel as though he was chopping birch chunks out at his deer camp.

"I'll send the Lieutenant over soon, Max," I said to the hovering Sheriff. "We want to talk a little."

"O.K., Polly," Max said, departing, and I saw that all was not yet lost—like Mary's little lamb the Lieutenant could still be trusted to find his way home.

"Lieutenant," I said, "I've been so damned preoccupied with other things I haven't been able to keep an eye on Mr. Dancer's pet psychiatrist. Have you observed him analyzing you with his telescope?"

The Lieutenant was his usual helpful and co-operative self. "I hadn't noticed," he grunted briefly.

"Well I have," Laura said. "The man positively gives me the willies. Every time I glance over that way he's looking not at Manny but at *me*. Once or twice I think he smiled."

"Perhaps he's trying to make a date," I thought. I bowed gallantly. "Well at least, Laura, he's picked out the most attractive woman in the room," I said, disloyally forgetting the pretty virginal jurywoman. Laura was closer to testifying than she knew, and I had to try to keep her in good spirits. Anyway this was no more than the solemn truth.

"Oh thank you, Polly," Laura said, coloring, and the Lieutenant obediently scowled, still wearing his jealousy for all the world to see.

"Please put on all your ribbons and decorations tomorrow, Lieutenant," I said. We'd been saving them for when he took the stand. "Tomorrow may be the big day."

"Right," the Lieutenant said with his customary garrulity.

I explained to the Manions that we would now no longer need to use the photographs of Laura taken by our photographer because the People's were so much better. It was just another example of the "waste" of a trial, like all the futile legal research Parnell and I had done to possibly prevent the People's psychiatrist from getting a crack at our man. It was much the same in trials, I thought, as that old lion Sir Winston had said about war, where "nothing succeeds like excess."

I asked Laura about the "barefoot-dancing" story and she denied it vehemently. "I didn't dance with anybody," she said, "and if I had I wouldn't have danced with that grotesque lurching Zippo or

Hippo or whatever he's called." She made a face. "They had him on the stand before—why didn't they ask *him?*"

"Probably little Dancer was saving it for a surprise," I said. "He loves surprises, you know. Anyway, at that early point of the trial the People wouldn't concede that a lady called Laura Manion ever existed—let alone had danced or been attacked. You can feel flattered that Mr. Dancer now permits you to breathe."

"Well, I feel better, at least."

"But did you remove your shoes playing pinball?" I pressed.

"Yes, Paul," she said, "I now remember that I did. I'd really forgotten. I did so for a few minutes during our last game so I could stand on my toes and aim better. But I didn't walk around that way and I didn't dance."

"Well, tell it that way," I said. The Lieutenant was frowning and I hoped this barefoot incident wasn't going to throw him or them into another emotional tailspin. "I think they made it up," I said reassuringly, "to pull you down and protect Barney."

"But why didn't they go through with it, then?" Laura asked innocently. "Why did they give up? Why was this bartender suddenly so truthful about the drinks and guns and all? You've been worried about that little bartender all along."

For a number of reasons I had not told the Manions about my visit with Mary Pilant. " 'Tis a waking mystery, Laura," I said, tugging up my brief case. "Maybe you've been praying. . . . I must go now."

The deserted back court corridors echoed hollowly, and I thought it fitting and proper that I should use Mitch's phone to call Mary Pilant.

"I've been waiting for your call," she said. "How did it go, Paul?"

"Like a dream," I said. "At times our little bartender was a reluctant dragon and at others he experimented gingerly with the truth. All in all though I think he definitely helped. Anyway, Mary, I am most grateful to you for unlocking as much truth as he told." I paused and lowered my voice, "And I want to thank you in person as soon as this mess is over."

"Please do, Paul, the whole thing has been worrying me terribly. I had not realized the danger to your case."

"The danger is not over yet, Mary, and I want to see you real soon."

There was a moment of silence. "So do I, Paul. I'll be thinking of you. Good luck and good-by."

Parnell was waiting for me in my car. Neither of us was very hungry and we decided to drive up along the north shore under the Norway pines. We picked up some potato chips and pop on the way. Parnell was by way of making a pop convert out of me. The trial was reaching a crucial stage and by common consent we did not talk much about it. I filled him in a little more on Mary Pilant; then, like men marooned on a desert island we discussed the news we heard on the car radio—all bad—and Parnell made some suggestions to me about my coming campaign for Congress. We parked at a secluded spot and ate our meager lunch and watched the lake.

I shook my head, mystified. "One of the most disturbing things in this case to me, Parn, is how vastly I miscalculated Mary Pilant. It bothers me. I thought I knew a little about people, and now I'm afraid I don't know anything. I shudder to think what that little fox of a bartender of hers might have said—rather have left unsaid— if you hadn't been inspired to send me to see her." As I stared out at the lake I thought I saw Mary Pilant's sweetly solemn face.

Parnell also stared at the lake. "The lack of knowledge of people, our lack of human communication, one with the other, may be the big trouble with this old world," Parnell said soberly. "For lack of it our world seems to be running down and dying—we now seem fatally bent on communicating only with robot missiles loaded with cargoes of hate and ruin instead of with the human heart and its pent cargo of love." Parnell still gazed morosely out over the lake. "And now—it seems, boy, almost as though a despairing God or nature or fate—call it what you will—has finally challenged mankind to open up its heart or perish. . . ." He paused. "Take our own situation in this case. All along we think that Mary Pilant is a calculating and avaricious female. She in turn thinks we're nothing but a lot of designin' bastards. Well, we were both wrong." He shook his head. "What chance is there for the world if people like us fall into the same old trap?"

"Yes, even take Judge Weaver, Parn. Both of us like and respect him, but all we know and probably all we shall ever get to know about the man is but three small hairs on his head. It's a solemn mystery."

"Ah, there, lad, now you've touched it. Yes, take our judge, Polly. Judges, like people, may be divided roughly into four classes: judges with neither head nor heart—they are to be avoided at all costs; judges with head but no heart—they are almost as bad; then judges with heart but no head—risky but better than the first two; and finally, those rare judges who possess both head and a heart —thanks to blind luck, that's our judge."

I nodded wordlessly.

"Alas, boy, we have plenty of words of bitter invective and scorn for people, but none to describe that man or our own Judge Maitland. It seems that humility and kindness and profound intelligence are so seldom blent in one man that the world—at least the English-speaking world—has never felt compelled to coin a word to describe it. If it has, that word has eluded me." He shook his head. "Our words are legion to describe bastards—Roget is simply a-crawl with 'em. Yet to describe this judge of ours I have instead to make a small speech!" He looked at his watch. "But come, Polly, better turn around—it's off to do battle again."

Every seat in the courtroom was taken and it seemed that there were almost twice as many people squeezed in the seats as the place could comfortably hold. Most of them were the same frizzy-haired, wall-eyed women who could have been turned out on the same lathe. The room grew perfectly still and Judge Weaver looked down at me and nodded. It was time for me to make the opening statement for the defense, the statement that Parnell and I had brooded over so long.

I arose and walked before the bench and bowed slightly and half turned toward the jury. "May it please the court and ladies and gentlemen of the jury," I said, in what was probably one of the shortest opening statements to a jury in the annals of Michigan murder, "the defendant proposes to show that he was not guilty of murder or of any crime growing out of the fatal shooting of Barney Quill; that he was actually and legally insane when he shot the deceased; and that he had a perfect legal right to go to the place of the deceased as he did and seek him out. I thank you." I turned and went back to my table and sat down.

"Call your first witness," the Judge said.

"The defense will call Dr. Malcolm Broun," I said. The curtain had risen on the third and final act of our courtroom drama.

Dr. Broun, a country doctor of the old school, hurried up to the stand in a kind of impatient sidewise lope. He was a large sandy craggy cliff of a man, almost defiantly untidy, and a stethoscope protruded ominously from the pocket of his wrinkled tweed jacket as though he were bent upon pinning down and thumping the Judge.

"I certainly do, young man," the doctor boomed in answer to Clovis' oath, sitting and squarely facing me. I briefly qualified him —everybody in the county knew old Doc Broun or Red Broun—the unabashed lover of county fair harness racing, Scotch whisky and newly born babies (though I was not quite sure of the order).

"Doctor," I said, "did you have occasion during July of this year to make a physical examination of Barney Quill in connection with his application for some policies of life insurance?"

"I did," the doctor boomed, and I could feel the Dancer panting softly on my neck. "July twenty-eighth in my office."

"And did you do so on behalf of Mr. Quill or the insurance company?"

"The latter, young man—and they paid me, too."

"And what kind of a physical specimen did your examination disclose Mr. Quill to be?"

"Objection. Irrelevant, immaterial. Anyway results of examination privileged," the Dancer cabled the Judge. "Too remote. No showing physical condition continued unchanged up to murder."

"Mr. Biegler?" the Judge said.

"I believe the privilege would be personal to the deceased or his fiduciary," I said, "and I am not aware that Mr. Dancer has now wormed his way in on the dead man's estate. Furthermore, this examination was made by this witness for the insurance company— he was not acting as Barney Quill's doctor. As for remoteness or possible change, I suggest that would be a question of fact for the jury; also possibly a proper matter for rebuttal by the People." I paused and glanced at Claude Dancer. "If Mr. Dancer wants to show that Barney Quill went into a wizened decline since July twenty-eighth he can call Dr. Raschid and the others who attended the autopsy to prove it—that, and by suppressing, if he can, all of the People's exhibits of the excellent photographs showing the deceased lying on the slab." I quickly found and held up the pictures of Barney, and waved them so that the jury could see the body-beautiful, superb even in death.

"The objection is overruled," the Judge said, rather unsuccessfully suppressing a smile.

During this exchange Dr. Broun had sat impatiently drumming his fingers on the mahogany railing of the witness box. His disapproving look declaimed eloquently that if all this infernal nonsense constituted the practice of law he for one would gladly stick to his stethoscopes and clattering bedpans.

"You may answer now, Doctor," I said.

"Incredible," he murmured. "Well, young man, I am a doctor of medicine and not of divinity," he growled. "Whatever this man Quill's morals may or may not have been, I can say this: they were lodged in the body of a Greek god. The man was compounded of whalebone and piano wire. He was a magnificent animal—like a blooded stallion." He stirred restlessly. "Any further questions?" It was more of a challenge than a question.

It was also a good question. "No further questions, Doctor, and thank you," I said. "Your witness, Mr. Dancer."

"No questions," Claude Dancer said from his table, to which he had returned, glancing up sharply and glowering at Dr. Broun as he loped past him.

"The defense will call Dr. Orion Trembath," I said. Dr. Trembath was the "lady" doctor who had examined Laura about a week after the shooting. He transported his big-shouldered field-marshal bulk to the stand with surprising ease and was sworn, sat down, and was examined by me as to his qualifications.

"Now, Doctor, do you have any specialties?" I went on, the preliminaries over.

"Yes," he replied. "Obstetrics and gynecology."

"And gynecology is what?"

"Female pelvic disorders."

"Did you have occasion to examine Mrs. Laura Manion recently?"

"Yes."

"When and where?"

"On August twentieth in my office."

"Will you please tell us the results of your examination?"

"Yes, I found several areas of discoloration, from former bruises and contusions, around both eyes, the left shoulder, both buttocks and a large area over the left hip. This last measured six by four inches."

"Were these discolored areas what a layman might call black and blue?"

"Yes, but turning yellow when I examined her."

"And what might that indicate?"

"The duration of the injuries."

"And have you formed an opinion on that?"

"Yes, upwards of one week old."

"Now, Doctor, have you any opinion as to how the woman might have received the massive discoloration on her right hip?"

"Left hip, sir. Possibly a hard blow or kick."

"Now, Doctor, if you were called, say to the county jail, to take a vaginal smear to determine the possible presence of sperm in a woman, what would you bring?"

"I would bring a vaginal speculum or dilator so the tract could be exposed and inspected, and a light to illuminate the area. And some applicators, which are slender sticks of wood with cotton on the end, to swab up any secretions which are present, and glass microscopic slides on which to transfer these secretions."

"And I ask you how many glass slides you would probably take."

"At least two."

"In what areas?"

"To be taken well up around the cervix, which is the mouth of the womb. Well inside the vaginal tract."

"And having obtained those slides what would you do with them?"

"I would either send them to the Michigan Department of Health at Lansing or to a competent pathologist."

"Under any circumstances would you send them to a laboratory technician who was not a pathologist or a medical doctor?"

"By no means, sir."

"I ask you whether or not it would be possible to examine a dead body of an adult male and determine whether or not he had recently ejaculated?"

"Yes. An examination of the seminal vesicles would indicate whether they were full of seminal fluid or not."

"And if a doctor or pathologist were trying to determine that fact would you say in your opinion that that should have been done?"

"I would think so."

"Is that your opinion?"

"Yes."

"Now I ask you whether or not you made any further examination of Mrs. Manion?"

"Yes. I examined her right knee and also did a pelvic examination."

"What, if anything, did you find about the right knee?"

"She complained of pain in the inner aspect of the knee. The knee was tender at that location."

"Any bruises?"

"There was no bruise apparent."

"Did she complain of tenderness or soreness in any other part of her body?"

"She complained of vaginal pains and disorders."

"And you made such an examination?"

"Yes."

"And I ask you, Doctor, whether or not such soreness could have been induced by a forcible act of sexual intercourse."

"I believe it could have."

"And what is the medical explanation of that?"

The Doctor hunched forward and spread his hands. "Well, ordinarily when a woman intends to have sexual relations there is a secretion of fluid, a natural lubrication. When the act is taken against her will there is no preliminary secretion, and consequently more friction and subsequent inflammation and pain."

I looked at Claude Dancer. "Your witness," I said.

Claude Dancer stood thoughtfully staring up at the skylight, rocking on his heels. "You did not specialize in pathology, Doctor?" he said.

"No."

"And that is a specialty, as much as your own?"

"Yes, indeed."

"And the pathologist is usually more experienced and schooled in post-mortem procedures?"

"Yes."

"And would you concede that an experienced pathologist would be more qualified to determine the cause of death in a dead body than yourself?"

"Freely."

Claude Dancer had stared up at the skylight during his brief examination. He now turned and gave me his Dead Sea scroll smile. "Your witness," he said.

"Doctor," I said, "would you equally concede that this experienced pathologist was more competent to test a dead male body for recent seminal ejaculation than yourself?"

Thoughtfully: "I should say that we were equally well qualified on that score and that if that were an issue, an examination of the seminal vesicles should properly have been made."

"Back to you, Mr. Dancer," I said.

"No further questions."

I turned and looked at Laura Manion and nodded. "The defense will call Mrs. Laura Manion," I said.

The Judge looked out at the clock and batted his sandy forelock out of his eye. "I think we'll take ten minutes before examining the next witness," he said. "All right, Mr. Sheriff."

chapter 18

"Lieutenant," I said, when we three were alone in the conference room, "I want you to go outside and have a smoke or something so that I can talk with Laura alone. The coach wants a final word."

Without a word the Lieutenant turned and marched to the door and out the room. I turned to Laura. "Well, young lady," I said, "this is it. I was hoping I could rush you onto the stand before you had time to brood about it, but the Judge didn't co-operate. How do you feel?"

Laura laughed nervously and felt her stomach. "The butterflies are flapping like condors," she said. "What's good for that, Coach?"

"Truth," I said. "All you got to tell is the truth. Remember what I told you before?—don't be led into anything that can throw any doubt on our rape story." I anticipated that the Dancer would go after her with hammer and tongs trying to shake her story and cast doubt on her morals and credibility and what not, but I did not tell her so. "Before you answer a prosecution question, Laura," I said, "*think*. Soft-pedal the jealousy business if you can, but if they get into it don't lie about it. And don't answer more than you are asked and if you don't understand the question or know the answer, simply say so. Truth must be the order of the day." I'd told her all this before, many times. "One more thing," I said, "when we get to the rape part keep it slow and simple—don't feel you must act and don't, for Heaven's sake, try to dramatize any emotions you don't feel. Those women on the jury will crucify you if you dare play-act." I patted her shoulder. "Have you got it, my dear?"

She nodded and smiled tremulously. There was a knock on the door and Max Battisfore put his head in. "So soon, Max?" I said.

"I'd like to see you for a minute, Polly," Max said. "Alone."

"Sure thing, Max," I said wonderingly, turning and nodding to Laura, who crushed out her cigarette and quickly left the room. I turned to Max.

"First of all, Polly, I got a telegram here for you," he said, handing me the sealed envelope which I put in my breast pocket. "Then I want to thank you for that nice courtroom sendoff you gave me and our department when you were questioning Deputy Lemon. I really appreciate that."

"That's all right, Max," I said, smiling but still puzzled as to his real mission. "You and your boys have been very nice to the Manions and me. We can't forget all that and especially how you threw out the life line on that psychiatrist business—having your top man drive the Lieutenant to lower Michigan. That was—could be—a lifesaver—"

"Listen, Polly," Max broke in, lowering his voice and speaking rapidly. "Recess is almost over and I got to talk fast. It's about the Lieutenant. I'm willing to testify for him."

"*Testify* for him?" I said incredulously.

Max nodded. "Yes, testify. I feel sorry for the man, and especially the way this guy Dancer is piling on him, trying to block and keep out the truth. Like that lie-detector test. I've known all along that the test showed his wife told the truth and the state police are fit to be tied the way this man Dancer has put them on the spot, making it look as though *they* were trying to hide the truth."

"Hm. . . . What would you testify to, Max?" I said thoughtfully, my mind racing.

"Insanity," Max pressed on. "Manion was practically a harness case that first weekend, like a man in a dream—he didn't eat or sleep and just wanted to sit and mope in his cell. When the bartender came and gave him that carton of cigarettes he absently handed them to one of our panhandling drunks. Didn't he tell you all this?"

"Lord, no, Max," I said. "You really mean you're willing to testify for the defense on these things?"

Max glanced at his watch and gave me his hand. "Any time, Polly, and now I must be going"—and he was gone. I tore open the telegram. It was from our psychiatrist, Dr. Matthew Smith. "Arriving your airport at 9:17 tonight. Please meet me," it said.

"Hear ye, hear ye, hear ye," Max intoned, and once more we were away. The Judge nodded at me and I arose and addressed the court.

"Your Honor," I said, "with the court's permission I would like to change the order of my witnesses, if I may, and call another witness at this time in place of Mrs. Laura Manion."

"Very well," the Judge said. "Call your other witness."

"Sheriff Max Battisfore!" I announced, and there was a rustle and stir in the courtroom as Max got up and marched resolutely to the witness stand and was sworn and sat down. I stole a look at Claude Dancer, who had his head bent in hurried conference with Mitch. Glancing the other way I found a perplexed Parnell leaning forward with his brows understandably knitted. "Your name, please?" I said.

"Max Battisfore," good old Max answered.

"Occupation?"

"Sheriff of Iron Cliffs County."

"And as such do you have custody of the county jail and its inmates, Mr. Sheriff?"

"I do, sir."

"Including that of the defendant in this case?"

"Yes, sir."

"And how long has he been—ah—living with you?"

"Since his arrest on August sixteenth."

"And have you seen him almost daily since he was first arrested?"

"I have, sir."

"Now, Mr. Sheriff," I said, "how did his appearance, deportment, and general behavior when he was first arrested compare with that of now?"

"Well—" Max began.

"Wait, wait!" the Dancer shouted, leaping to his feet. "Objection, Your Honor. Irrelevant and immaterial. If calculated to show mental state of defendant, then this witness certainly not competent to express an opinion."

I turned and looked at the little man, who was livid with rage that a law-enforcement officer should dare do anything to oppose the prosecution in a murder case. "Mr. Biegler?" the Judge said.

"Your Honor," I said, "the defense would not for a moment try to pit our Sheriff against the erudite psychiatrist for the People. In the first place our Sheriff appears to labor under the disadvantage of having seen the defendant over a longer period and much closer to the time when we claim he was temporarily insane. However, we do not offer this evidence as the Sheriff's opinion on the sanity or insanity of Lieutenant Manion, but as possible evidence by one of the few witnesses who was in a position to observe and tell, of certain symptoms, from which, persons who are competent to pass an opinion might do so. Mr. Dancer, with his characteristic tactics, seems bent on keeping this out as well."

"You offer the evidence, Counsel," the Judge inquired of me, "not as an opinion, then, on either sanity or insanity, but rather as evidence possibly bearing on those disputed issues?"

"Correct, Your Honor," I said.

"The witness may answer," he said.

"Well," Max said, "Lieutenant Manion was practically a harness case when he first came to my jail—"

322

"Objection, Your Honor, I am unacquainted with the argot, the terminology—"

"Strait jacket, Dancer," Max broke in, his gray eyes flashing ominously. "Then he went into a sort of gloomy depressed state, like a man in a dream, he didn't eat or sleep for two days and just wanted to sit and mope in his cell. We were so concerned I put one of our deputies as a phony prisoner in a cell near him to keep watch. When the bartender came on Sunday and gave him that carton of cigarettes he absently handed it to one of my drunks and in five minutes was himself bumming my jailer for a smoke."

"And how did the Lieutenant appear, say, during the latter part of his stay?"

"Much better. He seemed to get a grip on himself, like a man come out of a fog. After about a week he ate and slept well and has never given us any further concern or trouble."

"Thank you, Mr. Sheriff," I said, and turned to Claude Dancer. "Your witness."

Claude Dancer stood glaring at the Sheriff, who glared steadily back at him, and Dancer, sensing shrewdly that all he could do now was make matters worse by examining, murmured, "No questions," and abruptly sat down.

I stood for a moment silently reflecting that perhaps I had been culpably lame in not quizzing the Sheriff on all this long beforehand. Supposing Max had not come forward? All this testimony would have irretrievably been lost and it would have been my own stupid fault. But then again, perhaps no; getting sheriffs to testify for the defense in murder cases was something like bird-watching: if you hotly pursued and wooed the birdies they gaily flew away, but if you went calmly and unconcerned about your business the woods were apt to be alive with them. Good old Max. . . .

"Laura Manion," I announced, and Laura got up and walked to the stand, and held up her hand for the oath. The jurors, I noted, especially the women, were watching her closely.

"Your name is Laura Manion and you are Lieutenant Manion's wife?" I asked.

"I am," Laura replied quietly.

"Did you consent to ride and did you drive in an automobile with the deceased, Barney Quill, on the night of August fifteenth?"

"I did."

"Will you please tell us what happened," I said.

Without giving any background of how or why she had ridden with him Laura described briefly how Barney had first driven her and her dog to the gate of the tourist park; how he had expressed surprise on finding the gate closed and had said he would drive her home another way; and then how he had backed up to the main road and driven rapidly down the road and abruptly turned off to the right on a strange, heavily wooded side road. Parnell and I had planned it this way, first, to get her over the hard part before she possibly broke down, and second, so that the jury could judge the 1est of the story in the light of what had happened, and third (this was Biegler's corny reason), because of the greater impact that might be added by satisfying the curiosity of the jurors at once.

The courtroom had grown hushed. "What happened after Barney turned off on this strange side road?" I went on.

In a low voice Laura told what had happened: how Barney had grabbed her arm and driven furiously into the woods and suddenly stopped and turned out the lights and flung the dog out when it had whined; how he had told her he was going to rape her and would kill her if she resisted, of his pounding her on the knees and all the rest; and of how she had finally told him that her husband would kill him if he did that to her; how Barney had then bragged about his prowess as a pistol shot and Judo expert; how he had finally hit her hard with his fist and sworn and called her an "Army slut"; and how she nearly fainted but knew she hadn't because she could still hear the little dog Rover whining and scratching at the door.

"What happened then?" I said softly.

In the intensity of her recollection Laura seemed to have forgotten that she was being questioned or was talking in a courtroom before a jury; her green eyes glowed as she went on and described how she finally knew that the man had succeeded in his purpose; that finally she realized that the car was turned around and moving again and that little Rover was once again beside her; and how Barney had finally driven her back to the gate. . . .

At this point I asked her how she happened to have ridden with Barney that night, and she began at the beginning and told of how she had left her husband sleeping in the trailer and gone to the hotel bar to get some beer; of her playing pinball with Barney and, later, his asking her several times to let him drive her home; of his warning against the bears and strange men; of her final consent to let him drive her. She also admitted having removed her shoes to play one game of pinball, but denied having danced with Hippo Lukes or any man, with or without shoes.

I then led her back to the gate, after the rape, and the telling of Barney's second attack and her temporary escape, with Rover lighting her way through the stile; of the recapture and struggle and blows and her final frantic screams for help; of her making her way to the trailer and falling finally into the arms of her husband. Then, her entire testimony taking but little over a half-hour, she quickly recounted the rest of the events of that evening: the arrest of her husband, the ride to the jail, the attempted smear taken by Dr. Dompiere, her co-operation with Detective Sergeant Durgo and the other police and of her telling them the story several times, the last time at the state police post with various gadgets attached to her body and arms. I then turned and glanced casually at Parnell who arose and quickly left the court by way of the judge's chambers.

"And have you yet been officially informed of the results of that lie-detector test?" I asked her.

"I have not," Laura replied.

"Would you like to know the results?"

"I would."

"Would you for your part be willing that everyone in this room should know the results?" I said.

Laura nodded. "I wo—"

The Dancer was on his feet. "No, no! Objection!" he shouted. "Counsel plainly trying circumvent rule against admissibility of polygraph tests."

The jurors glared at the little man. "Pardon me, Mr. Dancer," I said. "I keep forgetting how zealous you are that nothing shall get in this case that could possibly harm a hair on the head of Lieutenant Manion. I withdraw the question." I addressed the court. "Your Honor," I said, "before I tender this witness I should like to bring in the little dog Rover for a demonstration to the jury, if I may."

"Demonstration of what?" the Judge asked, startled.

"First, that the dog is both small and friendly and was unlikely either to dissuade the deceased or protect the witness and, second, that the animal and its flashlight could indeed have lit the witness through the stile near the park gate, as she has testified." I paused. "And there is a third reason, Your Honor," I said. "To prevent Mr. Dancer from thereby making a slavering mastiff out of this little dog if we are not allowed to produce him."

Claude Dancer glared at me and leapt righteously to his feet but the Judge held up a warning hand like a traffic cop. "The request is granted. Produce the animal."

I turned to Laura. "If you please, Mrs. Manion."

Laura got down off the stand and went to the lawyers' door by the side of the jury, which I held open for her, and was back in a thrice carrying Rover, doubtless herself as surprised to have Parnell thrust the animal at her in the corridor as was everyone in the courtroom to see her back so soon.

"Please release the dog, Mrs. Manion," I said, and Laura put the dog down, with its flashlight lit in its mouth, and, wagging its tail furiously, it ran gaily up and smelled the Judge, who frowned and turned quickly away, and then—of all things—ran bright-eyed to the prosecution table, its tiny feet pattering, and tried to climb up on Claude Dancer's lap. The Dancer flushed and lifted his legs to prevent it, not unlike a maiden lady being suddenly wooed by a mouse, and even the jury tittered. Then Rover spotted Lieutenant Manion and ran to him in an ecstasy of wriggling and whimpering joy, whereupon the Judge, who evidently took as dim a view of dogs in his courtroom as he did of flash cameras, inquired of me in a rather pained voice whether our jury demonstration was done.

"I swear, Your Honor," I said solemnly, "I wasn't waiting for Rover to be sworn," and everyone laughed, even the Judge and Mitch—everyone but Mr. Dancer—and I nodded to Laura to fetch the dog back out to the waiting Parnell, and when she returned, turned and said, "Your witness, Mr. Dancer."

chapter 19

The Judge looked thoughtfully out at the courtroom clock and then down at the counsel tables. "Gentlemen, it's nearly four-thirty," he said, "which is too early to suspend for the day and yet perhaps too late to finish with this witness before five." He glanced at the jury. "I seem faintly to discern a chance to end this case tomorrow, Saturday, and I wonder if the jury and counsel would be willing to work a little overtime tonight, if necessary, on the off-chance that the case will not have to run over into next week."

Most of the jurors quickly nodded their heads and, swiftly getting our cues, Mitch and I perforce popped up and nodded ours. "Very well," the Judge said, "suppose we proceed with the cross-examination." He nodded at Mitch's table.

Claude Dancer quickly arose and padded up before Laura Manion with a sheaf of notes, his lips curled in a toothsomely amiable grin, much like a miniature panther about to pounce upon an unsuspecting rabbit. "Good luck, dear Laura," I murmured to myself. The lady didn't quite know it, but she was about to be sacrificed to the wolves.

"How long have you been married to the Lieutenant?" Claude Dancer purred silkily.

"Three years," Laura answered.

"And have you worked during your lifetime?" he purred on.

"I have, naturally."

"And what was your occupation?"

"Well, I was a housewife for twelve years before I married Manny —I mean, Lieutenant Manion."

"Oh," Mr. Dancer queried, in false surprise. "You mean you were previously married?"

"Yes."

"Hm. . . . And had you any other occupation beside that of housewife?"

"Yes, I once sold lingerie in a department store and another time demonstrated and sold cosmetics."

"Anything else?"

"Yes, I worked as a telephone operator and junior instructress."

"Anything else?" Claude Dancer pressed, appearing to consult a dossier he held in his hands, which indeed he might have held or, like a clever cross-examiner, it might have been only an old time-ta-

327

ble; on this score neither the witness nor opposing counsel could ever be sure.

"No, I think that's all."

Still consulting his notes: "Weren't you once a beauty operator?"

"No."

"You mean you did not graduate from a beauty course you took in St. Louis?"

"You didn't ask that. I had the training but never actually became an operator." (It was now plain to me that the little man did have some information on Laura's background—she hadn't even told me some of these things.)

"But you did sell cosmetics on the road?"

"Yes."

It was also plain that the Dancer was trying to show Laura up as a well-traveled bag, but I did not object, first, because I saw no valid grounds to do so and further because I wouldn't have objected if I could, because so far Mr. Dancer was doing precisely what I'd hoped he'd do: trying subtly to attack Laura's character but *not* her story of the rape.

"Now, how long after the death of your first husband did you marry your present husband?" little Mr. Dancer asked with disarming innocence. I caught my breath for this was one of those trick loaded questions that I had warned Laura against. His question was so framed that he might either deliberately lure her into a lie or she might innocently fall into one if she was not on her toes.

"Two weeks," Laura replied, and Claude Dancer could not resist shooting a look of triumph at me as my heart sank. Good Lord, she had fallen into the trap.

"So that two weeks after you became a free woman you got married to the Lieutenant?" the Dancer pressed, luring her on and nailing down her lie.

"Yes, two weeks after my divorce was granted," Laura said, and once again I was able to breathe.

"Divorce?" Claude Dancer said. "I thought you just testified that your first husband *died* two weeks before your remarriage."

Laura shook her head wonderingly, and I was sure then that her flub had been innocent, she had misunderstood the earlier trap question. "He was and is very much alive, sir. I have never told anyone he was dead. In fact he has recently written my husband and me offering to help." (This, too, I had not known.)

328

"Objection," Claude Dancer said. "The answer is irrelevant and unresponsive—at least the portion about the former husband offering to help. I move that portion be stricken."

"Yes," the Judge ruled, "the reference to the offer to help by the former husband may be stricken and the jury is asked to disregard it."

I arose. "Your Honor," I said, "now that three people have already drilled into the jury the import of the offending testimony, I might as well make it unanimous. We agree that the reference to the offer of help by the former husband may be stricken and disregarded. I am sure now that the jurors will resolutely banish it from their memories."

Claude Dancer glared at me. "I further object to defense counsel commenting on an objection after the court has ruled," he said.

"Mr. Dancer," I said, "I apologize for commenting on the fact that the former husband still wants to help. If it will comfort you I am willing to stipulate that he is jealously sulking or dead."

The Judge stifled a smile and lightly tapped his bench with his gavel. "Gentlemen, gentlemen," he said. "Time's a-flying. Let us get on with the examination. Proceed, Mr. Dancer."

Claude Dancer took his little setback like a little man; it was all part of the game; he would now bore in with something else. "How long had you known the Lieutenant before your marriage to him?" he pressed on.

"Five months."

"And where was your first husband during all this time?"

"With the Army in Europe."

"So that all the while your husband was in the service in Europe you and the Lieutenant were conducting your little romance over here?"

Laura's green eyes flashed behind her glasses. "I did not say that. You asked me how long I had *known* Manny, not how long he had courted me."

"Well, then, please tell us how long he courted you," Mr. Dancer complacently purred on.

"One month."

"In other words, you and he were going steady, then, before you were actually divorced?"

"Well, yes."

Claude Dancer glanced at the jury and I noted ruefully that several of the women were glancing significantly at each other. "Now, coming to the night of the shooting," the Dancer pressed on, "I believe you just told the jury you went to the hotel bar that night to get a six-pack of beer?"

"Yes."

"And that was for your husband?"

"Yes, I rarely drink beer myself." She smiled a little and glanced nervously at the jury. "Too fattening."

"I see," Mr. Dancer said and paused. "But if you went there for beer for your husband, why didn't you get it and fetch it home instead of staying there over two hours?"

The little man was giving Laura a bad time. I held my breath hoping she would have the wits to wriggle her way out of this question.

She did, and with a vengeance—she told the simple truth. "I did not go there primarily for beer, Mr. Dancer. If you must know, going to the bar to get the beer was more or less of an excuse to get out of the trailer. I had been ironing all afternoon and I was dying to get out."

"To get out so that you could go drink whisky and play pinball with Barney Quill?" Mr. Dancer pressed, no longer purring.

"No. Not at all," Laura shot back. "Just to get out. If you were a woman you would understand what I mean."

"But you did drink whisky and play pinball with Barney Quill?"

"Yes. I've already told that here today and many times to the state police." (Laura was getting her dander up and, I felt, was doing much better—if she would only keep her head.)

"And how many drinks did you have?"

"Four."

"Double shots?"

"No."

"And over what space of time?"

"About two hours, with a large glass of water. My dad taught me that."

"Did you feel the effects of these drinks?" the Dancer asked, and cleverly, since if she said no, she perforce made herself out a bit of a rum pot and if she said yes he would purr over that too.

"Well, yes, I felt relaxed and was enjoying myself."

Claude Dancer paused and rolled up another spitball. "Is it your practice to remove your shoes when you drink whisky?" he said, hurling it.

"It is not."

"Or when dancing?"

"No, I did not—"

"And were you served drinks with your shoes off?" the Dancer pressed on.

"Your Honor," I said, rising, "I don't want to spoil the gallant Mr. Dancer's fun—he's waited so long for it—but I wish he would let the witness complete her answers before he gets on to the next question. I object to his cutting her off."

"The objection is sustained. The witness will be allowed to complete her answer," the Judge ruled.

Laura glanced gratefully up at the Judge. "I was going to say that I did not dance with anyone and that I only removed my shoes once briefly during the last game of pinball."

"Are you sure you did not dance with anyone?" the Dancer pressed.

"I am sure."

"Didn't you dance with a tall red-faced man?" (At this point I began wondering whether the lurching Hippo Lukes had made another switch.)

"No, not even a short pale one. I danced with no one, not a soul."

"Are you sure?"

"I am positive I did not dance. I am a poor dancer and I do not particularly like to."

"Do you recall any man having your shoes in his pockets while you danced with him? Answer yes or no and leave out the comments." (Ah, this was the great Hippo, all right.)

"No."

"Now, after the shooting when your husband returned to the trailer did he then go to the cottage of the caretaker, Mr. Lemon?"

"Yes."

"Did you hear the conversation between them?"

"No. I only saw Mr. Lemon when he came to our trailer."

"Did your husband turn over his pistol to Mr. Lemon?"

"I don't know."

"Did you tell Mr. Lemon what happened?"

"Yes, I did; I said, 'Look what Barney did to me.' "

Claude Dancer appealed to the court. "Objection. The answer is unresponsive and I move it be stricken."

"But you have asked the witness what she told the caretaker," the Judge said, "and she has answered. If you have something particular in mind, then ask it. Your motion to strike is denied."

"Did you tell Mr. Lemon your husband had shot Barney?"

"I did not."

"Now did you and your husband ever go out socially in Thunder Bay?"

"Several times."

"And did you and he once attend a cocktail party in the hotel shortly after your arrival?"

"Yes."

"And at one of those parties did your husband have an altercation with a young second lieutenant?"

"Altercation?" Laura said. "My husband knocked him down."

"Why?"

"I cannot tell. You had better ask him. The young man kissed my hand."

Suavely: "Did you approve of your husband's behavior?"

"I did not and I do not," Laura replied.

Claude Dancer turned and beamed at me. "Your witness," he said.

I pondered the skylight but found no inspiration. "No questions," I said.

"Mr. Sheriff," the Judge said, "I guess we'll call it a day."

chapter 20

After the crowd had thinned out I gravely nodded my thanks at Max, who stood over by the door, discreetly waiting for the Lieutenant. I did not want to embarrass him by having anyone see me talk to him then; I could thank him later; but in the meantime, win, lose or draw, he had become one of my favorite sheriffs.

"How did I do, Paul?" Laura asked.

"Beautifully," I said. "Simply beautiful. I'm sorry I had to let the little man dig at you so, but there was no help for it. And it's all for the cause." I did not tell her that I felt Claude Dancer had scored heavily on us in his cross-examination, but indeed there was no help for that either. I had told Laura to tell the truth and that she had, as Parnell might say, the bad along with the good. I hoped that Parnell and I could dream up some medicine to counteract it, for it was apparent now that Mary Pilant or the bartender or someone from Thunder Bay had furnished Claude Dancer at least some of the material he had used (probably before the "big change"), else the little man could scarcely have asked some of the searching questions he had. Like the cocktail-party incident.

I patted Laura's shoulder. "Now you and Manny go over to the jail," I said. "The good Sheriff is waiting—and I'll be over after a bit for some final skull practice. Tomorrow's the big day."

After the Manions had left Parnell shuffled over and stood silently watching me stash my papers away. I looked up. He had been reading my mind. "Well, tomorrow's the day—the big pay-off, one way or the other. What do you think, boy?"

"What do *you* think, Parn?" I countered.

Parnell shrugged and held out his hands. "You've got most of the stuff in now, Polly. All we need now is for the Lieutenant to tell his story and our doctor to say he's crazy and I guess then it's in the lap of the gods."

"Yes, Parn, and for me to make a decent argument to the jury, and for the Judge to give the jury our requested instructions, and then for the jury to understand and heed them and give us a break—a hell of a lot of big ifs."

"You'll do it, Boss," the familiar voice of a woman said. "I—I'm almost proud of you."

I wheeled around. "*Maida!*" I said. "What the hell are you doing here? I thought you were home minding the till? Why—I—"

Maida snorted. "Till?" she said. "That's been repossessed. Stay home? Not on your life, Boss. Did you think for a minute I was going to sit around that empty old law office while the boss was on his way to rags or riches? And while the loveliest case that ever hit this county unfolds? I'll confess, Boss—I've been here every single day." She cocked her head defiantly. "Am I fired again?"

I glared at Parnell, who hung his head. "You—you villainous old man, stealing my stenographer, closing my office, wrecking my discipline. . . ." I paused, at loss for words.

Parnell drew himself up. "Have you forgotten we're partners in this case, Polly?" he said. "It was my considered judgment that Maida ought to be on hand. As a matter of fact we've still got important work to do."

"What's up now? Back to Green Bay—or is it clean down to New Orleans this time?" I glanced at my watch. "I've got to go see the Manions, maybe eat something, and then meet the damn plane tonight." I lashed my brief case together and stood up.

"Come, Maida," Parnell said, offering her his arm. He bowed gravely and he and Maida swept grandly out of the courtroom.

The plane swooped down out of the darkening autumnal sky like a great rigid bird and taxied up near the cluster of airport shacks and disgorged four passengers, three loud-talking rumple-suited half-potted men whom I dismissed after an envious glance, and, lastly, a tanned and nice-looking young man of moderate height who for a moment, in the glaring searchlights, I thought might be Mitch, crew cut and all. But he simply had to be our psychiatrist; if he wasn't we were in one hell of a fix; and as he passed the gate I took a deep breath and said "Doctor Smith?" and he said "Paul Biegler?" and I almost staggered with mingled surprise and relief as I took his bag and led him to my mud-spattered coupe. Crew cut or not, we at last had our psychiatrist.

Dr. Smith gestured at the three men ahead of us. "Reporters," he said. "Your little murder trial seems at last destined for immortality —for the weekend, that is. It seems that word of a little dog with a flashlight is what did it." The three reporters noisily commandeered a cab and whirled away.

"A little dog shall lead them," I murmured. "God bless our free and untrammeled press."

"An amazing trip," the Doctor remarked as we left the airport. "Your scattered towns are nothing but occasional scars set amongst the lakes and woods. I didn't dream of the remoteness and wild beauty of this place. 'See America first' is right."

"Perhaps, Doctor," I said, "perhaps you would join my committee to bomb the new bridge over the Straits of Mackinac? I'm enlisting recruits and the initiation fee is modest—only half a case of 40 per cent stump powder. Can I sign you up? Otherwise I'm afraid that before long the highways will be one continuous neon-lit hotdog stand, with serpent lines of cars locked exhaust to exhaust, like hound dogs following a bitch in heat. I shudder to think of it and have lately been eying my escape hatch, Alaska. For years the Straits stood as our English Channel against invasion from the south. And now this goddam bridge, which our gleeful chamber of commerce sturdies have now added to their nightly prayers."

The Doctor laughed. "All of us have our little fixations, haven't we?" he said. "Well, maybe I'll consider joining your demolition club, but in the meantime, tell me—how's our murder case coming?"

On the drive back to Iron Bay I filled him in on the trial situation: how the People had not made any psychiatric examination of the Lieutenant or seriously attempted to make one. I also told him the things, both good and bad, that had cropped up since he had talked with the Lieutenant. I was concerned over the testimony of Detective Sergeant Durgo as it might modify or even completely change his previous diagnosis of insanity. And also over the evidence of jealousy that the Dancer had dug out of Laura. Dr. Smith said very little, occasionally asking a question or two, and by and by we arrived at his hotel and got him registered and proceeded up to his room where I wryly noted that for the second night in a row I was finding myself adrift in a hotel room looking out upon Lake Superior. "Next week, *East Lynne*," I thought. I fell to musing over Mary Pilant, wishing I was back in her moonlit apartment.

After Dr. Smith tidied up I told him more about the case, including the whole tangled yarn of Barney Quill and his guns and drinking.

"You say that this Dr. Gregory proposes to testify as to the mental state of Lieutenant Manion on the night of the shooting merely from observing him in court?" the Doctor said.

"Well, I can't be sure, Doctor," I said, "but I certainly hope so. I can't see any earthly reason why they would have him here otherwise."

Dr. Smith shook his head. "I am sorry to hear that. Very sorry."

"Well I'm not, Doc," I said. "How can the People expect to rebut our proof of insanity based upon such counter-testimony? Yet they must do so under the law—and do so beyond a reasonable doubt. The cases are clear."

"That's precisely it, Mr. Biegler," the Doctor said soberly. "You see, I wasn't thinking so much of your man as I was of my own profession. The profession or art of psychiatry is still in its adolescence if not its infancy. It is precisely practitioners like Dr. Gregory who help keep it there, daring to pass a professional opinion on such a basis."

This crew-cutted young man, I saw, was as dedicated to his profession as old Parnell was to his. I shrugged. "I see your point," I said. "I'm dismayed for your profession, Doctor, but very happy for my client." I paused. "And do I assume from what you've just said that you still are of the opinion that the Lieutenant was legally and medically insane when he fired the fatal shots?"

The Doctor glanced at me quickly. "Yes. There is not the slightest doubt about that. What you've told me tonight only serves to clinch it."

"Would you feel disposed to discuss it more now?" I said.

He shook his head. "I would rather do so in court, if you don't mind. It might lend my testimony a little more spontaneity, if nothing else, and at the same time spare you from being bored twice instead of once. But I assure you that in my opinion your man was clearly insane and that I will so testify. Is that enough for now?"

"As you say, Doctor." I stifled a yawn.

Dr. Smith grew thoughtful. "I will say this, however—I believe that Lieutenant Manion's case is routine compared with the dead man, Barney Quill. There is a man whose mind I would really have liked to explore. There is a challenge."

"Yes, Doctor," I said, "the big thing that still perplexes and worries me is that a man of such unusual endowments as this man Quill could have done what he did. It seems to me he must have known that nothing but disaster would follow his rape and assault of Mrs. Manion." I shook my head. "My biggest worry is that despite all our proof to the contrary the jury might still doubt that the man could be capable of such an act. The thing was so utterly savage and primitive."

Doctor Smith looked thoughtfully out at the lake. "We must remember that for untold millenniums in the long history of the human race something very much like rape was probably the normal order of the relations between the sexes. Anthropologically speaking it was only yesterday that men ceased to club and ravish on the spot any female that attracted their passing whim."

"Yes, I suppose, Doctor," I said. "Life must have been one merry chase in those relaxed and informal old times. 'Nice day, madam. I love you madly. *Conk!* Oops-a-daisy, my little penguin.'"

Dr. Smith smiled. "And just as there are a surprising number of men today—so-called 'civilized' men—who somehow derive their greatest sexual satisfaction from colliding with the most depraved women they can pick up, so there are still many men who take their greatest pleasure from something not very far from rape."

"You make me feel so—so kind of old-fashioned, Doctor," I said. "So soft, so effete—imagining that a man should woo or possibly consult a woman's pleasure during such an enterprise. It's doubtless the unimaginative brewer in me."

"And I suspect," the Doctor continued thoughtfully, "that Barney Quill might have been one of them, a sort of frustrated throwback who suffered a sudden atavistic regression to type. When to his addled brain *his* manhood seemed to be at stake, he perhaps almost naturally descended to rape. He would show the whole world what a dominant masculine fellow he was. Most interesting."

"Whatever it was, Doctor, he really did himself a job."

The Doctor again looked out the window. "Yes, to me the dead man is by far the most fascinating character in this whole drama," he said musingly. "I would have loved to try to find out just what made *him* tick."

"Quite a character," I said, yawning and remembering that Parnell had once made pretty much the same observation. "Your main diagnosis, then, Doctor, is that the Lieutenant still was the victim of irresistible impulse that night, regardless of whether he remembered what he was doing or knew right from wrong?" I had at least to know that before I could possibly sleep that night.

The young Doctor nodded his head emphatically. "Exactly," he said. "Though we now call it dissociative reaction. In fact it is quite possible that the Lieutenant remembers more about the shooting than he admits. He may in fact remember all about it, have clearly known right from wrong that night, and think he is pulling the wool over your eyes and mine by now saying he doesn't." The Doctor shook his head. "It wouldn't make any difference—in my opinion he still couldn't help himself; he was nevertheless irresistibly impelled to do what he did and was therefore medically insane."

"But almost not legally insane, Doctor," I said, explaining to him what a cold sweat his diagnosis of irresistible impulse had induced in Parnell and me until we had discovered that Michigan was one of the comparatively few states in the country that admitted the defense, and about the only one among the northern tier of states. "Had the Lieutenant shot Barney just over the border in Ohio or Wisconsin it would have been curtains for his insanity defense, at least on your diagnosis. Consciousness of right and wrong is the sole test in those and most of our states."

Dr. Smith shook his head in dismay. "How primitive and medically unrealistic," he said. "It is precisely those victims who *know* they are doing wrong and who realize what they are doing and still cannot resist doing it who are most to be pitied and protected by the law—instead of having criminal guilt added to the torment of their conscious wrongdoing. Their suffering and agony is not only compounded by knowing, but tripled by being punished for knowing."

"Perhaps, Doctor," I suggested, "perhaps most states reject irresistible impulse because it can more easily be faked than the classic 'unremembering' insanity."

"No," the Doctor said, shaking his head. "In my opinion it is as medically hard if not harder to fake than any other form of serious mental aberration. As for fakery, the net result in most states is to force criminal defendants who might truly have been *medically* insane to fake symptoms of a form of *legal* insanity they actually did not suffer. The fake lies quite the other way. It is a callous and pitiably sordid state of affairs, medically unrealistic and legally an inducement to perjury and sham, involving defendants and psychiatrists and lawyers and judges alike in a squalid sort of make-believe."

"Amen, Doctor," I agreed and sighed, stifling a yawn. "God knows I'm with you. But right now I'm awfully glad we're in one of the few emancipated states that recognize irresistible impulse as a defense to crime."

Dr. Smith arose and held out his hand, smiling. "I don't want to appear to pass out diagnoses like a depot scales does one's weight and his fortune," he said, "but I suspect that the place you clearly belong, Mr. Biegler, is home in the sack. Your head has been nodding and your eyelids drooping for the past hour. What time is court?"

"Sharp at nine," I said, "and our judge doesn't fool. I'd like you to be there to hear the defendant testify."

"Sharp at nine," he said. "And now home to bed for you."

I shook his hand and yawned prodigiously in the poor man's face. "Sometimes, Doc, I think this damn case is getting me down. See you later."

"Alligator," he said, softly shutting his door.

The next morning, Saturday, the cars were parked solidly for blocks around the courthouse and I was glad that the thoughtful Sheriff had reserved parking space between the courthouse and jail. The line of people waiting to get in the courtroom, mostly women, stretched clean down the marble stairs and along the entire main downstairs corridor and through the door and down the cement stairs and out upon the leaf-strewn sidewalk. I recalled a picture I had once seen of a long straggling file of Alaskan gold-rushers toiling and plodding their way over Chilkoot Pass. These dedicated native pilgrims seemed to sense that this was the big day and most of them had paper bags and lunch boxes so that they would not lose their places, such was their passion as students of homicide, as Judge Weaver had wryly observed.

When I had fought my way upstairs the jurors and the Manions were already in their respective places; I nodded at Dr. Smith, who sat in one of the lawyers' chairs behind Laura; Parnell sat gravely by his door; and the Sheriff's men were just admitting the clacking advance guard of the thundering lunch-laden horde. A whole flock of city reporters was huddled earnestly around the press table talking with Bob Birkey, the local *Gazette* man; it seemed reinforcements had arrived on the night train. Rover and his flashlight had triumphed over all. . . . Laura leaned over and whispered to me, nodding toward Parnell. "That old man sitting over there just left this envelope on the table for you—the same nice old man who handed me Rover when I testified yesterday. Who is he, anyway?"

"He's my chief veterinarian, Laura, in charge of kennels and flashlight batteries in all my murder cases," I said, smiling and tearing the envelope open.

"Polly," Parnell's note read, "call the hotel desk clerk as your first witness. His name is Clarence Furlong. Credit Maida with a touchdown on this one. The rest of us clean forgot. Don't forget the money. Good luck. Parn."

I glanced anxiously over at Parnell and he winked and looked away like an innocent choirboy. What a man, what a man. . . .

The door to the Judge's chambers sighed open and the Judge came swishing out with long purposeful strides, followed by Claude Dancer and Mitch, like two altar boys in the wake of a priest. When the Judge had mounted to his place Max hammered us to our feet, bawling for his lost dogies, and the courtroom was finally seated. At length a bated silence fell over the courtroom, a sort of rustling uneasy hush, like a shower of autumn leaves. The Judge's nod at my table abruptly lit the wick of combat.

"The defense will call Clarence Furlong," I said, praying silently that Parnell knew what he was about.

Mary Pilant's little desk clerk padded his way to the stand, taking short dancing-master steps, not unlike the dog Rover, and it would not have surprised me had he held a lighted flashlight in his mouth as he turned timidly after the oath to face me from the witness chair. It was a curious sensation to be about to examine a witness one had never properly interviewed. I took a deep breath and plunged ahead on the assumption that we two had been raised on the same neighborhood sand lot.

"Your name please?" I asked.

"Clarence Furlong," the witness answered.

"Where do you live?"

"Thunder Bay, Michigan."

"Occupation?"

"Desk clerk at the Thunder Bay Inn."

"How long have you been so engaged?"

"Nearly four years."

"And were you so engaged on the night of the shooting in this case, that is, on the night of August fifteenth and the early morning hours of August sixteenth?"

"I was."

"And where in the hotel were you working?"

"At the desk in the main lobby."

"And I ask you whether or not your desk commanded a view of the main entrance?"

"Yes, sir."

"And also the stairway to the bar?"

"It did."

"In other words you could see any one who entered or left the lobby by either route?"

"That is correct, sir."

"Now I ask you, Mr. Furlong," I said, "if you saw your late employer Barney Quill in the lobby the night of the shooting?"

Quietly: "I did."

"When?"

"He came into and passed through the lobby at approximately midnight—possibly five minutes before."

341

"Using what entrance?"

"The main entrance."

"Was there anyone else in the lobby?"

"There was not. I was alone."

I paused and took the plunge. "Will you now please describe the general appearance of Mr. Quill when you saw him?"

Mr. Dancer was on his feet. "Objection, Your Honor. The appearance of the deceased would have no bearing on the issues of this case. Irrelevant, immaterial."

"Mr. Biegler?" the Judge inquired. "Why do you offer this testimony?"

I arose by my table. "Both the defense and certain of the People's witnesses have now clearly injected the issue of possible rape into this case. If there is anything to this, Your Honor, the deceased must have come fresh from his attack." I paused. "It occurred to me that the jury might be mildly interested in learning about the appearance of Mr. Quill. I shall of course abide by the court's ruling." I sat down.

I now felt that it did not make much difference which way the court ruled: if the Judge kept the clerk's story out, the jury would undoubtedly resentfully imagine it; if he let it in, well, then it was in. Perhaps it was even better to let it out, or at least safer. The Judge resolved the dilemma. "I am going to permit the answer," he ruled.

"Mr. Quill was disheveled and panting as though he had been running," the witness replied. "His hair was mussed and his trousers and white shirt were soiled as though he had fallen."

"Did he pause or speak to you?"

"No, he hurried through the lobby and up the stairs without a word."

"Did you see him later that evening—in the lobby, I mean?" I asked.

"Yes, in about ten minutes or so he came downstairs and, after pausing at my desk a moment, proceeded down to the bar. I never saw the man alive after that."

"What was his appearance then?"

"He appeared to have changed his clothes and washed and tidied himself up."

"How about his hair?"

"It was combed."

"How about his breathing? Was he still panting?"

"He seemed very calm and composed—almost icily so."

I paused and felt my way: "You have mentioned his pausing at your desk. Did any words pass between you?"

The clerk grew thoughtful. "No," he said. "Not any words."

The witness had stressed "words" and I still felt my way along. "Did *anything* pass between you?" Parnell had cryptically mentioned money.

"Yes."

"What?"

"Money. He handed—rather slid me—a twenty-dollar bill."

Ah, so Parnell had scored again. There was a rustle and stir in the courtroom and I paused to ponder the situation. The obvious thing was to press on and ask the witness why money had passed, but since no words had passed I sensed he could not very well testify to that but could only guess, which would only give Mr. Dancer a free pounce with another successful objection. Perhaps it was better to let it rest right there and let Mr. Dancer dig it out himself if he dared. There was one final question.

"Mr. Furlong," I said, "had Mr. Quill ever done anything like that before—silently given you twenty-dollar bills or any amount?"

"No, sir," the witness answered.

"Your witness, Mr. Dancer," I said.

Claude Dancer and Mitch were engaged in a whispered huddle while all of the jurors sat watching them with interest. I glanced at Parnell who sat staring pensively at the jury.

Mitch arose to his feet. "No questions," he said.

"Next witness," the Judge said.

I arose to my feet. "Lieutenant Frederic Manion," I said.

I had to admit that the Lieutenant made an imposing figure as he marched to the stand, erect and military looking in his fresh uniform, with all the colorful campaign ribbons and battle stripes; and the female contingent among the students of homicide evidently agreed, as their heavy sighs indicated. The Judge scowled and tentatively fondled his gavel as the Lieutenant was sworn and sat down and faced me. I felt like a tired old horse on a muddy track heading into the home stretch. "Don't falter now, Biegler," I thought. "Run, dammit, run."

"Will you please state your name?" I said.

"Frederic Manion," he replied.

"What is your business or profession?"

"Professional soldier."

"What is your rank?"

"First lieutenant in the United States Army."

"How long have you been a soldier?"

"Nearly sixteen years."

"Now, Lieutenant, where were you when your wife left the trailer for the hotel bar the night of the shooting?"

The Lieutenant went on in a calm low voice and told of his napping after supper; how Laura had awakened him to ask him if he wanted to go to the hotel bar; how he had told her to go along and he would join her later; and how he had then again fallen asleep.

"When did you next wake up?" I said, plunging into the midst of it.

"When I thought I heard the sound of screaming."

"Go on, tell us what happened," I said.

"Well, I got off the bed and went to the door and then Laura— my wife—fell into my arms."

"Please describe what you saw."

"She was hysterical; her face was swollen; her skirt was torn; her hair was in her eyes; she was crying and couldn't speak."

"What did you do?"

"I got her in on the day bed and got some cold cloths and tried to quiet her down and find out what happened."

"Did you finally find out?"

Quietly: "I did."

"Now, without going into details now, will you tell us what your wife told you had happened to her?"

"Yes. She told me she had been beaten and raped by"—the Lieutenant paused as though he hated to say the words, and indeed he fairly spat them when he spoke—"by Barney Quill."

"What happened then?"

"I stayed and tried to comfort her and quiet her down. Then I tried to get her out of her clothes—she was helpless and still half-hysterical—and then I—I saw the evidence on her legs."

"What did you do?"

"I wiped it off and burned it in our incinerator."

"Then what did you do?"

"I went to a little stand and took my pistol out of the drawer and put it in my pocket and left."

"Did you tell your wife you were leaving or to your knowledge did she see you take the pistol?"

"No, I said nothing and I don't think she knew I was leaving. She has already testified she did not."

"Then what did you do?"

"I stepped outside the trailer and stood in the dark for a few minutes to adjust my eyes. I also wanted to make sure that—that the deceased wasn't lurking around out there. Then I went to the tavern."

"Walk or ride?"

"I rode in my automobile."

"Do you remember opening the gate?"

"I do not."

"Or remember driving to the tavern?"

"I do not."

I paused. I was coming to one of the crucial parts of our case and I wanted to get it right and make sure the jury heard it. "Lieutenant," I said, "what was your purpose in going to the hotel bar?"

The Lieutenant flushed darkly as he spoke. "I was going to grab that individual, so help me."

"What were you going to do with him?"

The Lieutenant spoke rapidly. "I'm not quite sure. Grab him and hold him. A man like that could not be at large."

"I ask you whether or not you had any intention of killing or harming him?"

The Lieutenant breathed deeply before he spoke. "I had no intention of killing or harming him but if that man had made one false move I would have killed him."

I paused. Well, it was in now; for better or worse our man had now declared that he had gone to the bar to "grab" Barney Quill, an assertion which I hoped gave us sufficient evidence to warrant an instruction from the court on the right of arrest. If so, it would help answer many perplexing defense questions.

"Well, when you got to the tavern with your car what did you do?"

"I remember I got out of the car and walked into the tavern. It seemed almost as though he was expecting me. I wasn't even in the tavern when I saw him watching me through his rear bar window. I watched him. And he kept watching me. As I approached the bar he whirled around on me."

"What happened after that?"

Again the sighing deep breathing. "I can't—from there on it is a jumble. My next recollection is back in the trailer. My next coherent recollection is back in the trailer."

"Can you illustrate for us, Lieutenant, what position the deceased assumed when he turned around?"

The Lieutenant's words came in breathless spurts. "As I say, he turned . . . To the best of my recollection he turned to his right . . . his left hand on the bar . . . I cannot recall seeing his right arm."

"You say his left hand on the bar or arm and hand?"

"His left forearm. He kind of leaned."

"State whether or not you remember driving back to the trailer."

"No, sir; I don't."

"What happened when you got back to the trailer?"

"I guess I came to."

"What were you doing when you came to?" I pushed on.

"I was standing with the empty pistol in my hand."

"How do you know it was empty? Before you answer I would like to show you People's Exhibit Number Eleven, and I ask you if this is your pistol."

"It is mine, sir."

"Now how did you know it was empty?"

"This is a semi-automatic pistol—it is recoil operated. This gadget sticks up on the top of the magazine when the last round goes off—and there is not another shell. The piece here holds it back—you can't aim it and you can't release this."

"In other words by looking at it you could tell it was empty?"

"Yes, sir."

"Is that substantially as Detective Sergeant Durgo explained it the other day?"

"It was near it. I think he probably knows more about side arms than I do."

At this point I purposely did not get into how the Lieutenant had got the lüger; I had a little trap set out myself for this one, and if the clever Mr. Dancer evaded it I could still bring it out on re-direct.

"How many people did you see in the bar that night?"

"Only one—the deceased."

"There has been testimony here that a number of people were in the tavern and at the bar, and that some of them greeted you. Did you observe any of them or were you aware of their greetings?"

"I saw and heard nothing."

"Now you of course saw and heard these eyewitnesses testify here in court earlier this week?"

"Yes, sir."

"And did you know prior to that night some of those who claimed to have greeted you?"

"Yes, mostly by sight, but I had spoken to them on previous occasions. The people up there were very friendly."

"Did you speak to anyone at the bar that night?"

"No, sir."

"To your best recollection did any one speak to you?"

"No, sir."

"Including the deceased."

"That is correct."

"Do you remember leaving the tavern?"

"I do not."

"Or talking to the bartender or anyone outside?"

"No, sir."

"Do you remember returning to the trailer?"

"No, sir."

"What is the first thing you recollect?"

"I first recall sitting in the trailer with my wife and telling her I guessed I had shot someone, probably the deceased. Then I went over and told Mr. Lemon what I believed I had done."

"That is the deputized caretaker of the trailer park?"

"Yes, sir."

"Why did you go to him?"

"Well, he was the only one who seemed to be in charge, either there or in the village for that matter."

"Did you go to him because he was a deputy sheriff?"

"I may have. At any rate I went to him."

Claude Dancer was scribbling furiously and I knew he would pounce on all this deputy business. "Did you think of Mr. Lemon being a deputy before you went to the bar that night?"

"I did not. I did not think of Mr. Lemon or his being a deputy or about anything but grabbing that man."

I paused and I pitched a fast ball, as much for Mr. Dancer as anyone. "If you had thought of Mr. Lemon and remembered he was a deputy would you have gone to him?"

"No, sir, I would not have, any more than I'd have got my old father out of bed to go gather in this—this man."

347

"Do you recollect what you told Mr. Lemon?"

"Not exactly. I assume I told him what he has testified to here."

After that I quickly took the Lieutenant over his knowledge of Barney's prowess with pistols; his medals; the fact that it was common knowledge that he possessed pistols and sometimes carried them; his experience at Judo; and, finally, that the Lieutenant possessed this knowledge the night when he went to the bar to "grab" Barney. I purposely avoided his war record, feeling Mr. Dancer would glean more enjoyment rooting for it himself. I then brought out, over the Dancer's strenuous objection, that the Lieutenant had been obliged to retain an Army psychiatrist for financial reasons. Then:

"Lieutenant Manion," I asked, "on the night of this shooting did you love your wife?"

"I did, sir."

"Do you still love her?"

He frowned and breathed deeply, clasping the arms of his chair until his knuckles showed white. "Very much, sir."

I turned to Claude Dancer. "Your witness," I said and retired to my table.

Claude Dancer got his cross-examination under way with ominous calm. "You don't remember much about that night after you left the trailer, do you, Lieutenant?"

"Well, sir, just as I have already testified," the Lieutenant parried, and I noted that the People's psychiatrist had at last come to life and was making some notes.

"Have you ever had similar lapses?"

"None other than the ordinary lapses a man might bump into from combat."

"What do you mean?"

"Well, quite often after an action had been completed and we got back to talk it over, if there were ten survivors there'd be ten different stories of what happened."

"Can you give specific instances rather than generalities?"

Claude Dancer would surely have objected had I tried to bring out anything like this, and yet here he was, diligently wrapping the flag around our man on his own.

"Yes, I recall one incident in Korea. One of my half-tracks was supporting the infantry. I had eight men in this action and a Commie mortar round dropped in and wounded all eight. I happened to be far enough away to see what happened without getting wounded. Several more rounds came in. When we'd silenced the mortar fire and the meds could work on our men, all of them told a different story. They reported that from one to a hundred rounds had come in. There were actually four."

I glanced at my veteran juror and he was hanging on the Lieutenant's words, white-faced, evidently gripped by some private battle recollection of his own.

"How long did you serve in Korea?" the Dancer went on.

"Nearly sixteen months."

Mr. Dancer then obligingly took the Lieutenant through World War II, from Sicily up through France and Germany and wound him up on V.J. Day on an island in the far Pacific. As he pressed on I began to see what he was getting at, although the price he was paying seemed a little high.

"Now did you see action in all these places?"

"I did, sir."

"Were you in constant combat?"

"No, sir, no soldier is ever in constant combat. None that survive,

349

anyway. We were under constant to intermittent barrage, constantly in a sweat, you might say."

"And you had skirmishes from time to time?"

"Oh, yes."

It came to me that the Dancer was also, and not so subtly, demonstrating his own familiarity with combat conditions. The little man had evidently been everywhere and done everything.

"Did you participate in these skirmishes?"

"Yes, sir. As platoon leader I had to."

"About how long?"

"Sometimes a day, three days, even four. Again sometimes it was three or four days in the hole."

Claude Dancer paused to hurl another bolt. "And during this time did you experience any unusual mental state of any kind?"

"No, sir. I once had a concussion from shellfire but I was back in action the next day."

"Were you ever treated for mental disease?"

"No, sir."

"Were you ever hospitalized for mental neurosis or psychosis?"

"No, sir."

The Judge was busily engaged making notes, evidently preparing his instructions, and in his zeal Claude Dancer appeared inadvertently to have gotten between the Lieutenant and me. Rather than interrupt I instead got up and moved over and stood between Mitch's table and the jury, near the scribbling knot of reporters, where I could get an unobstructed view.

"You have testified, Lieutenant," the Dancer pushed on, "that after you found certain evidence on the person of your wife you immediately slipped your gun in your pocket and left the trailer, is that right?"

"Yes, sir."

The Dancer glanced over his shoulder and noting I had moved, glanced again and once more squarely got between me and the witness and shot his next question. "And were you angry, Lieutenant?" This last blocking maneuver was clearly no longer inadvertent.

"Some," the Lieutenant admitted. "I guess any man would be."

In the meantime I had moved back to my table, so that I could see my man, and once again the Dancer spotted me and, with elaborate care, again moved squarely between us—whereupon the attorney for the defense blew his stack.

"Your Honor," I arose shouting, as the startled Judge looked up.

"May the record show that on three occasions within the last minute the prosecutor has deliberately got himself between me and my client so that I cannot observe him."

The Dancer fairly leered at me. "Surely *that* wouldn't interfere with anything would it?"

"I further object to the implication that I am signaling or wanted to signal my client. This is the shabbiest courtroom trick I have seen in years."

"You haven't lived," the Dancer said, turning coolly back to the Lieutenant. "Lieutenant," he began, "when—"

"Your Honor," I interrupted, hotter than ever, "I ask the court's ruling on my objection."

The Judge was mystified, having been busy and not having seen the incident, a situation which the Dancer had evidently cleverly waited for and which only made me the madder. "What is there to rule on?" the Judge said curtly. "Go ahead, Mr. Dancer."

"Your Honor," I persisted, "I cannot let this pass. Please hear me out. I was seated here and Mr. Dancer got between me and my client. I thought it was inadvertent and rather than disturb you, since you were busy, I moved over by the jury. Again counsel got between us, and then I returned to my table. Once more it happened, and then it was clearly not inadvertent, anyone who saw it would know that. I ask that the court instruct this man not to do it again. I am sorry for the explosion but I won't sit and take that kind of guff from anyone."

I had now irked the Judge in the bargain. "You know very well where you should sit, Mr. Biegler," he said testily. "If counsel is in the way all you have to do is ask me and I'll move him. I must warn you against any further unseemly explosions. Go ahead."

The Dancer cocked his head back at me. "Anything else, Mr. Biegler?" he inquired sweetly.

"Yes, Dancer," I shouted, "you do that just once more and you won't *hear* the next objection—you'll *feel* it! I—I'll punt you clear into Lake Superior."

"Gentlemen, gentlemen," the Judge shouted, glaring at us and pounding his gavel. "This infernal backbiting has got to stop. The next man who speaks out of turn will have me to deal with. Proceed, Mr. Dancer."

After that Mr. Dancer did not get between me and the witness, but he bore in like a bulldog and grabbed the Lieutenant and fairly pelted him with questions. He brought out that the Lieutenant's military training included the cool appraisal and confirmation of reports; and he repeatedly stressed that the Lieutenant had stayed in the trailer only long enough to confirm this rape report and then had taken his gun and left. He was obviously trying to picture our man as gripped by a cold implacable rage.

"Was your wife reluctant to tell you about the alleged rape?" he purred on.

"Not reluctant; she was hysterical; she couldn't tell anything for a long while."

"But you questioned her carefully?"

"I did."

"You wanted to be sure, Lieutenant, that you did not kill the wrong man?"

"Grab, Mr. Dancer—grab the wrong man."

"Now you had a key to the gate, did you not?"

"Yes, Mr. Lemon gave it to me."

"And you knew the gate was locked at ten every night?"

"Yes, Mr. Lemon told me that."

"And your wife knew that, too?"

"Apparently not. I guess I didn't tell her. She had no occasion to use it alone and the few times we did together Mr. Lemon thoughtfully left it open."

"You knew he was a deputy, didn't you?"

"I don't think I did, but if I had it wouldn't have made any difference."

"Oh, so you preferred to take the law into your own hands rather than call on Mr. Lemon?"

The Lieutenant eyed Mr. Dancer coolly. "I'd no more have thought of calling on Mr. Lemon to do this job, sir, than I'd have thought of calling on you."

Mr. Dancer had not forgotten how to blush, and he did so now, to the vast amusement of at least two people in the room: the attorney for the defense and an ex-soldier juror. "Look, Manion," he rushed on hotly, "when you saw this stuff on your wife's leg you blew your stack and promptly went over to kill Barney Quill and did kill him, didn't you?"

Coolly: "I think we've been over all that, Mr. Dancer. I went over there to grab him."

"And you did so while carrying a concealed weapon?" Mr. Dancer said scornfully.

"The pistol was out of sight, yes, until I produced it."

"Concealed contrary to law?"

"I didn't think of that, sir."

Parnell and I hoped we had legal medicine for this last charge: medicine which I had not even confided to the Lieutenant, and for a moment I felt almost benevolent toward Mr. Dancer—a benevolence which fled with the next question.

"Didn't you tell Detective-Sergeant Durgo that a man who would do that should not live, that you'd first thought it all over from every angle, and that you'd do it again if the occasion arose?"

"I don't recall saying any of that. Nor do I deny saying it. I respect Mr. Durgo's integrity, but I do not recall saying it."

"You don't deny saying it?"

"No."

The Dancer had drawn very near the witness, wagging his finger at him in the best Hollywood tradition. "I ask you now, would you do it again?"

I arose laconically. "I am sorry to disturb Your Honor, but if counsel gets any closer to my client I'm afraid my man might succumb to an irresistible impulse and grab *him*. I object to counsel standing so close to the witness."

"Stand back, Mr. Dancer," the Judge ordered, and the Dancer quickly retreated, shooting another question as he did. "I ask you now," he pressed, "would you do it again?"

Coolly: "I rather doubt that I would dare, Mr. Dancer—now that I have met you."

There was a momentary giggle over this and then a sudden thumping commotion in the back court. I wheeled around and saw a weird scene, as in a surrealist frieze: a young man lurching to his feet, warding off the upstretched restraining hands of seated onlookers, yawing his mouth open, trying desperately to say something. "L—l—let him gug—gug g—go. . . ." he shouted in a grotesque parody of human speech. "L—let the p-pup—pup—poor-poor-poor . . ." he gobbled crazily, the rushing words finally spat with dreadful clarity. *"For Christ's sake let the poor bastard go!"*

The Judge's gavel sounded and a cordon of officers descended on the culprit and half carried and half dragged him outside. Cold with fury, the Judge sent the jury to its room and called the Sheriff and counsel into chambers.

The Judge glared at all of us. "Does anyone in this room know anything about this?" he demanded sternly, and since the incident was plainly pro-defense, I flushed and hung my head, feeling like a guest suspected of stealing all the mink and jewelry at a weekend house party.

"Not I, Your Honor, I swear," I said. "I like to win my cases but I wouldn't be a party to a thing like that for the world. I never saw the man before."

Claude Dancer glared at me as though I was lying by the clock and then the red-faced good old Sheriff came to the rescue. "Judge," Max said, "if anyone is to blame for this incident it is me. This boy was blasted to hell in World War Two but refused to die and we try to be nice to him around here and take him off his mother's hands for a few hours. We'd kept him out of the trial until today and only let him in when he promised to behave. I guess we guessed wrong—he unfortunately blew his top. It must have been all the war talk. In fact that is more than I've ever heard him speak. I am positive that none of the lawyers of parties had anything to do with it. I'm terribly sorry, sir."

Claude Dancer looked over at me and shook his head. "Even the disabled veterans throw you an assist, you lucky bastard," he murmured.

"The cause of righteousness shall prevail," I retorted piously.

"Let's take ten minutes," the Judge said, still frowning ominously. "I guess," he added slowly, "I guess there isn't a damned thing we can do. This is just one of the belated casualties of war, one of the lame chickens of our civilization come home to roost." He shook his head. "The poor, poor bastard," he murmured. It sounded like a benediction.

Back again after recess even Claude Dancer seemed somewhat sobered—as indeed all of us were—by the incident of the disabled veteran. He kept badgering and worrying the Lieutenant about what he had told Dectective Sergeant Durgo, and going over and over the story of the actual shooting in an effort to get him to admit remembering some fragment of the events that he had earlier denied remembering, but the Lieutenant, of all the people in the courtroom, seemed heartened now by what had happened, and his answers were if anything more cool and deliberate than they had been before.

"Is it true that you struck and knocked down a fellow officer who had paid some attention to your wife at a cocktail party?" the Dancer next led off.

"Yes, sir."

"Why?"

354

"Because he was intoxicated and was annoying her."

Softly: "Were you jealous, Lieutenant?"

"I wouldn't say so. I didn't like it and I resented his actions."

"Were you angry?"

Frowning: "Well, to some extent I was, yes."

"Do you have a quick temper, Lieutenant?" The Dancer paused. "Would you knock me down if I dared kiss your wife's hand?"

Lieutenant Manion stared up at the skylight and a half smile flitted over his face as he answered. "No, Mr. Dancer—but I think I might be sore tempted to spank you."

The courtroom tittered and Claude Dancer flushed with hot anger and stood biting his lips, fighting for self-control, as though he were counting to ten. He retired to his table and drank a glass of water and returned to the witness.

"Now, Lieutenant," he said, after a pause, winding up to pitch a fast inside curve (I was beginning to learn the signs) "take this lüger you used to shoot Barney Quill with."

"Yes, sir," the Lieutenant replied coolly, and I glanced quickly at Parnell and hoped the Lieutenant would remember the medicine Parnell and I had cooked up for that one.

Claude Dancer found the fatal weapon in the pile of exhibits and spun it on his finger like Billy the Kid. "This lüger pistol that you kept loaded in your trailer and carried unlawfully concealed on your person that night—it was not regular Army issue, was it?" he purred.

"No, sir," the Lieutenant replied, as I held my breath for the next question.

Still spinning: "You had not reported it to your C.O. and as far as your superiors knew you did not even possess it?"

"That's correct, sir," the Lieutenant answered quietly.

Pausing triumphantly: "Then please explain to the court and jury how and where you got it?"

"Yes, sir," the Lieutenant said obediently, and in accordance with my repeated instructions he began abruptly with the patrol skirmish he had told me about weeks before. "We had gone out on night patrol," the Lieutenant began, and without so much as mentioning the lüger he proceeded to tell the story of how the old gray timber wolf of a German lieutenant had sniped at his men from behind the battered stub of chimney; of how he, Lieutenant Manion, had crawled around behind the hidden German.

"Lieutenant, I did not ask you for a Cook's tour of your heroic adventures in World War Two," Claude Dancer broke in, at last sensing the trap he had fallen in. "I asked you where you got the lüger. Just tell us that." He dropped the pistol back on the pile of exhibits.

"I'm telling you, sir," the Lieutenant said calmly, and he proceeded on with his story of the death of the battered and wounded German lieutenant, telling it even better, I thought, than he had told me the first time. "And that is how and where I got the lüger pistol, sir," he concluded, looking coolly at Claude Dancer and respectfully awaiting the next question.

Claude Dancer shot me a grim nod of congratulation and swiftly changed the subject in an effort to cover up. "Do you and your wife have any children?" he asked abruptly.

"No, sir."

"And is this your first marriage?"

"No, sir, my second."

"And did either you or your wife have children by your respective previous—ah—adventures in matrimony?"

Scowling: "No, sir."

"And both of your parents are dead, I believe?"

"Yes, sir."

"And you have no dependents other than your wife, Lieutenant?"

"None, sir."

Claude Dancer was now cleverly showing the jury that there was no widowed mother or seven starving children standing in the way of the jury throwing the book at the Lieutenant by its verdict.

"And your wife has earned her living before and she is in good health and could do so again?"

"Yes, sir, if it came to that I believe she could, sir."

"The witness is back to you," Claude Dancer said, turning to me.

"No re-direct examination," I said, tugging at the knot on my tie out of sheer relief to at last have the Lieutenant off the stand and out of the clutches of this diabolical little man.

"We'll take five minutes," the Judge said to the Sheriff, plainly grown parsimonious of time in this case that all of us hoped would be over and done that day.

During recess Parnell told me that he and Maida had driven to Thunder Bay the night before, following Maida's inspired brainstorm over the desk clerk, and had dined at the hotel, overlooking the lake. After supper Parnell had had a long and friendly visit with

Mary Pilant in her rooms. When the night clerk had come on duty Mary had summoned him upstairs and, so she told Parnell later, for the first time had heard the full and significant details of Barney's appearance and actions the night of the shooting.

I cocked my head skeptically at the earnest old man but remained silent. "Ah, Polly," Parnell said, shaking his head, "you may find it hard to do, but I believe her; I believe she was moved by the highest of impulses to shut her mind to an evil thing. Don't think harshly of her, boy; she—she is such a sweet child, so grave, and now so penitent and concerned. She particularly asked me to extend you her warmest best wishes. I think you made a hit with her, boy." He blinked his eyes mistily. "Ah me—to think that I might have had a daughter like her. She—she reminds me so much of my own lost lamb."

I silently patted the old man on the back and ducked out for a drink of water. "You are a good man, Paul Biegler," this strange girl had said.

"Dr. Matthew Smith," I said, and young Dr. Smith arose and moved forward and was sworn and took the stand.

"Your name, please, Doctor?" I said.

"Matthew Smith."

"What is your profession?"

"I am a psychiatrist."

The jurors glanced at each other, surprised, and I was sure they were appraising his youth, evidently sharing with me the Hollywood notion that psychiatrists had somehow to look like first cousins to Svengali and Rasputin. "Are you duly licensed to practice medicine and surgery in the state of Michigan?" I went on.

"I am."

After that, in accordance with courtroom protocol, I took the young doctor on a quick guided tour through medical school, graduation, an internship in psychiatry here, a residency there, then some graduate work over there, then work on the psychiatric staff of a Detroit hospital, work with various health clinics, probate courts, the Veterans' Administration and the like, finally down to his present job.

"Are you a member of a board or organization devoted to your specialty?" I pressed on.

"Yes, I have been certified by the American Board of Psychiatry and Neurology."

"What does that mean?"

"That means that the American Psychiatric Association has put its stamp of approval on me as a specialist to practice psychiatry."

"And are there practicing psychiatrists who do not possess this certification?" I said.

"There are."

"How many years have you spent actively in the field of psychiatry, Doctor?"

"Over eight years."

"How old are you?"

"Thirty-five."

The Doctor's Army association had to be dragged out by someone, so drag away I did. "What is your status as to being a civilian or otherwise?"

"I am at present in the military force in the Army, stationed at Bellevue Army Hospital as chief of the neuropsychiatric service."

"With what military rank?"

"Captain."

"Now, Doctor, I ask you if you were recently assigned by your superiors to conduct a psychiatric examination of Lieutenant Frederic Manion, the defendant in this case?"

"I was."

"Did you conduct such an examination?"

"I did."

"Where?"

"At Bellevue Army Hospital."

"When?"

"From Thursday, September fourth through half of Sunday, the seventh."

"And will you tell us, Doctor, some of the things that were done in connection with this examination."

"This man received a complete physical examination, which means that he went through each of the specialty clinics in the hospital and he was examined by a specialist in the particular department. Then a complete social history was performed by a man specially trained and qualified in that field. He also received an electroencephalogram study."

"What is that?"

"Because there was in the history the fact that the Lieutenant had been unconscious as a result of a concussion suffered in military service efforts were made to determine whether or not there might be some residual effects—these would probably have shown up on an electroencephalogram. However it was perfectly normal."

"Go ahead."

"He also received the apperception test and was extensively interviewed on the three and one-half days he was there. This was my primary assignment during the period of the Lieutenant's hospitalization."

"I ask you if some of the preliminary tests were conducted by men working under you—by persons working under you?" I had to get this out in the open before Claude Dancer did.

"Taken by technicians trained for the purpose, yes. The responses were examined by me. The test itself, that is the various responses to the previous tests, were examined by myself and interpreted to the extent that they were interpreted."

"Now I ask you, Doctor, whether there are modern psychiatric facilities and equipment at the Bellevue Army Hospital?"

"There are indeed, sir."

"And how do they compare with other equipment of that nature in other hospitals?"

"Our facilities compare favorably with that in any hospital I am acquainted with."

I paused. We were coming to the crucial hypothetical question over which Parnell and I had worked so long and given so much thought. The hypothetical question was one of the law's more urbane fictions, a convenient sort of legal make-believe by which counsel, when examining an expert witness called by it, wrapped up all the facts and issues and pet theories of his case in a sort of neat legal grab bag and pelted it at the expert witness for his opinion and conclusion. It at least mercifully possessed the highly desirable quality of saving time.

"Doctor," I said, "I ask you whether you and I have heretofore reviewed together a hypothetical question based upon the issue of possible insanity in this case?"

"We have."

I advanced to the Judge's bench. "Your Honor," I said, "I hand you a copy of our hypothetical question." I walked over to Mitch's table. "I also hand counsel a copy." I returned to my table. "With the Court's permission I should now like to read into the record our hypothetical question."

The judge nodded. "Read away," he said, and the court reporter rolled up his eyes and seemed to brace himself for the expected flood of words, in which he was not disappointed.

"Thank you, Your Honor," I said, and began reading. "Doctor, assume that a man of thirty-six is a First Lieutenant in the United States Army; that he was a combat veteran of World War II and the Korean War; that he returned to his country from Korea in 1953 and for a time was assigned to special military duty in various places. That in July of this year he was assigned to duty in a remote logging and resort village in the Upper Peninsula of Michigan. That he was married to an attractive and vivacious woman five years his senior. That these two were and are much in love with each other. That they lived in a trailer in a public park in said village. That the social and recreational facilities of said village were limited. That one of the few public recreational places they could conveniently go to was a neighboring hotel bar. That because of his long overseas service and the further fact that he was on loan from his own outfit the Lieutenant had few acquaintances among local Army personnel. That he occasionally went to the hotel bar when off duty and that his social relations with the civilian proprietor were cordial though in no sense intimate. Assume further, Doctor, that at approximately 9:00 P.M. on Friday, August 15th the wife of this lieutenant went to this tavern to get some beer and play pinball and that the lieutenant went to bed and slept and that at approximately 11:45 P.M. he was suddenly awakened. That he hurriedly got up and thereupon heard a series of screams. That he then met his wife at the door of his trailer. That she was sobbing and breathless and hysterical. That she finally told him that the proprietor of the hotel bar had threatened her life and assaulted and raped her; that he had again just assaulted her and beaten and kicked her. That she was badly bruised and beaten. That her skirt was ripped and her underpants were missing. That the Lieutenant spent upwards of an hour attempting to calm and comfort and minister to his wife. That during this time she told him the details of the threats and assaults and beatings. That during this time he wiped a fluid from his wife's leg which he believed to be seminal fluid. Assume further, Doctor, that this lieutenant reasonably believed that the man whom he believed had just assaulted, threatened and raped his wife was an expert pistol shot and that he kept pistols about his premises and possibly on his person. That he himself kept a loaded lüger automatic pistol in his trailer for protection. That his mind was in a turmoil over what he believed had just happened to his wife and over her present condition. That he finally determined to seek out said hotel bar proprietor and grab him and hold him for the police. That while he felt considerable anger and loathing and contempt for the proprietor he had at no time any intention of killing or harming him but felt that if the man made one bad move he would have killed him. That he went and got his pistol without his wife's knowledge and left his wife in the trailer and proceeded toward this tavern. That he does not remember what time it was or precisely how he got to the tavern. That he finally got to the tavern and entered it. That he saw the proprietor standing alone behind the bar watching him. That he then advanced to the bar and the proprietor whirled around and the Lieutenant produced his pistol and pointed it at the proprietor and emptied its contents into his body, leaning over the bar to do so. That he had and has no conscious recollection of his act. That he then turned and left the tavern and proceeded toward his trailer. That he does not remember anything after he entered the tavern other than as indicated until he got home to the trailer. That he then first observed that his pistol was empty; that he then told his wife that he had shot the tavern proprietor. That he then notified a deputized caretaker of the trailer camp of what he had done. That he waited in his trailer for the police and was subsequently arrested and charged with murder. Assume further, Doctor, that this man had never before in his lifetime ever been arrested for or convicted of any criminal offense, including any civilian act of violence toward another human being." I paused and caught my breath. "Now, Doctor, assume all the facts herein stated to be true, have you an opinion based upon a reasonable psychiatric certainty as to whether or not it is probable that the hypothetical man was in a condition of emotional disorganization so as to be temporarily insane?"

"I have."

"What is that opinion?"

"That he was temporarily insane at the time of the shooting."

"Doctor, have you an opinion as to whether or not he was suffering from a temporary mental disorder at the time the deceased met his death so as to be unable to distinguish right from wrong?"

"I have."

"What is your opinion?"

The Doctor hesitated here as he had the night before in his hotel room. "That the hypothetical lieutenant was probably unable to distinguish right from wrong." He paused. "I do not think it makes too much difference," he added, and out of the corner of my eye I saw Claude Dancer scribbling furiously.

I pushed on. "Have you an opinion as to whether or not at that time he knew, understood, and comprehended the nature and consequences of his acts?"

"I have."

"What is that opinion?"

"That he was not."

"Was or did not, Doctor?"

"That he did not, I mean. Thank you."

"Do you have an opinion, Doctor, as to whether or not he was in such a state of mind that he did not have the benefit of his conscious reasoning mind, and rather was dominated by instinct and the unconscious mind?"

"I have an opinion."

"State your opinion."

"That he was completely dominated by instinct and the unconscious mind."

"Now, Doctor, I ask you whether or not you have a psychiatric basis or bases for these opinions you have just expressed?"

"I have."

"And is there in your opinion a condition presented here known to the profession of psychiatry?"

"There is."

"Would you please explain these bases and the condition, if any, which may be known to psychiatry?"

"The condition is known to psychiatry. It is not uncommon. At the present time the nomenclature of this condition is known as dissociative reaction. The condition that you describe certainly constitutes a psychic shock. This shock disturbed the mental and emotional equilibrium of the hypothetical Lieutenant and was responsible for creating an almost overwhelming tension. In this state the one object the Lieutenant would seek would be anything, something, that would reduce or alleviate the tension. His past history indicates he is a man of action and it was natural at this time that he should turn to action. It would mean that at this time he could not consider any alternative course. It would also mean he would not be fully capable of understanding the significance of any course of action he followed. Though he might very well have been told what that significance would be he was not at this time in a state where he could fully appreciate it. At such a time the only right that this individual may understand is the right that will reduce the unbearable tension. In this instance it was responsible for certain phenomena, in other instances responsible under circumstances having similar remarkable phenomena."

"Can you give us example?"

"This is a condition that I have seen and discussed with men who experienced it during combat. After they were out of it some time. Considerable time. Some of the most remarkable heroics take place in this state, as well as some of the most remarkable cowardice."

"Does this mental state of dissociative reaction you have been talking about bear any other tag or label?"

"It does. It has also been known as irresistible impulse."

The Dancer was evidently growing suspicious that irresistible impulse might be recognized as a defense in Michigan and he did not like the fatal words. "Object, Your Honor," he said. "That is invading the province of the court and jury. Move that it be stricken."

"Mr. Biegler?" the Judge said.

"Your Honor, the Doctor has called this condition one of dissociative reaction and I have asked him if it had any other name or label and he has just told us." I walked forward. "This is crucial to our case, Your Honor, and we will go to bat on that—"

The Judge held up his hand. "No need to make a speech, Mr. Biegler," he said. "The answer may stand."

"Doctor," I said, "I appreciate that as a professional man you feel naturally impelled to couch your opinions and conclusions in professional language. But I wonder whether you could, in capsule form, give us your opinion on the psychiatric condition you find here as it might be more understandable to a layman?"

"Yes, sir, I'll try. The situation described in this hypothetical question is one of massive shock; the mental and emotional equilibrium of the man would be profoundly disturbed; a tension approaching the unbearable would be created and he would, in his trance-like state or spell, be irresistibly impelled to seek immediate means of alleviating this tension."

"Now, Doctor, I ask you whether in your opinion this hypothetical man laboring under the mental state you have described would have been apt to have gone to an aging and unarmed deputized caretaker and instead asked him to grab the deceased and hold him for the police?"

Claude Dancer arose but the Judge silenced him with the upraised palm of his hand. Both the Dancer and I were wearing him down.

"Such behavior would have been incompatible with everything else you have enumerated in this hypothetical question," the witness replied. "The question indicates that this is certainly a hypothetical of honor, a man who would sense that personal security depends upon self-respect, self-esteem, ideals and honor. To have such a man at this particular point turn to an aging and unarmed caretaker would have been simply incompatible with the hypothetical man up to this point. I would not relish attempting to explain any circumstances under which such a hypothetical man could do such a thing."

"Doctor, I ask you whether or not he, the Lieutenant, would have gone to the bar to grab the proprietor—"

Mr. Dancer: "This is supposed to be hypothetical. We should keep it that way."

"I beg your pardon, Mr. Hypothetical Assistant to Prosecutor Lodwick," I said.

"Someone sounds hypocritical to me," the Dancer shot back.

"Gentlemen, gentlemen," the Judge broke in wearily. "Let us *please* saw some hypothetical wood."

Doctor Smith smiled. "In the state in which this hypothetical lieutenant was at the time he would have gone to the hypothetical inn, in my opinion he would have done so with or without a gun, whether or not the hypothetical proprietor had any hypothetical guns available, and whether or not he knew that they were there. In my opinion he would have walked into a cannon mounted on the bar. I think it is important to understand that the very essence of this hypothetical man's manhood was at stake here. It could countenance no alternative short of oblivion or death, and the presence or absence of an alternative course—consideration of its significance or of any other course of action—could not have prevailed against this overpowering need of alleviating the tension under which he labored. The need to alleviate this tension took precedence over everything else."

"Doctor, can you explain why this need involved the hypothetical tavern proprietor?"

"It was the most natural thing under the circumstances that the efforts to alleviate this tension would be directed against the hypothetical cause or precipitator of this tension. In your question you indicate only such conditions that would make it clear that this is a man of action. He could not suddenly have started to behave in a condition so completely foreign to him as to philosophically have pondered this matter. This man was no complex self-searching character out of Henry James. Action was the thing that was essential."

I wondered wryly how many students of Henry James we had on the jury. "You may state whether or not this hypothetical lieutenant might have done this while feeling angry toward the hypothetical tavern keeper?" (Dancer would surely harp on this, and I thought it better to try to becalm his sails in advance.)

"This man might have felt anger among all the other emotions he would be capable of feeling at that time. I would think it would be impossible to limit that emotion—there would certainly be an appeal to anger."

"Doctor, I ask you whether or not this mental state or condition of which you speak would necessarily interfere with the physical abilities or manual dexterity of the hypothetical lieutenant, as for example his ability to quickly produce a gun and aim it accurately."

"It would not. Indeed it might well even facilitate whatever activity this man was following."

"Have you seen such phenomena in your experience as a psychiatrist?"

"I have seen and I have heard—I have heard of it from those in whom the phenomena took place."

"Doctor," I pushed on, "you may state whether or not intensive and extensive psychiatric observation and examination of the individual is important in reaching psychiatric conclusions about his mental state."

"I would say they were essential."

"Can you explain that?"

"To understand that a particular experience would be a shock to one man or to another man does not necessarily require personal observation. To understand *why* the particular shock would result in a particular course of conduct or mental state in a given individual requires intense observation of the highest order. That, sir, is psychiatry."

"You may state, Doctor, whether or not you would venture or attempt to pass a psychiatric opinion on the past mental state of either the hypothetical lieutenant or the real Lieutenant Manion on the basis of merely sitting here during the course of this trial."

Doctor Smith shot a quick look at the People's psychiatrist. "I would consider it impossible to pass any valid professional opinion on the state of this man's mind on or about August sixteenth and immediately thereafter on the basis of such observations."

I turned to Claude Dancer. "Your witness," I said.

"Doctor, during your examination of this defendant did you find any psychosis?" Claude Dancer shot out before leaving his chair.

"I did not."

"Any neurosis?" he asked, advancing with his stealthy short-legged tread.

"That is a broad question. I found no history of serious neuroses."

Claude Dancer now paused squarely in front of the witness. "Now, Doctor, will you tell us what facts or factors in the hypothetical question you considered the most important?"

This was a cleverly loaded question: dynamite, in fact; the moment the doctor started isolating factors in our hypothetical question he was opening the gate to the possible tearing of our question—and of his opinion—to tatters. I had not anticipated this line of questioning or warned the Doctor about it and I drew in my breath awaiting his answer.

"The whole hypothetical question was important," the Doctor quietly answered as I began gratefully to breathe again. "It delineated a particular hypothetical man. No one, two, or three factors more or less could quite do so, so that I must say that my answers were based on the whole question."

Suavely: "Weren't there any parts that were a *little* more significant than others?"

"No part was so significant that I would like to take it away from the rest."

Still tugging: "You mean you don't recall the parts which were more significant?"

"I mean what I said, that the whole question as stated is significant and separating the question part from part would destroy the significance of the individual parts, like adding dimples or removing the smile from Mona Lisa. This is a question dependent one part upon the other and I would not care to take one part and call it more or less significant."

The Dancer was getting no place on that and he wisely changed the subject. "How is dissociative reaction classified by psychiatrists?"

"This is a temporary neurotic condition."

"It is not a psychosis?"

"It is not a psychosis nor is it ordinarily even a serious neurosis. This depends upon how you are referring to the reaction—it can of course be quite serious at the *time* that one is suffering it, both as to the consequences to himself and to others. But if duration is considered it is generally of a more temporary nature."

"Now, Doctor, just what tests were made when you conducted your examination of the Lieutenant?"

"He underwent all the usual laboratory tests."

"Was he given a Wechsler-Bellevue test?"

"He was not."

"Was there a Bender-Gestalt test?"

"No."

"What type of tests are those?"

"They are psychological tests."

"And no psychological tests were given?"

"The ones that I thought were indicated were administered and examined and appraised by me."

"What were they?"

"An apperception test was one."

"Is it a psychological test or projection?"

"Both psychological and a projection test. Projection test is a general heading for psychological tests."

"What is the purpose of the Wechsler-Bellevue test?"

"The Wechsler-Bellevue intelligence scale would, as its name implies, give some estimate of an individual's intelligence and it may also be used to determine the classification of some mental disorders."

"What type of disorders?"

"Well, it may contribute information about feeble-mindedness, where suspected, depending upon the skill of the person administering it. It could be of significant help in the field of educational psychology. I make no pretense of being an authority in that latter field, however."

"Did you have the facilities to administer this test?"

"Yes."

"And the Bender-Gestalt test?"

"Yes."

"Did you administer either to Lieutenant Manion?"

"I did not."

"Why?"

"Because I felt they were not indicated. The latter is a psychological test aimed largely at determining the accuracy of perception."

"Did you make a personality inventory study of the Lieutenant?"

368

(The Dancer had evidently taken a short cram course on the argot of psychiatry, and he was trotting out his knowledge with characteristic glib crispness.)

"I requested no such study. I made my own individual psychiatric study of this man. There are different tests that may be used. I did not use any of those you have mentioned."

"What tests did you use, then?"

"I tested his perceptions rather carefully and then I used an electroencephalogram. Then with my own rather intensive observations and study I felt I was qualified to make some observations about this man and perhaps understand quite a little about him."

Claude Dancer paused and referred to his notes and glibly tossed out some more tests. "Did you give him the Szondi test?"

"I did not give him a Szondi experimental diagnostic examination."

"A Rorschach psychodiagnostic examination?"

"No."

"A thematic apperception test?"

"No, sir."

"Or any personality screening tests?"

"I did not." The Doctor paused and glanced at the People's psychiatrist. "I may add, sir, in a general way that I happen to belong to the school of psychiatry that tends to stress individual study and appraisal rather than to that group that has sometimes lightly been referred to as the slot-machine or gadget school of psychiatry."

Claude Dancer ignored the thrust and pressed on. "From your examination of the Lieutenant did you find any history of delusions?"

"None."

"Or loss of memory?"

"None before this case."

"Or hallucinations?"

"No."

"Or conversion hysteria?"

"Well, the dissociative reaction itself embraces cases of what has been called such hysteria."

The Dancer paused triumphantly as though he had dug up a fresh bone. "In common language, Doctor, isn't the conversion hysteria also known as a fit of temper?"

"It is not. I know of no reputable psychiatrist or psychiatric authority who would so describe it."

"How would you describe it in common language?"

"I think I have done so already in the commonest language I could and still preserve accuracy," the Doctor replied coolly. "If you wish me to repeat it please ask the appropriate questions and I shall do so again."

Claude Dancer eyed the witness and then referred to his notes. "Doctor, on direct examination you were asked if the hypothetical lieutenant was able to distinguish between right and wrong and you answered that he *probably* could not have, adding that you did not think it made much difference. Do you still feel the same way?"

Quietly: "I do," the witness answered.

"Then he might actually have known the difference between right and wrong?"

"He well might have."

Triumphantly: "Then how can you possibly come in here and testify that the Lieutenant was legally insane?" he shot at the witness, and I now saw that Claude Dancer himself apparently did not know that irresistible impulse was a defense to crime in Michigan under a plea of insanity, a situation for which he could scarcely be blamed when one considered that Parnell and I—and I a D.A. for ten years—had had such a devil of a time to unearth it ourselves. Yet the situation was fraught with peril and I waited anxiously for the answer.

"I did not ever say here that anyone was *legally* insane, sir," the Doctor coolly replied. "I have said that I thought the hypothetical lieutenant was suffering from a medically recognized mental aberration known as dissociative reaction, sometimes known as irresistible impulse, and I say and repeat that a consciousness of doing right or wrong would not make much if any difference to a victim of that mental disorder."

Claude Dancer turned his back on the witness and shot a significant look at the jury and then over at me. Then, with his back still turned to the witness: "And you are willing to rest your testimony in this case, Doctor, on that answer?" he fairly purred.

"I am, sir."

Claude Dancer was going to have himself a little surprise, I saw, if only the Judge gave the jury our requested instructions on irresistible impulse and if only the jury understood and heeded them. Always there was the big uncertain *if.* . . .

Claude Dancer veered on to another subject. "Might this man have felt anger toward the hotel proprietor?" he pressed on, facing the witness again.

"Are you referring now to the real or hypothetical lieutenant, Mr. Dancer?" the witness countered calmly.

Claude Dancer was stung to be corrected by this cool young cucumber. "Either one," he snapped. "As a matter of fact wasn't the Lieutenant angered at the proprietor and didn't he go over there in a homicidal rage to shoot him to death?"

The Doctor grew thoughtful. "He might well have felt some anger toward the proprietor," he conceded. "It would have been rather abnormal if he hadn't. But we may be sure it wouldn't solely be anger." He paused and smiled slightly. "Just as you have now displayed anger at me, Mr. Dancer, yet your main desire and dearest wish is still the cool and calculated one—to trap me if you possibly can."

Claude Dancer glared momentarily at the witness and then evidently decided not to pursue the subject of his own anger. "But wouldn't the defendant's main desire and dearest wish be to vent his wrath and anger upon the hated proprietor?" he persisted.

The Doctor shook his head. "Abstract words like 'patriotism' and 'anger' and 'love' and 'hate' exist mostly as convenient and oversimplifying labels for the complex emotions that men feel, Mr. Dancer," the Doctor said. "The feelings of men do not exist because of the words. The feelings were there long before men had any words. Rarely if ever, in fact, are men's emotions confined to any mere word or set of words. To insist that the Lieutenant felt only anger is unduly to isolate and stress but one of the many complex and conflicting emotions he was doubtless feeling at the time."

"Very well, Doctor, please tell us some of the others," Claude Dancer said, smiling sweetly. "Perhaps love?"

The Doctor avoided the looming semantic morass of that clever trap. "I cannot say, sir. All we can be fairly sure of is that it wasn't anger alone, if anger indeed there was any. When we are discussing the ultimate personality of a man, the oppressed human psyche, driven and at bay, we do not hang a tag on it called 'anger' or 'love' and think we have described that man; when we do so we have only ignored the problem. Only in certain primitive tribes and in ancient Greek drama did men dare label the whole man by the use of masks. And everybody understood they were mere convenient tags, conventional symbols representing comedy and tragedy and the like —never the whole man."

I glanced at the jury, fearful that they might themselves be sinking into a hopeless morass of semantics. Instead they were sitting alert in their chairs and appeared to be having the time of their lives. "Hell's fire," their combined expressions seemed to say, "this beats the graven wisdom even of the *Reader's Digest* and the *Saturday Evening Post.*"

The Dancer veered away from anger. "Are neuroses considered insanity?" he said.

"Usually they are not."

"That is all," Mr. Dancer concluded, turning away.

"No re-direct examination," I swiftly put in. Then I took a deep breath and went on. "That is our case. The defense rests."

"Noon recess," the Judge said. "Please be back at one P.M." He glanced at Max. "Mister Sheriff," he murmured.

chapter 25

When, after the noon recess, Max Battisfore had notified me it was time, he lingered in the conference room until the Lieutenant and Laura had walked on ahead toward the courtroom. He spoke rapidly. "Look, Polly," he blurted, "something's cooking, I don't know what, but I just found out from Sulo Kangas that our friend Dancer's been interviewing my prisoners since yesterday. Sees 'em alone in Mitch's office, one at a time. Of course I suppose I couldn't have stopped him but I thought I'd let you know."

"Thanks, Max. Do you know what it's all about?"

"Not exactly, but I naturally figure it's about this case. You can expect just about anything from that little guy. And you can bet it won't be good. I gotta go."

"Thanks for the tip, Max. I'll be expecting anything." I closed my eyes and sighed and grabbed up my brief case and lurched out the door. What was the relentless Mr. Dancer up to now?

"Hear ye, hear ye, hear ye!" Max bawled out, and the crowd, conditioned now to the ceremony of the gavel, arose like a raggedly obedient congregation and then slowly ebbed back into a thrall of silence. The waiting Judge looked down at the People's table. "Any rebuttal?" he said quietly.

"Yes, Your Honor," Claude Dancer said, popping to his feet. "The People will call Dr. W. Harcourt Gregory," whereupon the People's psychiatrist unwound his considerable height and strolled languidly stoop-shouldered to the stand, was earnestly sworn by Clovis Pidgeon, and sat coolly facing the body of the crowded and hushed courtroom. It was a mildly enervating experience just to look at him. Claude Dancer advanced slowly toward the witness, smiling as though to say: "Here, ladies and gentlemen, here at last is a psychiatrist that *looks* like a psychiatrist."

"Your name, please?" he purred.

"W. Harcourt Gregory," the witness replied in a precise and high-pitched voice, fleetingly fingering the ends of his mustache.

"What is your occupation?"

"Doctor of medicine."

"Have you specialized in any particular field of medicine?"

"I have."

"In what field?"

"Psychiatry."

"For how long?"

"Approximately twenty-five years."

"Will you please outline for us, Doctor, your medical and psychiatric training and experience?"

Dr. Gregory thereupon, like Dr. Smith, got himself through college and medical school, various graduate and post-graduate courses (including some impressive-sounding hitches in Paris and Vienna), and thence, evidently as fast as he could, unto the salaried staffs of various public mental institutions.

"And what, if any, is your present position, Doctor?"

"Medical superintendent of the Pentland State Hospital in lower Michigan."

"And what kind of patients are treated there?"

"Those regarded as insane or feeble-minded."

"And are you associated with any national psychiatric groups?"

The witness cleared his throat. "I am a diplomate of the American Board of Psychiatry and Neurology," he replied with the softness of great pride.

Claude Dancer then raised a paper that looked suspiciously like his copy of our hypothetical question and began to read it. As he read on my suspicions were confirmed: the clever little man was shooting *our* precise hypothetical question at his psychiatrist, word for word. "Now, Doctor, assuming all the facts stated herein to be true, have you an opinion based upon reasonable psychiatric certainty as to whether or not it is probable that the hypothetical man was in a condition of emotional disorganization so as to be temporarily insane?"

"I have."

"What is that opinion?"

"That the information given regarding the hypothetical lieutenant is clearly not sufficient to warrant a diagnosis of insanity."

"Have you an opinion based upon a reasonable psychiatric certainty as to whether or not that hypothetical man under the facts stated in the hypothetical question was suffering from dissociative reaction?"

"I have."

"What is your opinion?"

"I do not believe he was suffering from a dissociative reaction," he said, thus calmly attempting to slay our main defense of irresistible impulse.

"What is your reason for that opinion?"

"A dissociative reaction is a severe type of psychoneurosis. Psychoneurosis is a condition of long standing. I feel certain that the hypothetical lieutenant would have shown either one or repeated upsets of a dissociative nature during the time or times of his combat service. None has been postulated."

Under the further adroit questioning of Claude Dancer the witness proceeded to attempt to demolish our case. Yes, the hypothetical lieutenant could distinguish right from wrong; yes, he could understand and comprehend the nature and consequences of his acts; yes, the lieutenant was in possession of his faculties and was not dominated by his unconscious mind. I glanced sidewise at our young psychiatrist, who had hung his head. Claude Dancer pushed on.

"Now, Doctor, if those instances in the question as set forth stating that the hypothetical lieutenant had no memory of certain events were eliminated and it was substituted that he did have a memory of those events would that change your opinion?"

"No, sir; rather it would accentuate my opinion."

"If in addition to the facts as stated in the hypothetical question it were assumed that the hypothetical lieutenant returned home and as stated in the question told his wife that he had shot the tavern proprietor, then went to the home of a deputized caretaker which was about thirty feet from his trailer, and told him that he had shot a man and that he wanted this deputy to take him into custody, and that a few hours later this same hypothetical lieutenant reported to a detective sergeant of the state police the details of an alleged sexual attack that had been previously related to him by his wife and stated that he considered it from all angles and made efforts to make sure that his wife was giving him true facts and that he had decided that a man who did that to his wife should not live, and then described how he had gone to the tavern, shot the proprietor, and returned home and turned himself in to the deputy who lived just thirty feet from the trailer,—assuming those additional facts, Doctor, would that change your opinion?"

"No. It would serve only to confirm that he was not legally or medically insane."

Claude Dancer looked back at me, beaming. "Your witness," he said. I glanced back at young Dr. Smith, who still sat with his head bowed and his hand over his eyes. His direst fears had been realized.

I arose and slowly advanced to destroy this man if I could. A grim thought suddenly assailed me. Though I had never held many illusions to the contrary, I was now struck solidly in the gut with the notion of what a snarling jungle a trial really was; with the fact that despite all the obeisant "Your honors" and "may it please the courts," despite all the rules and objections and soft illusion of decorum, a trial was after all a savage and primitive battle for survival itself.

"Doctor," I began softly, "so you're a diplomate of the American Board of Psychiatry and Neurology?"

"I am, sir," he said proudly, delicately fingering his luxuriant mustache.

"Since your colleague Dr. Smith belongs to the same outfit might he not, were he disposed, also refer to himself as a diplomate?" I went on. I had swiftly to square *that*.

Stiffly: "I assume so."

Twitting softly, in an ascendant questioning voice: "Perhaps, Doctor, perhaps there is a shyer and more modest class of diplomates in your club?"

"Objection. Objection. . . ."

"Sustained," the Judge swiftly ruled.

"How long have you been on the staffs of various public mental institutions, Doctor?"

The doctor pondered. "Twenty-one years," he answered.

"And you head the staff of one now?"

"That is correct."

"Isn't it a fact, then, Doctor," I pushed on, "that during most of your professional career, working as you have in public mental institutions, you have dealt largely with people who had already been adjudged insane by others?" (I had, if I could, to try to take some of the curse off his advantage in experience and years over our young psychiatrist.)

"Well, yes," he admitted, because he had to; he had already clearly so testified.

"And a major portion of your work and experience then has been in determining when and if those patients had recovered or been restored to *sanity*, rather than in determining if they were insane, the form of that insanity, or how they became so?"

"Yes, sir, that and in trying to cure them."

"And isn't it further true that all of the public mental institutions you have been connected with, including the one where you presently work, have had and now have long waiting lists of the mentally ill seeking admittance?"

376

I had struck a responsive chord. "It certainly is true, sir," he said, nodding his thin head with a languid sort of emphasis. "The lack of proper facilities to accommodate our mentally ill, and the consequent dire overcrowding of existing facilities, is a disgrace to the state and the nation."

My man was coming nicely. "And as a consequence of that overcrowding isn't it also true that only those persons with the most objectively advanced symptoms of insanity, those most socially difficult to handle or permit to remain at large, are precisely the ones most likely to be admitted to our asylums, including yours?"

He still did not quite see the drift. "Very true," he agreed. "We naturally get only the most advanced cases."

"So that it would further be true then, Doctor, would it not, that those psychiatrists who work in such public mental institutions would rarely if ever get to study or observe the more subtle and subjective types of mental illnesses?"

He saw the wind drift now but he was committed beyond all retreat. "Well," he said, frowning, "yes, I suppose that is so."

"There is no supposing about it, is there, Doctor?"

"Well, no, sir."

"And that would include persons allegedly suffering from dissociative reaction, would it not?"

Resignedly now: "Yes. They would rarely be committed to a public mental institution."

It was time now to get down to particulars. "Now, Doctor," I asked, "when did you first lay eyes on the real and not the hypothetical Lieutenant Manion?"

"On Thursday morning of this week."

I paused and pondered. "Let's see—up to now that's roughly two and one-half court days, is it not?"

Loftily patient: "It is, sir."

"And did you see him at all outside of the courtroom during that time?"

"I did not."

"Then may I assume, Doctor, that you did not conduct any personal examination of him?"

Dryly: "Rather obviously I did not, sir."

"Nor did you conduct on him *any* of the various tests and whatnot that have been mentioned here by Mr. Dancer or by your colleague?"

"I did not."

"Now you were present, Doctor, were you not, when Prosecutor Dancer cross-examined Dr. Smith this forenoon?"

"I was." Again his fingers strayed to his mustache, of which he seemed inordinately fond.

"And did you hear Mr. Dancer question Dr. Smith rather extensively upon his failure"—I paused and consulted my notes—"upon his failure to give a Wechsler-Bellevue test, a Szondi test, a Bender-Gestalt test, a Rorschach psychodiagnostic examination, a thematic apperception test, various personality screening tests"—I paused, dutifully panting, elaborately out of breath—"and possibly one or two others which in the rush may have escaped me?"

Aggrieved: "Of course I heard it. I was sitting right here."

"Yes, of course, it comes back to me now that you were here. And am I correct in assuming, Doctor, that Mr. Dancer got all this impressive-sounding lingo from you?"

Drawing back, offended: "Lingo?"

"Excuse me, Doctor—psychiatric terminology."

Grieved over my flailing of the obvious: "Why, yes—yes of course I told him. Many otherwise highly competent *medical* doctors wouldn't be apt to know those terms."

Crafty Claude Dancer saw the way the wind was blowing and he began stealthily to stalk me as I pressed on. "Then am I further correct in assuming, Doctor, that if you had had the opportunity to test and examine the defendant in this case you would have done the things and given the tests your colleague failed to do and give?"

Emphatically: "I certainly would have. In my opinion the necessity for them was clearly indicated."

"I see," I pushed on, nailing him down. "So that your main complaint, then, over the findings of Dr. Smith is that he failed to give the proper psychiatric tests available to him?"

The awaited objection came. "No, no, Your Honor. This witness has made no complaint. Question assumes something not in evidence. The witness—"

"The objection is overruled," the Judge quickly ruled. "Proceed."

"Yes," the witness replied, compressing his lips.

"So that it would be fair to say that your criticism of Doctor Smith's findings, Doctor, would largely be one of the methods he employed?" I pressed, pinning him down further.

"It would," the witness answered reprovingly, glancing darkly toward Dr. Smith and deftly combing his mustache between his fingers.

I paused to let all this sink in. I was aware that the world of psychoanalysis was split into almost as many squirming schools and theories and methods and warring cliques and splinter groups as the artists on the Left Bank. But I was not aware that any of these schools preferred no theories or no methods to any of those they quarreled with, and I went baying along the scent.

"Doctor," I said, "do you assume and want this jury to believe that no personal screening or observation or examination or tests of the Lieutenant whatever were better than the methods employed by Dr. Smith?"

The drift of things was impinging upon the witness, and he drew himself up tall in his chair. "I did not say that," he replied stiffly.

"I know you did not actually say it, Doctor; but you have plainly inferred it and that is why I am asking you now. Were no tests at all better than those given? Was it better to screen or not to screen?"

A light was beginning to dawn. "What do you mean?" the witness parried uneasily.

"I mean this, Doctor," I said, spelling it out. "Do you mean to testify here that the newly announced Gregory system of *no* tests or *no* examination whatever is better than Dr. Smith's test or even the tests Mr. Dancer so glibly inquired about?"

The full import of my question now struck the witness broadside. He shifted and glanced at Claude Dancer. "I would not say that." He frowned. "Are you trying, sir, to make a joke out of my profession?"

I drew closer to the witness and observed that there were large drops of perspiration on his long chin. "*Joke*, Doctor?" I said softly. "*I* making a joke out of your profession?" It was time to lower the boom. "Look, Doctor, I asked you a simple question and I'd like a simple answer: are no psychiatric tests or personal observation and examination *ever* better than where such an examination or tests are given? Is that what you want this jury to believe?"

"Objection, Your Honor—"

"The objection is overruled."

The witness was fairly trapped. "No," he replied, and it seemed to me that even his mustache wilted ever so little. He stroked the sweat off his chin with his hand and damped his hand in his limp handkerchief.

"No, what?" I dug away.

"No, it would have been better to have personally observed and tested the subject."

"So as a diplomate of the American Board of Psychiatry and Neurology you no longer claim or wish to infer here that your failure to examine and observe the Lieutenant would afford you the necessary scientific detachment so that it would be a positive advantage not to have examined him?"

"I have already answered that."

"Will you please answer it again?" I pressed harshly.

Curtly: "My answer was and is 'no.'"

"So that it was and is a disadvantage not to have examined him?" I hammered away relentlessly.

There was a long hushed pause. "Yes," he finally said, fairly hissing the sibilant, and I noted the jurors glancing quickly at each other.

"Did you make any request or was any request made on your behalf to examine Lieutenant Manion?" (This question was as shabby as anything Amos Crocker could have dreamed up in his finest hour: we would cheerfully have beheaded anyone who tried to examine our man.)

"No request was made."

My voice rose. "And yet you would dare come in here and pit your professional opinion against that of a reputable colleague who had actually examined him?"

"Objection, Your Honor. I—"

"Objection sustained."

My next question, like the last, was largely rhetorical, intended more for the jury than for the witness. "Perhaps, Doctor," I said, "since you were not inconvenienced by having ever even *seen* him— perhaps you would care to venture an off-the-cuff opinion on the psychiatric state of the dead man himself?"

"Objection! Clearly improper."

"Sustained."

I paused, noting a grin on the faces of several jurors. "Now, Doctor, let us forget all about hypothetical questions and hypothetical lieutenants and get to the real man"—I pointed—"sitting over there under a real charge of first degree murder. I ask you if you agree with your fellow diplomate, Dr. Smith, that the man is presently sane?"

"I do. It is obvious to a child."

"Thank you, Doctor. Now I ask you if you have an opinion as to whether the real Lieutenant was suffering from insanity at the time of the shooting? Now please forget any shadowy or fictional lieutenants."

"I object. That would not be proper," Mr. Dancer said.

"I asked your expert, Mr. Dancer, if he had an opinion?"

The witness remained silent, his face twisted into a sort of dark saurian frown. "Do you have an opinion or not?" the Judge pressed with a rare show of impatience. "Answer yes or no."

The witness tugged nervously at his mustache and seemed to slide lower in his seat. "I have an opinion," he answered, taking the final plunge.

"Good," I said. "Will you please state it?"

"Just a moment," the Judge broke in, turning toward the witness. "I want you fully to realize, Doctor, what you may be about to venture. Now if you have a real opinion I will permit you to state it. But I don't want any guess. And you must be prepared to back your opinion up. I want you to be sure you understand the situation exactly before we get into it. Are you still prepared to offer an opinion?"

The Doctor was hopelessly committed now. "I am," he said, sitting bolt upright and again wiping his sweat-beaded chin.

"What is your opinion?" I asked.

The unhappy doctor clasped the arms of the witness chair and went sled length. "My opinion is that the real Lieutenant Manion was not insane at the time of the shooting," he replied.

Softly: "And upon what psychiatric bases do you ground that opinion, Doctor?"

"From what I have seen and heard here."

"You mean to venture an opinion on the sanity of this man that night without the benefit of any personal observation or tests or history whatever?" I shot at him.

The answer was now inevitable. "Yes, sir."

I paused for nearly a minute. "Doctor," I said slowly, "is that the normal and accepted psychiatric practice for a diplomate of the American Board of Psychiatry and Neurology?"

"I object to that," Mr. Dancer quickly cut in. "Counsel asked a question and got the answer and now he doesn't like it."

"I'll show you how much I like it, Mr. Dancer."

"The objection is overruled," the Judge said shortly. "Answer the question."

The Doctor seemed to sink even lower in his seat, his fingers gripping and gripping the chair rails. "No, it is not normal psychiatric practice to make a psychiatric diagnosis without the complete history and personal examination of the individual," he said, patting his wet chin.

I stood looking at the man for several moments. "No further questions," I said. "Your witness, Mr. Dancer."

"No further questions," Mr. Dancer quickly said.

"Call your next rebuttal witness," the Judge said to Claude Dancer.

Claude Dancer arose with his air of invincible aplomb and portentously cleared his throat. He made me think of a Japanese wrestler as he hunched his shoulders, preening his coat collar tight against the nape of his squat muscular neck. "May it please Your Honor," he said quietly, "at this time the People wish to move to endorse the name of Duane Miller on the information as a rebuttal witness. His identity and testimony have just come to our attention. I respectfully so move, Your Honor."

Judge Weaver blinked in surprise and looked down over his glasses at me. "Any comment, Mr. Biegler?" he said.

"This is it," I thought wildly, scrambling to my feet. "This is the little surprise package we've been waiting for." Duane Miller? Duane Miller? Who the hell was he? What could he rebut? What was back of this sudden last-minute move?

"Mr. Biegler?" the Judge prodded gently.

"Counsel inquires who the new witness may be," I said lamely, my mind racing. I knew that I could not successfully object to the addition of a good-faith rebuttal witness whose identity was previously unknown to the People; yet I could not bring myself to consent blindly without some sort of clue. The Judge looked inquiringly at Claude Dancer.

"The name is Duane Miller," the little man repeated loudly, affectionately mouthing the name with irritating articulation. "Presently an inmate of the county jail. Iron Cliffs County jail, Iron Bay, Michigan."

"Thanks, Dancer," I grated harshly at him. "I once heard of the place."

"Back to you, Mr. Biegler," the Judge hastily cut in.

"This witness is being called to rebut what?" I said, sparring for time—both time and inspiration.

Claude Dancer grinned amiably and glanced knowingly at the jury. "That, Mr. Biegler, still remains to be seen. Wouldn't it be a pity to spoil your little surprise? I renew my request, Your Honor."

"Ruling, Your Honor," I said, not daring to risk a losing objection at this crucial stage of the trial.

"The motion is granted," the Judge said dryly, glancing at the clock. "Mr. Clerk, you will please endorse the name of Duane Miller on the information as a witness for the People. Proceed, Mr. Dancer. Time's a-fleetin'."

"The People will call Duane Miller to the stand," Claude Dancer announced, grabbing up some papers and moving briskly toward the witness box. The side door by the jury breathed open and a lean sallow ravaged-looking man clad in blue denim shuffled into the courtroom accompanied by a watchful sheriff's deputy. The surprise witness stood there blinking uncertainly, swallowing his generous Adam's apple. I had never seen him before.

The deputy pointed at the witness box. "Up there, Duke," he murmured, as Duane Miller shuffled forward and was sworn and sat down, the Adam's apple bobbing like an eccentric toy.

"Your name, please?" the Dancer shot at him before he fairly got the seat warm.

"Duane Miller, sir. Folks mostly call me Duke."

'Call me Ishmael,' I thought wildly, restraining an impulse to cackle.

"Where do you presently reside?" the Dancer pressed.

The witness gestured toward the jail. "Across the alley—over in the jail, sir."

"Do you know the defendant, Frederic Manion?" Claude Dancer purred on.

The witness kept glancing over at me, plainly apprehensive of his impending cross-examination. "Well, sir, kind of, sir, it's this way, sir. For the last week I've been in the cell next to his." I felt the Lieutenant suddenly stiffen and grow taut at my side. "I can hear him and him me but I've never really laid eyes on the man."

"Have you had any conversation with him during this trial?"

The witness again swallowed and glanced at me, and Claude Dancer repeated the question. "Oh, yes, sir. A little, not very much. The man ain't much of a hand for talkin'." (Well, I'd buy that one, anyway.)

"When was the last conversation you had with him?" the Dancer pressed.

"During this very noon hour, sir."

Claude Dancer paused and glanced back at me, grown fairly elfin with delight. "Will you now please relate that conversation to the court and jury?" he said.

The Judge glanced quickly down at my table. I sucked in my breath so hard and fast that I thought that my gut was glued to my backbone. This was clearly an improper foundation for rebuttal, as the Judge and Dancer and I all knew. The little man was plainly luring me into a temporary winning objection so that he could save his surprise and eventually clobber me twice. I could also have questioned the identification of the Lieutenant by the witness but that would only have been an annoying delaying tactic at best. I breathed deeply and shook my head almost imperceptibly.

"Go on," the Dancer prodded the witness. "For once Mr. Biegler is miraculously wordless."

The witness gulped and then spoke rapidly, glibly. "I heard the Lootenant chucklin' to himself durin' this noon hour an' I says, 'Things lookin' up, Lootenant?' and he chuckles some more an' says, 'You damned tootin', Buster,' or words to that affect, and I says, 'Buck up, Lootenant—I'll bet you my tonight's coffee ration you won't get more'n manslaughter outa this rap,' an' then he laffed out loud an' says, 'You got yourself a bet, Buster. I've already fooled my lawyer an' my psy—' I can't say it but he meant his brain doctor— 'an' I'll bet you my pet lüger against this awful swill they call coffee here that I'll fool that bumpkin jury too an' beat this rap all the way.' " The witness paused. "That's all him and me said."

"You're sure he called you Buster?" Claude Dancer inquired inno cently, stroking his chin.

"He called me Buster," the witness answered firmly, as my heart dropped to my belly.

Lips pursed, Claude Dancer glanced back at the clock, rocking on his heels. "Mr. Biegler," he said, still looking thoughtfully at the clock as he strove manfully to hide his rapturous glee, "the witness is all yours."

An aching fractured sigh swept through the courtroom, a sort of rueful breath-catching, like that of a street crowd seeing a stranger suddenly tossed and mangled in traffic before their eyes. I sat very still and closed my eyes. "Oh Lord, oh Lord," I thought, over and over. I glanced at the Lieutenant. "Lieutenant!" I whispered sibilantly.

The color had drained even from his hands. Waxlike, he sat very still, only the muscles of his jaw quivering. "*Lieutenant!*" I repeated. He turned slowly and his eyes glowed like a lynx's. I felt every boring eye in the courtroom upon us. Slowly, slowly he shook his head. Then he sat staring stonily at the other wall, the maximillary muscle still leaping and twitching. "Dear Lord," I thought, rising and facing the witness. "What am I ever going to ask this sorry bastard?"

"What you in for, Duke?" I began.

"Arson," he answered tonelessly, resignedly folding his hands for the ordeal.

I lifted my brows. Arson was a felony for which prison not jail was the normal site of atonement. "Hm. . . . Confined in the county jail for arson?" I said.

"Waiting sentence. I copped out last Monday."

"I see. Where you from? We two haven't met before, have we?"

"No. I usually belong around Detroit. There and Toledo."

"Ah, so Ohio has shared the wealth," I said. "Ever happen to have been in jail or prison before, Duke?" I asked, swiftly sure of the answer.

Tonelessly: "Yes, sir."

"How many times?"

The larynx bobbed and the witness blinked out at the clock. "Let's see—two, no three prison raps an'—an' I can't remember about the jails."

"Anything else?"

"I guess maybe that's all."

"Are you sure you're not being too modest, Duke?"

Firmly: "That's all, Mister. A guy ought to know how many times he's been in stir."

"Of course. Please forgive me, Mr. Miller." I turned to Mitch's table. "I request that Prosecutor Lodwick produce and loan me this man's official criminal record to assist me in cross-examination," I said. "As an ex-D.A. I know he has one. This man is a surprise witness whose very existence I did not know about until a few minutes ago." Mitch and Claude Dancer fell to whispering. "Your Honor, I repeat my request."

Claude Dancer arose apparently to give battle but the Judge held up a warning hand. "Do you or do you not have in your possession a copy of this man's official criminal record, Mr. Lodwick?" the Judge asked

"Yes, Your Honor," Mitch said, flushing.

"Please produce it for defense counsel," the Judge swiftly ruled

Mitch dug in one of his pregnant brief cases and finally pulled out a three-page criminal identification record which he walked over and handed to me. I sat poring over the imposing document.

Mr. Duane "Duke" Miller had really lived. His record went back to early depression years, starting in juvenile reformatories in Ohio. He had been in Midwest prisons five (not three) times for offenses ranging from aggravated assault to indecent exposure and on through perjury. He had dwelt in various scattered jails countless times for offenses ranging from common drunkenness to window peeping. He possessed more aliases than a moderately fastidious dog has fleas—although Buster was regretfully not among them. . . . Consulting this alarming dossier I brought all this out from the witness. He denied nothing and, both his pride and memory being stimulated, even recollected for me that he had deserted from an Army labor battalion during the War, a peccadillo which his record failed to disclose. Duke Miller was by way of being one of society's finer little assets. Yet he had just testified that the Lieutenant had told him his defense was a hoax. And, almost worse yet, that he had called him *Buster* while doing it.

"How come you so promptly told the prosecution about this alleged conversation this noon with Lieutenant Manion?" I pressed on.

"How do you mean?" the witness sparred uneasily.

"Did they ask you or did you go tell them?"

"They asked me. I unnerstan' they been quizzin' prisoners the last coupla days."

"When did they quiz you?"

"Just before court took up here after dinner."

"Who quizzed you?"

The witness looked at Claude Dancer. "That little bald-headed guy sittin' there. Prancer or Dancer, I think his name is called."

"You're quite sure it wasn't Dunstan?" I asked, remembering the People's photographer.

"Huh? Yes, positive."

"Where did he ask you?"

Gesturing: "Back in the D.A.'s office behind this here room."

"Who brought you over to see him?"

"Charlie, the deputy there."

"Is it fair to say, Mr. Miller, that if nobody had asked you you would not have mentioned this alleged conversation to anyone?" I held my breath awaiting the answer.

"Nope, I spose not. I got troubles enough of my own."

"Perhaps little troubles like awaiting sentence on your plea of guilty to arson?"

"Well, yes."

"And of course nothing, not a whisper, was said about your pending arson sentence when you talked to Mr. Prancer or Dancer?"

Claude Dancer half rose and the Judge frowned and waved him down.

"Nope, nary a word."

"And of course no promises were given you?"

"Nope."

"And of course, Duke, you weren't thinking even faintly about your impending sentence for arson when you told the People the kind of story you thought they might possibly be panting to hear?"

Claude Dancer again shot up, bristling, and this time the Judge glared him back down.

"Nope, nary a thought."

I paused. There was still some unfinished business, Buster business. If this man was lying he had doubtless dredged the name Buster from jail gossip or the newspaper accounts of the bartender's testimony at the trial. *Buster.* . . . Wasn't *that* an inspired diabolic touch? I stroked my chin, my mind galloping. Perhaps I could trap him into a transparent lie. "Where'd you find the name Buster?" I demanded suddenly. "I suppose from the newspaper accounts of the trial, didn't you?"

"No."

"You mean no newspapers were available in the jail?" I pressed softly, trying for a demonstrable lie. I knew that during the trial the place was awash with newspapers.

The witness glanced quickly at Claude Dancer, then the Judge, then back at me, the Adam's apple gyrating. "Oh, yes, plenty of newspapers," he answered. "But I haven't read any accounts of the trial. Bum eyes." His voice rose. "The man called me Buster, I tell you."

"And of course you also didn't discuss the trial with any of the other inmates."

"What? Oh, no. No, I got troubles enough of my own."

"So I suppose the bet you claim you made of your precious coffee ration with Lieutenant Manion was based solely upon intuition?"

"What's that there?"

"Guesswork."

Swallowing: "I s'pose," the witness answered, spreading his hands. "Musta been."

"Tell me, Duke," I said. "If you didn't read the newspapers or discuss the case with your fellow inmates how did you know that the prosecution was 'quizzing' inmates, as you have already testified?"

"Well, we did discuss that some."

"So for at least a day before you yourself were quizzed you knew the prosecution was asking prisoners what they knew bad about Lieutenant Manion?"

"Well, yes."

"And you're as sure of this alleged conversation you claim you had with the Lieutenant as you are that you were previously in prison only three and not five times?"

Sullenly: "I flubbed that part about prison. I told you what the man said."

"Thank you, Mr. Miller," I said with a show of assurance I did not feel. "This has been a most illuminating encounter. It is always nice to meet a man of such varied talents and broad experiences. Especially one with such an intuitive and dedicated concern that the processes of justice shall prevail."

The witness answered as Claude Dancer arose to object. "You're welcome," he said, with a final parting swallow.

"Your witness, Dancer," I said, abruptly sitting down.

"No further questions," the little man said, bestowing on me one of his more winningly toothsome grins.

The courtroom had grown as still as a convention of enchanted mice. All of the jurors were avoiding my eyes and I quickly glanced away. I could still sense the curious air of ruefulness all about me, an air of puzzled and even faintly horrified resentment. Up to now this murder trial had been within the rules of the game, it seemed to whisper; now something disturbing had been added, something that didn't belong, that wasn't quite cricket. True or false, there had been a switch to strange dialogue that somehow didn't belong in this play. . . .

"Oh Lord, oh Lord," I thought. "Can this egotistic bastard of a soldier man of ours have possibly been so stupid?" I choked back a sudden welling impulse to retch and again closed my eyes. Was all Parnell's and my weeks of work and worry to be in vain? Was our case shooting straight up through a shattered courtroom skylight?

"Call your next rebuttal witness," the Judge said to Claude Dancer.

"No further rebuttal," Claude Dancer said.

The Judge looked at me. "Any rebuttal for the defense, Mr. Biegler?" he said, well knowing that I simply had to recall Lieutenant Manion.

"The defense recalls Lieutenant Manion," I said, prodding him in the side.

The Lieutenant, terse and grim, categorically denied having talked with Duke Miller, that noon or any time. No, he had never called him Buster or anything. No, Claude Dancer did not care to cross-examine, thank you.

"Any further rebuttal, Mr. Biegler?" the Judge inquired.

"Nothing further, Your Honor," I said.

"Both sides rest?"

"Yes, Your Honor," Claude Dancer and I said.

"Let us take ten minutes before the jury arguments," the Judge said. "Mr. Sheriff."

I wheeled around and looked at the courtroom clock. It was 2:17 —Wechsler-Bellevue time—on Saturday, September the thirteenth. The battle was nearly over. Was the battle also lost?

I sat alone in the conference room staring out at the lake. This was the lowest moment of the case. After all our work and toil were Parnell and I to lose on the word of a convicted felon? Had the Lieutenant really told him that? Why hadn't I warned him to clam up?

The door opened and Parnell joined me, his eyes rolled up in his head. "There's only one more thing you might have done, boy," he said softly.

"What's that, Parn?"

"Asked the Lieutenant during rebuttal if he was willing to take a lie-detector test on whether he talked with this lovely Miller character."

I nodded my head glumly. "I thought of that, Parn, but rejected it for two reasons. First, the jury and everybody now knows that the results would be inadmissible, and Dancer could then argue that the offer was just a safe and cheap grandstand play. Then there's an even bigger reason."

"What's that, boy?"

I stared at him a moment and sighed and lowered my voice. "Because the People might just possibly have taken us up," I said. "Just between us, Parn, I was and am deathly *afraid* of what a lie-detector test might show."

"Yes," Parnell said thoughtfully, nodding his head. "I see what you mean, boy. Ah yes, I see exactly what you mean. Please forget that I ever mentioned it." He shook his head. "May the Lord save us from the claws of a cat and seven horny animals."

The door opened and Dr. Smith hurriedly joined us. During recess he had discovered he could catch a plane home if he hurried. Parnell, bravely hiding his disappointment over missing any of the argument, gallantly volunteered to drive him to the airport; we could do no less.

"I've never seen a shabbier performance in my professional life," the young doctor said, shaking his head sadly, referring to the testimony of his fellow diplomate. "But at least I think your scorching cross-examination will discourage him from venturing an early repetition."

"Thanks, Doc," I said, grasping his hand. "You were our rock and I'll surely send you word. As for Doc Gregory, I intend in my argument to burn his soft diplomatic ass."

"To a crisp, I hope," Dr. Smith said with feeling.

"Let's hurry, gentlemen," Parnell said, looking at his watch. "I want to get back for the arguments. I've waited over three weeks for this hour."

"Two minutes," Max said, popping his head in the door, and I sighed and grabbed up my brief case.

Recess was over and the whispering thronged courtroom slowly fell silent. The Lieutenant and I sat alone at our place (I had purposely retired Laura to one of the lawyers' chairs behind us), and our long table was bare except for the accumulated dust and the notes for my jury argument and a small scratch pad. The pad was small because I guessed that Mitch would probably open, saying little or nothing that I could gnaw on; then would come my turn; and then, I suspected, the little giant-killer Claude Dancer would arise and wind it all up.

The tense courtroom grew as hushed as a graveyard and the Judge nodded at the People's table. A mote-streaming shaft of sunlight penetrated the skylight. Mitch got up and formally addressed the court and jury and walked up to the court reporter's table, where he rested his pad of notes. He then proceeded to make a very capable review of the People's case, very capable and very dull: capable, because it was all there and yet gave me little or nothing to argue about; dull, because all of us had heard all of it at least once and much of it almost a dozen times. He briefly outlined the elements of murder and reviewed the possible verdicts. He pointed out that the People would speak twice and the defense once; that the People had the privilege of making the opening and closing argument; that I would speak after him; and that the People, doubtless meaning Claude Dancer, would then finally close.

Significantly enough Mitch made no direct mention of the rape or of Laura's lie-detector test. About the only mention of this argumentative area he made was in asking the jury to ponder why Barney would ever have driven Laura to the tourist-park gate in the first place if he had meant her any harm. At that point I scribbled my first fresh note: "Slam damn gate!" I wrote.

"Ladies and gentlemen, there has been a violent killing in this county," Mitch continued soberly, "and we believe that the People have shown beyond any doubt that that killing was done by the defendant here. We further believe we have shown beyond any reasonable doubt that the killing was done deliberately, maliciously, and in a fit of homicidal anger, and that it was done without legal justification or excuse.

"If you tell this man he has done nothing wrong," Mitch continued soberly, "aren't you thereby telling the forty-nine thousand people of Iron Cliffs County and indeed all of Michigan that they may safely go and do the same thing?"

Mitch turned and gathered up his notes and marched to his table where Mr. Dancer rather ostentatiously arose and congratulated him; the little man was always in there pitching, he never missed a trick. The Judge looked down at me and nodded. "We will now hear the argument of the defense," he said quietly.

"May it please the court and ladies and gentlemen of the jury," I began, advancing before the jury rail. I lowered my voice and solemnly launched my argument. "When, in Kipling's phrase, the tumult and the shouting dies, and this tall old courtroom empties and falls silent, and our patient long-suffering Judge returns to his concerns in lower Michigan, and, yes, when Mr. Dancer goes back to Lansing—when all this has happened, ladies and gentlemen, I wonder what will have become of Lieutenant Manion?

"This is the time when we lawyers, we men of many words, continue to indulge the amiable fiction that anything we can say here will possibly change your minds. For in all truth if we have done our work well there should really be nothing more to say. I sometimes think in these cases that if at this point counsel would retire and play cribbage or go fishing—and I can scarcely wait to do both with Mr. Dancer—while the Judge gave you his instructions on the law, all of us might be saved considerable time, and you certainly infinite boredom. But our system is otherwise, this is the time when we lawyers must traditionally trot out our little verbal wares, however tarnished; and I only hope that I can suggest a point or two which you might otherwise have possibly overlooked. For surely it is impossible in the brief time allotted us here to cover all the facts and angles of this tangled case.

"Most of you know that I was formerly a prosecutor of this county. During that time, under the wise guidance and example of our own Judge Maitland, I conceived it to be the duty of the People in a criminal case to bring out all relevant and admissible evidence bearing upon the guilt or innocence of the defendant, the bad along with the good. I had been led to understand that it was *not* the duty of the People to at any price convict all defendants charged with crime, but rather to lay the entire transaction fairly before the jury so that they, guided by the Court's instructions, might try to reach a sensible and just verdict. Our own good Judge here will correct me if I am wrong. I may add that so firm was my belief in this procedure that never in my ten years as prosecutor did I once ask a jury to convict a defendant charged with crime. And I don't think anyone ever fairly accused me of being a softie.

"Now I do not think it is necessary for me to rescue the American jury system from Mr. Claude Dancer, but under it no one is either freed or rushed to the gallows without a full and free inquiry. But that means inquiry to all the facts, not just part of them, not just the part that helps one side or hurts the other."

I glanced at the People's table. "It seems that my views, if not wrong, are at least not entirely shared by the strolling representative of our Attorney General's department. Speaking of Mr. Dancer, there is no question that your young prosecutor, Mr. Lodwick, had a right to ask for assistance in trying this case. His right is clear and plain and I make no issue whatever about that." I paused. "But I say that that assistance should be that and not usurpation. You have sat here for days now and watched this case stolen away from our young prosecutor before his very eyes. You have watched a deliberate and at times brilliant effort made here by the People—but not the police officers, I hasten to add—to suppress or pervert evidence that it was the clear duty of the People and not the defendant to produce. Now I am not talking about routine objections on procedural matters or the form of a question or about evidence which the court has ruled inadmissible. I am talking about the studied and deliberate suppression of *truth*, about fundamental and important matters of truth which it was the People's clear duty to bring out, not keep out."

I turned to watch my time and observed Parnell sitting white-faced and grave over near the door. The old boy must have driven to and from the airport like a demon. "But enough of vague generalities, let us get down to cases. The unfair tactics of the prosecution have been double-edged: to keep out the truth, where possible, and to insinuate that certain things were so without bothering to prove them. In fact this latter tactic seems to be getting quite a settled procedure—almost an act of patriotism—in some quarters these days. . . . As a glaring example of the first tactic, let us take the People's biggest and sorriest fiction of all, the grotesque assumption that Laura Manion was not brutally beaten and raped by Barney Quill that night. Yes, for days now you have watched Mr. Dancer fight the fact of that rape tooth and nail, with all the pettifogging and delaying brilliance of a filibustering Southern senator. But more of that later.

"As a lovely example of the second tactic of perversion and sly insinuation let us take the incident of Hippo Lukes having supposedly danced with Laura Manion with her shoes in his pocket. Yet I ask you now: who in this whole courtroom has ever once testified she did that? Who alone has inferred it but Mr. Dancer himself? You will recall how he clawed away endlessly at Mrs. Manion on that score. The waltz of the dancing shoes, one might call it. Yet if that had actually happened could not the great Hippo Lukes have testified to it when he was first called? Would the clever Mr. Dancer have missed that chance to smear our lady? And if he forgot to then could not Mr. Hippo have been called in rebuttal after she had denied it?" I turned and pointed out into the body of the courtroom. "Behold Hippo Lukes sitting there now," I said. "Temporarily forsaking the dance, for which nature has so splendidly endowed him, he has been sitting here all week as a witness paid by the People. If this thing actually happened Hippo should remember it. Or if he forgot, surely there was *someone* in that barroom that night who would have recalled it.

"But the most interesting thing about these tactics is the *why* of them. So what, you may be tempted to ask yourselves, so what if she did or didn't dance that way? Well, I'll tell you why. Because the clever Mr. Dancer was trying slyly to plant in your minds the picture of a Laura Manion as an abandoned and willful slut who would drink whisky neat and dance barefoot with beefy strangers and thus presumably go out and lay up with the first man that came along. Because Mr. Dancer, who dares not meet this rape issue head on, seeks subtly to confuse you and make you think this brutal rape was a mutual affair, that is why.

"Consider if you will his terrier cross-examination of her personal life while she was on the stand: his gallant raking over of her background, bringing out the fact that she was divorced, the awful revelation that she once sold cosmetics and worked as a saleslady and even dared answer telephones. What does the little man mean by all this? What does it signify? Does he mean to stamp all divorcées as immoral? Does he infer that all beauty and telephone operators are abandoned sluts? If he didn't mean that, then why did he buzz away at her like a gnat to bring all that out?

"Yes, ladies and gentlemen, he hammered and clawed away at this woman in every clever and insinuating way he could—and his talents for insinuation are impressive—to show her up as a bag and a flirt and, more, a casual and easy lay. But, remark you, never once did this knight exemplar of the law refer to anything as coarse as the brutal assault and rape she suffered at the hands of the dead man. Never once did he mention anything as crass as a lie test. If he didn't and still doesn't believe her rape story then why in Heaven's name didn't he *examine* her about the rape? Do you think for a moment he was gallantly trying to spare her feelings? Do you think he wouldn't have assaulted her with every offensive weapon in his arsenal if he didn't know full well that she had told us the brutal truth?

"What does Mr. Dancer need to become convinced of this rape —Technicolor? I wonder how much proof he would need if, with his fine sense of detachment, he were instead *defending* this case? Ah, then the proverbial shoe might be on the other foot—or perhaps I should say, in Hippo's other pocket."

I turned and pointed scornfully at Claude Dancer just as Amos Crocker used to point at me. "Ah yes, this is the able little man who has come up here into the brambles to show us bumpkins some of the sly city tricks he has learned so well from experts. Have any of you so soon forgotten how, when the Judge was not looking this morning, he several times got between me and the testifying Lieutenant? Why? I'll tell you why. In order to get me angry—in which he so richly succeeded; then in order that I might incur the Judge's wrath, which I so beautifully did; but mostly in order to plant in your minds the sinister notion that I was signaling lies to my client." Still pointing. "For shame, Mr. Dancer! You brought only discredit and tarnish on your own considerable talents." I turned back to the jury. "You may have also observed that the man didn't do it again."

I paused. "But after all this case is not a gladiatorial contest between Mr. Dancer and me. Your verdict is not a television giveaway prize to be awarded the side that puts on the best show. No, ladies and gentlemen, the stakes here are far bigger than Mr. Dancer and Paul Biegler. They have to do with some old-fashioned things, big things like truth and justice and fair play. They have to do with the fate and future of a tormented lonely man who sits here so uncertainly among us strangers."

The Sheriff brought a glass and pitcher and put it on the court reporter's table, and I nodded gratefully and poured and hurriedly gulped a glass of tepid water—courtroom water is always tepid—and turned back to the jury, again eying my favorite juryman. "I wonder if any of you would ever have known that anyone had been raped in this case if I had not kept hammering away through the buzz-saw objections of Mr. Dancer? And what purpose has all his objections served? Jurymen, we could have been done with this case many hours if not days ago if the People had faced up to the reality of this rape, which like dwellers in a sort of enchanted dream world they still do not admit. We didn't and we won't deny the shooting; we have never denied it. That was obvious from the start of this case and the People knew it long before that, ever since we filed our written plea of insanity 'way back in August. Yet they have spent hour after hour and witness after witness—and incidentally dollar after public dollar—flailing the gory details of that dead and undisputed issue. Just as Mr. Dancer has used up hour after dreary hour trying to hide and suppress this rape, the rape that surely no fairminded person in this courtroom can any longer doubt took place."

I then reviewed in detail the evidence pointing toward rape, reminding the jury that practically all of it had got in the case over the repeated objections of Mr. Dancer. I advanced close to Mitch's table and again pointed down at Mr. Dancer. "You still do not admit this rape! You still want to picture Mrs. Manion as a slut! You are still obsessed with your pathological lust to go home with the Lieutenant's carcass lashed to the fender of your state-owned car. Well, Mr. Dancer, I dare you to admit the rape!"

I returned before the jury and took up and reviewed the harmful portion of Detective Sergeant Durgo's testimony. That had frankly to be faced; it would not go away by ignoring it. "People," I continued, "maybe the Lieutenant did say these things. The fact that Sergeant Durgo says so is pretty good proof that they were said. We cannot have our cake and eat it, too: we cannot fairly pick out the parts of the Sergeant's testimony that please us and reject the rest. Only the hardy Mr. Dancer seems able to undertake that miracle. But supposing the Lieutenant did say these things? Was he still not in the shock of his mental lapse, still gripped by the massive blast to his psychic personality, still groping his way back to reality, still trying to put a rational face on the dreadful thing he was slowly realizing he had done? In any case I believe that the Judge will instruct you that you may acquit this man, even if he said these things and realized he was saying them, if at the actual time of the shooting you believe he was in the grip of what is known as irresistible impulse."

I again checked my time and hurried on. I pointed out that Mitch was right in warning the jury not to invoke the defense of "natural law" (the Judge would do so anyway); and how, under our law, if the Lieutenant had awakened and come upon Barney raping his wife and had killed him, there would doubtless have been no trial and the Lieutenant would instead have got a new medal to add to his combat decorations. "But here," I went on, "the difference is that the woman was not discovered in any act of adultery or *while* being raped, but had, however mistakenly, trusted a wolf who had offered to drive her home. Ah yes, instead she was assaulted, pounded, choked, raped, mauled, tripped, kicked, repeatedly struck—the last time practically within a stone's throw of her sleeping husband—but now the killing becomes murder.

"Ladies and gentlemen, some of you may be asking yourselves why?—why have I been spending so much time here trying to show the obvious truth, namely that the dead man Barney Quill was drinking heavily, that he was acting peculiarly, that he was an awesome physical specimen who knew Judo and all manner of the dark arts of self-defense and offense, that he was an expert who possessed pistols and knew well how to use them? Some of you may also have been wondering why our friend Mr. Dancer has so strenuously sought to keep these truths out."

I paused. "Well, I'll try to tell you. If Mr. Dancer could suppress these truths he could then argue that Barney Quill was unable physically to overpower and rape this woman and do to her the things he did; that in any case she should have put up more resistance and that therefore this sexual collision was not rape; that Lieutenant Manion did not need to take a gun when he went to grab and hold this man for the police; that he therefore did so solely to slay him; and, last but not least, that the little old unarmed caretaker, Mr. Lemon, was just the man he instead should have sent to gather in this dangerous wild man." I again paused. "These I believe are the answers in a nutshell; this is why our Mr. Dancer has spent days here trying relentlessly to baffle and block any attempt by me to show Barney Quill as anything other than a nice quiet harmless outdoor boy."

I hurriedly gulped another glass of water. "Yes," I ran on, "the People, so zealously represented by Mr. Dancer, will doubtless argue that the Lieutenant should have hunted the little old unarmed caretaker out of his midnight bed to go over and arrest this man crouching in his lair, behind his bar with his arsenal of weapons he so well knew how to use. Wouldn't that have been the fine, manly, legal thing to do?

"People," I said, "to be competent jurors you need not check your brains in the jury cloakroom. There is no mystery about your role here—it is to use your heads and also your hearts. If Barney Quill did this thing to Laura Manion there were exactly three courses open to him. One, he could have given himself up. He didn't. Two, he could have run away or destroyed himself. He didn't. Three, he could have stayed and determined to brazen it out. He did. The great Barney Quill, running true to form, chose the latter role, he returned to his lair and sent his bartender scuttling, whether as lookout or whatnot we shall probably never know. He quickly surrounded his bar with a protective cordon of unsuspecting humanity—his buffer as well as his witnesses—and waited confidently for the showdown, primed by his whisky and his enormous ego, surrounded by all his pals and his pistols and medals and his ever-faithful lookout. Barney could not stand behind the bar staring at the door—he had desperately to play the part of the cool and calm one. That is why he had to give his tired bartender a "rest" so he could *stand* nearly an hour over by the door and give him the signal.

"But, you may ask yourselves, if Barney was waiting for the Lieutenant to come, with or without a lookout, why didn't *he* plug the Lieutenant the moment he entered the door? Ah, folks, that would not only have been murder, but murder added to a tacit confession of rape. That would have given the show away. Barney was on the spot. Barney knew what he had done but the others didn't. Had Barney mounted a Tommy gun on the bar and shot the Lieutenant down as he entered the door he would by that very act have confessed his rape. Don't you see? Barney *had* to wait for the Lieutenant to advance into the room so that when the expected showdown came, the big scene, the accusation, the argument, the attempted laying on of hands, even a hostile move for a gun, then the great marksman Barney could shoot the man down in front of witnesses and plausibly claim the whole thing was done in self-defense. He had to gamble that he was faster on the draw than Lieutenant Manion. Can't you see—this tense barroom drama was all carefully staged?" I lowered my voice. "The only thing that went wrong was that Barney forgot, or didn't know, the Lieutenant was left-handed—that and the fact that at last he had met his match. He lost his grim gamble, he at last lost his first pistol shoot. This time the medal he lost happened to be his own life."

Time was fleeting and I rushed on. "No, the Lieutenant didn't send a sleepy unarmed old man, but went himself and did so legally, as I believe the Judge will so instruct you." (This was the instruction Parnell had toiled over so long.) "Surely, people, this Barney was either a dangerous maniac at large or at least a dangerous criminal. In either case he was a man who had just committed, in aggravated form, one of the gravest felonies on our books. I believe the Lieutenant had every right to go there and grab that man. I believe the Judge will tell you so. Because the taunting sight of his wife's tormentor may have unhinged the Lieutenant's reason, you are now asked to ruin his life."

I looked at the clock and stepped forward. One of the constant and worrisome defense problems in any criminal case—since it has but one chance at the jury argument while the prosecution has two—is not only to cover its own case in the allotted time, but to try as well to anticipate and cover the possible arguments the prosecution might advance in its still unheard and forever unanswerable closing argument. About all that Mitch had given me to fulminate about in his routine opener was the business about Barney and the gate. Claude Dancer had graciously tossed Mitch that solitary forensic bone, thoughtfully saving the rest for himself. I moved quickly on to that.

"Our prosecutor has pointed out in his opening argument that if the deceased had intended any harm to Mrs. Manion he would not have bothered to drive her to the park gate in the first place," I said. "The implication of that argument is, of course, that some mysterious thing happened between the bar and the gate that led Barney to believe his romantic advances would not be unwelcome, that Love and Four Roses finally conquered all. Now that argument has a certain glib plausibility, a surface persuasiveness, but I wonder if it will stand analysis? I wonder, people, whether this is not the true reason why Barney Quill drove her first to the gate: He knew the gate was locked. He had already formed his design to have at this woman. He already knew that she was reluctant and nervous about riding with him. By first driving her to the gate, which he well knew was locked, he could thus allay her suspicions and hide his real intentions. If on the contrary he had simply driven past the gate road without turning in—a point which the chart shows is still right in town—she would immediately have become suspicious and could have raised an effective hue and cry while still in town. His plan worked; when he made his final turn off on the "rape" road, far down the main road, it was too late, any screams then would have been futile, she was finally in his power." I paused. "Is that not more probably the real reason why he drove her in to the gate at all?"

My favorite juror was all but nodding his head at me. Embarrassed, I looked at the woman next to him, a plump, pop-eyed, folded-armed, middle-aged lady who, doubtless through some wry trick of the thyroid, had sat wide-eyed during the entire trial, watching or rather beholding the proceedings, a look of perpetual astonishment stamped on her face. She stared at me, oily-eyed and unblinking, and I wondered vaguely if she had any pulse. . . .

I swiftly reviewed the testimony of the bartender concerning Barney's drinking and the guns and all the rest; the revealing wolf designation he had pinned on Barney; the unsought sympathy he had bestowed on the Manions; the gift of cigarettes and the expression of regret over the broken mirror and bottle of "white-vest" bourbon. "Surely this crafty shifty little man must have known when he did and said these things that they would come back to haunt him if he had not really meant them."

My argument was verging on a sensitive area and for Mary Pilant's sake I had to try to cover it obliquely. "And who was it that dragged whatever truth of these things we finally got out of this witness? Not our Mr. Dancer, certainly. You will recall how hostile this bartender was when I first cross-examined him. At first he would have nothing unusual with Barney, either in his drinking or otherwise. The Thunder Bay Inn was the setting for a summer idyl."

I glanced back at the frowning bartender and then returned to the jury. "I wonder why the witness changed? Could it have had something to do with Barney's estate or his insurance? Or was someone growing afraid of perjury?" I paused. "In any case, when I got him back again on the stand *something* certainly had changed, for whatever reason. I then dragged out of him over Mr. Dancer's trip-hammer objections that things had been so normal, indeed, that Barney was still gulping his double shots as hungrily as ever; that his behavior was still normally queer; that things were so placidly normal and fine, in fact, that some of his arsenal of guns had to be locked up while at least two others were unaccounted for. Yes, that's how really *normal* things were around that seething hotel and bar." I paused. "And isn't that what the bartender really meant when he told Mrs. Manion it was too bad they had come to Thunder Bay when they did? Weren't the Manions indeed like two lost characters who had wandered unwittingly onto the stage of some dark Greek drama they knew not of?"

I turned toward the clock; my time was rapidly running out. "We now come to our defense of insanity, to the battle of the psychiatrists. Doubtless Mr. Dancer will call our young doctor a charlatan and a faker for failing to use the impressive-sounding tests that he, Dancer, had so glibly learned by heart from the People's doctor. In this connection I ask you why, if this young man were no good at his work—why would this able and poised young doctor be put in charge of all this modern psychiatric equipment by the U.S. Army itself?"

The jumbled mosaic of evidence pointing toward insanity had to be reviewed, and I swiftly reviewed it, along with the testimony of young Doctor Smith. "Now Dr. Smith has told you of his intensive examination of the Lieutenant upon which he based his opinion," I went on. "This is flatly opposed by the testimony of Dr. Gregory. There is no way to reconcile their opinions—one of these men is dead wrong." I paused. "If the stakes here were not so high I might be tempted charitably to overlook Dr. Gregory's testimony and pass it by. This poor man in one breath tells us *our* Doctor's tests were no good, that he would have given a whole flock of others. Then in the next breath he dares to pass a professional opinion on this man's sanity without *any tests whatever!* Then in his final breath, when he was cornered he reluctantly admits, over a final barrage of Mr. Dancer's protective objections, that this is not normal or recognized psychiatric procedure."

I turned and looked at Dr. Gregory. "This is the same diplomate who made no attempt to examine the Lieutenant although he has been here for days. I wonder whether he meant by his testimony that no man could *ever* go off his rocker when such a thing had happened to his wife? He does not tell us. If he meant that none could, then I wonder when and under what circumstances *any* man could ever be expected to lose his mind from sudden emotional or psychic shock? If the Doctor instead meant that *some* men might go insane over such a shocking event, but not *this* man, then I wonder what psychiatric basis of observation or examination he used to arrive at that conclusion? He does not tell us. And you observed how our four-day expert in the argot of psychiatry from Lansing, Mr. Dancer, couldn't hustle the poor man off the stand fast enough when I had done examining him.

"If the doctor meant that he believed the Lieutenant was sane that night because he, the doctor, didn't believe his wife had been raped, then, along with our two die-hard prosecutors, he is possibly the lone holdout in this room on that score. In any case I believe the Judge will tell you that it is not what actually happened that is the guiding test in these insanity cases, but what the insanity victim reasonably believed had happened. And this is true both psychiatrically and legally. People unfortunately go insane every day over mere figments of their imagination. Does Dr. Gregory mean that men must never go insane when faced with the real McCoy?"

I paused and shook my head. "There is something sad about this performance we have seen here. If a regular doctor had done a thing like this he would be called a quack, a lawyer a shyster. When a man will blithely pervert and make a mockery out of a whole profession, one to which he has presumably dedicated his life, then the lie takes on large dimensions of sorrow and wonder." I pounded the mahogany jury rail so hard with my fist that I wondered vaguely if I would ever again be able to cast a fly. "And a lie of that kind is all the more vicious and reckless and cynical because we ordinary mortals lack the training to appraise and nail it." I shook my head. "It makes one reflect that a man must doubtless first be a good man before he can be a good psychiatrist; that if he is a timid or gutless or cynical or arrogant man, then—when the squeeze is on, the chips are down—that is the kind of professional man he will be.

"Ladies and gentlemen," I pressed on, "I take no pleasure in having to be so harsh on this doctor. His testimony would be laughable if the stakes weren't so high and the attempted use to be made of his testimony so ruthless and cynically bold. But when any man dares to come into court and tinker with the destiny of a man charged with first degree murder, then he is treating us as fools and he warrants our scathing censure and scorn."

I paused and mopped my brow. Both my temperature and voice were rising and I turned and again pointed at Claude Dancer. "But however we may censure this poor doctor, it is the man who master-minded his coming here to testify on such a pitifully inadequate professional basis who deserves the full blast of our contempt. Was poor Doctor Gregory sacrificed here on the altar of the insatiable ambition of someone in this room to hang up still another legal scalp? To someone for whom law and justice and freedom is merely a cynical game? Is poor Lieutenant Manion again to be caught in the vise of some squalid desire of some ambitious lawyer or doctor to get a better job? Did Mr. Dancer need the scalp of a veteran of two wars to round out his growing collection? And is this jury going to give it to him?"

I glanced back at the clock. "So much for Wechsler-Bellevue." I rested my notes on the court stenographer's table and moved empty-handed close to the jury rail. "We come now to the astounding testimony of our own domestic duke—to one Duane Miller, ex-convict, confessed arsonist, eager stool pigeon, last-minute key witness for the People in this murder trial. Ladies and gentlemen, I scarcely know what to say to you. There is no use denying or evading the fact that the testimony of this bombshell witness can blast our case wide open if you believe this man."

I turned and gulped some more water. "Consider the timing here. Isn't it strange that the People waited over a day to ask this man what he had on the Lieutenant? Remember, he was the man in the cell nearest our man. If the People sought only the truth why didn't they ask him *first*? Wouldn't he be the most likely initial candidate for questioning? By questioning all the other prisoners first were the People trying subtly to give this witness time to learn what was cooking and thus make up a whopping good story when his summons to Parnassus came? But no, they saved him for the last, they let this convicted man alone to soak in the growing jail-gossip knowledge that they were searching, seeking, looking for bad news, any bad news, to use against the Lieutenant."

I shook my head. "And, Lord, how beautifully the plan worked; how well their man came across—even to adding 'Buster'—this lost sheep of society with his dreary record of crime that speaks so eloquently of a warped personality; this convicted perjurer, this frightened trapped creature crouching in his cell awaiting sentence, wondering what there might be in it for him; this driven pliant soul who even lied about the number of times he was in prison and then told us he 'flubbed' when I trapped him at it. Do you think that this man would hesitate an instant to trade the truth even for a broken cigarette, especially if he thought it might remotely help save his own hide?"

I shook my head wearily. "I cannot tell you precisely when this trial degenerated from a search for truth into an inquisition." I again raised my fist and, remembering, lowered it. "But I can tell you that degenerate it did—and that *this* marks the lowest descent of all. All of us are now gliding helplessly downward, mired and sinking in the bottomless ooze and slime of the Big Lie."

I turned and looked at the Lieutenant, who had bowed his head. "I shall not dwell on the inherent improbability that Lieutenant Manion would even pass the time of day with such a character, much less have risked confiding his very future to this cunning man by telling him what he says he said." I widened my arms. "No, people, it is your baby. You've got to grapple alone with this one."

Swiftly consulting my notes, I raced on: "Let us dwell briefly upon Lieutenant Manion's wife before Mr. Dancer gets lovingly to paw her. There may be those among you who may question the wisdom or propriety of her conduct that night. If any such there be I ask only that you consider this: here was a healthy, vivacious woman cooped up in a strange logging and resort village among strangers; she is an Army wife, used to being alone, shipped around, amusing herself, making do, living much among men—living a sort of easy and informal gypsy life, if you will. Can you fairly or charitably judge her by the prim standards of the ordinary sheltered housewife and mother?

"In any event I remind you that there is not the slightest hint of immorality or looseness on her part, no shred of evidence that she was more than a normally friendly woman duly appreciative of the deceased's false concern for her safety. There is no breath of proof that she knew she was trafficking with a roaring wolf." I wagged my finger at the jury. "Surely if the lady went out with the great Barney just to romance with him, as the People have tried so hard to insinuate, then why on earth did he have to treat her as he did? Why, why, why? When has it become necessary for wolves to beat up and maul and nearly kill a willing victim?

"But if you still have any doubts about her conduct or her story, I ask you to remember that it is Lieutenant Manion who is on trial here for murder and not his wife; that it is what *he* believed that counts; that it is how *his* mind reacted; finally that it is *his* freedom and future that is at stake."

I glanced at the clock and saw that my time was running out. "I haven't time to go over the testimony of the little doctor who tried to take the smear in the jail. I say only this: If he didn't take the smear right even Mayo Brothers couldn't have worked the slides. Or if he did take the smears right they still wouldn't show if the person who worked them up wasn't a competent technician."

I paused and again glanced at the clock. "We've had everything happen in this trial but an old-fashioned balloon ascension. We've even had a trained-dog act. I refer of course to the little dog Rover and his flashlight. Mr. Dancer will doubtless try to tell you that bringing the dog in court was a corny side show, nothing but sly defense tactics calculated to tug at your heartstrings, an act of cheap showmanship. But I wonder if little Rover could have fit in this courtroom if we hadn't produced him here? Do you think for a moment Mr. Dancer would not then have invested little Rover with the temper of a crocodile, the fangs of a spring-tooth harrow, the proportions of a buffalo? Yes, Rover was an important defense witness on at least two grounds bearing on Mrs. Manion's story of the rape: one, that he was a friendly little animal who likely would not and obviously could not have prevented this rape; two, that he could indeed have shown his frantic mistress through the trailer-park stile with his flashlight.

"Both his friendliness and training were well demonstrated here in court. You saw him pattering around with his little tail wagging, running here and there as proud as Punch." I paused and smiled. "But Rover must learn to be more discerning of those who are friends or enemies of his master and mistress. Surely all of you saw him try to leap into the lap of the benevolent Attorney General from Lansing."

The Judge tapped his gavel lightly and spoke quietly as I turned to him. "Time runs out, Mr. Biegler," he said. "About three minutes more." I nodded my thanks and quickly turned back to the jury.

"There are things in this case we will never know," I raced on, "things which seem to have nothing to do with the Manions, and I have time but to suggest a few. Why was Barney drinking so hard? Why was it necessary to lock up his guns? Why did he apply for more life insurance a few weeks before that terrible evening? Was he tired of life? Was the man suffering from some progressive disease of the body or mind? Was he somehow maddened and driven by the idea that he was no longer top dog of Thunder Bay? Was he gnawed with jealousy over someone? Was he trying to pay back the Army for some real or imagined hurt?" I paused. "Finally, ask yourselves why—*why* did this man single out and rape and degrade and nearly kill the wife of the sort of man he should have had every reason to expect would retaliate swiftly? Would it not take a whole panel of psychiatrists to have sifted the mind of that driven man? I paused thoughtfully and lowered my voice. "It is almost as though he *sought* death, much as a burning meteor soars across the sky, searing and destroying all in its path.

"Consider soberly if you will the enormous sense of betrayal that must have afflicted Lieutenant Manion that night. Why do I speak of betrayal? Not only had he the knowledge that his wife had been raped and foully abused—but the almost as bitter knowledge that all this was done by a *civilian*, by one of those lucky ones for whom the Lieutenant had risked his life in two wars so that Barney might continue to drink double shots and blithely play wolf and shoot up empty whisky bottles. I do not try to wave the flag or enfold my man in patriotic bunting. These are brutal facts. A sleek, whisky-addled, wolfish *civilian* betrays the Lieutenant and his wife the first chance he gets. Wasn't that alone enough to make the mind reel? Wouldn't any man in the Lieutenant's place feel the very hiss of mankind against him? Yet Mr. Dancer and his diplomate ask you to scoff at the idea that such a paltry incident should have bothered the man at all."

There remained something more to be said about Claude Dancer; I could not in good conscience take leave of him this way. "If I have been harsh on Mr. Dancer then all I can say is that he has asked for it." I paused. "Rarely if ever have I met an opponent in the courtroom who possessed larger endowments and more formidable talents as a trial lawyer." I shook my head. "Never have I collided with one who by his sly deceits and shabby little tricks has so gratuitously demeaned and tarnished those splendid gifts." I lowered my voice. "Heaven help us, none of us is infallible; all of us are vulnerable, weak, partisan, and childishly avid for victory. But if this earnest man would only put away his courtroom toys and bring a little more humanity and heart to his endeavors I believe that for him the sky will be the limit—if sky indeed is what he seeks.

"My time is practically up," I went on. Most jurors expect and thirst for a final flight of purple prose in a closing argument and I paused and reflected a moment and then soared into the wild blue yonder. "Can you possibly find it in your hearts to add to the woes of these sorely tried people, of this tormented man? To subject him to the sentence of this court, ruin his military career, shut off his sole means of income? To send Laura Manion back to peddling beauty lotions or to her 'immoral' switchboard?" I paused. "How much ruin are you going to permit this Barney Quill to leave in his wake? Hasn't he wrought enough havoc for one man during one lifetime? Whatever happens here has brought lasting degradation and shame on himself and his family. He has beat up and raped and nearly killed another man's wife. He has set in motion the Lieutenant's arrest and this harrowing and expensive trial." I paused. "Can you possibly want by your verdict to let the great Barney work one final bit of mischief from the grave?"

I lowered my voice and held up my cupped hand. "People, you are not dealing with a hypothetical lieutenant now but a living, pulsing, suffering human being, a man whose destiny you hold in the palm of your hand." I turned and looked at the Lieutenant who sat white-faced, staring at the opposite wall. "Look at this harried, lonely man, up here on trial for his freedom among strangers—friendless, broke, foully betrayed by one of the first civilians he encountered. Look at him well. Surely it would be an act of Christian charity, as well as your legal duty, to show by your verdict that up in our neck of the woods all decency is not dead, that justice is not a mere lawyer's game played by a big voice from Lansing, that all our traditional friendliness is not a false prelude to betrayal."

I shook my head and lowered my voice almost to a whisper. "Can you possibly find it in your hearts not to send this tormented and tortured man back to the Army that needs him—yes, and back to the woman he loves?" I bowed gravely and returned to my table. The Lieutenant still sat staring straight ahead. I heard the dry click of the electric clock behind me. My work was done and I was weary, weary. . . .

There was a prolonged whistling expiring sigh from the courtroom behind me, like the sound of a truck tire going flat, and I looked around and saw that one of our more faithful lady students of homicide had swooned dead away. Her arms were held rigid at her sides and her legs pointed stiffly out straight before her as though she were ready for crating and shipment. Her mouth sagged comically open on one side like that of a carnival barker making his pitch. Her neighbors were busily fanning her while the Sheriff rushed her the remains of my old water. I speculated wryly whether she was overcome by Biegler's eloquence or rather by boredom. She hiccupped with fervor and then her eyes rolled open, heavy and slow like a doll's eyes, and suddenly she clamped her bosom and glared glassily at a red-faced Max, who had, it appeared, inadvertently spilt some water down her neck.

The Judge cleared his throat. "Perhaps we'd better take five minutes," he said. "Perhaps, too, Mr. Sheriff, you can open more windows."

"Yes, Your Honor," Max said, abruptly abandoning his ungrateful charge and scrambling back to his gavel.

After the court had recessed Laura Manion came forward and

pressed my hand. "You were wonderful. Thank you, Paul," she said, and there were tears in her green eyes.

The Lieutenant gruffly cleared his throat. "You did good," he said, nervously sipping his mustache.

"Thank you," I said, rising and making my way out of the courtroom. As I groped my way out to the conference room Parnell fell in by my side and grasped my hand in both of his. "Good boy," he whispered huskily, and then turned away, thoughtfully leaving me to sit alone in a chair by the window looking out over the lake, meditatively puffing my pipe, until Max Battisfore reminded me it was time.

"You sure gave the little bastard hell, Polly," Max said. "Good boy."

"Yes, Max," I said, knocking out my pipe and grabbing my brief case. "But don't forget, Dancer has the last word."

chapter 28

The Judge nodded at the People's table and Claude Dancer arose and walked slowly before the jury. During Mitch's argument and the earlier phases of mine I had observed him busily taking notes, but now he carried nothing and stood thoughtful and empty-handed before the jury, speaking in a low, almost conversational tone of voice. "First of all, ladies and gentlemen, I want to compliment my young associate on the way he has conducted his case. It was a pleasure to assist such a sterling young man." Having gracefully tried to give the case back to Mitch he paused and turned, looking at me. "I also want to compliment Mr. Biegler on his spirited and thorough defense of this case. If he thinks I am tough, then it has indeed been a good match. In any case, whatever happens, whatever you may decide, Lieutenant Manion should never have any regrets over his choice of a lawyer or over the capable and astute way that lawyer has fought for him."

I nodded gravely as Claude Dancer turned back to the jury. "But I must remind you, ladies and gentlemen," he went on, "that it is not I who am on trial here; nor is the dead man, Barney Quill, on trial here; nor is the People's psychiatrist, Dr. Gregory, on trial here —however adroitly defense counsel would lead you to believe that we are. It is Lieutenant Manion who is on trial, and if you will bear with me I shall briefly review the elements and proofs in this case that in our view tend to show his guilt of murder beyond a reasonable doubt."

Claude Dancer then defined murder as the deliberate, malicious and premeditated killing of a person without legal justification or excuse. He then proceeded to make a masterfully concise presentation of the detailed testimony tending to show that the shooting was just that: the elapsed time between Laura's return to the trailer and the Lieutenant's trip to the bar; the fact that he himself admitted he left the trailer almost immediately after discovering the alleged tell-tale fluid on Laura's person—"Was not this the action of a man gripped by a cold and implacable fury?" he asked—; the fact that the woman herself had correctly predicted that her husband would kill Barney; the quick temper and jealous nature of the defendant as shown by the time he had struck a young fellow Army officer for kissing his wife's hand; the "Buster" testimony of the bartender when the Lieutenant had asked him if he wanted some too. . . .

"As though all this alone were not enough," Claude Dancer went on quietly, "we have in addition the revealing remarks he made to Detective Sergeant Durgo shortly after the shooting," and he went on in one, two, three order and brought all that out, quietly, forcefully, inexorably. "Are these," he demanded, "are these the actions and statements of an insane man or rather are they those of a man —penitent, remorseful, resigned—after a homicidal outburst of anger over the behavior of his wife with a strange man?" (For a moment I had thought Claude Dancer was tacitly admitting the rape, but no, he was back in the realm of fantasy once again.)

"Here is a man who deliberately and knowingly took a loaded gun —there is no question but he remembered doing that—and drove swiftly over to the hotel bar and, looking neither left nor right—and surely if he *intended* to kill this man, as we claim, he would keep his eye on him and not be greeting those who spoke to him—and shot the man down like a dog and then returned to his trailer and told his wife what he had done and then gave himself up unerringly to the only deputy sheriff in Thunder Bay, telling him that he had shot Barney." He paused. "Now if he was insane how could he have known he shot Barney? And if he remembered shooting Barney then he wasn't insane."

The jury listened intently as Claude Dancer quietly poured it on. "And if he was able to recount and remember what happened right before and again right after the shooting, why should he later and now conveniently forget the damaging and significant things he told Sergeant Durgo upwards of an hour later?" he demanded. "Isn't this rather the picture of a calculating man who conveniently forgot whatever might be harmful to him?" Several of the jurors involuntarily nodded and I rolled my eyes over at Parnell and lifted my shoulders in a shrug. "And remember, this, good people, this man took the law into his own hands. If the deceased had even done the things the defense claims, which we do not admit, there were legal ways to deal with Mr. Quill rather than shooting him. In any case it is no legal defense to this case, as I am sure the Judge will instruct you. And in taking the law into his own hands the Lieutenant broke the law in another particular by secreting and carrying a concealed weapon on his person; his actions began in wrongdoing."

On this last again the little man was due for disenchantment, as we hoped some of our requested instructions would show—provided only that the Judge gave them, and provided further that the jurors listened to and understood and heeded them. Claude Dancer then moved on to the insanity issue and, in his adroit and plausible way, did a rather remarkable job of rehabilitating the People's mauled and tarnished psychiatrist. "Even the defense's own doctor found no psychosis, no neurosis, no delusions, no hallucinations, and no history of insanity or dissociative reaction." He pointed out that Dr. Gregory was an old experienced hand while our man, however sincere and dedicated, was still learning his trade. "The Army should not have sent a boy to do a man's job," he rolled on in his melodious voice.

"As for counsel's comment that we did not request a personal examination of the Lieutenant, I may add that no chance or opportunity to do so was offered." He paused and glanced back at me. "I have a grave premonition, a dark suspicion, that had we tried to examine this man Mr. Biegler would have used everything but his client's lüger to have prevented it." I glanced wryly over at Parnell as Claude Dancer continued soberly: "In fact the sorry predicament of the People when they are met with a defense of this kind has been so forcibly borne upon me during this trial that I expect to speak to my superior about it upon my return to Lansing. I believe new legislation should be recommended to plug this breach. Under our present procedures there is grave doubt in my mind that, however timely or hard we had tried to examine this man, we could legally have compelled him to submit to one. That is a serious situation, both in this case and for the future."

I sat shading my eyes with my hand, musing, listening to the dedicated little man with half my mind, drifting into a sort of waking reverie as he chanted on and on with that persuasive voice, skillfully drawing the noose of argument ever more tightly about the neck of Lieutenant Manion. There was something at once admirable and frightening in his naked singleness of purpose. Here was a relentless prosecutor in the classic tradition: he sought only to convict. And, I had to admit, he was doing no more than I myself had done so many times for so many years. Who was I to cast the first stone? Weren't all of us prosecutors and ex-D.A.'s adrift in the same boat? And hadn't it finally taken the detachment of an eloquent and outraged non-lawyer, John Mason Brown, to utter the last devastating word on the subject?

"The prosecutor's by obligation is a special mind," he had written, "mongoose quick, bullying, devious, unrelenting, forever baited to ensnare. It is almost duty bound to mislead, and by instinct dotes on confusing and flourishes on weakness. Its search is for blemishes it can present as scars, its obligation to raise doubts or sour with suspicion. It asks questions not to learn but to convict, and can read guilt into the most innocent of answers. Its hope, its aim, its triumph is to addle a witness into confession by tricking, exhausting, or irritating him into a verbal indiscretion which sounds like a damaging admission. To natural lapses of memory it gives the appearance either of stratagems for hiding misdeeds or, worse still, of lies, dark and deliberate. Feigned and wheedling politeness, sarcasm that scalds, intimidation, surprise, and besmirchment by innuendo, association, or suggestion, at the same time that any intention to besmirch is denied—all these as methods and devices are such staples in the prosecutor's repertory that his mind turns to them by rote."

Claude Dancer pressed relentlessly on, abruptly rousing me from my reverie. "Defense counsel and the Army psychiatrist make light of the fact of whether the defendant knew what he was doing and whether it was wrong. They tell you blandly that it makes no difference. Perhaps as an abstract legal and medical proposition that may at least be arguable. But what do we have in this case? We have a defendant here charged with murdering a man who has testified on his solemn oath that he *didn't* remember doing it." Claude Dancer pointed up at the skylight. "I say to you that if *in fact* he did know and remember what he was doing and lied to you about it, then he has not only lied to his lawyer and doctor but deliberately perjured himself on a material issue in this case. If so, as I believe the court will instruct you, you are entitled to disregard all of his testimony, including his defense of insanity, unless it is corroborated by other and credible witnesses whose testimony you do believe. So it makes a whale of a big difference whether this man lied."

I found myself nodding involuntarily at the brilliant cogency of this argument as the little man continued to bore in. "Remember, none of us can peer into the mind of this cool stranger we find among us. The fact is that we know little or nothing about the man. Now it is quite possible that he *has* fooled his able lawyer, that he *has* fooled his youthful psychiatrist. As Mr. Biegler has so well pointed out, none of us is infallible. This brings me to the testimony of Duane Miller, the defendant's cell neighbor. Like Mr. Biegler I am quite content to let you grapple alone with that one. To use one of his more elegant expressions, it's your baby. I'll say only this: in this grim business of crime and punishment it sometimes takes a thief to catch a thief, as the old saying goes. Sometimes, indeed, it is the only way."

Claude Dancer paused and glanced at the clock. "Yes, Duane

Miller is a confessed arsonist awaiting sentence, a man with a criminal record as long as my arm." He smiled grimly. "Believe me, I would much prefer to have had him the head of a theological seminary. But may I remind you, as Mr. Biegler's Kipling also said about fun, that the People must take their witnesses where they find them; they cannot pick and choose them as the defense can. Surely neither Mr. Biegler nor you intelligent jurors expected us to produce a live bishop who might have heard this revealing boast from a cell neighbor. And just as surely he and all of us here know that our just and good Judge will not in his sentence for an instant spare this witness because of his testimony here or because of any alleged promise I may have made him—of which, please remember, there is not a shred of proof."

I glanced ruefully at a white-faced Parnell and then looked up at the Judge, who smiled faintly. "Ladies and gentlemen, I am nearly done," Claude Dancer went on. "Please keep in mind the difference between insanity and passion. Consider if you will how easy it is to simulate the one and twist the other into a symptom of mental aberration. Indeed homicidal passion and murderous anger is in itself a form of mental lapse but, fortunately for the peace and welfare of society, one that the law does not recognize as a defense to cold and brutal murder."

The little man had not yet raised his voice, not once had the thunder rolled, and yet his argument was logical, pointed, and, I was growing afraid, rather devastating in its persuasiveness. He now put out his hands and modulated his voice even lower. "This is a serious case. Certainly it is serious to the defendant. It is equally serious to the People—one of our number has been shot down in cold blood. Ours is not the law of the jungle and it illy behooves you to lightly get abroad by your verdict the impression that it is." He held out his hands. "Listen well to the Judge's instructions. Then bring in a verdict that accords with your hearts and your minds. That is all we ask. I thank you." Claude Dancer bowed gravely and returned to his seat.

chapter 29

Judge Weaver looked down at Mitch's table. "Are there any requests for instructions, gentlemen?" he said.

"No, Your Honor," Mitch said, rising.

The Judge looked over at me. "Any requests from the defense?"

"Yes, Your Honor," I said, grabbing up a manila folder and moving up toward the bench. "At this time I hand the court written requests for seventeen instructions which we conceive to properly bear upon the issues in this case." The Judge looked at me questioningly. "I may add," I went on, "that they are in all respects identical with certain draft requests submitted to the court earlier." I walked over to Mitch's table. "At this time I also tender the prosecuting attorney true copies of our requests."

"Very well, gentlemen," the Judge said, looking out at the courtroom clock and opening a leather portfolio before him, tilting his head back and peering through the bottoms of his bifocals. He turned to the jury and cleared his throat. "Ladies and gentlemen," he began, "under our law you are the sole triers of the facts, but I am the sole giver of the law. You will take your law not from the Sunday supplements, not from your favorite cops-and-robbers programs on television, not from the family almanac, not even from the attorneys in this case, but solely from me.

"Embraced in the information filed in this case are three separate offenses," he went on, "and the law makes it mandatory that the jurors shall be instructed as to the different elements which constitute each offense so that you may determine the grade or degree of crime, if any, which was committed. Murder at common law and as charged in this information, may be defined as where a person of sound memory and discretion, willfully and unlawfully kills any human being against the peace of this state, with malice aforethought, express or implied. This common law definition is still retained in our statute. So if you should come to the conclusion that the respondent is guilty of murder, as I have defined it, it will be your duty to determine whether he is guilty of murder in the first or murder in the second degree, which I shall now explain to you."

The Judge carefully defined and explained the difference between first and second degree murder—lack of premeditation in the latter; he then defined manslaughter as a killing without either premeditation or malice; he then defined the presumption of innocence and moved on to reasonable doubt. The Sheriff came forward with a fresh pitcher of water.

The Judge paused and slowly sipped some water, thoughtfully turned a page of his notes, and then went on. "A reasonable doubt, then, is a fair doubt, growing out of the testimony in the case; it is not a mere imaginary, captious or possible doubt, but a fair doubt based on reason and common sense. It is such a doubt as shall leave your minds, after a careful examination of all of the evidence in the case, in that condition that you cannot say you have an abiding conviction to a moral certainty of the truth of the charge here made against the respondent."

As Parnell and I had anticipated he would, the Judge next quietly blasted the notion that the jury could acquit the defendant under so-called "natural law." "There is no such animal in our law," he dryly went on. "It exists only in public bars and on street corners and I charge you to dismiss it wholly from your minds." He then went on explicitly to instruct the jury that they could also not acquit the defendant simply because Barney had allegedly raped his wife, even if they firmly believed that he had. The Judge dilated on this subject much as I had done with the Lieutenant weeks earlier, and some of the jurors blinked uncertainly, having rather plainly thought otherwise up until then.

The Judge looked out at the clock and turned his papers and again spoke. "In defense of this charge the defendant has pleaded insanity and I now instruct you on the law of that subject." I glanced down at my copy of our requested instructions so that I could determine when and if he started giving any of them. We had numbered our instructions consecutively and my heart leapt as I saw that he was now giving the first of them, word for word.

"At the outset there is a presumption in cases of this kind that the respondent is sane, but as soon as evidence is offered by the respondent to overthrow this presumption, the burden shifts and it then rests upon the People to convince the jurors beyond a reasonable doubt of the respondent's sanity, as that is one of the necessary conditions upon which guilt in this case may be predicated. When any evidence is given on behalf of the defendant which tends to overthrow that presumption of his sanity, the jurors should examine, weigh and pass upon it with the understanding that, although the initiative in presenting the evidence is taken by the defense, the burden of proof in this part of the case is upon the prosecution to establish all the conditions of guilt, of which sanity is one. Where there is any evidence in the case by the respondent which tends to show that at the time of the commission of the offense he was laboring under either permanent or temporary insanity, it then becomes the duty of the prosecution to prove the sanity of the respondent beyond a reasonable doubt, as I have just defined that term, and unless they have done so the defendant must be acquitted."

The Judge flipped a sheet and, obviously reading, but looking up occasionally like a competent TV newscaster, proceeded to give our second instruction verbatim. "It is claimed here on behalf of the defendant that he was insane at the time he fired the fatal shots. His defense, as I understand it, is one generally known as temporary insanity, and I charge you that such a defense, if proven to your satisfaction, is just as valid as though the defendant were shown to be totally and permanently insane. In other words, the duration of the defendant's insanity is not the controlling test, but the issue is whether his insanity, however brief, was of such a nature and character as to render the defendant incapable of either (1) exercising his own free will and volition or (2) of appreciating the difference between right and wrong. If you should find that at the time he fired the fatal shots he was suffering from either such insanity, then you should acquit him, despite the fact that prior and subsequent thereto he may have been as sane as you and I."

I glanced over at Parnell, who sat leaning forward tensely listening with his eyes winced shut. It was now apparent that the Judge was going to give our requests on insanity, at least, and he had already injected irresistible impulse into the case. "One of the important incidents of legal responsibility for crime," he went on, "is that the defendant must have had his wits about him, that is, that he must have been a sane person. And in the absence of proof to the contrary all men are in the eyes of the law presumed to be sane. But where the sanity of the defendant has been put in issue in a criminal case, as it has been put in issue in this case, then the burden of proof shifts to and falls on the People to prove the sanity of the defendant beyond a reasonable doubt. It follows, therefore, that if you should find (1) that the defendant here was insane at the time the fatal shots were fired or (2) that a reasonable doubt remains in your minds as to his sanity at that time, then, in either case, you should acquit him on the ground of insanity."

The Judge continued his charge on insanity exactly as we had prepared our requests. "As I have said, the main matter of defense offered here on behalf of the defendant is that he was insane at the time of the alleged offense and was therefore not legally responsible for his acts. The defendant has introduced evidence on his behalf tending to show that one of the contributing factors to such alleged insanity may have been his belief that his wife had just been threatened and assaulted and raped by the deceased."

The Judge paused and I held my breath waiting to see if he would give the next part. "In this connection I charge you that if you believe that the defendant was insane, as I have defined that term, it is not controlling on this issue of insanity that you should first find that the defendant's wife was *in fact* actually threatened, assaulted and raped by the deceased or indeed that any of these things had happened to her. It is enough that you should find that the defendant actually *believed* that these things had occurred to his wife and that the deceased was guilty of them and that this belief of the defendant was based upon reasonable grounds.

"In other words it is sufficient that you find that the defendant actually believed his wife's story and that this belief was based on reasonable grounds and that it actually contributed to any alleged insanity on the part of the defendant, if you should find any such insanity, even though in fact no such threats, assaults or any act of rape may ever have actually occurred."

I again glanced at a tense white-faced Parnell, who seemed to be moving his lips with the Judge, as the Judge then delivered Parnell's pet charge on irresistible impulse. "Expert medical testimony has been offered on behalf of the defendant that he was insane at the time the fatal shots were fired, and that it was a form of insanity generally known to the law as 'irresistible impulse.' I charge you that such a form of insanity is recognized as a defense to crime in Michigan and that it is the law of this state that even if the defendant had been able to comprehend the nature and consequences of his act, and to know that it was wrong, that nevertheless if he was forced to its execution by an irresistible impulse which he was powerless to control in consequence of a temporary or permanent disease of the mind, then he was insane and you should acquit him."

The Judge paused and then quoted verbatim from the old Durfee case that Parnell and I had simultaneously run on to during our research. "As was said in an earlier Michigan supreme court case on this subject: 'It must appear in this case that the defendant is a man of sound mind. Now, by "sound mind" is not meant a mind which is the equal of any mind possessed by any mortal in the world. We all know that there is a difference in the minds of our acquaintances. Some men are very bright, others are very dull; but they are held accountable. Perhaps it would be enough to say—and to leave it right here—that if, by reason of disease, the defendant was not capable of knowing he was doing wrong in the particular act, or if he had not the power to resist the impulse to do the act by reason of disease or insanity, that would be an unsound mind. But it must be an unsoundness which affected the act in question, and not one which did not affect it. There is a simple question for you.' "

I again stole a look at Parnell and he rolled his eyes up in his head as though in silent thanksgiving as the Judge rolled irresistibly on. "Even if you should find here that the defendant knew the difference between right and wrong, then, if at the time of the shooting he had by mental disease or insanity so lost the power to choose between right and wrong that his free-will agency was at that time destroyed, and the act was so connected with said mental disease or insanity as to have been the sole cause of it, then the defendant would not be responsible, and your verdict should be 'Not guilty because of insanity.' "

The Judge cleared his throat as he came to our crucially important request on the relative opportunities of the respective psychiatrists to obtain the knowledge upon which their opinions were based. "There has been expert medical testimony offered here on the question of the sanity or insanity of the defendant. In this connection I charge you to consider the testimony of the doctors and their opinions on the subject. Also consider what opportunity the doctors had to obtain knowledge upon which to base their opinions."

This was taken whole from the old case I had dug up, and I had wanted badly to dilate and enlarge on it but dared not; that was one of the ticklish things about requested instructions: a lawyer found authority for a proposition but if he sought to extend or inflate it too much to fit his case he ran the risk of shaking the Judge's confidence in *all* his requested instructions and, worse yet, the further risk that the Judge might not give the particular request at all.

But here, for the first time, the Judge on his own motion went beyond the letter of our request, and my heart leapt as I heard him resonantly rumble on. "Considering the opportunity of the doctors to obtain knowledge of course includes the physical opportunity to examine the man whose sanity is in question; what tests if any were given; a consideration of the prevailing practices in the field of psychiatry, so far as they may have been shown; and finally whether there was any sufficient opportunity at all upon which to base any opinion."

The Judge loosened his collar with his broad middle finger. "I have already told you that the fact that the deceased may or may not have raped the defendant's wife does not, in itself, afford the defendant legal justification or excuse for taking the life of the deceased. But, as we have already seen, we must nevertheless consider the question of rape in this case as it might bear on the possible insanity of the defendant and as I shall further presently explain. Before I pass to that I must accordingly first define rape.

"Rape is a felony and is defined to be the carnal knowledge of a woman by force and against her will. Force is an essential element of the crime of rape and in order to convict a man of rape a jury must be satisfied beyond a reasonable doubt that the offense was accomplished by force and against the will of the woman, and that there was the utmost reluctance and resistance on her part or that her will was overcome by fear of the defendant or the consequences of her refusal.

"In cases where rape is an issue, then, the jury must believe that the offense was accomplished by force and against the will of the woman; and that there was the utmost reluctance and resistance on her part or that her will was so overcome by fear that she dared not resist. If consent to intercourse is made by the woman through mere lust or weakness of will, without any threat being made or without fear of consequences if she resisted, then the offense would not be rape; but if sexual intercourse is had with a woman and she did not willingly submit to such intercourse but submitted because of threats made against her if she did not yield to such intercourse and through fear and apprehension of dangerous consequences or great bodily harm, and her mind was so overpowered by fear that she did not dare to resist, then the offense would be rape, although she may have made little or no overt physical resistance to such connection."

The Judge glanced at the clock and went on with our requested instructions, speaking faster. "There is also evidence that later the same evening the deceased may have again assaulted the wife of the defendant with intent to rape her. The statute creating and defining this offense, so far as the same is material here, provides: 'Any person who shall assault any female with intent to commit the crime of rape, shall be guilty of a felony.' An assault is defined as an attempt or offer, with force and violence, to do corporal hurt to another. The essential elements of this offense, then, are an assault made with intent to commit the crime of rape. In such cases the jurors must be satisfied, before they could find such an offense, that the man intended to gratify his passions on the person of the woman at all events, notwithstanding her lack of consent and any resistance on her part. Where such an assault has been made with the unlawful intent mentioned in the statute, it is no defense that the man thereafter abandoned or failed to accomplish his purpose.

"If you are satisfied from the circumstances detailed in evidence here that the deceased did later make a further attempt to have sexual intercourse with the defendant's wife, and that he did this with the intent to accomplish it at all events by his strength and power, against any resistance which might be offered to him, then he would have been guilty of assault with intent to commit rape, no matter whether he actually committed the rape or not."

The Judge droned on. "There has also been some medical and other testimony here on the subject of whether or not any seminal fluid or male sperm did or could pass from the deceased onto or into the body of the defendant's wife. In this regard I charge you that the presence of seminal fluid or sperm is not controlling on the question of whether or not the deceased raped the defendant's wife. Under the legal definition of rape that offense may be complete without the presence of seminal fluid or sperm because any male penetration, however slight or fleeting, is sufficient to constitute rape under our law provided that the intercourse was had against the will and without the consent of the woman. On the other hand the mere presence of seminal fluid or sperm does not of itself necessarily make every sexual intercourse a rape where the intercourse is in fact had with the consent of the woman. Once, however, that the sexual intercourse amounts to rape, as I have defined it, I charge you that it is not necessary that the man reach a sexual climax."

The Judge sighed heavily and took another drink of water. He had now given thirteen of our requests and if our luck held he should now pass to the right of our man to go and "grab" Barney that night. As the Judge droned on all I would have needed was to watch the spreading grin on Parnell's face to know that all was well.

"It is claimed here on behalf of the defendant that he left his trailer that night and went to the hotel bar with the intention of apprehending and arresting the deceased. In this connection I charge you that it is the law of this state that a private person—that is, a person who is not a policeman or other peace officer—may make a legal arrest without a warrant when the person to be arrested has actually committed a felony even though such felony did not occur in the presence of the private person seeking to make the arrest.

"Therefore, if you believe here that the deceased did actually commit one or more felonies earlier that night (and in this connection I repeat that rape and assault with intent to rape are both felonies) then the defendant here had the legal right to go and seek to arrest the deceased without a warrant, and this right would apply to the defendant even if he were a perfect stranger to the proceedings here and was no relation whatever to the woman victim in this case.

"A private person may also make an arrest without a warrant on suspicion of a felony, but in such a case he must be prepared to show in justification that a felony actually had been committed, and that any reasonable person, acting without passion or prejudice, would have fairly suspected that the person sought to be arrested had committed it.

"I further charge you that both an officer of the law or a private person may in such cases as outlined above use such force as reasonably seems to him to be necessary in forcibly arresting a felony offender or in preventing his escape after such an arrest, even to the extent of killing him. He must, however, first announce his purpose to arrest the person he seeks to arrest."

Claude Dancer stirred and glanced uneasily over my way as the Judge continued. "On the other hand there is no claim here that the defendant actually did arrest the deceased, or announce his purpose to make such an arrest, or that he shot the deceased in order to make such an arrest or to prevent his escape. Rather it is claimed that the defendant here in the meantime became temporarily insane with the fatal results that followed. However, you should carefully consider the foregoing charges I have just given you bearing on the subject of the right of the defendant to arrest the deceased as bearing on the important question of the *intent* with which he went to the tavern. If he went there with the intent to kill the deceased rather than to arrest him, then, if he were otherwise legally responsible, the offense is murder; but if he went there with the lawful intent to arrest him and not with the intent to kill him, and thereupon became insane as I have defined that term, then you should acquit him.

"While I am on the subject I should also charge you and do, that whatever the intent or motive you should find the defendant possessed when he went to the tavern, and even if you should find that he went there with the unlawful intention of killing the deceased, that if you should further find that he was legally irresponsible at the time the alleged offense was committed, that is, insane, then you should acquit him."

It was my turn to glance at Claude Dancer as the Judge pressed on about the right of the Lieutenant to carry a gun the night he shot Barney. "There has been some testimony offered and argument made here that the defendant might have been guilty of carrying an unregistered and concealed weapon on the night in question contrary to the law of Michigan. Now it is true that in this state it is required by law that the average citizen register any pistol possessed by him and it is also made a felony for the average citizen to carry a weapon concealed upon his person or elsewhere without first obtaining a license to do so.

"But in this regard I charge you, regardless of what you may have heard here to the contrary, that the Michigan pistol registration and concealed weapon laws do not apply to the defendant in this case. They do not apply here because our Michigan statutes on these subjects expressly provide that the provisions thereof, and I quote, 'shall not apply . . . to any member of the army, navy or marine corps of the United States . . .' In other words Lieutenant Manion as a member of the United States Army was exempt from the provisions of these laws and he had a lawful right to carry an unregistered and unlicensed concealed weapon upon his person on the night in question, and under the law it made no difference whether he was on duty or off duty. So I repeat that regardless of what you may have heard here to the contrary, that is the law in this state."

The Judge closed his portfolio and removed some papers from another folder. I glanced at Parnell and he grinned and looked quickly away. The Judge had not only given all seventeen of our requested instructions but had measurably improved on one of the crucial ones, the one about the psychiatric examination.

The Judge proceeded to charge the jury on some necessary legal odds and ends, including the expected charge on how the jury might treat the testimony of a witness it found to be lying. "At least," I thought, "this can work as well against the testimony of Duke Miller as it can against the Lieutenant's."

The Judge sat erect and placed his big hands out flat in front of him. "I now draw near the end of my charge. I charge you that you cannot find this man guilty of anything if you find him insane as I have defined it. On the other hand you must not infer that because a man acts frantically or in a frenzy that he is therefore laboring under irresistible impulse or any other form of insanity. Insanity must always be separated from passion or anger or our courts will simply become public arenas wherein to acquit murderers."

The Judge glanced at the clock and pressed on. "Your first duty upon retiring to your jury room will be to elect one of your number foreman." The Judge smiled. "In view of the lateness of the hour and the oppressive length of my charge—not to mention the dilations of counsel—I suggest you sharply limit your respective electoral campaigns for that office. . . . Your foreman will announce your verdict.

"Next you should discuss all of the facts in the case. Then you may consider and apply the law as I have given it to you, to the facts as you may find them, and thus try to reach a verdict. You may reach one of five verdicts. If you find the defendant guilty of murder in the first degree, then bring in such a verdict; if not you should next consider murder in the second degree. If your decision is guilty of this then bring in such a verdict; if not you should next pass to manslaughter. If after due deliberation you cannot find guilt here, then bring in a verdict of not guilty by reason of insanity or plain not guilty."

The Judge looked down at Clovis Pidgeon. "Mr. Clerk," he said, "please reduce the jury from fourteen to twelve."

Again Clovis' hour had arrived and he arose, white-faced, and returned all fourteen of the jurors' name slips to his box and shook it elaborately and drew out the first name. I held my breath hoping my favorite juror would not be banished. "Mrs. Minnie Leander," Clovis called out, and the thyroid-afflicted lady with the look of perpetual astonishment was doomed to pass forever out of my life.

"Thank you," the Judge said as, uncertainly, she left the jury box, perhaps for once during the whole trial at last truly astonished.

Clovis again shook his box and pulled out another slip. "Arsene LaForge," he called, and poor Arsene was also hustled off to the showers along with the Judge's thanks.

"Swear an officer," the Judge said, and Max's chief deputy, Carl Vosper, marched forward and raised his hand and was sworn by Clovis in words that were probably ancient when Sir Thomas Malory was a child. "You do solemnly swear that you will, to the utmost of your ability, keep the persons sworn as jurors in this trial in some private and convenient place, without meat or drink, except water, unless ordered by the court; that you will suffer no communication, orally or otherwise, to be made to them; that you will not communicate with them yourself, orally or otherwise, unless ordered by the court; and that you will not, until they shall have rendered their verdict, communicate to anyone the state of their deliberations or the verdict they may have agreed upon, so help you God."

"I do," Carl Vosper said, and he turned and beckoned the remaining jurors to arise and follow him to their room.

"Mr. Sheriff, will you please see that the jurors are fetched some supper," the Judge said, "after you recess the court."

"Very well, sir," Max answered, and he arose and pounded the crowd to its feet. "This Honorable Court is recessed until the verdict of the jury or the further order of the court."

chapter 30

After the jury had filed out I manfully resisted the impulse to crawl up on my table and stretch out and sleep. The nightmare was over: for weeks, and especially since the start of the trial, my goblin-ridden slumber had been little more than a fleeting and uneasy doze. I felt too weary even to talk, and I sat there with listless arms hanging at the sides of my chair, staring up vacantly at the pigeon-spattered skylight. Laura and the Lieutenant were restless and excused themselves and went out to the conference room for a smoke. My head nodded forward and then I sat bolt upright in my chair. Parnell came hovering over me like a brood hen and bent and whispered to me. "Better go sit in the car for a while, boy," he said, nudging me. "I'll keep the vigil and call you." He plucked away at my coat sleeve. "G'wan, scat you now, lad, before you up an' start snorin'."

I nodded my head gratefully and silently got up and lurched downstairs through the buzzing and milling knots of people and out to my car. I slumped down and sat staring sightlessly out at the stone foundation of the courthouse boiler room, studying the fudge-like whorls of ancient cement oozing from between the massive foundation rocks. I was both worried and desperately tired. After a long arduous trial one is not only physically exhausted, but the overchurned mind itself grows buttery and numb; the goaded emotions are whipped to a watery whey; there is simply nothing more to give—one is at last not unlike a battle-scarred old boxer finally reduced to a sparring bag. Added to all this was my growing anxiety over the outcome of the case. I yawned until I thought the state was permanent; my eyelids grew heavy; my head nodded on my chest; and, lo, it was twilight and I was lying on a pine-scented hill overlooking a beautiful trout pond. . . . Ah, the dimpling plash of the trout made such pretty out-curling rings. . . . But how had the sweetly solemn face of Mary Pilant suddenly blotted out the scene . . . ?

Someone was shaking me. Darkness had fallen. "C'mon, Polly, the wake is over, the jury has knocked. They've finally reached a verdict." It was Parnell, chucking me under the chin. "Come, boy, up—this is it. The Judge an' everybody's waitin'."

The courtroom was deathly still, bathed in an eerie coppery glow from the old serpent-headed brass chandeliers foaming out of the ceiling. The frugal statesmen on the board of supervisors refused to replace them; they had provided us noisy garrulous lawyers with a free public arena for our fulminations, hadn't they? Surely we didn't also expect to see . . . ? It was ten minutes past nine. Everyone was in his place, as tensely still as spectators at an execution. As Judge Weaver saw me speed to my table he nodded quietly at the bailiff. "Bring in the jury," he said, and the bailiff departed.

Tension had hung over the courtroom all week, sullen and heavy, like a blanket of smog, but now it sprang suddenly alive, almost intolerably so, leaping and darting, obscenely fingering and probing the farthermost crannies of the tall chamber with the speed of forked lightning. Tension . . . I seemed plainly to hear its high electric whine, sounding so much like the siren song of my childhood, the piping of my private Pied Piper, when, disobeying my mother, I had been repeatedly drawn by a magnet to the forbidden iron mines, a tiny but resolute trespasser, there to stand hour on end listening dreamily to the music not yet written—the strange troubled music of the humming high-voltage transmission lines. I moistened my dry lips. My knotted stomach relaxed convulsively and suddenly I had burped, mightily and unmistakably, putting to shame the recent glottal indiscretion of the hiccupping lady onlooker. But no one heeded, so lost were all of us in listening to the wild ascendant banshee wail of mounting tension.

It seemed an eternity before the bailiff breathed open the heavy jury door and stood aside for the jurors to file in. My heart leapt as I saw my favorite Finnish juryman heading the procession. The leader, I knew, was usually the foreman. But, good God, could I have been wrong about him all the time? Could he have been one of those weathervane jurymen, those chameleon sponge-like ones who absorbed and held best the last argument he was exposed to? Had the testimony of Duke Miller caused a last-minute big switch? A thousand doubts assailed me, my thoughts shuttled and fluttered like those, it is said, of a drowning man. The tired jurors formed a ragged semicircle across the front of the Judge's bench, a jaggedly fateful half-moon.

The Judge held up his hand. Despite the crowd his voice boomed out hollowly like that of a midnight train dispatcher in an empty depot. "I warn all those present not to interrupt the taking and acceptance of the verdict," he declaimed sternly. "I will stop the proceedings and clear the courtroom if there is any demonstration or interruption during that ceremony. I have warned you. Proceed, Mr. Clerk."

Clovis Pidgeon arose and faced the jurors. This was his final role of the case. His high tenor voice rang out unnaturally loud in the tall courtroom. "Members of the jury, have you agreed upon a verdict and, if so, who will speak for you?"

"We have," my juryman said, taking a step forward. "I am the foreman."

"What is your verdict?" Clovis said, the frowning Judge still holding up a warning hand.

"We find," the foreman began, and his voice cracked, and he cleared his throat and began again. "We find the defendant not guilty by reason of insanity."

There was a stifled punctured sigh as Clovis quickly pressed on. "Members of the jury," he intoned, "listen to your verdict as recorded: You do say upon your oaths that you find the defendant not guilty of the crime of murder by reason of insanity? So say you, Mr. Foreman? So say you all, members of the jury?"

The twelve jurors solemnly mumbled yes and nodded their heads affirmatively. The lowering of the Judge's hand seemed a signal for chaos: the courtroom suddenly burst alive like a sea in a lashing typhoon. The dikes of tension had finally broken. The clamor pounded in on mounting wave upon wave. Everybody was standing now. Laura threw her arms about the Lieutenant and wept. The flushed Lieutenant held out his hand behind her back and I took it. I glanced back at the clock. It was 9:17. A strange beady-eyed little woman who looked like an unkempt French poodle suddenly vaulted the lawyer's rail—she wore no pants, I observed with fascinated horror—and threw her arms wildly about Laura and the Lieutenant and tried to waltz them around. She turned and lunged at me but I ducked and, frustrated, she tackled the jury foreman, who grinned and winked at me over her shoulder. Parnell stood white-faced and blinking by his chair, biting his tremulous lip. The court reporter sat bowed over his desk working a crossword puzzle and looking endlessly bored.

Claude Dancer was the first to reach me. He pumped my aching hand and cupped his free hand to my ear. "Congratulations, Biegler!" he shouted. "You're a worthy opponent, damn you."

"Thanks, Dancer," I shouted back, smiling. "That goes for you, too —double."

Mitch gave me his hand and smiled and said something and backed away. He grabbed the Lieutenant's hand and pumped it and turned away. Then the city newspaper men were upon us, exploding their flash bulbs like happy anarchists, either oblivious or heedless of the

428

Judge's earlier injunction. "Over this way, Lieutenant, *please.* . . ." "Hey, look this way, Biegler . . ." their plaintive exhortations ran. "Can't you smile, man?—you won, damn it, you won. . . ." "Will you please take off those glasses, Mrs. M . . . ?" "Let's get a pic of the jury. . . ." "Where in hell is the neon-lit dog? . . . Let's go find the goddam mutt. . . ."

The Judge, shaking his head ruefully, was monotonously banging his gavel amidst the fitful heat lightning of the photographers. Smiling Max was banging his gavel wildly, anywhere, like a hopped-up vibraphone player at a pre-dawn jam session. The swells and organ rolls of noise gradually, spasmodically, subsided; the stormy courtroom finally fell silent. The silence grew oppressive, almost worse than the noise. The Judge addressed the jurors.

"Thank you, ladies and gentlemen, for your loyal and attentive service in a long and difficult case," he said soberly. "You have deported yourselves well in one of the highest duties and privileges of citizens in a democracy." He looked at the clock. "I guess there is no more to say. You will be excused from further duty until Monday morning at nine o'clock."

The Judge nodded his head gravely and looked out at the milling newspaper men. "I admonish the worshipers of Daguerre present to please transfer their photographic calisthenics out of this room," he said wryly. "Perhaps I should add that any who disobey this order will spend at least the night as the guests of our hospitable sheriff whose amiable motto is, I am informed: 'An innerspring mattress in every cell.' "

As the jurors slowly filed out their door, followed by the eager wolf pack of retreating photographers reloading their cameras, some of them glanced back at the scene. I nodded slowly at my favorite juryman and he grinned and lifted and shook both cupped hands at me. When the tall door finally closed behind them the Judge cleared his throat and addressed counsel.

"Gentlemen, as all of you well know, the law now enjoins upon me, under this verdict, the unpleasant duty of sending this man away until he is pronounced sane. It is a dilemma all the more sharpened by the fact that two otherwise violently disagreeing psychiatrists agree on this one thing: that the man is now sane. It so happens that I too think he is sane, as I believe you do, and it strikes me as a travesty on justice that I should be compelled to send this man away." The Judge paused. "As a matter of fact I don't intend to do so; and I don't intend to do so because the law also wisely says that no one shall be compelled to do an idle thing. Certainly it would be idle to send this soldier away; moreover it would be vicious and vengeful. Yet this man is technically still in custody." The Judge again paused and drew a deep breath. "Gentlemen, I shall be glad to entertain a writ of habeas corpus for his release from custody. Despite the lateness of the hour I am willing to proceed with it now if you men are also willing. The jury has spoken and I personally greatly dislike seeing this man spend another night in jail."

I had flopped in my chair but I quickly arose. "I already have such a writ and supporting papers filled out and ready to serve," I said. (During the week the ever-planning Parnell had prepared them on a hunch.) "If the People will agree I am willing to proceed now."

Claude Dancer whispered briefly with Mitch and quickly arose. "We agree, Your Honor, that this man should not be sent away," he said. "We further agree that he should not spend another night in jail. I therefore suggest that we proceed." The little man paused and hacked his throat. "Moreover, in the interests of speed I further suggest that counsel now stipulate and agree upon the record that a transcript of the psychiatrists' testimony given at the trial to the effect that he is now sane be filed in the habeas corpus proceeding and that the man be released tonight. For my part the court and Mr. Biegler and Mr. Lodwick can complete any further papers and proofs at their leisure next week."

"A generous and sensible suggestion, Mr. Dancer," the Judge said, nodding. "We will proceed at once. Mr. Court Reporter, if I may impose upon you to temporarily forsake your crossword puzzle and take a stipulation. . . ."

In seven minutes by the courtroom clock Lieutenant Manion was a free man. Detective Sergeant Durgo came over and shook hands all around and then smilingly thrust the lüger at the Lieutenant. "This belongs to you, fella," he said dryly.

The Lieutenant blinked his eyes and quickly drew back. "Give it to my lawyer," he said. "As a memento. . . . I—I guess maybe he's earned it."

I found myself standing holding with two fingers the gun that had killed Barney Quill. "Thanks," I said uncertainly, gingerly dropping it in my brief case. "I trust, Sergeant," I said, "that you and Claude Dancer will let me smuggle this thing home without pinching me for carrying concealed weapons."

The Sergeant nodded and wryly laughed and, saluting, went on his way. Laura and the Lieutenant went over to the jail to get his things and check out. We were to meet later. The courtroom was now nearly deserted except for a straggler or two and Smoky Madigan and his mop and steaming pail and Parnell and Maida and me. I lit a cigar and sat stoically stashing my papers away.

Parnell was at my side. "Well, boy, you did it, you really did it," he said huskily, resting his hand gently on my shoulder. "You were magnificent."

I looked up at the tired old man. "We did it, Parn," I said quietly. "Never forget that, my friend. We did it."

The Judge appeared in the tall doorway of chambers in his street clothes and topcoat, wearing his large square-set gray fedora hat and carrying his scuffed and swollen brief case. As he stood there, silent and thoughtful, he looked like a granite personification of Law. I left Parnell and went over and took his extended hand.

"Congratulations," he said, squeezing my aching hand in his paw. "Congratulations on winning one of the strangest and most oddly brilliant criminal prosecutions I've ever witnessed. And I've seen a few."

I glanced at him quickly. "Prosecutions?" I said, puzzled, fearful that the poor man had grown daft and punchy from trial fatigue. Good God, he didn't take me for Claude Dancer, did he?

"Prosecutions," the Judge repeated, smiling broadly. "I've known for years, of course, as you doubtless have, that murder juries invariably 'try' the victim as well as the killer. Did the rascal deserve to be slain? Should we exalt the killer . . . ? But this is the first time in my legal career that I've seen a dead man successfully prosecuted for rape. This is a new one. Quite incidentally, I may add, you seem also to have acquitted a man called Manion." He paused. "I—I guess you're just an old unreconstructed D.A. at heart."

"Thank you, Judge," I said, smiling with pleasure. "I never thought of it that way. It was a pleasure and privilege to work with you. If I may now say so, sir, without being suspected of polishing apples, you're a judge in the high tradition of our own Judge Maitland."

"Thank you," the Judge went on. "That is high praise indeed; I have heard much of your Judge Maitland and his good works. I also want to tell you that I am keeping your set of requested instructions as a model. As I hinted before they are among the best I have ever seen."

I flushed with mingled pleasure and embarrassment and turned and motioned Parnell to join us. "Judge Weaver," I said, "I want you to meet the man who was most responsible for those instructions—and for that matter, for much else that happened at this trial —my new law partner, Parnell McCarthy."

The Judge pumped Parnell's hand warmly. Parnell, grown suddenly white and drawn, kept staring at me uncomprehendingly. "It always delights my heart to meet a real lawyer, Mr. McCarthy," the Judge said, still pumping away at Parnell's limp hand. "I wish you much pleasure and success in your new partnership with still another good lawyer. You two should make quite a pair. You should complement each other nicely."

"Thank you for the compliment, Your Honor," Parnell punned absently, still glancing at me questioningly.

The Judge finally spotted Smoky Madigan and his clattering mop. He lowered his voice. "I may add, Mr. Biegler, that I've decided to give your man over there a break." He stood musing a moment. "Perhaps we can blame it all on our friend William Hazlitt." He paused and blinked his pale blue eyes. "Well, gentlemen, good luck and good night," he said. He turned suddenly away and was gone.

Parnell stood biting his lower lip, his glasses heavily misted. "Did you mean it, boy?" he said in a small voice.

"Did I mean what?" I said gruffly, knowing.

"About—what you said about you and me after bein' partners?"

"Why sure, damn it, Parn, of course I meant it. That is if you'll have me. I'd consider it a privilege and high honor, my old friend. If you'll be my law partner I've already picked out the new firm name: McCarthy and Biegler. I'm figuring to order the new stationery and formal announcements Monday. As for the rest, I've already drawn all the agreement we'll ever need; I hold it here in my empty hand. Everything fifty-fifty, the good and the bad. Just say the word, pardner."

I thrust out my hand and Parnell took it. His lips worked and tears welled up in the old man's eyes. A solitary drop hung trembling on the tip of his nose. "C'mon, Maida," I called out in the hollow and echoing courtroom, "we're all going out and celebrate the big case and our bigger new partnership. Here come the Manions now."

"It's nice I got *two* bosses now to fire me," Maida said, laconically joining us. "Are we all going out and watch you play a drum solo for us at the Halfway House?"

"You guessed it, Maida," I said, patting her gently on the fanny.

"You run find a phone now, like a good girl, and tell 'em to chill up a batch of champagne—lots of it. I didn't dare ask 'em to before. Wait! On second thought go use Mitch's phone."

"I see," Maida said. "Poetic justice rears its ugly head."

During the long hectic evening, during which it seemed a gay and sparkling Parnell must have toasted and been toasted in at least two cases of orange pop, the Lieutenant several times tried to draw me aside and bring up the subject of my unpaid fee. I kept brushing him off and finally silenced him by agreeing to call upon them next morning at their trailer in Iron Bay. After all, the winner of the big murder case, the junior partner in the new law firm of McCarthy and Biegler, the champagne-glowing candidate for Congress, yes, the best non-union drummer in the U.P.—surely this man had no time for the mundane and paltry. . . .

"What time will you plan to be at our trailer?" the Lieutenant insistently inquired. "We want to be sure to be up."

"Oh, ten or eleven or thereabouts," I answered airily. "Don't worry —I'll be there."

"Bring a form of promissory note," he said. "Don't forget, now. We'll be up and waiting for you." He frowned. "I want to get this thing off my mind."

"We'll be there," I promised, and then on an impulse I moved swiftly over to the telephone booth and closed the door and found a coin and phoned Thunder Bay. "Bing-bong," the phone went. "Mary," I said when she answered. "I know that by now you must know the result of the trial but I wanted you to hear it from me." There was a silence and I continued awkwardly. "I know it's late but I just wanted to talk to you is all. Didn't have the nerve to call you before." The silence continued. "Is everything all right, Mary? I'm sorry . . . I—I guess maybe I shouldn't have called."

When she spoke her words came rapidly. "Thank you for your call, Paul. I've been sitting up waiting for it—sitting here alone in the moonlight. Of course everything is all right but it wouldn't have been if you hadn't phoned. I'm almost too happy and relieved to talk—over the trial, now over your call."

"Mary?" I repeated questioningly. "Mary? Mary?"

"Good night, Paul," Mary said. "Please come and see me soon. *Please* do. . . ." The phone clicked softly in my ear.

Parnell stood eyeing me skeptically as I floated dreamily from the phone booth to rejoin the party. "Ordering the stationery for our new partnership, no doubt," he said, crowding and bumping his way into the booth I had just vacated.

"More champagne!" I crowed, moving over and pounding the bar with my benumbed fist. "Boy, oh boy, oh boy!"

It was nearly noon before Parnell and I threaded our way into the Manions' trailer court on the outskirts of Iron Bay. I had slept the sleep of the drugged, and anyway thoughtful Parnell and I did not want prematurely to disturb the reunited lovers. . . . A tall silver-haired man with a drooping tobacco-stained silvery mustache, like a character out of Owen Wister, emerged from what appeared to be an office trailer and crunched across the dirty white gravel to the side of our car, shaking his head.

"We only park trailers here, folks—this here ain't no motel. Sorry," he said.

"I'm looking for Lieutenant Manion's trailer," I said.

"Sorry, boss, you're jest too late—they pulled out last night about three A.M. Seems like they was in a kind of a hurry."

The thumping pall of silence ticked like a time bomb. "Did—did they leave any message?" I said in a small voice.

"Well, yup, if you can call it that. Just as they took off the man leaned out an' tole me if anyone comes lookin' for him to tell 'em he'd had an irre—what the hell—an irresistible impulse to get the hell out of here. Said you'd understand."

"Anything else?" I murmured.

"Yes, they was movin' when the woman called back for me not to deliver the message I jest now delivered. Said that was too cruel, I think she said. I kinda think mebbe she was bawlin' some."

"Was that all?"

"That was all, boss, an' I hope it makes some sense to you folks 'cause it sure don't make none to me. Oh, yes—he was a kind of a sassy fella—he also called me Buster."

"Thank you," I said. "I'm afraid I understand—even to the part about Buster."

Parnell took over. "I trust," he said dryly, "I trust, sir, that the gentleman paid you up in full?"

The proprietor turned and spat a stream of tobacco juice on a bed of frostbitten limp-stemmed dahlias. "Never fear about that," he said. "Old George Roebuck allus gets paid in advance. You see, folks, my motto is: 'Never trust a stranger—an' treat everybody as strangers.' As the fella said, if you don't never trust nobody you don't

434

never get stuck. Sorry I can't help you." He spat again and, his message delivered, crunched back to his trailer.

I thoughtfully lit a cigar. "A pragmatic philosopher," I mused after him. "Just another representative of the vast gentle breed that shall one day inherit the smoking cinder of the earth."

Parnell was silent for a time. Finally he spoke. "In a way, boy—don't you see?—the Lieutenant used you and you used him. He got his freedom and you got whatever it is you've got." He paused. "Maybe," he said slowly, "maybe in a certain sense you two are just about square. Maybe, as Maida said, maybe this is a kind of poetic justice."

I slowly nodded my head. "Anyway I've got a new partner," I said. "A new partner and a big headache."

"Headache?" Parnell said sharply.

"Headache, pardner," I said. "What'll I ever tell Maida? Lord, Parn, I'll never be able to face her."

"What'll *you* tell Maida!" Parnell snorted. "What'll *we* ever tell her? As your new partner, lad, I share in the headaches, too. Fifty-fifty you said."

I smiled wanly. "Yes, Parn, I guess you can share the new wealth."

Parnell cleared his throat and stirred restlessly. "Well, boy," he said, "let's be on our way an' not settin' around here mopin' all day. I'm anxious for you to get runnin' and lose this Congress race and get *that* bug out of your bonnet so we two can settle down and practice law like we belong." He shot me a tart sidelong glance. "Though I must say, boy, I'm gettin' a little worried lately about your drinkin'. . . ."

"Get the goddam money and trust no one," I mused aloud, slowly putting the car in gear. "What a beautiful soaring philosophy of life." I shook my head and smiled. "Well, at least we got a German lüger out of it, partner." I grunted. "Maybe the Lieutenant intended I should play Russian roulette with it. But I guess they can only do that with revolvers."

Parnell patted my knee and spoke softly. "Forget this graspin' trailer man and his peasant motto, boy. Forget the Lieutenant, too, just put him totally out of your mind. Don't you see?—he's gone to prison anyway, locked away forever in the squalid prison of *himself*. . . . You'll never see or hear from him again, of course, so forget him, simply expunge him from your memory. I knew something like this would happen, boy, and I think you knew it too, if you'd only let yourself think. . . . Now let's speak of it no more." Parnell sat suddenly erect and stared straight down the whirling, leaf-strewn road. "Let's to the future, lad, you and me together—maybe makin' a little money, surely havin' a barrel of fun, practicin' our profession together, occasionally helpin' bastards and angels alike, between whom, always remember, our Lady Justice has never distinguished."

I nodded my head and stepped on the gas.

Parnell reeled down his window and turned to me. "Now supposin' you drive us up along the shore line toward a village called Thunder Bay? 'Tis a beautiful autumn day, lad. We'll have our Sabbath dinner at a nice little hotel I know up there, overlookin' the lake."

We drove along in silence. I observed Parnell watching me out of the corner of his eye. He fidgeted and cleared his throat.

"Let's have it, Parn," I said.

"In fact, boy, she's expectin' us, she is that. You see, she and I been in touch."

"Who's expecting us?" I said, suddenly knowing and feeling very glad.

"Why our Mary, of course, lad," he said softly. "I meant to save it as a surprise but I guess maybe you've had enough surprises for one day. The sweet child invited us to dinner for today when I phoned her the result of the trial last night as I'd promised. Miss Maida will be waiting there for us." The old man smiled privately. "But I thought maybe I'd already told you. My, my, I must be getting forgetful."

"No, Mr. McCarthy, you hadn't told me," I said, stepping hard on the gas. As the battered old car leapt forward I began to feel free as a bird; a curious sense of relief and release came over me. And expectation. We sped along, finally shedding the last scars of town, and at length climbed a long granite-girt hill. Gaining the top we seemed breathessly to hang in mid-air. Spread out far below us was the tremendous expanse of the big lake: beautiful, empty, glittering, cold and brooding, gull-swept and impersonal; always there, always the same—there for the grateful and the ungrateful, there for the bastards and the angels, there for the just and the unjust alike.

"Amen," Parnell murmured huskily, spreading his plump hands and shaking his head in awe. "Sometimes, lad—sometimes when I behold a sight like this I—I just want to stretch out my arms an' soar like a bird. Can you understand a silly arthritic old man thinkin' much less sayin' such a thing?"

"The unfettered spirit," I thought. "Yes, Parn," I said, again stepping on the gas, and as we fled down the steep hill the soaring words of William Blake came surging back to me, so Saxonly muscular and bleeding: "The pure soul shall mount on native wings, disdaining little sport, and cut a path into the heaven of glory, leaving a track of light for men to wonder at."